# NOBLE WARRIOR
### Becca Ketelsleger

*Dedicated to the hero in all of us*

When a person looks back on their life they will inevitably decide if it was meaningful. As they examine, they will weigh the good and the bad, trying to find out which the balance falls in favor of.

I'm nearing the end of my life. It has been long, and the list of deeds to weigh lays heavy on my shoulders. I've seen more than my fair share of good and evil in life and in people. Looking back, it is much easier to divide the people who have populated my life into those who were worthy and those who weren't than it has been to determine my own place. Some were valiant, kind and inspiring. Others were tormented, frightened and cruel.

When most people look back they will come to a final decision of their worth.

I find that I cannot.

I cannot reduce my life to a tally sheet of wrongs and rights. So, instead of trying to convince myself that I am a saint or a sinner, I have decided to write down my tale before it becomes too late.

Maybe someday someone will read this and objectively analyze my actions and my passions. Perhaps they will come to the same conclusion as I have . . . That every moment is unique and conclusions about them are merely pale and meaningless reflections.

# CHAPTER ONE
## Saving Father

The blades sung out as they came together, a startling and jarring sound that mimicked the feeling of the jolt running up my arms. My opponent was stronger than I, but I was faster. Ducking to the left, I slid my weapon to the right, redirecting his blade away from my body. Circling behind him, my sword slid effortlessly to contact his right shoulder.

The blunt blade made a thud against his flesh, and he stumbled slightly before catching his balance. I saw him take a deep breath, his fingers loosening from their white knuckled grip on the hilt of his weapon.

Turning towards me, his flushed face broke into a large grin. "Well done, Aceline! That might have been your best attack yet!"

Pushing my hair back from my glistening forehead, I couldn't keep a smirk from my own face. "I think I'm just getting to know your weak spots too well, Father."

Slinging his arm around me, we walked back across our modest yard into our even more modest home.

"Or you just have a knack for winning a fight. Who says I need a son, when I have the best swordswoman in the land for a daughter?" Father slid his sword into scabbard, and handed my leather sheath to me.

"Well I'm not sure about that," I replied as I walked to put both swords into the chest at the foot of my father's bed. "But I have certainly had more practice than any other woman in all of Bryton."

Returning to the common room, I swiftly lit a fire in preparation for the evening meal. The days were beginning to grow shorter, and the orange streaks of the falling sun slid through the cracks in the door.

Father sat down to remove his boots with a chuckle. "I firmly believe that a woman should be able to defend herself. And as much as we both will hate it, I feel that soon it will be less and less appropriate for a traveling merchant to bring along his only daughter with him on all business trips." I turned to acknowledge what he had just said, and he gave me a knowing look. "Although, without your company, I will feel quite lost."

I sighed as I returned to cutting potatoes. "But what will I do here all alone? It's not as if I have any friends or suitors to remain for. With all these years of travelling and returning here only for brief respites, it's not much of a home without you."

Placing his boots to the side, father stood and came to place his hand on my shoulder.

"Sometimes I fear that I have done you a disservice by keeping you so much to myself. If your mother was still here it would have been different. Without her, I feel as if perhaps we have had to rely a little too much on one another. And because of that, you have missed out on many things." His voice had a hint of melancholy as it always did when he spoke of my mother. I suppose that cannot be helped when the love of your life has been taken from you.

Pausing from my duties, I reached my hand up to place it upon my fathers and glanced over my shoulder to give him a smile. "I wouldn't have had it any other way."

Returning my smile, he replied, "I'm very glad to hear that my daughter. Hold tight to that, no matter what change may come."

**********

A few days later, I was alone at home catching up on chores. My mindless flitting around the house was less out of necessity than needing to take my mind off the news that soon Father would be departing on a lengthy business trip, without me.

I grew up with my Father. My mother died when I was four and I barely remembered her, except as a creature who had been born to be adored.

My Father, John Grosipan, had been born to a lower class and had worked his way to becoming a well-respected merchant with many important friends. When he was still a struggling and ambitious youth, he had met a beautiful servant girl on one of his many adventures. He said he had loved her from first sight, with her sunshine hair and sky-blue eyes. Her sweet disposition caught his attention next. He always said she was like a breath of fresh air. I could hear his love for her in his voice even then, 13 years after her death. He had never married again, or as far as I knew, bedded another woman.

Though the life that he had wanted with his bride had been taken away, Father was nothing if not resilient, and in me he saw the last glimpse of happiness left from my mother.

Father loved to tell me that I was like her in many ways. Not in looks, for I had mousy hair and hazel eyes, but in spirit. Although I was often quiet and unsure of myself, once I had reached a decision I became unflinchingly headstrong.

As far as my father, I gained many things from him, but that did not include his outward appearance. He was a passionate man and that was plain to see from first glance. He had wild red hair and flashing green eyes.

I always wondered how a simple and plain girl like me could have come from two such beautiful people as my parents. Because of this knowledge that I was not as alluring as a young girl might hope, I was more than happy to remain sheltered by my father, the one man who didn't seem to notice that I wasn't a beauty.

To my father, I was the perfect daughter. I was intelligent enough to understand his business dealings and tough enough to accompany him on even the most grueling journeys. I was pleasant enough and interesting enough to be introduced to his business partners, but I was respectful enough to leave them to their bartering and trading. He never told me that I wasn't good enough or raised a hand to me.

Because of this, I had never been exposed to the true cruelties of the world, even though I had been warned. Father had always trained me with the sword so that I could protect myself, whatever the cost.

Lost in my thoughts of what it would be like to remain at home alone for such a long period of time, I did not notice a darkening near the front window of our small home.

I nearly screamed when all of a sudden I heard the ominous crack of wood being broken. I dropped the wooden plate I was cleaning and looked cautiously through the open doorway like a scared animal. The soldiers walked in through our shattered wooden door and filled our bare living room.

Unsure of what was happening, I froze. It is often said that in situations where there is danger, the two natural responses are to fight or flee. I maintain that there is a third option: to freeze.

While there had not been many occasions of true fear in my life up to that point, I had already learned this important facet of myself and I had ever since been trying desperately to overcome it.

My legs shook unsteadily as I tried to force myself to grab my sword, so that I could defend my home against these intruders. My skills would never be any good if I couldn't find the courage within myself to use them.

Though at least a minute had passed, the men still appeared not to notice me. After another moment of them rudely prodding through our things and breaking many of my Fathers priceless trinkets, I finally was able to take one small action. I cleared my throat.

That was when the soldiers of King Aidan Penhalion, son of the late King Umber, finally noticed that I was standing there.

"We need to speak to John Grosipan, maiden," the man who appeared to be in charge stated gruffly. He looked around with his eyes narrowed behind his unadorned helmet.

It was clear that these men did not merely want to speak to Father, so I hesitated in answering. I wanted to tell them that he had already left for his next business venture. I wanted to tell them that he wasn't here and wouldn't be for some time. In reality he was out buying produce and was due back any moment.

"He is not here right now, but I am his daughter Aceline Grosipan. May I ask what business you have with him?" I tried to look the leader in the eyes, but he would not even give me the courtesy of looking at me. Instead, his eyes skimmed around the room, trying to find any nook or cranny where my father could have been stuffed.

"My business with your Father is confidential." He sounded extremely unamused with finding a whimpering girl instead of the man he was sent for.

My mind was racing. Unsure of how to get the men to leave, I did not know how to proceed. I could sense that my Father would not be safe if he came back to these visitors, but they were men of the King and I had no sway over their actions.

Unfortunately, even if I had there was not enough time.

There was a startled gasp in the doorway, and I looked past the soldiers to see my Father standing there with a wild expression painted across his face. He held a basket of vegetables in his hand, which he promptly dropped with a sickening thud. Before my father could make another move, the soldiers quickly snatched his arms and twisted them behind his back.

"What are you doing!?" I screamed as I flung myself at my Father. A large guard pulled him out of my grasp and then clamped chains around his wrists.

"John Grosipan has been involved in a treasonous plot to kill the young King Aidan. He is to be taken to the castle and jailed immediately." The guard's words were cold as he and his followers pushed Father out the door without even a second glance at me.

"Father!" I screamed, following the soldiers out onto our busy street of Calentto. I could feel the people milling around staring at us and whispering. I pushed my way through them with no regard to the scene that we were making. The soldiers were moving swiftly, hauling my Father along and I was barely keeping up even though I was pushing people out of the way left and right.

"Aceline, go back!" He yelled before I lost sight of him in the crowd. "Hide or they will come for you also!"

"Father! Father! What is happening?" I screamed, but there was no reply.

I kept running through the streets crying, even though I could no longer see them. The faces blended together and finally I stopped, out of breath on a street corner that I barely recognized.

I was scared senseless, frightened for my father and myself. I had never felt so completely and utterly helpless and alone. Treason most always meant hanging. I could not believe that my father would be involved in anything illegal. My Father had never broken a law in his life.

Heeding my father's words, I quickly ran along the streets that had once been a haven, but were now filled with treachery. I quickly shut the back door and nailed some boards across the remainders of our front door. I stayed barricaded in our two room home for two weeks, stepping out only to dump my chamber pots and get water from the well in the common courtyard. I was frozen with fear and uncertainty. By the end of the second week the food supply of dry goods in our pantry was running out.

Though I knew that the whole town would be talking, I also knew that I needed to buy some provisions. Hopefully, a trip to the market would provide me not only with supplies, but also with news of my father.

**********

In order to avoid recognition, I put on some of my father's clothes and then wrapped an enormous cloak around me, concealing my hair and most of my face. There was no way anyone could possibly know who I was. I walked quickly for two blocks until I reached the peasant's market. I looked around and saw all my friends. Sal, the butcher, and Anita, the fruit vendor, whom I had known my whole, life both looked happy and fresh. I envied them, living a simple life, but a safe one. It seemed so long ago that I had stood next to them laughing and joking.

Now everything seemed dangerous. I felt like a caged animal and could not even imagine what my father must be experiencing.

I was a quiet observer as I went to Phillip, the bread man's, stall. I picked up a loaf and examined it while listening to the chatter. For once in my life, I was glad that Callento was filled with gossips.

"They say that he is to be hung in a fortnight," Phillip said with a sad shake of his head.

"Aye, I never would have suspected John Grosipan of treason though," a strange man replied.

"John always did have strange ideas. I've heard him talk on several occasions of a new revolution. I always thought he just meant a new religion or something, not a new King!" Philip sighed.

Anger welled in my chest at this man who my Father had called a friend. Father would have trusted Philip if he was in trouble, he would never doubt a friend. How could this man that I had grown up around give up on my Father so easily?

"I suppose one of Aidan's new knights will be doing the job. Talk is that they are going to be the only ones Aidan trusts to see to prisoners. I suppose the new King has a right to be paranoid though, seems like there is more unrest in the kingdom now than ever."

I cleared my throat loudly and the two men looked at me, aggravated that I was interrupting their conversation. I dropped my voice down an octave and started to talk.

"I have heard tales of the knights. Is it true that the King will be taking any qualified knight into his service?" Since I had been holed away, I had heard nothing of the knights. They didn't have to know that though, as long as they gave me the information I needed. It was refreshing to finally know what was happening around me. All my life I had been kept informed about my surroundings. Father had never believed that girls should be left ignorant.

"Well, any knight is qualified to try and get into his Highnesses personal guard, but the tournament on the Usk River will decide. Only the top fifty knights will be invited to sit at the round table. You wouldn't be thinking about entering the tournament now would you, lad? You sound a bit young," Phillip said jokingly. He gave my arm a nudge and smiled at the other man, who grinned also.

"No, I'm just curious sir," I held out my meager coins for the bread and quickly walked away. I could hear the two men joking from behind me and wished that I could spit on their shoes. Good friends they were.

As I walked home, I thought about what the two men had said. It appeared that I only had two weeks before he would be lost to me forever. I shivered at the thought and blinked the tears from my eyes. I was foolishly hoping that he would be kept alive. I had been hoping that the situation was not as dire as it had seemed, but it had turned out to be worse.

The only hope that my father had was to escape before his sentence was carried out, and if what they said was true, then only a knight could save him from the gallows. I had already counted all of the gold I had found hidden away in the house, and we would not have enough to effectively bribe anyone. I was not attractive enough to seduce anyone. The more and more I pondered the problem, the more my thoughts were drawn towards the swords laying in my father's chest.

An idea was forming, as crazy as it might have been.

However, when I got an idea in my head, I didn't easily let it go.

**********

The next day, I stood in the bedroom I had shared with my father and held the sharp knife to my hair. I had never cut my hair, and it hung to the middle of my thighs. Most men wore their hair short and ragged but some wore it long. I had decided to cut my hair to just below my chin. Even though it was a small consolation to keep an inch or two, this was still a big change, and I knew that once I did this there would be no going back.

It seemed silly to think about such a trivial thing, but my hair had been my only physically beautiful feature that I had cherished. I felt a tear roll down my cheek, even though I don't remember actually crying it. Before I had time to change my mind, I quickly started to hack at my brown locks.

My hair was so thick I had to saw the knife back and forth. Every time I drew the knife I saw more hair fall to the ground and my head felt lighter. I looked down at the disembodied locks that had been part of me for as long as I could remember. When I was done, I gathered the lengths of hair and stuck it under my bed with one last loving caress. I should have thrown it away, but I just couldn't bring myself to do that. It seemed almost inhumane.

Next, I got undressed, took a long piece of linen, and started to bind my chest. Since I had to look as flat as possible I bound very tightly. Considering that I had a rather large chest, it felt like knives were stabbing into me every time I tugged on it. By the time I had tied the linen, I could barely breathe and the splintering pain had turned into a steady ache. I couldn't imagine how much pain I was in before I was even on the road. I just hoped that I wasn't doing all of this for nothing. If I did not make it into the fifty . . . well, I had to try not to think about that.

I walked over to my father's chest and opened it slowly. I was taller than my Father and probably a little chubbier, but fortunately all of his clothes were large so they fit. I pulled out some breeches and a shirt. Then I strapped a breastplate onto my chest, arm and leg plates onto my extremities and put a helmet on my head. All of the armor looked pitiful, since it was all mismatched pieces that Father had kept over the years.

After I put them on, I pulled out our lone silver plate and looked at myself. I thought I could pass as a boy once I got some dirt on my face. For once I was glad that my face was plain and I was not a beauty.

Finally, I reached into the chest and pulled out my Father's sword. It was a fine piece of craftsmanship and had been my father's pride and joy. Father had traded a lot of swords in his day and had found me a beautiful one to keep as my own. But, beautiful and well-made mine was, it could never compare to Father's blade.

He always told me stories about our ancestors. My great-grandmother had been forced to defend her younger siblings from a rogue group of Rebels when she was not even 15. The only reason that she and her siblings survived was because her father had taught her how to use a sword before he had died of illness. One of the Rebels had been wielding this sword, and my great-grandmother kept it in remembrance of that day. It had been passed down in the family ever since.

This sword had a silver hilt with one lone blood red stone placed in it. The actual blade had Old-Language markings on it that my Father said meant "Bring Blood Noble Warrior." I had only ever held it once.

The first time that I had ever beaten father during our sparring, I was only a young girl of about 14. In my aggression and excitement, I had accidently knocked father to the ground in my attempt to be victorious. Instead of being angry, as any other father would have been, my father slowly got to his feet and offered his sword to me. As I held it, he told me the story of how it had come to our family, and that I had the spirit of my great-grandmother.

Pulling myself from my memories, I put it gently into its decorated leather scabbard and placed it around my waist. Taking one last look around my childhood home, I grabbed my bread, a flask of water, and all the coins I had left. I took a step outside of the door and did not dare to look back, because I knew that I would turn around.

For a moment I was beyond embarrassed and disgusted with myself for putting on such a show of going to save my father. How could a stupid little naïve girl change the fate of even one man?

But I knew that it was too late to turn back.

Sir Andrew Banidere was on his way.

**********

After I got five minutes out of town, rain started to pour down. Bryton was prone to such changes in weather and it was the only thing about this lush and diverse land that I did not like. I went off the road after thirty minutes of trying to walk through ankle deep mud, which was left from the last rain, and took refuge under a tree on the edge of a small grove. Despite feeling hypocritical, I grumbled and complained aloud to myself the whole way.

The funny thing about aggravation, is that somehow it manages to be just as potent and tangible as the emotions upon which stories and songs are written, without being near as beautiful.

As I sat staring out into the rain, I heard a small noise behind me. At first I didn't turn to look. I had played here as a child and knew that many forest creatures lived among the branches. I had never been here alone, though, and I shivered. Father had always accompanied me when I played here. These branches were filled with happy memories and I soon became lost in them.

"Hello," came a voice right behind me.

At the sound of the voice, the hairs on my arms raised and my eyes widened in fear, but at first I made no movement. Yet again, I froze in the face of fear.

"Hello?" The voice came again.

I took a deep breath, pushing aside the momentary panic that had overcome me. My hand flew to my blade as I jumped to my feet and swiftly turned to face the voice.

Standing in front of me was a man. His dark curly hair and trimmed beard were wet, and water clung to eyelashes which framed brown eyes. He was smiling, but had his hand on his sword hilt as well.

"Don't be afraid Lad. I won't hurt you. I am Leonard, here from Fraunc for the tournament on the Usk River." He leaned against a tree and his hand slid from his sword. Apparently, he did not think that I was a threat. Based on my reaction to his presence, he was probably right.

"I am Andrew Banidere, and also am heading to the tournament." My voice was shaky but I managed to keep it low.

"Well, I suppose we should travel together then!" His eyes lightly glanced over my mismatched armor, thin arms and pale face. "Although I think that if you are trying to impress your family, or perhaps a girl, there might be more appropriate avenues than fighting the best swordsmen in the kingdom." The man was not joking, I could see it in his eyes, but his tone was light and jovial. Still, I felt the heat of anger swell up in me.

"I have as good a chance as any, maybe even a better chance than you!" My voice trembled despite the defiant tilt of my chin.

The knight was amused, based upon the sparkle in his eyes. "Well then, boy, since we might end up fighting each other anyway why not have a trial run? So that you are prepared when the real thing comes." Leonard pulled out his sword and pointed it at me. I was shaking, but still managed to pull out my sword.

"First hit wins," Leonard said before lunging at me. I held my sword to block him. He pushed down on my sword and I realized how weak I was. My muscles screamed and Leonard did not even look like he was using any effort, in fact, he was still wearing his cocky grin.

Using old skills I knew well, I pulled my sword out and sprung to the right. Leonard followed and lunged at my stomach. I moved to the left. I knew I was on the defense, where a swordsman never wants to be. Suddenly I lunged and was a hair away from nicking Leonard's leg when he blocked and pushed me away. Before I knew what was happening, I was on the ground with the stranger's sword at my throat. My chest was heaving even though we had only fought for a few seconds. As I closed my eyes I prayed that he was a good person and would not kill me.

"You should know lad, that I am Leonard from Fraunc. I have heard shouts that I am second only to Aidan. I'm here to test that claim." He drew his sword back and held out his hand to help me up. I eyed the hand wearily before accepting it. The man's hands were large and callused. I hoped that he did not notice that my hands were white and soft, at least compared to his.

When I got up, I dusted myself off before speaking, searching for the right words to use. "I did not know who you were," I said gruffly. My pride was a little wounded. He knew that I was a gullible youth and he took advantage of it to make a point. I sighed and let my anger cool off. He probably saw me as a cocky young dandy, which to some degree I was.

Leonard laughed. "If it's any consolation you fight well, for a lad. You almost have right to be prideful." I was shocked and pleased, but refused to let it show.

"You call me a lad but you aren't too old of a man yourself." This man probably meant well but he was getting annoying and the rain had stopped. I wanted to get going, without him.

"You are right, I'm only thirty but when you have seen as much blood as I have it feels like many more years than that."

In that moment, I was able to really see him, and saw that though his disposition was cheerful; his eyes were wise and sad. I was sorry that I had even brought up the subject of age; because of the new look in those eyes.

Suddenly, I was not so aggravated. I coughed; I would never be a good man if I had such a soft heart. I bent down to pick up my pack and slipped my sword back into its sheath.

"Well, it's off to the Usk River, I go. Are you going to join me or not?" I started walking towards the road.

"You still insist on entering the tournament? There will be at least 400 men and boys," Leonard was jogging to catch up. When he came up beside me he started to walk, but his stride was almost twice as long as mine. He was a fairly large man, and it was hard for me to keep up.

"Then there are only 350 men I must be better than," It was straining my voice to talk so low and I cleared my throat softly.

Leonard chuckled. "I hope you do make it. We could be good together lad," he clapped me on the back. I looked over at him. I was going to have to get used to men touching me. I did not greatly enjoy being touched.

We walked for at least two hours with Leonard's sporadic chatting. My legs started to get weary with the large amounts of mud coating my shoes and I kept dropping my bag. Finally, we went over a rise and below us was a long glittering snake of water surrounded by tents and pens.

"The Usk River," I whispered, filled with a mixture of dread and anticipation. My Father's future was is my hands.

**********

I stood before the long table that took our names. The area was mass chaos and I had been waiting for such a long time that my back was sore and I didn't want to stand anymore, let alone fight. But, it was only about an hour till noon so the day was still young.

Finally, I reached the front and stood before a small, thin man. "Sir Andrew Banidere." I delivered the lie with confidence even though my insides were in turmoil. What if someone found out I was a girl? What would they do? A smile tickled my lips, maybe then they would take me to be with my Father.

"Lad, you are to fight Sir Hector in the northernmost pen at noon. Be there or you will be disqualified." He waveded me off with his hand as if I was a fly, and I was glad to oblige. I slipped away while Leonard was busy signing up so that I wouldn't have to continue listening to his jokes and annoyingly deserved confidence.

The tournament had the same air as the Callento summer fair. There were a lot of people selling their wares and there were even jugglers and fire blowers. After a while of wandering and gawking at the goods I looked at the sun and decided that it was time for me to start heading towards my ring.

The area around the rings was a mess of people. Sweaty, stinky men were all over the place. I weeded my way through the crowds, trying to breathe in the smells as little as possible. I knew that I would have to get used to the stench, if I made it into the knighthood. I reached the last pen and stared at the people already fighting.

It was obvious that the short bald man in the pen was beating the tall red-headed youth terribly. I wondered if I would look like that while fighting Sir Hector. Leonard had said I was good, but was he just being nice? He had wished me good luck and that had to count for something. Suddenly, the red headed lad clutched his uncovered arm. First blood had been drawn and the bald man had won the fight. The rules had said that it was a single elimination tournament.

Suddenly, I heard my name being called. I shivered and took a deep breath, trying to calm the butterflies in my stomach and the ache in all of my muscles. I walked into the pen and saw my opponent for the first time. Sir Hector was an old man with long gray whiskers and hard eyes to match. He snarled at me and pulled out his sword. I pulled out mine also and threw the scabbard aside. Many people had gathered on the side lines and I heard the man in charge yell to begin.

I quickly lunged, hoping that since I started out on the offensive I would stay there. Hector moved and my blade swung harmlessly past.

Hector swung at my back but I turned in just enough time to duck beneath the blade that was aimed for my head. I knew that this man had been trained to kill, not just draw blood or give someone a whack with the flat end of the sword. I lunged again and I was so close that I could almost smell the blood. Hector let out a yell of rage because of his near defeat. We both crouched low, my toes digging into the soft dirt. I did not want to be the one to spring first, so I let him go. He did and as he launched at me, I swung around and almost clipped him again. Suddenly, and without warning he lunged at me again and I fell back, avoiding the blade. I lost my balance and fell to the ground. Hector stood over me and started to bring the sword to my throat when I jumped up and swung at him. Our swords clanged together loudly but he pulled away quickly. I jumped back and raised my sword above my head to bring it down on the man's shoulder. I sighed when I missed and clutched my arm as a sudden pain shot through it. I looked down and was glad to see that there was no blood and that the pain must have just been a cramp.

Hector had experience and strength on his side and I had the speed and agility of youth. Besides that, fear is a powerful motivator, and I had never before been so afraid in my entire life.

Sweat trickled into my eyes and made it hard to see. My head felt as if it was frying inside of my too-big helmet. But, I could see that the old man was getting tired. I saw my opportunity, and I lunged. My sword surged past him once more. My muscles screamed with a fiery pain and I didn't know how much longer I could hold out. Hector was struggling as well, and was trying to catch his breath. In a moment of weakness, he lowered his sword an inch in an attempt to take a deep inhale.

It was now or never.

With one final lunge I slashed his unprotected shoulder between where his breastplate and arm plate met and I could see the torn cloth start to turn red. I remember being utterly shocked that I had won. The crowd cheered and I smiled. I was sorry for Sir Hector, but so very proud of myself. I held out my hand to give his a shake but he glared at me and spit near my boot. The crowd gave a murmur of surprise. The older man pushed past me and I clenched my hand, trying very hard not to turn around and slap him across the face. Maybe men were used to being treated like this, but I was not.

"You had better go give your name," a man shouted. I picked up my scabbard, wiped the minimal blood off my blade and jumped out of the ring.

For a moment I was in utter disbelief. It was as if the moment the fight ended, all the pain and fear was gone and all that was left was an ecstatic feeling of being complete master of one's own body. I could feel every muscle and tendon working together in perfect harmony. I felt unstoppable, though moments before I had been worn almost to exhaustion. I worked my way to the table and could see that the recorder was shocked to see me back. His eyes were wide and he almost dropped his pen.

"Sir Banidere for the second round," I said and I knew that I sounded cocky, but I was so proud of myself that I just wanted the whole world to know that the underdog had won. The man looked down and muttered something.

"It looks like you will be fighting Lord Tremet at half past one in the second pen to the left," he motioned me off again and I couldn't help smirking. Since it was a single elimination tournament that meant there were roughly only around 200 men left. I wandered around again for a while before reporting to my fight.

I watched several fights before my name was finally called. I unsheathed my sword and walked into the ring, with a slight bounce in my step. I was still nervous but at least now I really knew what to expect. I had already gotten farther then I had realistically thought, and I hoped that my luck would continue. I almost stopped in my tracks when I saw my opponent. Lord Tremet looked even more battle hardened than Sir Hector had and I felt all my pride and assurance drain from my body.

The man was a lean, tall pillar of coiled muscle. A large scar ran down one cheek and the only armor that he wore was a light breastplate and leather gauntlets. I felt like a scared little rabbit next to a large and ravenous wolf.

"Get ready to bleed boy!" His accent was Romeni and I wondered why he was here. I heard that King Aidan had lived in Rom for a time and that he had at one time considered it his home. Once again I heard the leader yell to start. Tremet lunged before I moved, he missed and while his face was turned away from me I swung at his back and hit flesh before his swiftly moving sword intercepted my blade. My sword came away bloody. I smiled, shocked and please that the match had been so easy. Suddenly, I was knocked to the ground. All the air was knocked out of me and I tried to breath but couldn't. There was a pair of hands around my neck choking me beneath my helmet. I brought up my fist to punch Tremet but he was pulled off by someone. I lay on the ground breathing hard with my eyes closed.

"What reasons did this man have to attack this youth?"

"Your Highness, this youth, Sir Banidere, just defeated Lord Tremet."

**********

Finally, I caught my breath and edged up on my elbows, slowly opening my eyes. "Your Highness . . ." Here I faced the King, the man who had sentenced my father to death, but I could say nothing for I was in awe.

His eyes, the most piercing blue, wandered over me. His dark blonde hair was cut closely above his ears and he had not shaved that morning. He held out his hand to me as Leonard had done earlier. I took it and immediately felt as if lightning was coursing through my veins. Like Leonard, his hands were strong and warm without being clammy. Then he smiled and I was breathless again. "I hear that you, Sir Banidere, are one of the last few knights. Quite an accomplishment for one so young," he pulled me to my feet and I brushed myself off, but I could not tear my eyes away from him. "Tomorrow you will face the best in all Bryton. But for tonight, do you have a place to stay?" His voice was friendly. I shook my head no.

His smile made it almost impossible to believe that this was the tyrant accusing my father of treason. I had to remind myself that wolves often come in sheep's clothing.

"Well then, you can stay with me and the other one hundred odd men," he patted me on the back, "Come along. Tomorrow will be a big day." I followed Aidan across all the rings until we reached an enormous, colorful tent. "Go on in Banidere, most are already inside. I have some business to attend to." And with a nod and a grin he walked off.

I stared after him for a moment, utterly confused. That man could not have been the King. I pictured the King as a spoiled brat who ordered men to be beheaded without a second thought, and didn't mind turning young girls into orphans.

This man was anything but the villain I had imagined. He seemed remarkably normal, but in a way that made normal seem to be more than I had ever thought it could be.

Unsure of myself, I walked slowly into the dim and uncomfortably warm tent. Once my eyes adjusted I saw many men, most of which were staring at me. "Banidere!" I heard a voice call from my left. I turned and saw Leonard sitting at a small, crudely made table with cards on it. I walked over slowly, wading through the masses of men. Most were nearly twice my size, with full beards and ample body odor. But I wasn't the only one who noticed that I was out of place here, everyone stared at me as if I was an infant crawling through their midst.

"So glad, and shocked, that you made it lad! Come, play some cards," Leonard made room for me. I grabbed a chair from a vacant table and plopped down in it, still nervous. The only real reason that I sat was that I was exhausted.

"Leonard, did I surprise you?" I managed to get out. As much as I hated to admit it, it was nice to have someone that I knew among the large throng of unwelcoming men.

Leonard smiled. "That you did." I could tell he was intoxicated despite the fact that it was only midafternoon. "Oh, so sorry for being rude. Here are Sir Gerard, Gladwin, Garvan, and Gair; we like to call them the brothers, even though they all aren't related. Gladwin's the odd one out." He talked as if he had known these men for ages, when in reality he must have met them just a few minutes before. All four men were huge with red hair and rather large noses. I still saw that one man, that I assumed was Gladwin, had a different face from the rest; slightly more handsome. The other three looked exactly alike. They reminded me of the big friendly giants I had often heard fairy tales about.

"Sir Bran." Bran was the bald man I had watched before my first fight. He had a large scar running the length of his plump face. His arms were huge and I knew that if I ever fought him, I would lose just as easily as the red-headed boy. I realized I had just been lucky in getting easy men to fight all day. I sent up a silent prayer of gratitude.

"And last but not least Sir Teague." It was Teague my eyes stayed on the longest. He was tall and blond with deep green eyes. I had heard of him before. It was said that Teague was a man of many talents and fought well on the battlefield. He had been the King's man long before this and everyone knew that, even if he didn't make it legally into the fifty, he would still sit at the Round Table as an equal.

"Hello good sirs," I said before turning back to Leonard. "Leonard, where do the men sleep around here?" I did my best to cover a yawn but couldn't quite help it. I had never worked so hard before in my life.

"Going to bed? What about the wine . . . and the women?" Leonard laughed. He turned to look at Bran. "There are at least a few women around here aren't there?" I imagined he was the type of man who enjoyed wine and women a great deal.

"I believe I need sleep more than wine or women right now," I was getting tired of being around so many men. I wondered if I did make it, if I would be able to keep up with their hectic schedule.

"You can sleep over there. It will be a little rowdy and loud though. I suppose if you are tired enough you will be able to sleep through it," a deep, melodious voice answered. I turned to see Teague staring at me.

"Thank you, sirs," I nodded.

"Cut the titles, we all piss the same," Bran voice was rough and loud. I smiled as I walked away, little did they know. I found a quiet corner and curled up in my cape. My last thoughts were of traitors and kings.

**********

I slept for a few hours until the noise became too much for my exhaustion to allow me to ignore. I got up drowsily and wiped my matted eyes. There was a large fire in the center of the massive tent and I silently made my way over to it, pushing through the throngs of intoxicated men.

When I finally got next to the blaze I held my hands close in order to warm them and looked around me. Some of the men were singing rowdy war songs and one had even managed to produce a flute that he was playing skillfully.

I heard someone shout above the crowd but it didn't register for a few minutes that it was my name that they were screaming.

Looking across the fire I saw Leonard beckoning me towards him. I smiled and waved before wading my way through the masses of men.

Once I had finally managed to reach him he roughly placed a hand on each of my shoulders.

"So glad that you could wake up and enjoy the festivities," he slurred with a grin. "Unfortunately, there are no women so I have been reduced to mere drinking."

I looked around. "Where have all your fellow drinkers gone?" I laughed.

"Well, being as most of them are rather serious gentlemen they have retired," he answered as we started walking towards the doorway. "Teague is apparently my only fellow troublemaker and unfortunately he has been stolen away by the King."

We walked out into the clear night and I was relieved to have a breath of fresh air.

"I have heard tell that they are close," I replied quietly.

"Yes," Leonard shook his head wistfully, "So it is a rather grand thing that you and I have become such dear friends." He was talking rather loudly and I smiled as I looked at him. "We're going to be like brothers, you and I. Isn't it wonderful?"

"I suppose it is," I agreed.

We stood in silence for a few minutes listening to the din of the crowd and staring at the multitude of stars. My breath created clouds that seeped silently from my lips. I had slept in my armor for fear that it would be stolen, and the metal against my skin had grown cold.

Suddenly Leonard turned to face me with a grin. "Do you wanna go stir up some trouble?"

"And how would we do that?" I asked warily. I had never had the chance to be a prankster, and the idea had never much appealed to me.

"Oh there are thousands of ways," he began. "We could

temporarily relocate some horses, or undo a couple of the tent ties. My personal favorite would be to replace all of the whiskey with muddy water but I think we would need a few more people for an undertaking as large as that."

I looked at him skeptically. "Doesn't that seem cruel?"

He let out a great laugh. "You are not like other boys," he clapped me on the back and the metal rung loudly. "Come on and let's live a little."

The gleam in his eyes wasn't malicious, merely amused, so I finally nodded.

"That's the spirit lad!" he smiled as he took off running through the night.

\*\*\*\*\*\*\*\*\*

The next morning I woke up stiff but with a smile on my face. My chest was aching but I knew there would be no time to take the linen off till we got back to Calentto, whether I made it or not. I sat up and looked beside me. Leonard was laying there and I noticed that he looked even younger in his sleep than he had in our escapades the night before. The lines that were etched all over his rugged face disappeared. I was smiling at him when suddenly his eyes flew open. His mouth flew open just as swiftly, and he vomited a chunky green liquid all over my sack.

Any good thoughts I had about him vanished. I had to plug my nose because of the awful stench, or else I would have lost the contents of my stomach as well. I had seen my Father drunk before, though, and I knew what to do. I carefully approached the ill man and wiped his mouth with his cloak. Then I ripped off a piece of my tunic. I wetted it down with water from my flask and placed it on his forehead, which was slightly warm.

When Leonard fell asleep again, I tried to clean up the vomit with my cape and some water. The result was a mess. I put my bread and water in my pocket and headed down to the river bank.

When I got there, I dipped my cloak and sack in the water. The quickly moving river washed away the vomit but not the smell of whiskey. I looked down into the water and saw my dirty reflection. My hair was greasy and tangled while my face was dirty and scratched. If I was at home I would have taken a nice hot bath, even though it was a luxury, and washed away the memory of everything that had happened. I wished that I could be clean and free. For a moment I thought that it had been a bad idea to come. I thought that I was not cut out to live the life that I had head-strongly walked in to. I only hoped that I would be 'man' enough to finish what I had started.

By the time I was done, the sun was up.

As I walked back to the tent I heard a man yelling at another man. "I told you I did not steal your horse! I woke up this morning and this horse had replaced mine! I still have no idea where my horse is."

"Of course because horses just magically disappear all the time,' the other man grumbled.

I couldn't help but smile.

I walked back to the tent and saw that most everyone was up and getting ready. I walked over to Leonard and gently shook him.

He grunted and swatted at me. "Leonard, it's time to get up," I said loudly. He opened his eyes.

"No, I do not know the King personally!" he said before letting out a snort and rolling over. Most of the men were leaving. I shook him again but he still didn't wake up. I had to decide if I should leave him and get there on time or wake him up and be late. I tried to shake him again, to no avail.

I had no choice, I punched him firmly in the mouth.

Leonard sat up quickly with a hand to his lip. I shook my hand with tears in my eyes. I think it hurt my fist more than it hurt his lip.

"What in Hell?" Then he let out a long stream of obscenities that I will not repeat. Slowly he started to calm down and his eyes looked like they were getting heavy.

"Leonard," I pinched his cheek, "It's time to get up." I looked around; we were the last people in the large tent. He looked dazed but managed to stand with my help. He was a lot heavier than he looked.

I practically dragged him to the main ring. When we walked in, found an empty spot, and I finally got Leonard sitting up by himself, I pulled out my sword and started to polish it. Father would be angry if he ever learned that I wasn't taking care of his sword properly. I had to try and be more responsible. Leonard sat propped up against me as I watched the fighting take place. I quivered with excitement and fear. This was going to be by far the hardest fight that I had yet done.

"Nobody else would have done what you just did. It was a very noble thing to do," the deep voice from last night returned. I turned to look behind me.

With his golden hair framed against the sun, Teague looked like an angel.

"It was the right thing to do," I said before going back to my sword. I was glad that he was so bold. I really wanted to get a chance to talk to the handsome man, but I didn't know how to start the conversation. Now I just had to think of something else to say. I had to remember that I wasn't a girl and I couldn't act like a lovesick little child. I was only allowed to show an interest in our friendship, not in him as one of the most handsome men I had ever seen.

"You would think that knights would always do the right thing, but they don't," Teague settled down next to me. Even sitting down, he was an imposing figure.

"When I am one of the fifty, I will always do what is right," I said boldly. Freeing my Father was what was right, I was sure of it. Knights might do the wrong things, but I was sure that at least one king had done something hideously wrong.

"Things aren't always black and white, but you have spunk. I think that you'll make it." Then we both fell silent for a moment.

"Why are you here Teague?" I whispered, finally working up my courage. I didn't look at him but pretended that I was more interested in the fight than anything else.

He glanced over at me. "Probably the same reason as you, Noble. I want to go down in history as someone who did something good. Is that why you are here?"

I bit my lip and then nodded. "Yeah, I want to be remembered," I lied, but I didn't sound convincing. I could sense him looking intently at me, but didn't flick my eyes up to meet his.

If it was obvious to a complete stranger that I was lying, I wondered how bad at it I really was. I hated lying and I knew it was going to eat me up, but I it was what I had to do.

I was called before Leonard. I was glad that I had not been called out to fight any of the men that I had met the night before. I knew without a doubt that I would have lost. There was barely any hope that I would win as it was.

I stepped out into the arena with my sword drawn. Across from me another man stepped out. He was a youth roughly my same age, but he looked twice as confident as I must have. I shuddered.

Suddenly there was a hand on my shoulder and Teague whispered in my ear, "I watched him yesterday. Make sure that you watch out for his high blows, they're strong, but his left side is weak. You can win if you get him there." I felt his warmth disappear from behind me and I took a deep breath. A horn blew, beckoning for us to start.

We made our way towards each other, low to the ground, not knowing what to expect. When we were close enough so that I could see the color of his eyes, the youth lunged. He swung at me low first, feeling me out. I deftly avoided his blade and swung at his right, knowing that it would do little good. He let me come close, but I could see from the glimmer in his eyes that he was only playing. We circled each other, continuing the charade, not knowing who was going to give way first.

There were shouts from the crowd to hurry. My eyes drifted up to where Teague was sitting. For a moment our eyes locked before his eyes opened wide. "Noble, watch out!" He bellowed.

My eyes darted back to my opponent just in time. His blade was so close that the tip of my blade barely caught his before it hit my throat. This boy was not going to be content with a tap on my armor. He was in for blood, probably thinking that it would somehow prove his manliness.

I held him there for a moment before we both pulled our blades away. I swung at his right side repeatedly, and every time he blocked it. He fell into a rhythm of blocking my hits and then pushing forward again.

Suddenly, I lunged at his left side while his sword was already going to defend his right. I caught him on the underside of his arm. I could feel a few layers of flesh tear. There was a general roar of approval from the crowd. They hadn't expected me to win. I hadn't expected it either, but I wasn't going to question it.

A grin plastered across my face as I walked back to sit down next to Leonard while the defeated man left the stadium kicking angrily at the dirt. Teague and Leonard clapped me on the back. For the rest of the day that silly grin stayed painted across my face, and I felt as if I could not sit still. Leonard fought, and thankfully he was sober enough by that time to win relatively easily. He probably could have even beaten the man even had he been intoxicated.

At the end we had to line up to give our names. Every knight's name would be carved into the legendary Round Table. I saw that all of the men I had met the night before were part of the fifty. I was glad that I recognized faces and was not completely unknown among the people who were going to be my companions for the near future.

Leonard had finally escaped fully from the trap of the whiskey he had consumed and was proud to give his own name. I smiled as he did. I felt pleased for him.

"Sir Andrew Banidere," I said proudly and felt like screaming at the top of my lungs for joy. I couldn't believe that I had made it! I had conquered over almost impossible odds. My Father would soon be freed and I would live happily knowing that I had helped him. It seemed that all life was good. I even drank with the men. I had never had whiskey before and it felt like swallowing fire, but oddly enough, I liked it. I drank as much as Leonard, which is more liquor than should ever be consumed. In the early morning, before the sun came up I finally fell into my sleeping space, exhausted, drunk, and ecstatically happy.

**********

I woke up sicker than I had ever felt before. But even that couldn't stop my excitement at being able to return to the castle above Callento with the chance of saving my father. I rode on an extra horse beside Leonard, who was sicker than yesterday. It was a lot faster on horseback, and we reached the castle in prompt time. Entering the courtyard of the great castle, which I had only seen from a distance, I couldn't help but stare in amazement.

While the castle looked massive from far away, it was even more impressive up close. The grey stone towered above us as solid as the mountain from which it had been stolen. Statues of martyrs and kings littered the courtyard effortlessly. No one else seemed taken aback by the grandiosity as we paraded through archways carved with dragons, on carpets woven to look like a meadow forest.

Aidan led us all up to the second floor which held the conference room. We were all shocked to see that the table was already inside. The table was massive and made of a light wood that seemed to suck up all the light pouring from large windows situated all over the room.

"Everyone find your place," Aidan echoed. I walked the entire circumference of the room, not finding my name etched into the wood. Everyone else had already sat down when I saw an empty chair on the other side of the table. I blushed and everyone laughed at my embarrassment. Nothing like a little humiliation to encourage friendship, I thought to myself.

I walked over and saw my name on the table beside Leonard's. To my right sat Teague. I felt privileged to be sitting between two such strong and well-known men. Despite myself, I couldn't help but notice that I was only four seats to the right of the king himself.

"My brothers in arms, I hope that you find the castle of Calentto to your liking. If you need anything at all just call for a servant and they will help you. I know that you will all enjoy it here." He paused with a smile and I noticed that he had a small dimple in the left corner of his mouth. He gave a small chuckle. "I have many fond memories of growing up here with most of you." A majority of the men chuckled. I looked over at Leonard who was smiling also. His smile was infectious and I couldn't help but grin.

Then Aidan became more somber. "Unfortunately, the time here will be short for some of you. A quest has already arisen for a few of my untried knights. There is news of feuding villagers near our southern coast. This needs to be stopped, immediately. During my reign, Bryton will be a land united, not divided as it was during the time of my father. I won't stand to see provinces and townships turning against each other when they could be learning from each other and trading goods. I think we will need at least four knights to go see if they can talk some sense into the villagers. Now, I know that this is not at the best time and you are all tired but I need someone to volunteer to take on this opportunity."

The room was silent for a few minutes. I wanted to raise my hand just because no one else was, but I did not want to be the first. Then a booming voice called out, "I, Gladwin, volunteer myself and my three friends." Of course everyone knew who his three friends were; the people that he considered his brothers. I turned to look at the man. I knew enough about the court to know that he was brave to volunteer. Watching villagers was very demeaning and would lower the four brothers in many people's eyes. In my mind I thought it was a very honorable thing for the man to do. I would have liked to have gone with them.

"Then you will all leave for Lipton tomorrow morning. I think it would be best for the rest of you to stay in Calentto and train, get to know each other. There is word of the Scarcillans building a large army. I do not know if this is true or not but it's always good to be prepared and in order to fight together, you need to at least know each other's names. You all have free range of the castle. Go wherever you wish. The only doors in the castle that are locked are those to the armory, which holds all of the castles' weapons, and the dungeon where our minimal amounts of prisoners are kept. You will find a single key to both of those on your bed. You are the only men, besides myself, to have keys to these places and I expect you all to be trustworthy and chivalrous as your new position demands." He smiled. "Now, I know that you are all ready to begin your training so I'll let you go, but I want you to remember one thing." His gaze wandered evenly around the table, making sure that none felt neglected. As his eyes swept past me, I looked down at my name, carved forever into the table in front of me. "You will all go down in history and I want you to act like it. You should all make your every moment count for something. From this day forth you are King Aidan's famous knights, the knights of the Round Table." With that, Aidan stood up. As was custom everyone else stood as he did. Then he walked out the door with a small nod . Slowly, everyone started talking as they made their way out the door.

"Do you think that the Scarcillas will really invade? They have been under suspicion for as long as I can remember," Leonard asked curiously. I stood, running my hand over my name engraved in the table. It felt as if magic flowed through the carved wood. Somehow, as I was touching my name engraved in the wood, I had the sense that my name would also be engraved in history, as the king had just said.

I sighed as I realized how ridiculous the whole thought was. Even though my Father was innocent, I would soon be a traitor when I freed him. Any attachment to this new found opulence and inspiration was almost laughable.

"Noble?" I was pulled out of my trance by Leonard. He was staring at me. "Are you alright?"

"Yes, um, I'm going to go find my room," I said hastily and walked quickly out. I needed some alone time. From a young boy I found out that my room was on the second floor, not far from the conference room. When I got inside I summoned a servant, something I had never done before, and asked him to draw me a bath. When the hot water was waiting I locked all the doors and stripped down. When I looked down at the linen, I couldn't help but gasp. The cloth held spots of blood that had soaked nearly all the way through. Even though it hurt to unwrap it, I undid the linen slowly. When I was done I saw large bloody places where the linen had rubbed my chest raw. When I was fully submerged into the water, the sores stung but it felt so good to be clean that I didn't care much. Normally, I only got a bath once or twice a year, but usually I wasn't as dirty as I had become in the last few days. I scrubbed till I sparkled and when I was done I was sad to put the newly cleaned linen back on. It hurt worse than it did the first time but somehow I muddled through. Fighting had been hard on the first day but I had felt it even more the next day when I was just sitting. It hadn't helped either that on the day after I had a hangover from all my drinking.

Thoroughly exhausted, I laid down. I knew that tomorrow I had to free my Father. It was better for Aidan to suspect everyone, because he knew none, than to suspect few. I was full of worry, and my sleep was troubled.

**********

I awoke to a loud knock on my door. "Training will begin in the courtyard in half an hour Sir," someone called. I sat up slowly and pulled on my clothes and my breastplate, still groggy from my heavy slumber. Walking out into the hallway unsteadily, I saw Bran also staggering out of his room across the hall.

"Well Lad, is this what you expected the life of a knight to be like?" Bran's voice was heavy with sleep. His eyes were almost completely matted shut.

"I don't know. I guess that I'm still not thinking of myself as a knight." To tell the truth I was intimidated by this man. I had learned that he was Aidan's cousin, and said to be a great and fierce warrior. This was a man that people feared. This was a man that women dreaded their husbands fighting, because they wouldn't come home.

"You fought better than 350 men. You have as much a right as any man here to call yourself a knight. Don't be afraid to take credit when credits due," he clapped me on the shoulder and I flinched. When I turned to look at him I blushed.

"It is true that you are a strange lad, Noble!" I wondered how the nickname had spread so fast. By that time we were in the courtyard where very few were waiting. Bran wandered off towards Teague and they started dueling. I watched them. I felt so inadequate against these skilled men. They sparred with a certain grace and elegance that came from years of practice.

"Care to duel?" a voice from behind me asked. I turned to see a man with long black hair, a narrow pale face and dark sparkling eyes. Somehow I felt like I had seen this man before. In the dark recesses of my mind, I *knew* that I had seen him before, I just did not know where. He didn't appear to be much older than I was.

"I am Sir Andrew Banidere. Do you have a name?" I answered, trying not to sound rattled. The man gave a smile with teeth that were as white as his skin.

"I am Sir Morgan." I had heard of him of course. Everyone in Bryton had. He was Aidan's nephew. On the day of his birth Merick, Aidan's mentor who had died years ago, had made a prophecy that Morgan would steal the crown from Aidan. Most people thought that it was just an old wives tale. I agreed with them, until I saw him. While there was nothing outwardly alarming about him, his stare was enough to chill to the bone. His eyes were almost black and I felt as if they were stealing the warmth from my skin. Children probably had nightmares after they saw this man.

"First hit," I whispered. This man had the same training with a sword as Aidan. Morgan nodded and then lunged. I moved and it felt as if I was fighting Tremet all over again. I lunged at his shoulder but unlike Tremet, he ducked below my blade and lunged at my knees. I felt the warmth of blood and my legs buckled. Morgan stood over me and said in low tones, so that nobody could hear, "Watch your back Banidere."

With that he walked away and I struggled to stand up. Anger welled up inside me, as well as wounded pride for being beaten so easily. I was still holding my sword and used it as a crutch to pry myself up and get to the nearest bench, flinching at the sound of the metal scraping across the stones.

I sat down and rolled up my loose breeches. The cut on my knee was not deep but it was bleeding heavily. I sighed and let out a mild curse, I was already learning from the men.

"Do you need help cleaning that?" I looked to my right. There was a short man with balding hair and a pockmarked face. "I am Sir Kade, one of the knights."

"I am Sir Banidere and yes, I would appreciate your help," I answered and turned away from the crimson sight. In truth, I hate the sight of my own blood. I don't mind animal blood or others' small wounds, but my own blood made me queasy. The ugly man pulled out a small bottle and poured some of its contents onto my leg. I bit my lip as the sting washed away the blood.

"It's whiskey. It helps to clean the wound," the man said in explanation as he pulled a small piece of linen out of a pocket in his shirt.

"Do you normally carry bandages and whiskey around?" I asked, trying not to wince as he pulled the bandage taunt and tied it. The pain was intense, but I was determined to put on a brave face. It was just a scratch compared to most of the wounds these men must have already suffered.

"Well, I am unofficially the knight's doctor. As far as fighting in the battles I am sufficient but not a genius like most here." The man certainly sounded scholarly and friendly. I looked down and saw that, though ugly, his face was open and warm. I decided that I liked this man and wanted him as a friend.

"I'm sure that your part is as vital as that of the brilliant swordsman," I said sincerely.

"Thank you Noble." And with that the odd man was off. I stared after him for a few minutes before pulling my pants back down and standing up. Now that the cut was bandaged it did not hurt badly at all.

"Will you fight me?" I turned around to see yet another strange face. This man was of medium height with brown hair and hazel eyes. His large mustache made him look comical and yet mature. While he stood there he stroked it as though he was very proud of it. There was no other word to adequately describe him besides jolly.

"First hit," I replied. I lunged first to meet his blade but he held me strong. I pulled my sword out and backed up. The knight lunged at my left but I took a small step right and missed his blade. I deftly swung and missed his side but managed to hit his hand. His blade fell to the ground and he did not move to pick it up. First blood had been drawn and I had won the duel. My blood was racing with the victory, however small it might have been.

"Well done, Lad! I am Sir Patrick and I am awed to find a youth that is so adept with a sword. You have natural talent!" Patrick bent to pick up his sword and smiled at me again. I noticed that he had a charming gap between his front two teeth. He looked just like a little kid with a pasted on mustache.

"Thank you," I replied and looked down at my feet, pleased.

"It's the truth lad!" The man gave me a pat on the back and then walked on to the next match. It amazed me how so many different types of men could all be on the same side. It called to mind Aiden's words about a country united.

For as long as I could remember there had been strife throughout Bryton. It had never been enough to divide the country, but it had certainly been enough to divide families. Even King Umber's own beloved daughter had turned from him. She was rumored to have been a pagan, and to have raised her son, Morgan, in the pagan beliefs. Though King Umber claimed to be a Christian, there was little evidence to support such statements. He had believed in nothing more than taking what he wanted and stifling what he didn't. His attention was often swayed though, whether by impending invasion or a new mistress, and he had been ineffective enough to do little harm. However, deep rifts had formed between those who were in his favor, and those who weren't.

If my father was evidence of anything, it was that Aiden was shaping up to be much like his late father.

I looked around and saw that everyone was preoccupied and that no one was looking at me. Seeing that my time had come to put my plan in motion, I moved silently back into the castle. Walking around as inconspicuously as possible, I finally saw a flight of stairs heading down to what I assumed must be the dungeon. I followed the stairs till they reached the bottom where there was a large wooden door with a lock. I met no one along the way and I started to realize how easy it was going to be to free my Father. I pulled the key that Aidan had supplied each of us with out of a pocket in my pants and stuck it into the lock. It turned easily and I pushed it open slowly before sticking my head in.

I looked around but saw no guards. I knew from gossip that Aidan rarely executed or even held prisoners. Most cells were empty. There were a few men sleeping on the floor in cells but when I got close I saw that none of them were Father. They would all look up at me and then turn quickly away in shame. I was saddened by the conditions that these men were living in. There was barely any straw on the floor and the smell was horrible. I heard rats squeaking and I prayed that they were only occupying the empty cells.

Rage welled up in me at the King. What sort of man could smile and clap men on the back, while still doing this to his subjects? This was inhumane and I am sure that the prisoners would have rather chosen death than to live in this hole for the rest of their lives.

When I got to the last cell I was shocked to see a man who was only a ghost of my Father. I nearly walked right past him. After almost three weeks in prison he was gaunt and his complexion was gray. He was sleeping near the back of the smallest cell in the dungeon and I could see the rats crawling over the thin form of his legs. I gasped and struggled to hold back tears. This was even worse than I had imagined. I knew then that even if I died for freeing my Father it would be worth it. It would be worth it to know that he was out of this terrible place.

Oh how I yearned to go to him, to comfort him as he had comforted me so many times over the years, but I kept my emotions in check and walked past without another glance at him. That night I would free my Father.

**********

I ran back out into the sunshine where everything was just as I had left it. I looked around and saw that no one appeared to even have noticed that I was gone. Suddenly I felt a hand on my shoulder and spun around to face Teague, who was grinning.

"Want to fight?"

I shivered, relieved that's all it was. "Of course." We both got into position. "First hit," I mumbled nervously and lunged at the sturdy man. Teague was said to be almost as good as Aidan himself. I had already fought one man with that claim to fame and I had lost badly. It had felt nice to win and I really didn't feel like losing again.

My first swing was wide and Teague ducked underneath the harmless blade. While he was down, he took a stab at my leg and I just barely managed to get out of the way before he slit open my newly acquired bandage. As he was pouncing back up, I swung at his shoulder and missed. He turned and struck my back lightly with the tip of his blade. I felt the sword rip through a layer of skin but I doubted that I would have to bandage it. I stumbled though and fell heavily to my knees.

I saw Teague extend his hand and grabbed it to pull myself up. "You have natural talent but you need to develop your technical skills quite a bit. Mainly you just need to always be sure that when you lunge you still keep up your own personal defense." The man smiled knowingly and I blushed.

"You really are as good of a fighter as everyone says," I smiled shyly.

Teague just kept grinning in a way that I was growing accustomed to. "Someday they will talk about you too, Noble." With that he walked over to Leonard and they started to duel.

I stood alone in the middle of the courtyard, feeling awkward and alone. Yes, people would talk of me, but would what they were saying be good?

The rest of the day went on monotonously; I kept fighting until I must have fought at least half of the men, and forgotten most of their names. The only break we had all day had been a short one for a simple lunch. The hot autumn sun was burning a hole in my skull and my face was turning pink. That night I fell into bed exhausted, but I knew that I could not fall asleep. I had to stay awake so that I could do what I had come to do in the first place. I had to remember that I was here for my Father and not for the glory that I had not even known that I craved.

I hid in my room until the safe cover of silent darkness fell. When I finally stopped hearing noises out in the hall, I stood up and walked over to the door. I stuck my head out into the hall and looked around. It didn't appear that anybody was still awake and out in the castle. I quickly ducked back inside and grabbed the key that Aidan had given us to the dungeon. Taking a deep breath, I stepped out into the hall. I walked quickly and silently along until I came to the stairs. Jogging down the stairs I didn't bother to grab a torch, the dungeon was so simple that I could not get lost in it. I silently unlocked the door and walked inside cautiously. As with this morning, there were no guards. I grabbed the keys which I had noticed were hanging on the wall and ran to my Fathers cell. There were around 20 keys on the ring and I took one and stabbed it into lock. My mind was numb, devoid of all logic. I was so close to doing what I had come to do.

"What are you doing?" My Father's voice was raspy as he came to the bars stiffly. His leg appeared as if it was injured. I cringed at how terrible he looked.

"I am freeing you from this terrible captivity, good Sir." My voice cracked with sadness. This might be the last time I would see him. If anyone ever found out that I had freed him I would either die, or have to live a life of hiding. I would be considered a traitor.

"But why would you free me? You are a knight and I committed treason!" He was looking hard at me as I accidentally dropped the keys. They made a heavy noise on the packed dirt floor.

"They accused you of treason. I know that you are innocent." I stammered as I bent down to pick up the ring. Tears welled in my eyes. Had they tortured him so much that his thoughts were addled? I wanted to kill Aidan for what he had done to my poor father!

"Believe what you will," Father said softly. We sat in awkward silence as I continued fiddling with the lock. I finally found the right key after trying about half the ring. The lock popped open and I let it fall to the floor with a clang. I looked around nervously, but heard no sound. None of the other prisoners had awakened. Father pushed the door open as I stood back. I saw a large blood stain on his loose pants just below his knee.

"Thank you my dear Lad," Father said as he patted me on the back and then silently crept away. I stared after him, but he was moving swiftly and soon he was lost in the shadows.

     I should have felt happy. My poor father was free from his unfair and untimely death. Instead I felt empty, what was I to do now? I couldn't just leave the knighthood, and besides I felt sort of at home with these men.

     I had never really had any friends besides my father, but the men that I had met had been nothing but friendly to me. I had never had the freedom to make my own decisions, and to associate with who I chose. These men might not have been the most intelligent or well-mannered, but they might have been the only people in the world who had accepted me for who I was, not what I was. These people had not even asked where I was from! I could have been a criminal and they would have still called me their friend. Surprisingly, I realized that I already thought of them as my friends even though I had only known them for such a short time.

     I ran up the stairs and numbly locked the door before making my way to my room, not caring if anyone saw me. When I got inside I locked the door and threw myself on my bed. All of a sudden tears were streaming down my face and my body was wracked with sobs. For a moment I lost myself, not even recognizing why I was crying. But then the truth hit me. My beloved Father had not even recognized me.

# CHAPTER TWO
## The Brotherhood

We were all called to the Round Table the next morning for a meeting. Slowly all of us knights made our way to the large room and took our seats. Everyone was whispering about the reason for our gathering. Only I knew why we were actually there. When we were all sitting down, Aidan cleared his throat. All eyes turned to him and everyone stopped talking. He was surprisingly and subtly regal. But down in the dungeon I had seen a completely different side of him. I had seen how much he truly loved his citizens.

"It has been brought to my attention that two important things happened yesterday. I am a fair man and I feel that if something affects one of the Brotherhood, it affects everyone. We are banded together and if one of you does something wrong, they must amend it within themselves, before God and their brothers. Having said that will Sir Banidere and Sir Morgan please stand up?" His voice was tense and you could see in his body language that he was angry. I shivered and did my best not to cry even though tears were welling up in my eyes.

I stood up slowly and felt all eyes on me. Feeling as if I might faint, I found that I could barely breathe. Did they know? They must have found out. I didn't want to be arrested for treason and hanged. I placed my hand on my name carved into the table. I don't know why but the hills and valleys of my name calmed me slightly, though my heart was still racing. Somehow I felt as if it would always be there.

"Morgan has informed me that you verbally attacked him at training yesterday, Banidere. We will not tolerate that kind of behavior here. What have you to say for yourself?" Aidan and everyone else were staring at me. For a moment his words did not register. My eyebrows scrunched together in genuine confusion while I let out a sigh of relief.

"I did not attack Morgan in any way. He challenged me to a duel. I told him 'First hit'. We fought, he won, and he left. That is what happened Sir," I was stammering and started to sweat. My adrenaline hadn't kicked in yet. Aidan stared at me and I looked away. The blue of his eyes was just too much to handle. I might break down. I was innocent of the charge he had just accused me of, but not of others.

"Morgan, is this true?"

Morgan stared at me and I shivered. "Would you trust a youth you hardly know over your nephew?" He was glaring daggers at me. If I would have caught his eyes I would have fallen to the floor, but I cast my eyes downward. Why did this man hate me so much? Why had he done such a stupid thing in lying to Aidan about the duel? What good could have possibly come from that?

"I am only trying to be fair Morgan." Aidan sounded resolved and weary. "I do not know which of you to believe, but from now on there will be no more rudeness exhibited from any of you at any time. Now, on to the second piece of business."

I sat down; this had to be about my Father.

"Last night a prisoner escaped from the castle dungeon. Sir Grosipan, a man known to have committed treason against me, was obviously helped by inside forces. The keys to his cell were found on the floor along with the lock. I'm sorry I have to suspect you all, but it is the only logical explanation, as you are the only people with the key to the dungeon and the lock into the area was not forced. I am afraid that I am going to have to confiscate the keys that were handed out." There was a general murmur of displeasure as people pulled their keys out of their pockets. I pulled mine out also. I had no need for it any longer. "I don't want to know who it was. Instead I want an oath. An oath that will ensure you will no longer fight among yourselves but vow to protect yourself and the whole of Bryton. Swear that you will do what is best for this country. Swear that you will be loyal to Bryton and its ruler in everything that you do. Raise your hand and swear!" He raised his right hand. I was glad that I was sitting because I felt my knees go weak. I was not going to be killed! He did not know that it was me. I had succeeded.

Bran was the first to raise his hand. "I swear."

Leonard raised his right hand. "I swear it."

I didn't want to swear my allegiance to this man, but there was no other way. My hand shot up. "I swear!" My voice was strong and assertive. This went on until all the knights had sworn. Sir Morgan was the last to swear and he said it almost unwillingly. There was obvious resentment in his gaze. How could the King trust this man, even if he was his nephew?

"Now that we have that out of the way you are free to go about your business." Aidan started tapping his fingers. looking ill at ease.

Leonard was the first to stand. "Come, let's work on our swordsmanship. Morgan, I challenge you to a duel." He looked over at me with a smile and a wink. I smiled back. It was good to have such a strong ally in Leonard.

"First hit," Morgan sneered.

As everyone stood up and meandered out of the room I glanced back once more at Aidan.

He sat with his head in his hands.

\*\*\*\*\*\*\*\*\*

Over the next couple of weeks all of us became very close. I soon distinguished Leonard, Teague and Sir Kade to be my closest friends though. They were always there for me when I needed them. They treated me as brothers would and they gave me reason to forget my depression concerning my Father.

During that time I became much more practiced in my swordsmanship. It seemed that I had natural talent, and through working with all of the best swordsmen in the nation the skills that I desperately needed began to seem like second nature to me. Eventually, the only men that I could not beat were Leonard, Teague, Bran, Morgan and Gladwin, who had returned unharmed with his three friends. All of these men were legendary though, and my pride was not wounded whenever I took the first hit in a duel against them.

Out of all the men I was the youngest and everyone liked to tease me. It seemed that my official name was now Noble and I was the mother hen of the group, despite the fact that I was by far the youngest. I still drank with the men and gambled with the exceedingly generous pay Aidan supplied, but they all knew that I was the voice of reason. I never let things get too far. The men trusted me to keep them in line. I had found my role amidst the clan.

Despite my steadfast nature, Leonard always tried to corrupt me. Every once in a while he would succeed in luring me out on some wild escapade. No one could make me laugh like him.

One day I was sitting off by myself in the courtyard when Aidan walked up to me. He often came down to watch the training and would sometimes even participate. He had to keep himself in practiced as well as the rest of us.

"Noble, you are a bit different than the rest aren't you?" He smiled and sat down beside me. I was still unsure of my feelings for Aidan. Tried as I may, I could not bring myself to hate him. Since I had arrived, I had seen him be nothing but kind and fair. And yet . . . I had seen the proof that there was a part of the father in the son. He was really the only man, beside Morgan, who I felt uncomfortable around. The rest I all felt at ease with by now. "You keep to yourself."

"I'm always with the men," I argued. "We've all become good friends."

"But even when you're with them you always look somehow alone," he tried to explain. "It's like you can't ever be fully present and engaged."

My eyes darted up briefly to meet his. Somehow he had explained it perfectly.

"Being alone lets you figure out who you really are. It clears the noise in your head." I said, watching Teague and Leonard fight. They were both so good that the matches ended up lasting for a long time. It was never certain who would win. Lots of bets were placed on the duels between the two. I never gambled on them. It would have been too hard to choose between two of my best friends. I would have felt like I was betraying one of them.

"It also keeps you isolated and distant," Aidan fidgeted with his sword. He sounded slightly troubled, as if he knew what he was talking about. He was a King though, he had friends from all over the world. It was hard to imagine that he could be lonely.

"I would not call finding out who you are and keeping your heart safe being 'isolated and distant.' I would call it being smart," I replied absentmindedly. I was unwilling to connect with this man more than was neccessaey.

Leonard had Teague pinned against a wall but Teague pulled out and lunged.

"You must ask whether the joy is worth the risk though. You have become attached to these men; will they in the end betray you? Do you have to keep your heart safe from them? In the end I suppose it comes down to either fear or trust," He looked at me and I risked a glanced at him before turning away. I knew that I could not answer. "Will you duel me?" I was not expecting this question and turned to look at him. He already had his sword out.

"First hit," I said slowly and unsurely. I had never fought the King before and I did not know if I should let him win or not, or if I even had a chance to win. I stood up and pulled out my blade. Aidan stood up and almost immediately I lunged. He blocked and bore down on me. I swung to the right and almost slashed the King's side. But he pulled back and gave a light swing at my right side; I blocked and moved forward so that we were nose to nose. He smelled intoxicating and I quickly pulled back so that not even our swords were touching. Aidan lunged and I ducked. The blade whizzed over my head. I stabbed at Aidan's knees but he blocked. I stood up and turned a complete circle, bringing my sword down on Aidan with all my strength. The move left me defenseless though and Aidan moved right and poked my side behind my breastplate lightly with Elamoneir, the sword that had been passed down from Penhalion to Penhalion for ages.

The jab hurt and I clutched my side. "Did I injure you?" Aidan asked genuinely. He looked concerned. I looked up and saw that most of the knights had gathered to watch the King and I fight. I was sorry that I had been so disappointing.

I straightened up. "No, it's fine. I was just shocked," I was trying to keep my voice steady. My side was hurting way more than it should have from just a simple cut. My whole side was throbbing and the warm blood was making me feel queasy. "Um, suddenly I don't feel so well, I think I'm going to go lay down," I practically ran up to my room without even looking back at the men. I locked the door and pulled off my shirt. The cut wasn't deep at all; it was more of a scratch then anything.

Suddenly I realized why my side hurt. I suddenly noticed that there was wetness between my legs and I knew I had my monthlies. How stupid was I? The ache in my side was cramps. The pain was always worse when I was more physically active than usual, and I had gotten more exercise in the past few weeks than ever before in my life. I ripped some linen off my bed and took care of my needs. When I had finished, I sat on the bed with my head in my hands. How was I going to deal with this? I needed to be out there fighting, not lying in here having female problems!

When I was done I heard a knock on the door. "Noble, are you in there?" It was Leonard's voice. He sounded as if he was worried.

I ran to the door and threw it open. "Yes, I tended the cut and am ready to go back down," I said running out the door. I stopped and looked back at him. I wanted him to believe that everything was alright. "It's just that blood sometimes makes me queasy and it was just the heat and . . . everything. I'm fine now."

Leonard eyed me suspiciously, and then finally patted me on the back with a smile. "I just wanted to check on my brother," he finally grinned. I smiled. It was at that moment that I realized just how much I loved that man and that I had no fear left towards him.

*********

Two days later we were all called to the Round Table again for some other unknown reason. I sat at my place beside Leonard drumming my thumb impatiently. I had been up all night practicing a complicated move in my room and I was ready to try it out.

We all sat in uncomfortable silence until Aidan walked in. I had not seen him since our duel and he had changed drastically in that short time. Something was wrong with the pallor of his skin, and it looked like he hadn't slept the nights before. The King sat down with a loud thump and everyone could feel the tension in the air. My finger stopped its tapping and everyone else stopped all of their movement also.

"It has reached my attention that the settlements made in Lipton have not been kept. There is another uprising. This time there are over 200 men prepared to fight their way here. I have decided that we will go to the rebels instead of having them come to us. We must show that we are stronger than their treason. I have to do this because they would have destroyed villages and recruited men along the way. Gladwin, what did the men seem like to you?" Aidan's voice was raspy and strained; he had bags under his eyes and the lines in his face were more pronounced.

"Your Highness, the traitors seemed eager and untrained. In my opinion that is a bad combination, but if we strike hard and fast we will win the battle without much damage." Gladwin had stood up to talk and now sat back down. The big man did not sound afraid, just a little worried. I trusted his opinion and if he said that we would be alright, I had no choice but to believe him.

"Do you all agree with my decision? We will have to leave in the morning. Does anyone have any better ideas?" I could see that Aidan genuinely cared about our opinions. There was a general murmur of agreement. "Good, be ready by dawn tomorrow then." We all stood up.

"Is battle frightening?" I asked Leonard in a whisper as we walked out, leaving Aidan with his head in his hands once more.

"You've never been in battle before?" Leonard looked surprised. "I have been fighting battles for Fraunc since I was 13!" He shook his head in astonishment. Then his face grew serious. "I suppose I could say that your first battle is worse than your most terrifying nightmare, but I have a great deal of faith in you, lad, and I know that you will be brave. Since this is a small battle I assume that you will kill a few men and then run off to vomit. Do not be bothered by it, even I sometimes get sick nowadays. It is a terrible thing taking another human's life. I wish I could say that you get used to it but, knowing you, it could take a while." He then grew silent and appeared to be lost in his thoughts. Leonard had been fighting for over half of his life already, so he had seen his share of blood. I hoped that I never saw as much as he already had. By then we were almost at my quarters. Though I was shocked by Leonard's blunt opinion I was glad to be going in prepared. I knew that everything would have been much worse if I had been caught unaware.

"Thank you for telling me the truth Leonard. I appreciate it," I answered softly as I pulled open my door.

"I just wish I would have had a man to tell me about battle," Leonard said before walking over to join Patrick, who was putting on a brave face even though I could sense his nervousness. I sighed, and then closed and locked my door. I took off my linen because it looked like I would have to be confined for a while. I sighed in pleasure when I slipped into my bath and hoped that everything would go well at Lipton.

\*\*\*\*\*\*\*\*\*\*

We were awakened at dawn to start our march towards Lipton. It was freezing in the early morning and everyone was plump with layers of clothing. It started snowing heavily and I wondered if it would be snowing even in the south.

As I rode along in silence I thought of the last time my father and I had gone sledding. It had been years ago, back when I was still a small child. He had pushed me down the hill and I had fallen off the sled, landing hard on the frozen ground. Father had rushed to my side but I was laughing with abandon. The rush of the air past me as I had flown down the slope, and the hard pressure of the ground beneath me had made me feel more physically alive than ever before. It had been one of the best days of my life.

Suddenly a snowball hit me in the back.

I turned around to see Leonard grinning at me wickedly. I shook my head at him with a smile and turned back around.

Within a few minutes another snowball hit me in the back of the head. I swiftly jumped off my horse, gathered a handful of snow and spun around, throwing it in the direction of my friend. Unfortunately, my aim was hindered by my bulky clothing.

The snowball hit Teague full in the face.

My mouth fell open as Leonard let out a tremendous laugh. Teague slowly wiped the snow from his eyes.

I ran over to stand next to his horse.

"Teague I'm so sorry," I mumbled, my cheeks flushing with embarrassment. "I really didn't mean to. Leonard threw a snowball at me and I was trying to hit him but . . ."

Teague slowly turned to look down at me. For a second my breath caught in my chest. There were crystals caught in his golden hair and they glimmered in the sunlight. His lips were red and swollen and water clung to his eyelashes.

At first his face was angry and I opened my mouth to apologize again. Suddenly, he launched himself off of the horse and tackled me into a snow bank on the side of the road.

"Don't think that you can get away with that," he laughed as he stuffed snow down the back of my tunic.

I yelped and tried my best to wriggle free but I was trapped underneath him. One of my arms broke free and I grabbed a handful of snow and pushed it into his face. For a moment he pulled back and I pushed him off me and tried to stand, but I slipped and fell down on top of him.

I started to laugh and then opened my eyes to see that his face was a mere few inches from mine. He was laughing too, and his green eyes sparkled. His laugh was deep and untroubled. For a instant I just laid there staring at him, before I finally remembered myself and sat up.

I stood up and then grabbed his hand to help him up. I let go as quickly as possible and started to walk back towards my horse.

Then I felt his hands softly touching my shoulders, I jerked away and turned to look at him with a shocked expression.

"You still have snow all over you," he grinned. "Sorry to say it but I think I won that little battle."

I licked my lips and then brushed the hair out of my eyes. His smile slowly faded.

"I think you're right," I finally laughed nervously. I couldn't meet his eyes before turning around and walking away.

It only took us three days to get to the edge of Lipton. By then the snow was about 4 feet high and we were all chilled to the bone. The traveling had not been all that hard, but it made us weary to just march all day. All night we slept together in one big tent trying to keep warm. Every morning I would wake up with ice on my eyes lashes and stiff bones.

On the night we arrived we were sleeping outside of Lipton, which turned out to be a small town on a wide open plain. We were supposed to attack the rebels the next morning. Messengers from both sides had met, and it had been decided upon. Aiden couldn't bring himself to attack his own people without warning. He was a negotiator before a fighter.

I could not sleep because I was filled with fear, edged with a sick anticipation. I wanted to get my first battle over with. If it was out of the way then I would never have to feel this anxiety again. Or at least I hoped that I wouldn't.

All of a sudden there was a loud yell. Since I was awake I jumped up to my feet quickly, hand on my sword hilt.

"ATTACK!" Someone yelled.

The rebels were attacking us! Battle cries sang through the frigid evening air. We all rushed out sleepily to see a wall of two-hundred men running at us. Though all the other knights rushed forward in bravery, I was frozen in fear just outside the tent with them pushing past me. I tried to move but couldn't. The world was tilting crazily in front of me and I could already smell the sickening scent of blood. I had to cover my nose so that I would not retch.

Suddenly a sneering rebel stood in front of me, sword raised. He did not move though and I realized that he was staring down at my chest. I looked down and saw that my shirt had flown open in the bustle of the attack. My linen was slightly twisted and it was obvious to tell what I was. With a gasp I quickly pulled it shut. The man's face changed into something more evil than it had been before, and now I knew that he did not just want to kill me. I pulled out my sword and swung. My mind was still numb from sleep and fear and I did not even place the blow.

Something thumped at my feet. I looked down to see a bloody, severed head staring up at me. Looking over, I saw the man's headless body slump to the ground as well. I screamed in my normal voice but no one heard me through the din of the battle. I felt lightheaded and almost fainted. Instead I shook my head and looked forward, shivering. I wrapped my arms around myself with my sword still in hand. The steel against my arm was bitterly cold. The blood smeared across it was sticky.

I heard a loud yell to my right and turned. Morgan was on the ground, pinned down by his cloak, which had an arrow through it. A rebel was lunging at him. Morgan pulled at the arrow and tried to rip the cloak but it would not budge. He kept deftly rolling around to avoid the angry man's sword. I could see that he could not hold out much longer.

"The oath," I said softly and wearily. Almost mechanically, I gave a battle cry and charged at the rebel. I interrupted his blade just before it hit Morgan's chest. The rebel turned his attention to me, pulling away and then lunging again. I stepped left and then plunged my sword into the villager's stomach. He doubled over as I pulled it out with sickening ease. The man fell to the ground in a pool of blood. I quickly slit his throat so that he would not suffer. I couldn't bear to look at his face.

I turned to Morgan, who was still on the ground. I slashed his cloak free and kicked his sword to him. He glared at me, his stare colder than the midnight air. As quickly as possible, I turned away. There would be no thanks from the King's nephew.

There was fighting going on but most of our men were just wandering around, we had made fast work of these villagers. I saw Leonard and walked over to him unsurely. It was hard to breath and my steps were unsure around all of the dead bodies of the villagers.

"How many men did you kill?" Leonard asked softly when he put a gentle hand on my shoulder.

"Two," I muttered before leaning over and vomiting away from my friend. When I stood up and wiped my mouth I was embarrassed to find that I was crying. The tears streamed down my face and I could almost feel them turning to ice in the early morning air. I looked over and saw that the sun was coming up. I stared at it so that I didn't have to look at Leonard.

"I chopped a man's head off! What if he had family and I ruined their lives too?" I could not keep quiet. It was as if my mind was numb from the cold. Silently I sobbed. How had I ever though that I was cut out to be a killer? Leonard leaned in closer to whisper in my ear.

"Noble, by killing two men you saved countless others," The older man's voice was soothing to me. I wiped my eyes and attempted to calm myself.

"Did you see if any of our men were injured?" I asked between hiccups. I held my chin up.

Leonard smiled. "Bran got a nasty blow to the head from falling over, but he'll be fine. I've heard that nobody else was even scratched." He stopped and stared past me. I turned and saw Aidan. Large circles were under his eyes and there was blood on his sword also.

"Are you all right Noble?" His voice sounded slightly distracted but still concerned. I guess that I looked as bad as I felt.

"I'm fine Your Highness," I said before wiping my nose on my sleeve. I looked down as an after thought and saw that my shirt was still closed. I could not allow myself to be as careless as I had been ever again.

"It was his first battle sir," Leonard said quietly in explanation.

Aidan nodded. "Was battle what you expected?" He was cleaning his bloody blade but was still looking intently at me.

"I don't really know what I expected but that wasn't it." I was shivering from the cold and shock. My thin shirt was doing nothing to ward off the chill now that my heart rate was returning to normal.

"I suppose it never is." He sighed and looked at the newly risen sun. "I came to tell you that we are going to burn all the bodies and then move out after I speak to the townspeople. I need you all to help." With a brisk nod Aidan moved on to the next group of knights. I turned and started to pick up a body. Leonard grabbed his feet. I tried not to look down at his mutilated face while we carried him over to a pile of other men. Everyone helped until all of the dead rebels were in a large pile. Aidan doused them with whiskey and then threw a torch on them. I hoped that the family of these men could see the flames. I hoped that they knew that we were giving their husbands, sons and fathers a proper burial. I hoped that they would know that it was not smart to betray their King again.

The deep snow around the burning bodies melted, and the smoke, mixed with the blizzard, made it nearly impossible to see. I heard the crunch of snow behind me and turned around.

"Don't think that this changes anything boy," Morgan sneered into my face before disappearing into the snow again. I turned back towards the fire and stepped closer to it. Morgan scared me more than any battle I could possibly imagine fighting. I knew that I had seen him before, and thus he was a threat from my past, come to haunt my future. If only I could remember from where.

I stared back into the fire and only one thing came to mind. "Bring Blood Noble Warrior."

\*\*\*\*\*\*\*\*\*

Traveling home took longer than it had taken coming to the south. The snow was deeper and slicker as the weather warmed and cooled. The slush was hard for the horses holding the supplies to walk in, and one broke his leg. I hated seeing Bran kill the animal, but it was for the best. When we finally got to Calentto, we were all frozen to the bone. I went directly to my room to take off my linen and thaw out. When I was done I decided to go into town with the men. They were all going to celebrate our victory and I thought that I deserved a part in that. I hoped that the wine would erase the horrible memory of battle from my mind.

Frequently after our days of sparring, everyone would go into town and enjoy the wine and the women. Aidan and Morgan were never among them, but no one really cared. Morgan was disliked and Aidan was the King. I did not go all of the time and when I did I made sure to keep myself in line. A few times my tongue had become loose with drink and I had almost told my secret. It was also hard to stay away from all the loose women that pestered us knights. I always fended them off until most of the men in the room were gone, but then I always had to leave because they became very persistent.

I really didn't care that evening though. I wanted to drink away the nightmare of battle that was still freshly engraved in my mind. We all walked together, joking and pretending that we had not just seen death, and caused it. I knew that it really didn't even bother some people anymore, taking life, but others, I knew, it still affected greatly. I was among the latter.

Our favorite place was Mimi's House, a place where drink was cheap and company cheaply given, even though the last part did not appeal to me. We all sat and drank heavily. I stayed until most of the men had gone off with their chosen women. Knowing I was going to be next, I decided to brave the cold and walk around to all the merchant shops and see what they had to offer.

The air outside was freezing, but with my heavy cloak wrapped around me I was pleasantly warm. The alcohol didn't hurt either. Most all of the stores I passed were closed, but a few were still open with their lights on. I entered a few but just wandered around looking at their goods briefly before going back out into the streets.

I abruptly stopped and looked at the familiar store front. I knew the man who owned the shop that I stood before. His name was Sir Jonathan and he had been a close and personal friend of my Father. I hesitated before walking into the shop and looking around. I had been here a few times before, but then I was with Father and I had never really had time to look. I walked around until something caught my eye. There in front of me was a beautiful dress. The blue cotton seemed to glow in its elegant simplicity. Despite the freedom that wearing breaches gave me, I missed being able to wear a dress. The color must have cost a fortune to produce and it was clearly well crafted. And though we had been well off enough, I had never worn a dress so beautiful in my entire life.

A wicked, dangerous idea popped into my head. Oh how fun it would be to be a woman for a night! Nobody had to know, if I kept the dress under my mattress no one would find it. If I went out once or twice it really wouldn't matter. I would avoid all of my friends. In a rash moment I pulled out my money from my pocket and pulled the dress off the shelf. I browsed until I found a head covering that would help to disguise my short hair, as well as obscure my face slightly.

Unsure of myself, I slowly went up to the counter. Behind it was Sir Jonathan himself. I ducked my head so he wouldn't recognize me, even though I doubt that he would have anyway. "I would like to buy these items Sir," I said gruffly, throwing my purse on the counter. I saw Jonathan eyeing me wearily and curiously, but he counted my money anyway. I always remembered the man as being a busybody who had to know everything, but his greed had always been his most prominent feature.

"Thank you for your purchases," He said as he pushed the extra money back at me.

I walked quickly back out the door. As I hurried along the snow filled street I tried to keep my purchases under my cape. If any of the Brotherhood saw the dress I didn't know how I would explain myself. I guess I could have said that they were for my woman, but if that was said I knew that I would have no peace until the men had seen her.

When I got back inside my room I shed my manly clothes and tried on the dress. The soft cotton felt so luscious against my skin that I sat there for a minute simply reveling in the happiness it gave me. The dress was beautiful and it made me feel and look striking. It fit perfectly and when I pulled on the head covering to see the combination, I saw that, though modest, the covering highlighted my hazel eyes nicely! I felt as if that this was the best I had ever looked. Reluctantly I pulled the dress off and folded it. After stashing the dress under the mattress, I fell into bed excited about the next night and the chance that I was going to have.

*********

The next day seemed to drag by. We all practiced archery and axes, which were my worst skills. I hated practicing them with a passion, I just couldn't get my wrist to flick the right way to get the axe to stick and the arrow always snapped me in the wrist. Most of the men had hangovers and could only talk of the women they had been with last night. I tried to stay away from them when they talked like that; it always made me feel uncomfortable. I hated to hear them talking about women as if they were just playthings for them, even though in truth that was what the whores were. Regardless, they were often too graphic for my naïve self to understand.

When darkness fell and the men had gone into town again, I ran up to my room excitedly. I pulled on my feminine things and my spare cape that I had been given. There was nobody out in the hall and I got out of the castle as fast as I could, hoping that no one would see me. If they did, they might place two and two together and my secret would be found out.

I decided to spend my time as a woman at a fairly secluded hangout called My Bryton. It was a respectable place and I thought that everyone would be at Mimi's House. I hurried through the cold streets, making sure that the covering stayed firmly on my head. I hoped that none of my own hair was poking out.

I went in and sat down at a table off by myself. When a bartender came up and asked "Madame, what will you have?" I almost didn't answer. I was so used to being called Sir that I was caught off guard, but it felt so pleasant. It felt normal and I found myself slipping back into the ease that I once had as a female.

"I'll just have a glass of wine please," I hadn't known I had liked being a woman until I had to pretend I wasn't one. I sat quietly, sipping my wine, reminiscing about the old days. Father and I had never really gone out on the town before. I had mostly spent my time at home or the homes of father's associates. I realized now how secluded I had been, despite all my travels around the country with Father. I was glad that I was experiencing these new things now. Lost in my thoughts, I suddenly heard a voice behind me.

"Mind if I sit with you, pretty lady?" The voice was slurred with drink but I still knew who it was.

I froze, my heart pounding. Would he recognize me, even in his drunken state? I knew that he hardly even knew his own name when drunk so I decided to chance it, at least until I could slip away.

I turned slowly around and smiled a delicate smile, one that I hoped was not at all like my smiles that I had while I was pretending to be a man.

He was wearing a green tunic that matched his eyes. He had a shadow of a beard and his cheeks were flushed.

"You may sit wherever you want, Knight," I batted my eyelashes and turned back to my wine with a big gulp. He sat down beside me. I saw that he looked at me warily for a few seconds and I wonder if he recognized me, but he just seemed to shrug it off.

"What's your name, fair maiden?" my friend asked as he grabbed my hand and kissed it. I shivered; I had only been kissed on the hand by my father's old friends. It felt good, but knowing him, I was scared of where it would lead. He was the kind of man who expected a lot from women when he was drunk. When we were out on the town, I had never seen a woman refuse him and I wondered what he would do if one did. Did he think that I was one of the women who often entertained him? I found myself slightly offended. It was hard for me to admit that I was also slightly jealous of those women for a brief moment.

"Aceline," I said as I pulled my hand away. He was silent for a few minutes and then started talking again. I had hoped that we would just sit there until I got up enough nerve to leave. It was too strange knowing that one of my closest friends wanted something like that from me.

"I'm Sir Teague, one of the fifty. One of the best too!" He snaked his hand onto my shoulder and started to massage it. I pulled away, trying hard not to get pulled in by my friend's charm. And he most certainly was charming.

"Are you so sure? I've never heard of you before." I was trying to act flippant despite my pounding heart. No man, drunk or sober, had ever acted like this around me. I had no idea what to do.

"You've never heard of me! I'm as famous among women as I am on the battlefield! Let me prove it to you," he said with a grin as he leaned forward. I stood up quickly, almost knocking my chair over, and started to walk out. Everything was going so fast that I was barely aware of what he was really asking.

All I knew was that what he wanted could never happen. It would ruin everything. And if I would have admitted it to myself I would have realized that I wanted to be with him too much. Teague was an amazingly attractive man, but I knew that one night wasn't worth throwing everything away for.

And then I heard his laugh and the way that he said my name and a smile crossed my face. As soon as it appeared I quickly pushed the thought away.

I walked out into the blowing snow and cursed myself for putting on the dress and going out. I couldn't blame him, it was all my own fault. Once again, his smile flashed across my mind, that silly, cocky grin that I often wanted to wipe right off his face. Those smooth lips . . .

I heard the heavy crunching of snow behind me and I turned around slowly to see who it was, even though I already knew. I looked up into his bright green eyes. In that moment he saw me for what I really was, a scared little girl who did want to be with him, but was far too afraid.

"I'm sorry if I frightened you Aceline. I really didn't mean to. Sometimes I get a little too drunk and the whiskey starts talking for me." He drug his toe lightly in the snow, not daring to try and meet my eyes.

"It's alright," I whispered and stared down at my feet also. We stood there for a few moments letting the snow fall around us, not knowing what to do.

"I really should be going now," I whispered with every intent of walking away and forgetting everything. But I had to look at him one last time. I had to see the want in his eyes for one more moment, because it was the last time such a look would ever be given to me.

In the life that I had chosen, there would be no love for me.

So I glanced up and in his eyes I saw all the loneliness and longing that were hidden in my own.

And then I kissed him.

He tasted of whiskey and was warm when he pulled me close. His body shielded me from the cold snow. I stood there with my head pressed against his chest for a few moments after his lips parted from mine. In that moment I blissfully thought of nothing at all.

Slowly, I untangled myself from Teague's arms.

"I have to go," I said hoarsely before turning around.

"When can I see you again?" He sounded slightly breathless.

I turned so that I could see him out of the corner of my eye.

"I'm sorry but that's not possible," I whispered with trembling lips. Tears clogged my throat and my knees were weak as if they might buckle at any moment.

"Aceline," he whispered, "My heart will break if I can't see you again." For a second I almost believed him.

I smiled bitterly and walked back to the castle as quickly as I could without another backward look at the amazing man that I left standing in the snow. Tears rolled down my face but I also felt a guilty twinge of ecstasy. It had been my first kiss, and it had been beyond all expectations that I had ever held.

When I reached my room, I quickly shed my feminine garments and hid them away. I sat on my bed shivering. Why had I even turned to look at him? I had invited trouble to myself. I hated myself for what I had done and yet I wouldn't take it back for all the money in the world.

I closed my eyes and let the tears slide down my cheeks.

I felt like I was doomed whether he recognized me or not.

**********

I got up bright and early the next morning, though I wanted to hide under the covers forever and never come out. I didn't want to face what I knew was coming. When I got to the training yard nobody was there yet and I decided to work on my archery. I was horrible enough so that I could hit the mark roughly twenty percent of the time, and with other things on my mind I was finding it even harder than usual.

"You're out early," I heard a voice behind me say. I turned around and saw Kade taking out his bow.

"Yes," I offered no explanation because I had none. I had needed some time alone and I was annoyed that Kade was out here ruining that. I sighed and let it go, though. I did not want to fight with my friend. I felt as if I needed all the allies I could muster together at the moment.

We shot in silence for a while before he spoke again, "I hope you know that I'm your friend and you are free to tell me anything that is troubling you." He let loose an arrow that hit his woven target dead center. I let one fly that went wide and did not even hit the target. We both laughed a little.

"I do tell you everything, Kade. You are one of my dearest friends, even though sometimes you are too smart for your own good," I let another arrow fly and this time it hit the target on the outermost edge.

"I'm glad that you feel you can tell me everything," Kade stopped shooting and looked at me. "I'm glad that you trust me."

"Why are you talking to me like this?" I asked nervously. I fired an arrow and miraculously it hit the target dead center. Why wouldn't Kade just leave me alone? Was I really that transparent about my feelings? Was there any way that he could know?

"I just want you to know that I am on your side no matter what," his voice was low.

"Please tell me if you know something that I don't because I hate it when you make me feel stupid." I saw that other people were starting to come into the yard and I began to put away my bow. My jaw was clenched.

"I'm sorry. I didn't mean to make you feel stupid. It just seemed to me that something was on your mind. I wanted to help." The man looked genuinely sorry.

I smiled at him in relief and patted him on the back. "I'm sorry also. I am fine, Kade, just tired, I have been worn down lately."

"Well, if you ever need to talk to someone, then just call on me and I will always be there Noble." And with another pat on my back he walked away to join Patrick. I had never known Kade to be so caring; he was always the scholarly one who needed nothing except his books. Even when he was tending the wounded, he managed to be quite efficient and matter-of-fact. I wondered what had gotten into him. My bow was put away and I pulled out my sword.

I had to let out my anger, about everything. I realized that anger had been building up in me. Ever since my Father had been taken, I had been mad at the world. Why me? I always asked. Why couldn't my life just have been simple? I had to learn that life wasn't simple and that it wasn't just me. Every one of the men around me had their own problems, and my problems were even those of my own choosing.

By noon that day, I had dueled five other men and was starting to feel as if my adventure last night would not have any consequences. My actions became more focused and I was not watching over my shoulder all of the time. I had not seen Teague and had started to hope that maybe he was too drunk to practice. If he was too drunk to practice then he was definitely too drunk to remember a stupid little girl that had kissed him.

But then, I turned around and saw his profile against the sun. He was talking to Leonard and looked a little pale, but not sick. I stared; maybe he hadn't been as drunk as I had thought. Maybe he would recognize me.

Then his green eyes were on me, finally really seeing me. His jaw fell open and his eyebrows scrunched together in confusion.

Suddenly his eyes were full of disgust. Teague's chest rose and fell quickly before he turned and jogged out of the courtyard, his face even paler then it had been before. Making a rash decision, I sprinted after him with Leonard staring after us.

"Teague wait!" I kept my voice low even though I knew it didn't matter to Teague. I rounded the corner and saw him on the ground against the stone wall with his head in his hands. He was visibly shaking.

"Teague," I said in my regular voice, it was scratchy but felt good. Teague didn't look up but just groaned. I knelt down beside him. "Teague, I can explain." I put my hand on his shoulder but he shrugged it off. I could feel how tense he was.

"I kissed a man!" He groaned, "I hate myself! I think that I am going to throw up again." My mouth flew open in shock and I fell backwards slightly. In my mind that had not even been an option. I blinked and sat there for a moment before I started to laugh hysterically. Teague looked up with anger in his eyes. I had to tell him, even though I really didn't want to.

"Teague, I'm not a man." His bloodshot eyes finally lifted and he stared at me. "I'm a girl." By this time I was crying. I had just told my secret. I might have ruined my life, but I couldn't let my friend hate himself. I cried harder.

He stared at me in confusion. "Please don't cry, Noble, I mean, Aceline." He stumbled over the unfamiliar name. Gently he put his hand on my shoulder. When he said my real name I cried harder. I was being a silly little girl, something that I hadn't been in a very long time. In a way it felt good.

"Please don't tell anyone," I whispered while I wiped my eyes. I looked down at his hand, which had somehow made its way into mine. It made me feel more confident. Slowly, though, I pulled my hand away from his.

Turning away, I slowly stood up and started to leave but heard Teague's voice, "Noble." I turned. "Is your real name Aceline? Why did you do this? Please explain!" He looked so innocent with his tearstained face; I wanted to tell him everything but held back. I needed some time to sort everything out with myself before I sorted everything out with him. I didn't even understand everything that I had done so far, so why would he?

"My name is Aceline Banidere. Please don't tell anyone. I don't know what I would do with my life now if it turned out that I can't be here, doing this. . ." I was trying not to hiccup and sniffle, but it was futile. Teague stood up slowly and hesitated a moment before reaching out to wrap his arms around me. At first I was rigid, unsure of what to do, but then I realized that he really didn't mean me any harm.

"You do belong here," he smiled into my short hair and I felt all the feelings from the night before oozing back into me.

At that moment, I was glad Teague knew my secret.

\*\*\*\*\*\*\*\*\*\*

Teague and I spent a lot more time together after that day. I found out that it was easier to talk to a person after they knew what you had to hide from everyone else. I felt as if a great weight had been lifted from my shoulders. I didn't have to bite my tongue at all around him.

He continued to teach me a lot of little details that would help me in battle. But during this time I also felt that I learned a lot from him about my life, and what it could be. The only thing in the world that I could not tell him about was my Father, but Teague knew my heart, and never asked me about my family. He understood that some things were private. I wanted to tell him, but I could not. I was too afraid to.

Over time and with Teague's help, I even started to like Aidan more. Teague and Aidan had grown up together, and he knew a different side of Aidan than we saw now. He knew Aidan the man, not Aidan the King. Teague often told me stories of how Aidan had always been wise beyond his years. From a young age he had tried to learn from his father, and eventually help his father when his rule began to crumble. Umber had rejected Aidan's help though, and now Aidan was trying to make it up to the people. Aidan also hadn't always been quite so serious, and Teague had some amusing stories about misadventures from when they were younger. When I looked at Aidan after that, I could no longer just see my father in the dungeon. Instead, I also saw a son and friend not unlike the rest of us.

Aidan always came out to practice with the men and was truly as good of a fighter as all the tales had said. It was hard to dislike the man because he genuinely cared so much about all of us.

Despite all of it, I still did not fully forgive him. I couldn't, at least not then.

Leonard and I drifted farther apart the closer I got to Teague. As we spent less and less time together, it seemed that he was getting closer to Aidan. The King would tell him things and then he would tell us. Some of the knights thought this unfair and complained. I was too busy falling in love to notice anything.

Falling in love for the first time is an experience hard to explain. It feels as if your feet are stuck to the floor every time that you kiss him, and your heart has fallen to your feet whenever he's not kissing you. It's like when you look down into the face of a baby and he smiles at you. You feel as if something completely pure and innocent has chosen you to bestow its grace upon. You are floating on air and you can't stop smiling because you know that there is something beautiful in a world that has so much ugliness.

The more time that I spent with Teague, the more I felt that I really saw him. I held his hand and I knew his heart. For that brief period of time there was nothing else that I wanted.

I was ecstatic when the King sent Teague and me to patrol the woods outside of Calentto for a few days. Apparently there had been quite a few bear sightings, and Aidan was worried that the animal would terrorize the farmers that lived outside the wall of the town.

Teague and I rode around the forest all day and spotted nothing. We pitched a single tent and lit a fire. Teague pulled out a flask of whiskey and we passed it back and forth.

"When I was little, my father always made fun of me because I wasn't as skilled of a swordsman as my older brothers, so every night I would go out and practice in secret, slowly growing stronger and more adept in my skills. They had no idea I was doing it, until one day I challenged father to a duel and he laughed, not expecting a real fight. I won that match, and I have lost very few matches since. I like having the power of holding someone else's life in my sword hand," Teague sighed as he took a swig.

"My father was the one that taught me how to fight. He believed that girls should be educated and know how to defend themselves. I miss him every day," I whispered finally. That was the first mention that I had ever made of my father.

"Does he know where you are?" Teague stared at me with his bright green eyes and for a second I lost my train of thought.

"No," I turned back towards the fire. "He probably thinks that I ran off with some country boy."

Teague stood up and walked over to sit down next to me. He wrapped his arms around me and I leaned against his sturdy body. We often found excuses to hold each other.

"Well, if he knew what great things that you have already accomplished, I'm sure that he would be very proud of you," he whispered softly in my ear.

"I hope so," I took a swig of the whiskey and buried my nose in the folds of his cloak. It was cold out and our fire was not big enough to completely ward off the chill.

"And he should have enough faith in you to know that your virtue is still in tact," he laughed, "At least for now."

A shiver went up my spine and he held me tighter and we both sat, lost in our own thoughts for a few moments.

"Teague?" I finally whispered, breaking the heavy silence. "Have you ever been in love?"

He let out a big breath. "Yes, but let's not talk about that now."

His breath was warm against my cheek. We hadn't kissed since he had discovered my true gender. I had longed to, but I had waited for him to make the first move, and it had never come.

I remembered the feel of his lips against mine and let out a shaky sigh. I needed to tell him how I felt.

I pulled away slightly and turned to face him. "Who was it?" I held my breath, hoping with all my heart that he would say that it was me that he loved.

His eyes reluctantly met mine and he opened his mouth to speak.

Suddenly there was a crack from the woods behind us. Both of our eyes widened and slowly we pulled away from each other and stood up, hands on our swords. I shivered from the cold and fear. Teague and I looked at each other and nodded. He started to move forward and I followed right behind him. The cracks were getting louder and louder, coming from the very edge of the woods.

Suddenly a large, squealing raccoon lunged out of the trees straight at Teague. He lost his balance and fell back onto me. I tried to hold him up, but I lost my balance too, and we tumbled to the ground in a heap of arms and legs.

For a moment we just lay in silence, not moving. Then I looked over at Teague and we both broke out into laughter. I started rolling on the ground trying to catch my breath and Teague had to sit up so that he could breathe. Our guffaws rang through the silent night air for quite a while before we finally quieted down and just lay back on the frozen ground.

"Nobody hears anything about this," Teague commanded. I nodded. He smiled a lazy grin at me. "How about we go to bed?"

I yawned as if on cue.

"I'm exhausted," I said as Teague pulled me to my feet. I brushed the dirt off and then glanced up to see that he was staring down at me. I started to smile but then he took another step towards me and my lips parted slightly as I struggled to breath. His hand slipped behind my head and tangled in my hair. For a moment he just stood there, his face less than an inch from mine. My eyes kept flickering from his dark green eyes to his lips. Finally, after what seemed like an eternity he leaned forward and pressed his lips to mine. His tongue slipped into my mouth for a moment before he pulled away.

"Actually, I was hoping that we wouldn't be doing much sleeping," he smiled down at me.

My heart fluttered. His hand slid from the back of my head lightly down my back . . . down and down. . . And I pulled away. My mouth was suddenly dry.

"Teague, I'm really tired," I mumbled as I looked at the ground. For some reason I couldn't look him in the eye. I had dreamt of him kissing me . . . of his hands touching me, but in those dreams those things had always followed Teague whispering softly in my ear that he loved me.

He let out a laugh. "A minute ago you were just laughing like a maniac. Don't be scared, I'll be gentle," he whispered and brought his hand up to stroke my cheek. For a moment I just stood there. I wanted him. It was hard to resist.

I pulled away so that we weren't touching anymore. "I said no, Teague. There's nothing you can do to change my mind."

He looked down at me for a moment like he didn't believe me. Then he saw from my face that I was being serious. A petulant scowl crossed his normally beautiful features, making him ugly.

"I hate it when women lead me on," he leaned down to whisper in my ear. "Teases are worse than sluts." I stood there, staring straight in front of me. I would not let the tears fall when he could see them. "I hope that you don't get too cold out here tonight. If you decided that you want me to warm you up come on in." And with that he walked into our little lean-to. He was nice enough to throw my blanket out at me. I grabbed it and went back to sit by the fire.

And with that all of my dreams were shattered. The taste of his lips on mine had soured.

He had been far worse than I would have thought. I had seen him acting that way to many tavern whores before, being unnecessarily rough and crude when he was intoxicated, but I had never thought he would act that way to me. I was supposed to be his best friend, if nothing else. The tears fell silently until I slipped into a frozen sleep next to the slowly dying flames.

In the morning I woke to the smell of meat frying over the fire. I opened my matted eyes to see Teague sitting across from where I laid. His hair was sticking up at all angles and there was a line on his face from the cloth that he had laid on. I couldn't be mad at him, even though I should have been. I should have been furious and hurt, but I wasn't. I just wanted everything to be normal between us.

He looked over to see me staring at him. He blushed a bit. "How did you sleep?"

"I slept well," I whispered, pardoning him from the crime of making me sleep out in the cold. I just wanted to forget all that had happened last night. I didn't ever want to remember him like he had been.

"I had a little too much to drink," he said gruffly as he turned the meat.

I just nodded. He had only taken a few swigs. He hadn't been drunk. I pushed the thought away, but there was one thing that I could not forget.

He had not even attempted to say that he was sorry.

"Teague," I whispered as we were riding home the next day. "I'm so glad that you know about me. I was so lonely." Things between us had been very awkward all the day before.

"I'm glad that I know too. You are the best friend that I have ever had Noble." I looked up at him and smiled a sad smile. Teague always called me his friend.

I should have known that he didn't love me, but I wanted to hear those words so badly.

"I think that we are best friends because we are different from the others. We both have secrets," I whispered. I knew that Teague did have secrets, but I did not know what they were. He was always sneaking off places. I hoped that he was not in any trouble, but if he was I would still stand beside him. It made sense that he was going off to see women, but I never wanted to believe that.

"I think that we are best friends because we understand each other. We don't push each other," he replied. He wasn't hinting at anything; he knew that it was true. I never asked where he went and he never asked why I was here or about my family.

After that night, I stopped waiting to hear him say that he loved me.

Every once in a while I would slip and say that I loved him. Instantly the mood would change, his smile would fade. I tried to play it off but I couldn't help it. It went on like that for many months. I became more and more dependant upon him. I knew that I was smothering him, but I could not stop because I did love him so much. He was a disease that consumed me. I was like a dog who had been kicked by her master, but kept coming close again and again.

He found his own way to take advantage of the situation though. Despite the fact that I never allowed him to bed me, he always kept trying. He never again asked outright, but he would sometimes caress me or kiss my neck.

It was hard to resist at times. Sometimes I started to believe that if I just let him have his way he would realize what I was worth. Perhaps if I let him have what he wanted, he would come to love me.

Of course I knew it wasn't true, and somehow I managed to find the strength to refuse the one thing that I wanted most in the world.

\*\*\*\*\*\*\*\*\*\*

"I love you," I whispered absently as Teague's lips glided softy along my collar bone.

My comment was met with silence.

We were sitting in My English and I was wearing a green cotton dress he had bought me for my eighteenth birthday, which had been the day before. I was sipping wine to try and sooth my nerves. I had known that things were going to be clarified here tonight, they needed to be or I would go mad. I couldn't stand having him push me away while all I wanted to do was be closer to him.

"I won't apologize," I gulped. "You know it's true. You've known all along."

"I know it," he growled as he took a large swig from his mug. Tonight his mood was worse than usual and he had been drinking for hours.

"Why don't you ever say that you love me, Teague?" I whispered and I wrung my hands together. "Even as a friend would be enough . . . I just need to hear it."

Teague grabbed my hands and warmed them in between his larger ones. "Aceline, as I have said many times before, you are special to me." He never told me the truth. He avoided it, because he knew that it would change everything. He was so open about everything else but this.

"Do you love me, though? I have to know. I have to hear you say it."

He looked into my eyes, knowing that I knew him better than anyone else. Knowing that I already knew the answer.

"I love you in my own way," he replied, choosing his words carefully. My eyes welled instantly, pain pulsing through my fragile heart. That almost hurt worse than him just saying that he didn't love me at all.

I tried to blink back the tears but he saw them.

Suddenly his face flushed and his jaw clenched. He grabbed my arm roughly and began to pull me towards the back of the stairs.

"Teague what are you doing," I asked tiredly, ready to run away to my bed for a long hard cry.

He didn't answer but instead pulled me up the back stairs. I knew that there were bedrooms up here for the customers to use.

"Teague just let me go," I snapped at him. "I'm not in the mood for this." I tried to pull away from him but his fingers were like iron.

He pulled me into one of the bedrooms. I grabbed hold of the door frame and wouldn't let go.

"God damn it Teague, stop," I cried, suddenly starting to become afraid.

He pried me away from the door and threw me towards the bed so violently that my temple cracked against the wall and I had to blink a few times to clear my mind.

Teague slammed the door shut and locked it.

I tried to stand up but he pushed me back down.

"Teague please stop," I stuttered, "You're scaring me." I looked past him towards the door.

"I'm so tired of your whining and your pleading!" He screamed into my face, pinning my arms down onto the bed.

"I promise I won't ever mention it again Teague, please," I sobbed. I didn't want to fight him.

"You say that every time but you never mean it! It's pathetic and I loathe you for it," he snarled into my face. He laid one arm across my chest pinning me to the bed, his other hand reaching down to undo his breaches.

I stopped crying and looked up into his face, more wounded by his words than I could ever be by his hands.

"You are the most worthless woman I've ever met. I don't even desire you for pleasure. I just want to have you and let it be over," he whispered into my ear. "Then I will be completely done with you. You can return to being a sexless nobody with nothing but your delusions of love and grandeur. I could never in a thousand years love something as gross and ugly as you."

I couldn't breathe. I just laid there trembling.

Suddenly I realized that he was crying. My eyes flicked up to his.

For a minute his tortured eyes met mine and then he flung himself off of me.

"Get the hell out of here," he yelled at me. "Just get out."

I stood up slowly and walked over to the door on unsteady legs. I looked back once as I shut the door behind me to see Teague curled up in a ball on the bed, unmoving.

I walked through the city streets as if in a daze. I had forgotten my cape at the tavern and my scarf had fallen off in the bedroom. I didn't even realize that if someone saw me it would be the end of my secret. The melting snow made the dark city look dismal.

I was too numb to feel dismal. I was too numb to feel anything.

As I walked through the castle I heard voices. Standing in the middle of the hall were Patrick and Leonard, talking. I quickly backed out of sight, regaining some of my awareness.

"Well, they say that she is the fairest maiden around," Leonard said loudly, as was his custom.

"Yes, but the Lady Iseult is married to Teague's uncle. He wouldn't do this as just another one of his conquests. He can already have any woman he wants, and probably has!" Patrick's voice was jolly and joking as usual.

That's why Teague didn't love me. His heart was already taken. She must have been prettier than me, and smarter, and more interesting. She must have been better than me. I wasn't good enough to have the one thing that I had truly wanted.

"I think he must love her. That must be where Teague always is, with Iseult," Leonard yawned. I couldn't think, I felt as if I was barely breathing. In the background I heard the two knights go into their sleeping quarters.

I stumbled into my room and fell onto my bed in exhaustion.

I couldn't cry anymore and I couldn't feel angry. It seemed as if I couldn't feel anything.

\*\*\*\*\*\*\*\*\*

I felt as if I was in a dream the next morning. The sun seemed endless and my hands felt dry, which made everything I touched seem scratchy. Feeling empty, I walked around my quarters preparing for training. I tried as hard as I could to block out what had happened the night before. The sun was pouring through the window, but everything was wrong. All the joy that I had felt was gone; it had even been slipping away for a long time.

I laughed and joked with all of the men but still felt hollow. I practiced my moves without heart but no one seemed to notice. Couldn't anybody see that there was something wrong with me? Was my façade so effective that my real feelings did not show through? Once I had thought it so thin that anyone could have seen through my guise, but now it was so thick that I wasn't sure where it stopped and I began.

I could feel my heart turning cold and I had to keep myself from getting physically sick.

I kept hearing him screaming in my face and grabbing my arms. I imagined him whispering sweet words and gently caressing some golden girl with long flowing blonde hair and slightly parted rogue lips . . .

I ate my dinner and supper but it all felt like oil, sliding down my throat and coating the inside of my mouth. I drank with the other men and kept drinking longer. The now familiar taste of whiskey felt like fire and pulled my thoughts away from the pain. Teague was sitting across from me at our large table at the tavern but I had been successful in avoiding his nervous eyes all evening.

". . . What do you think, Noble?" Kade's meek voice broke me out of my drunk, pitiful trance.

"What do I think about what?" My voice was slurred and it was hard to focus on anything. My head was bobbing all over the place.

"Does Teague love this Lady Iseult or is she just another sexual conquest?" All the men laughed. Suddenly I was angry. I was boiling with rage.

How dare Teague tell me that I was worthless . . . How dare he make me feel like I was inadequate. I looked him up and down with such contempt that I felt as if my skin was on fire.

"This is a trick question, for Teague loves none other than himself and his conquests!" All the men broke into laughter. I saw Teague go from as pale as a ghost to red as the stone in my sword. He looked at me in anger.

There was to be no apology from him. No bit of remorse at all would show through his arrogance.

I wanted a fight with him. It was a good thing that I didn't have my sword because I would have caused even more of a scene than I already was.

"This is high praise from a man who detests the thought of sleeping with a Lady!" The entire table went silent because he had just accused me of a horrendous thing in the eyes of my comrades. My eyes narrowed. That had been a very low blow.

"You're right! I'd rather feed a poor whore than bed a married Lady!" I sneered. I had not lied and yet had gotten myself off the hook.

"You are nothing but a selfish pig that wants to bed every woman in Calentto, married or not." I was starting to become sensible again. I wanted Teague to feel bad about what he did to me, not just embarrassed in front of everyone. "It doesn't even matter if she's willing or not," I finally hissed.

"Calm down Noble," Leonard said softly. I felt tears welling behind my bloodshot eyes and just wanted to go lay down in my own bed. It felt as if everyone in the room was against me.

"No, he has a right to be angry. He is jealous of Iseult and I. Noble just wishes he had someone, anyone, that loved him that way," Teague smiled the special insult just for me. I felt as if I had been punched in the gut over and over again. I stood up slowly and I felt all eyes on me. I wanted to fight him; I wanted to cut his heart out and feed it to him.

"Go fuck yourself," my voice sounded choked as I walked erectly out of the room. Once I was out on the street I started running and I kept running till I got to my chambers. I pulled the dress Teague had given me out of its hiding spot and proceeded to rip it to shreds. The rest of the night I was busy being sick into my chamber pot. I remember still feeling woozy when I walked to training the next morning. It was aided by the fact that I had not slept a wink. I had been up cursing Teague and hating myself for allowing this to happen. Also, despite my better judgment, I had proceeded to drink another entire flask of whiskey that I had stashed in my room.

As I stepped out into the courtyard, my head started to spin. I put my hand onto the stone wall to steady myself. I should have just stayed up in my room. I knew that I would not make it through the practice.

"Are you all right Noble?" Patrick's normally jolly voice sounded concerned.

I looked over at the fuzzy face of my friend. "I'm fine," I croaked.

"I think that you should sit down," he grabbed my arm and then tried to pull me to the nearest bench. I followed along slowly. I sat down and then felt my eyes starting to roll back in my head.

"Noble," Patrick yelled, "Noble!"

I could see the dark forms of my other friends gathering around but it was too late and my head cracked back against the stone wall while my world went dark.

**********

When I woke up, Teague was sitting on my bed next to me, staring out the window. I blinked a few times, groggily.

"Teague," I whispered through my dry throat. He jumped a little and then turned to look at me. His eyes were red. I stared up into the face I was supposed to hate and started to experience those feelings dissolve. He looked horrible. He looked horrible because I was sick.

"Aceline," his voice sounded cracked also and he reached down and gave me a hug. He pulled back. I looked down and realized I was wearing an oversized shirt. My eyes fluttered closed.

"Does anyone know?" I tried to calm down. Would they all be mad at me for keeping this from them? I knew that I would not be able to keep fighting with the men if Aidan knew. I wanted to stay so badly.

"No, I told everyone that your body was badly scarred and that you wouldn't want anyone to see it. They let me change you and everything." He turned away.

"Thank you." I kept my eyes down.

The thought of him seeing my naked body made me want to claw my own skin off. I couldn't help but wonder how it made him feel.

"You had a terrible fever for a week. You couldn't eat anything and I just had to sit here and watch you waste away. You screamed so loudly sometimes about things that I couldn't understand. I couldn't help you. . ." He stopped and I realized that he was crying.

For a moment I just clenched my jaw, not caring if he cried until there was no water left in his body. He deserved no less for what he had done to me.

But then the sunlight streaming through my window shone in his hair and I couldn't help catching my breath.

Through it all I still loved him. It was a fire that I couldn't extinguish, it burnt me beyond recognition and yet it fueled me to live on.

"Please don't cry," I said quietly. Teague reached up and wiped his eyes with his dirty hands.

"I really do care about you, Aceline, but Iseult consumes me. She's in my soul. I hate her for it and I look everywhere trying to find something that will make me feel the way she does . . ." I could hear his heart breaking. I reached over and stroked his back as a mother might. It was killing me to see this man in so much pain. He was killing me.

"I hate myself for the things that I said to you and trying to use you to make me feel better. Every time I think about how I touched you I want to . . . I don't know what's wrong with me. I want to do the right thing, but I never do." I thought that Teague had always been honest with me, but I never really knew what honesty was until that moment.

"I'll always be there for you, Teague. It doesn't matter about Iseult and I understand why you acted the way you did." Tears ran down my face.

It hurts so badly to love someone that's wrong for you, and it can kill you to love someone who doesn't deserve to be loved.

"You forgive me then Aceline? Forgiveness is one of your great virtues." He took my hand tenderly. He was back to being the sweet talker that I had fallen in love with that night on the street. It was all about appearances with him.

I knew that I would never again see the honestly that he has shown me only moments before.

"Or my greatest fault," I said unsurely with one last tear running down my cheek.

Suddenly, the door flew open and Aidan strode in. He looked haggard also but smiled when he saw me. Teague dropped my hand like it was a hot coal. I hastily wiped the tear away. "Noble, we were all so worried about you! How are you feeling?" He moved closer and laid a hand on my forehead. "It seems that your fever is gone."

"I feel alright, Your Majesty." In truth, I felt like I had been run over by wild horses. All I wanted to do was sleep some more. At least while I had been delusional and sleeping, I hadn't felt any pain.

"Well, please recover quickly. We need you out there." Aidan smiled and it seemed that I felt a little better. He was a kind man, for the most part.

"I'm sure that I will be up by tomorrow, Sir," I answered, smiling back slowly. This was the man who accused my Father of treason. I couldn't like him. Aidan nodded and strode out of the room. Teague and I sat in silence for a few minutes.

There wasn't anything for us to say to each other.

"He's going to tell everyone that you are alright. Soon everyone will be in here." He left that last sentence hanging thickly in the air.

I quickly leaned forward and kissed him on the cheek.

"I'll always love you," I whispered. "But it's okay if you forget it."

"You'll always be special to me Aceline." But nothing he said in that moment would have meant anything. I had already heard it before.

The door flew open a second time and Leonard, Patrick, Kade, and Gladwin rushed in. They all patted me on the back and talked loudly but my eyes were still on Teague. Maybe forgiveness was my greatest fault, but I couldn't live without it.

## CHAPTER THREE
### War

I recovered slowly over the next few weeks. I had lost a lot of weight and muscle. My stomach hurt all the time and it was hard for me to eat for a few days because it had shrunk so much. I was always lightheaded and it was hard to concentrate. Teague and Leonard sat by me most of the time and gave me anything that I asked for.

When I finally felt well enough to train, I worked slowly. Everyone knew I had to take it slow and didn't push me. Despite what everyone else said, I knew my limits but always tried to push them a little farther. As it was, it took me a few months to be as efficient as before.

I rarely saw Aidan after the day that I awoke. He was always shut away in his quarters. When he did come out he appeared exhausted and wasted. His eyes were red and the dark circles under them made the rest of his skin look sallow. I could tell that, though they tried to hide it, everyone was worried about him. Leonard, in particular, always snuck anxious glances over at him. I knew that Leonard really did care about Aidan; they had become each other's best friends.

I missed having a best friend.

Though I had forgiven Teague and we were cordial, things had reverted back to almost exactly how they were before he had found out my true sex. There was always the truth lingering in my mind, and I presumed his as well, that I loved him and he could never love me. I had not been deemed worthy by him of that.

Finally, one day at the end of summer, we were called to the Round Table. I sat down at the massive piece of wood and ran my hand over my name as had become customary for me to do. Andrew Banidere was who I was now, Andrew, not Aceline. Aidan finally walked in once everyone was seated. He looked truly terrible. I couldn't help but feel somewhere in the back of my mind I thought that he deserved this somewhat. He couldn't be perfect for them all of the time. I had seen the darker side of him and knew that he was not perfect, not even close.

"My friends, brothers, I come to you in a time when our country is in danger. I have learned that a massive Scarcillian army has formed and landed on our eastern shore. I have held this back because I did not know if war would be necessary. Apparently it is. I have sent out word to all our troops. They are all moving towards the east. We need to get ready to go also. I'm sorry," Aidan hadn't even sat down. He walked out the door as quickly as he had come in, just a flash of misery and fear.

A war? The battle against the rebels had been bad enough. Since that day, the country had been peaceful and none of us had to fight. I had been trying to forget how it felt to end someone's existence.

I looked over at Leonard. "Have you ever fought in a war before?" I didn't want to die and I knew that this would be harder than anything I had ever faced before. There was a wavering in my voice, though I tried to keep it steady.

Leonard gulped, "Once." His voice cracked. Leonard was the bravest man I knew, and if he was scared I knew I would be petrified. His face was grey and I wanted nothing more than to comfort him. Maybe it was a good thing that I had never fought in a war before; I did not want to be as scared as everyone else was.

"How is it?"

"Horrible." He got up, wiped a hand across his eyes and walked out. I stared after him, wishing that he had stayed to elaborate. I needed to find someone brave, someone brave enough to tell me what this war was going to be like.

I looked across the table at Teague. His eyes looked empty. He was looking past me. I looked around the table and saw that everyone looked like him. There was no one here that was going to be rational about this. Fear had taken over everyone.

I knew that war was a big event but these were huge, brave warriors. What would the coming months hold? What horror would the battlefield bring? Was I strong enough to handle the emotional struggle of war? And most importantly would I be able to take orders from a man that I didn't really believe in? Would I be able to follow Aidan to almost certain death?

**********

By the time that we had all the necessities, we had fifteen wagons packed full of our supplies. They were filled with armor, weapons and food for the troops we would meet at the front. We all marched briskly towards the west. Along the way we met thousands of men coming to fight for Bryton. With all the men it took us a week to get to our position. The march was terrible. We all took turns riding the few horses as much as we could, but there were not that many and some got sick or hurt and had to be killed. The weather was muggy and everyone was miserable.

Finally we reached our destination, with the Scarcillas in view. We were surrounded on all sides by soft and rolling hills. The grass was so green that it was almost painful to look at and small wildflowers dotted the landscape. The sky was a brilliant blue and there was nowhere to hide from the sun that beat down on us. Exhausted, we made camp and then went to bed before darkness even fell. I slept between Kade and Leonard but the latter's snores kept me awake. All I wanted to do was fall into a dream world and forget the horror that awaited me.

I stood up and quietly walked outside. I stared at all of the Scarcillian fires and shivered, even though it was still warm. A shuddering sigh escaped my lips. I was so frightened. We would fight tomorrow and in a way I was glad that we were going to get it over with. Fear was a hard partner. I hoped that I would not die, hoped that I would get to see my beloved Father one more time.

I sat down for a few minutes, thinking, until someone sat down beside me. I flicked me eyes over quickly to see Aidan staring into the night. I turned back to the fires and my jaw slackened slightly. I was so tired and scared and it was nice to have company, even if it was Aidan.

"Are you scared Noble?" Aidan's deep voice broke the void of silence.

"Yes, scared to die, scared for my friends." I didn't care what Aidan thought of me. For a moment I gave into childish self-pity. I was tired of being the only one who still had a brave face on. I was the youngest. I shouldn't have been fighting in this war! I shouldn't even have been there. I should have just left with my Father.

"While you worry about just your friends, I worry about everyone. Sometimes I wish I was just a common soldier. The weight of being a King is almost more than I can bear. Would you be me? I would give up everything if I could be you." Aidan finally looked at me. His blue eyes looked haunted. How I wanted to be his friend and comfort him, but I could not forget. I could not forgive, at least not yet. I wanted to, but it felt so much like betrayal of my father.

"There's no use in wishing for things that you have no chance of getting. We are all here because of you, and every man that dies here, dies because you brought us here, regardless of the cause." My words were harsh. I saw him flinch a little. Inside I recoiled also. Why did I have to be so good at hiding my feelings?

"Why don't you like me Noble?" he pleaded. I shuddered slightly. How little he knew. He sounded tormented, as if he wanted everything and by trying to grasp more, he was letting everything escape through his fingers. He wanted me between his fingers, under his thumb. When he looked at me with those eyes, I wanted to be in his grasp. I wanted to be like the others, who followed with blind trust.

"I don't understand you," I whispered, and I didn't. I had only started to take hold of who this man was, and yet he was still so much a man of mystery.

"What don't you understand?"

"How can you be one person on the surface and another underneath it all? You put on this façade of the perfect King, but you are really just a scared, lost little boy looking for someone to actually care about you," I choked on the words. How could I be saying this to my King? How could this man I was supposed to hate be the most interesting and caring man I had ever met? My first loyalty was to my Father, wasn't it? Why did I feel closer to Aiden at that moment than I did to my own father?

His face fell. "Am I really that horrible?"

I held back my tears as I shook my head no and then stood up. I walked back into the tent and sat down between my friends. I had to hate Aidan. He had put my Father in jail, accused him of treason. Why was I even still here? I could walk off and never have to beat myself up over this again. But could I leave my friends?

Was Aidan my friend? The second that the thought crossed my mind I knew that it would never leave. I took a deep breath to try and calm myself. Aidan had been nothing but kind to me. He had taken me into his home and let me build a life there. He had helped me build a better version of myself.

And all that he wanted was for me to care: about the knighthood, the kingdom and the man beneath the crown.

Suddenly, in that moment, the hatred was gone. As easily as it had come into my life, I had decided to let it go.

I looked up to see Morgan across the tent, lips curled in a snarl. I shivered and lay down. I could feel his hard eyes on me as I fell into a restless, nightmarish sleep, but at least the coldness of hate was gone from my heart.

\*\*\*\*\*\*\*\*\*

I woke up the next morning to Leonard shaking my shoulders. "Wake up sleepy head. It's time to prepare for your first war." The last word on his tongue held certain bitterness. I got up and slowly put on the armor that Kade had shoved at me. Though it was early morning I was sweating heavily, mostly from nerves.

Gladwin came up behind me and patted me on the back. "Good luck out there Lad!" I smiled. Gladwin had become a dear friend over the last year.

"Come back in one piece," I said jokingly. I heard somewhere that Gladwin had never even been injured in a battle. He smiled and walked away. I stared after him, hoping that it was not the last time that I would ever see him. I imagined his smiling face and it gave me courage.

On the long march out we had been instructed on the battle plan. Since we would be fighting on the open western plain, there would be little strategy involved in this war. Our companies would meet the enemy straight on. Aidan wished for us knight to be interspersed throughout the enlisted men, helping to give them courage and hold the ranks. He trusted us more than his commanders to make sure battles were won.

Slowly and without orders the men started to form into rows and columns facing the Scarcillans. Aidan, Leonard and Morgan rode on horses in the front. It was reassuring to know that the best of the best were our fearless leaders. I stood in the back next to Patrick and some other military men I didn't know. I didn't know where any other of my friends were. I scanned the crowd for them but could not see another familiar face. Aidan started giving a pep talk that I couldn't hear. After a while he turned forward and pointed his sword into the sky.

"CHARGE!" The whole army of Bryton moved forward. Arrows flew over us from the archers in the very back. Some of the arrows were lit with fire. Then I heard the unmistakable sound of shields and swords clanging. Our front line had hit the Scarcillas. I walked forward for what seemed like forever but was probably only a few minutes. Then we were in front. All of the other men had moved to the side to fight their own Scarcillans. The whole field was already a mess of bloody bodies.

The man five feet in front of me was huge with exposed muscles and long blond braided hair. In his hand he held an enormous double sided axe. He snarled, exposing teeth that were almost black as he walked slowly towards me. I could hardly concentrate because the beating of my heart seemed to be echoing inside my helmet and breastplate. The Scarcillans eyes went wide as he let out a great roar and brought the axe over his head. My brain switched into gear and I plunged my blade into his bare stomach. He still roared and brought down his axe. I moved in closer to the large smelly body and the axe swung behind me. I pushed the sword in harder. He swung the axe at my head again but I ducked. My sword was three-fourths of the way into my enemy but I still pushed harder. The man's mouth turned red as blood started to seep from behind his gritted teeth. His eyes were so angry that I felt as if my flesh might catch fire with his stare. His axe dropped to the ground. I pulled my sword out and he fell with a thud at my feet. His blood covered my breastplate.

I turned around and saw another man with a braided beard and balding head coming at me. He held one of the large broadswords native to his land. I quickly took him down by slashing his side. I looked around and saw men strewn all along the battlefield. Most were Scarcillans but there were a good number of us also. I saw Scarcillian men retreating while we still held the field. Far in the distance, Aidan sat atop his battle horse, surveying the field. Our first battle had turned into a success. Men were still fighting all around me but I weeded my way along and looked for my friends. I walked past a pile of bodies that looked mostly Scarcillan. These men hadn't made it far from their starting line.

"Aceline," I heard a cracked whisper. For the first time since the battle begun, I felt afraid. I slowly turned around. Lying on the edge of the pile of dead Scarcillans was Teague.

I felt all of the breath leave my body. Feeling faint, I knew that I had to help him.

I ran over and knelt beside him. His face was covered in blood and his eyes were barely open. I surveyed his body and almost screamed when I saw that both of his legs were gone. The ground was dark red with blood. "Teague!" I whispered. I thought quickly and ripped a strip off of my breeches. "We have to stop the bleeding." I started to move towards the disgusting stump of his left leg but he put a hand on my arm.

"Stop, it's too late."

"No, no it's not," I was sobbing and shaking, trying to move closer to his legs so that I could stop the bleeding.

"Yes, it is. Please don't cry Aceline," His voice was growing softer and I stopped moving towards where his legs had been. He reached out to me and pulled my hand to his cheek.

"Don't talk like that Teague. You'll be fine, you have to. I need you," I could barely talk, "I . . . I love you Teague." He smiled a little and then took a deep breath.

"Noble, you're the one worth loving," his voice faded slowly. Then he shut his eyes and his hand fell from my loose grasp. I put my head on his chest and stroked his angelic curls. My bottom lip quivered and I put a hand on his shoulder.

"Teague," I whispered. "Teague!" For a moment I sat there in disbelief.

"God damn it! Damn everything!" I screamed as I lifted my head. "Why did it have to be him!? He doesn't deserve this! Kill me! Strike me dead God, just don't leave me hear alone." I put my head in my hands and sobbed over the body of the man I loved, and one of my dearest friends. "Please don't leave me alone."

I don't know how long I sat there but it couldn't have been long because there was still fighting going on everywhere. I wiped my eyes and stood up slowly. Suddenly there was a Scarcillian in front of me. I fumbled for my sword but wasn't quick enough. The big man drew his axe from my navel to the base of my throat, cutting clean through my breastplate. For a moment I just stood there in shocked silence before I screamed and clutched my midsection. The Scarcillian was preparing to take another swing when suddenly there was the glint of metal and the enemy's head was lying on the ground. Behind the body stood Aidan covered in blood.

"Noble!" He rushed forward. He grabbed me and I slumped up against him. It felt like I was on fire. I could feel the warm blood seeping all across my front. "I need to get you to the medic tent." He scooped me up in his arms and started to jog to the back of the lines. I saw his horse standing forlornly next to Teague's forgotten body.

"Teague!" I whispered once more.

My head was pounding. I bounced up and down in the King's arms and I was very close to passing out. Finally we got to a tent and Aidan set me down. He looked around and then looked back at me. "I need to stop the bleeding or you will die." He started to pull off my breastplate, which was basically in two separate pieces.

Suddenly it hit me. He would know that I was a woman. I started trying to push him away with my heavy arms but he kept fending off my feeble attempts. "No!" I managed to croak. By now he was working on my tunic. I grabbed his wrists but he kept undoing the ties. Then there was only a shirt between him and me. The shirt was cut in half from the Scarcillian so he just pulled it away. Aidan paused for a few precious seconds staring at my slashed linen.

"Is this cloth for another wound?" he asked before reaching down to pull it off.

"NO!" I cried again but it was too late. My bare chest heaved and Aidan went white. I quickly crossed my arms over my chest, covering them with sticky blood. Aidan stared at me for a few more awkward seconds before averting his eyes.

"You'll die if I don't help," his voice cracked, harsh and cold as iron. He looked around and then walked to the other side of the tent. He came back with a flask. I moved my arms but managed to situate my shirt so it hid most of my chest. I looked away from him with tears streaming down my pale face. Taking a deep breath he uncapped the bottle and poured its contents along the cut. I realized it was whiskey when it hit me. I screamed and blacked out.

\*\*\*\*\*\*\*\*\*

I woke up with a large bandage wrapped around my whole midsection. I was in a tent by myself. Sitting up dizzily, I could feel dozens of stitches pulling my tender flesh together.

Running the events of the last few hours through my mind I started to feel sick. Teague had died in my arms and Aidan knew my secret. My whole world was falling down around me. Slowly I stood up and pulled on some clothes that had been put beside my make-shift bed.

I walked out into the fading sunlight and looked around. The battlefield was filled with men dragging our dead behind some tents. I saw Leonard and walked over to him. His brown eyes looked bland and empty as he stared at our massive amounts of dead. I knew how he was feeling.

I put my hand on his shoulder. "Teague died," I whispered with tears streaming. I hadn't thought that I had any tears left.

"I know," Leonard's voice cracked, "He's over there." He pointed to a place a little bit away from the rest of the men. I quickly hugged him and tried to ignore the tears in his eyes. His body was cold and I knew that he was in almost as much pain as I was. I didn't even know what I wanted to do. Everything was wrong. It was as if nothing existed except for my misery.

I walked over to where Leonard had pointed and kneeled down beside Teague's lifeless form. I ran my hand down his cheek and bit my lip to keep from crying out in desolation.

"I'm sorry. I know that you two were close," someone whispered from behind me. I turned to see Kade. I looked back down to Teague's body. I couldn't even bear to look at Ksde, because I wished that he was dead instead of Teague. Anybody but Teague.

"He was one of the people that I loved most in the entire world. I was with him when he . . ." I couldn't go on. Kade Bent down and put a hand around my shoulder. "He was the best! How is it that I survived and he didn't? It just isn't fair," I wailed into Kade's shoulder when I turned to face him, needing comfort more than anything. I finally stopped crying and started hiccupping. Then I pulled away and stood up. Kade looked embarrassed and I gave him a small smile. He nodded at me and then pointed with his chin to behind me.

I slowly turned while I wiped my eyes. Standing in front of me was Aidan. Embarrassed and scared I averted my once again tearful eyes. He was the last person that I needed to see.

"Kade, I need a moment alone with Noble please," Aidan seemed to feel awkward also. I felt Kade brush past me and walk away. "Can we go somewhere a little less public?" His voice was not angry, just tired.

I nodded, not trusting myself to speak and followed him as he started to walk towards his tent. He ducked inside and then held the flap open for me. I entered slowly and squinted in the darkness. He stood there, framed against the grey fabric of the tent and I felt some of my resolve slip away. I bowed my head.

"Who are you, really?"

"Aceline Gro . . . Banidere," I almost used my real last name. Even though I was forced to be honest with Aidan about my gender I was not going to tell him everything. I had not even had the chance to tell Teague everything. I wished that I could have had more time so that I could have trusted him with it all.

"I suppose that you thought the life of a knight of the Round Table would be glorious."

I looked up at him in honesty. "It is glorious, my King. There's no place I'd rather be."

He stared at me until I felt as if I was being forced to turn my eyes away.

"How can you say that even when you have just seen your best friend die?"

"Are you saying that he didn't die for something glorious?" Teague's death would be remembered, I would make sure of that, he would not be just another body on that field.

Aidan shook his head and looked away from me. "You are very young, Aceline Banidere."

"I am old enough to know what I am doing sir. You saw how I fought out there. I want to stay here!" I burst out and took a step closer. "I am still the same person, even if I am a female."

He looked down on me cautiously. "You were almost killed, and it will happen again if I allow you to stay with us. The next time you might not even be so lucky. You will stay here until we the next convoy returns back to Calentto and then you will go back home, wherever that might be." He sounded as if his mind was made up. My head sagged. All I wanted was to stay here now. These men were all that I had, and I had also found out that they were all that I needed.

"Sir, I'm a good fighter. You've seen me. I belong here. I'm valuable and the men like me! Please let me stay," I clasped my hands in front of me. I had no life to go back to. I would be utterly alone. "It's all I have," my voice cracked and I blinked back the tears.

"I'll think on it," He turned with a set jaw that stated exactly the opposite and disappeared from the tent.

"Wait!" I called as I burst out into the grey sunshine once again. The King turned around and I jogged toward him. "Please don't tell anyone," I grabbed his hand without thinking and the electricity that I felt at his touch flew through me once more. He studied my face for a moment and then gave a brief nod before slowly pulling his hand away. He walked away and I smiled a bitter smile, simply because there was absolutely nothing to smile about.

The next day there was no fighting while we made sure that we had gathered all of our dead and in the mid-afternoon they burned them all. Teague was the only knight to have died but 52 soldiers had perished also. The forty-nine of us left decided to burn Teague after everyone else was gone. Aidan poured whiskey all over the body. I ran my hands through Teague's hair one last time before Aidan threw a torch on his body. I stared into the flames. I felt somebody watching me. Through the fire he looked demonic. I looked down and realized that I was more afraid of the King's nephew than anything else in this world.

**********

That night I slept alone in Aidan's tent. The King had told the men that Teague's death had really upset me and that I needed time alone. I tried to tell him that I was fine with sleeping with the men, but he wouldn't listen to me at all. When I woke up the next morning I put on the armor that was sitting beside me. I presumed that Kade had put it there during the night. It was a nice set that actually matched and fit together well. I was almost done when Aidan walked in.

"What are you doing?"

"Preparing to fight," I said while polishing my sword on my breeches. I would not look at him; I knew that I was defying his wishes. I slid the clean sword into its scabbard.

"No, you aren't. I have thought it over and do not believe that you should be fighting with us. We are supposed to be protecting women like you, not fighting beside you." He stood there looking at his feet. "I told you that yesterday and you deliberately defied me."

"I am going to fight!" I answered heatedly, "I'm still Noble, the knight who fights beside her friends, for her country." I moved towards the door but Aidan stopped me. His arm grasped my forearm tightly, and I stiffened like a caged animal.

"I am not going to let you out that door," His voice was still even and patient, but edged with an iron will.

I just stared at him for a moment. I let out a sigh and looked down at my feet, not daring to acknowledge that I was about to beg.

"If you don't let me out that door I really don't have anything to live for anymore," I finally whispered. "It's all I have in the entire world."

I took a deep breath, still refusing to meet his eyes.

For a moment he didn't say anything, but I could feel him staring at me, assessing if I was being truthful or not.

"Alright," he finally began gruffly, "You can fight but the first drop of blood I see will be the last one you ever shed here."

I raised my head and nodded. "Thank you sir."

Aidan turned swiftly and walked out of the tent without another glance at me.

I pushed the hair out of my eyes wearily and smiled.

Walking out into the sunlight I was blinded. The whole world seemed a lot brighter and harsher the last few days.

I remembered the sun glinting through Teague's hair and his charming grin . . .

A hand came down on my shoulder and I shook the thoughts away.

"Ready to fight another battle for Bryton?" Bran's rough voice had come to be a fatherly sound for me. I had realized after a while that he was gruff, but he could also be really caring in his own way.

"Is anyone really ready?" I asked with a weak smile.

Bran seemed thoughtful. "No, I guess that I have just been doing it for so long that I am used to the sick feeling you get just before a big battle. I suppose that you aren't used to it yet." He pulled out his sword and rubbed it across his leather jerkin. Bran never wore armor; he said that it weighed him down too much. He did just fine without it. I had the feeling that I would not survive without my heavy armor. I certainly would have died without it two days ago.

The thought of that day sparked so many other thoughts that I was trying to push away.

"No, but I think that I'll get there eventually." I hoped that I would be around long enough to be as experienced as Bran. I hated the feeling of cold hard fear in your belly, making it hard to think, making your heart pound.

"Let's hope that you don't have to see as many battles as I have, Lad," His eyes sparkled as he walked away. He didn't seem sorry to have seen so many battles. He was one of the few who seemed a better man from it.

I looked around and saw men starting to line up again. I was closer to the front and was next to one of the four brothers. I couldn't tell them apart except for Gladwin. The brother standing beside me was not Gladwin. I looked closer and thought that it might be Gair; the youngest of the brothers. I looked forward and saw Aidan yell "CHARGE!" As we walked I thought of everything and anything but the fact that Teague wasn't out there. I was relieved when I was at the front and could concentrate on fighting.

I swung my sword at the man standing in front of me. He met my blade and I swung again. Every swing that I threw at him he blocked with amazing force. I started to tremble with weariness. I felt one of the stitches tear and I started to bleed. It had been stupid to even try to fight in my condition. I knew that I would not last much longer if my attacker kept up at this pace.

I stumbled upon a rock and almost fell to the ground but caught myself. By the time I looked up my foe was on the ground dead. Aidan suddenly caught my arm to steady me. There was blood on his sword.

"I could have done it myself," I whispered unconvincingly. I pulled feebly away.

"You shouldn't be fighting at all, let alone when you are injured. That's what I was trying to tell you earlier," he replied and slung his arm around my waist. He pulled me forward and held me so tightly that I was barely touching the ground.

"You have an army to lead! Let me go, at least let me walk back by myself. What will everybody think?" I struggled against him and he stopped walking.

"Fine, but promise that you won't fight on your way back to camp," he smiled slightly.

I didn't even bother to answer before walking as quickly as I could manage back to the safety of Aidan's tent. When I got inside I stripped off my armor and fell onto his bed exhausted, and hoping that soon I would be able to prove Aidan wrong.

*********

It took a month for the stitches to fully heal, but I stayed in Aidan's tent far longer than that. If people wanted to see me, they came into the tent. I didn't move an inch. I lay facing the sturdy fabric of the wall and listened when they talked, but didn't say anything. It felt as if nothing was worth my time.

The only thing that was worth my time was dead, and while I was recuperating I had nothing to distract me from my depression.

One night it was raining. Everyone had just come in from fighting and the blood was running in streams along the ground, a few trickles even came through the tent. My eyes were open and I was awake but I wasn't even thinking. I just sat there with one single mantra running through my mind. *Teague is dead and now so is Andrew Banidere.*

There was a ruffle of fabric at the entrance but I didn't turn to look. Someone sat down in one of the makeshift chairs beside my bed.

"Noble, the men are all worried about you. I think that you are well enough to fight now. I think that you need to fight." Aidan's voice made me tremble and I almost closed my eyes. I couldn't stand to listen to this. I couldn't stand to do anything.

"You were the one who didn't want me fighting, remember?" I feebly replied in a monotone voice.

He rested his hand on my shoulder and I was surprised when he pulled me over so that I faced him. I didn't move at all, not even to resist. I tried to stare past him but he grabbed my face and turned it to look at him. I stared into his eyes.

"Noble, we can't lose you like this," he pleaded.

My lip trembled. For the first time since I had stopped moving I felt something besides the emptiness. I felt pain, and anger and grief. My face crumpled and I sobbed into my hands. Aidan wrapped me in his strong arms and I grabbed his shirt, pulling him as close as I could. He whispered gently into my hair. I cried for a very long time. It had stopped raining and the sounds of the men outside had stopped. I pulled away feeling another emotion, embarrassment.

"I'm sorry, my King, tomorrow I will fight," I whispered.

"You have nothing to be sorry for. I know that you loved Teague. He was dear to me also, but I cannot just hide in my tent. I have to keep fighting and so do you," he gently wiped the tears from my cheeks. He stayed sitting close to me. I was glad that he was there. If he wasn't then I might just roll over and forget everything that I had just felt.

"I'll keep fighting because Teague would have wanted me to. He was so brave." No more tears came. My eyes were dry and it didn't feel as if I would cry for a long time.

"You are brave too Noble. It takes a lot of courage to keep going when everything inside of you screams that you should stop. When my father died I had to face that screaming every day. I know how you feel."

I realized that he did. He had felt what I was feeling and had cried just as I had.

"I just can't go back to being the person that I was before though," I started. "That person isn't here anymore. . ."

"Of course she is," he replied firmly. "He didn't make you who you are. He just made you feel like a better version of yourself. Please don't sell yourself short by saying that Teague was the reason you were strong and brave and kind."

I glanced up to meet his gaze. "Before he died Teague said that I was the one worth loving," I whispered.

"I don't know if I've ever met someone so deserving," he softly answered without hesitation.

I blushed and looked down at my hands. "Thank you, King."

He smiled at me gently. "Please, call me Aidan."

\*\*\*\*\*\*\*\*\*

I pulled on my armor the next morning with purpose. The sunshine felt brighter and the day even more glorious than it ever had before. I realized that because I had seen death and almost known it, every day had to be better than the one before or living was not going to be worthwhile. I had to live for Teague as much as for myself now. I had to feel everything that he never would again, for the both of us.

There was a tap on my shoulder and I turned to see Aidan smiling at me.

"I'm glad that you are here," he cocked his head slightly.

"I said that I would be here, didn't I?" I asked.

He looked around at the people all over the place and he leaned down closer to me. "Can I talk to you alone for a minute?"

I nodded and followed him once more into his tent. Over the last month we had spent a lot of time there together, me wallowing in my misery and him trying to pull me back into the world of the living.

He turned to look at me in the dim light. "Do you promise that you will be safe out there?"

I smiled and let out a soft laugh. "Of course! Why would you even worry about me when you were the one convincing me to go out? Besides, you have an entire army to look after,"

His look softened slightly. "I worry about everyone out there, but you are different. You belong out there, even though you shouldn't, and I will always be afraid for you. Somehow I was afraid for you even when I thought you were a man. I can't help but think of you as having an air of innocence and vulnerability."

"I promise that I will be safe," I whispered and gave him a reassuring smile. "And I can assure you that I am neither innocent nor vulnerable."

"Good, I suppose there's nothing else I can do then," he looked around as if he was nervous.

I nodded and stood awkwardly there, waiting for him to move out of the doorway or say something else. "I'll be fine . . . Aidan," I finally prompted, using his given name for the first time. I was eager to get out and begin.

He stared at me with a troubled look on his face but slowly stepped to the right so that I could make my way to the door. I started to walk forward and was beside him when I suddenly felt a hand on either shoulder that was pushing me to turn around. I turned and looked up into my King's eyes with genuine surprise.

"There is something else that I can do," he said with firm resolution. Then his lips bore down on mine savagely. My eyes stayed wide open because I was so shocked. He pulled back harshly and let go. I stumbled back, trembling.

He was shivering also. "Noble, I . . ." he took a step closer to me with his hand outstretched. I could not read his eyes.

"Get away from me," I hissed. I ran out of the tent, pushing him aside. When I touched him, I felt nauseous. The sun was hot and I stumbled around, thinking about everything and nothing all at the same time. My fingers went to my lips absently and I felt that they were tender.

I fell into place in the ranks and when I heard the familiar order to charge I moved forward blindly. When a rival stood in front of me I hacked at him efficiently and with rage. They all fell without me so much as working up a sweat, despite the fact that my muscles had greatly deteriorated.

What had Aidan been thinking? How could he have done that to me! He had taken advantage of my weak situation and I had not even tried to ward him off. I was even madder at myself than at him. Why hadn't I yanked away? Why hadn't I slapped him? Why hadn't I done something? Anything?

I let out a roar and decapitated the large Scarcillian in front of me. There were no tears running down my face, there were none left. Aidan had been my one ally and now he had betrayed me.

Suddenly there were no more Scarcillians to battle and there was no place to let out my emotions. I turned to see Leonard leaning on his sword, winded. I walked over, every muscle in my body tense.

He saw me and gave a slight smile. "How was your first day back on the battlefield?"

"It was fine," I whispered, surprisingly quietly.

"What's wrong?" He knew me too well.

"Nothing," I whispered and stared with tired eyes at the birds circling around in the sky. I looked at his concerned face once again. "I need a drink."

He let out an unsure laugh. "Last time you needed a drink you almost died."

I actually smiled when I looked at him. "That's true." I was almost angry as I had been the last time. I took a deep breath. "Leonard, talk some sense into me."

"I don't even know what you are senseless about."

I sighed. "Let's just say that I compromised myself."

He looked around at all of the dead bodies on the field. "Don't worry about it Noble, every man out there will never get to see another day to compromise themselves in. They are staring down from Heaven right now wishing that they could feel all of the emotions that you are feeling right now, just one more time."

I looked around at the littering of the dead all over, some already being picked apart by the birds that had just been in the sky. I slowly put a hand on my best friends shoulder. "Thank you Leonard."

He smiled softly at me. "You have to know that I would do anything for you Noble."

"I'd do anything for you also Leonard. I don't know what I would do without you. Please don't ever leave me," I looked down at my feet, embarrassed at how I knew that I must have sounded. I felt horrible about what had happened, but I would not cry. I had cried over Teague, who I had loved, I would not cry over Aidan. He wasn't worth it.

"I think that I will be around for a while Noble, if you promise that you will always be near-by," He put a hand on my shoulder which reminded me of Aidan. I fought not to stiffen and pull away, but then stopped. Leonard cared about me. I knew that he would never hurt me.

"I missed having my best friend around," I grasped his hand in my own, in a brotherly way. Leonard always brought out the best in me. I just hoped that he was enough to stop the tide of self-loathing that had risen within me.

**********

I was still there in that camp two years later. The Scarcillians were proving to be an even more formidable foe than we had first envisioned. There was no hint at anything like surrender, and both of our men kept coming to die. The death toll was high, and it grew worse day by day.

Both sides had their advantages. Since we were an island, the enemy had to cross the sea to get here, which took time and could be dangerous in and of itself. Additionally, we had to work hard to keep them from surrounding us. Our navy had begun to grown, but it was still in its early stages and many of our ships were needed for trade. While we had the home advantage, we were also a much smaller nation than Scarcilla. While their fresh men kept coming, ours were merely being recycled. Most men came for a few months and then went home for a month before coming back to fight again. I stayed the entire time along with Leonard; after all, what did we have to go back for?

One morning I awoke, not even concerned with the idea of fighting. It's amazing what two years of constant killing can do to a person. I pulled on all my armor and walked out into the drizzling rain. These were the worst days to fight because the mud was almost impossible to walk through. I sighed. At least it added some variety.

Leonard smiled down at me as he rode to the front on his horse. Aidan was away at Calentto attending to matters of state and while he was away Leonard was in charge of the army, with Morgan and Gladwin as his advisors. I walked to the front of the army and stood next to Bran. We didn't speak. There wasn't anything new to say. We had been living the exact same life day in and day out.

Leonard gave the order to charge and I jogged forward with a fearsome sounding battle roar. My adrenaline started to kick in as I cut down my first opponent with very little opposition. I moved on, making my kills without any major difficulty. It barley even bothered me that I had killed hundreds of men in this war. I had come to think of them as villains instead of humans, or at least that's what I had convinced myself. Doubt led to hesitation, which would eventually lead to my death.

I swung around to see a huge Scarcillian cut down a man that I recognized, but couldn't remember his name. His family would miss him. The victor looked up and caught my eyes.

"Looking for a real fight?" I called as I sized him up. He was big as a bear, easily the biggest man that I had ever fought. My eyes skimmed over arm muscles as big as my legs, and I hoped that at least he was slow. His long tangled red hair and bright green eyes made him look crazed, which would make things interesting. I never thought about dying, but I did think about losing, and I wondered if I might have gotten myself in too deep.

He gave me a grin that was much handsomer than that of most of his countrymen. As he walked over I glanced down at his weapon. It probably weighed about as much as all of my armor combined. It was an enormous broad sword that gleamed even though the day was wet and muggy.

I looked at the area around us. I didn't think that the mud would be too big of an issue. It wasn't very deep and I was used to using the mud to my advantage in some cases.

"Is Bryton sending their women to fight us now?" the man asked when he was close enough to talk in a normal voice.

For a moment I stiffened, and then I realized that it was just an insult and nothing else. "Is Scarcillia breeding giants nowadays to fight us mere mortals?"

"We actually train to fight in my country, instead of sending farm boys to die," he said pleasantly. It was almost as if we were having a normal conversation instead of preparing for one of us to perish.

"Believe me, I've been training for quite a while," I smiled.

He nodded. "I have been hoping to have a decent fight."

"Well then lets stop playing this game of cat and mouse and get to it, shall we?" I held my sword up and he raised his also.

"I thought that you would never ask," he said as he began to circle me. I followed his every movement.

I lunged to test him out. He knew what I was doing and hid

everything that was not absolutely necessary. He was giving nothing up. We circled for what seemed like forever, casually jabbing at each other, never really expecting anything. I had to fight to keep myself focused.

"Is the big soldier scared?" I finally asked flippantly. I was growing weary of this game. If he did not strike soon then I would, even though it went against all that I had learned in the past couple years. I had other battles to fight, and I could hear my stomach growling.

Suddenly, he lunged at me. He had seen evidence in my face that my mind was wandering. He swung at me again and again and again. I blocked everything, but only just barely, and I never had any time to strike at him. He was circling around me at a quick pace and I was getting slightly dizzy from following his movements. Each blow he rained down was bone jarring and I could feel my muscles start to give a little more with each hit. Once my blade chipped. My breathing was raspy and every once and a while my knees would start to buckle beneath me.

I missed one of his swings and it sliced all the way up my cheek and through my eyebrow. Thankfully, he had missed the hollow of my eye. I didn't falter, even though the pain was intense. The warm blood ran so heavily into my eye that it was hard to see.

I was faced with the fact that I couldn't hold on much longer. I was going to die if I didn't think of something quick. I looked down at the ground for a split second and saw a large rock sticking up. It was a miracle that I hadn't tripped over it already, but maybe I could move slightly so that he would fall over it. It seemed like my only chance. I saw no opportunity to attack, and I would not run, even if it would have been possible.

Then the worst thing that could have possibly happened occurred. I tripped over the rock that I had just been planning to use against my opponent. I fell flat on my back with a loud thud, barely missing falling onto the Scarcillian's singing sword. I instantly raised my sword, prepared to use my last ounce of strength, but the man already had his sword to my throat. The sharp point made it difficult to swallow. I set my jaw in a firm line, refusing to show the fear that was welling up in me.

"Go ahead," I whispered. "What's one more dead Brytish man." I met the man's eyes for a minute before staring past him.

I stifled a gasp that threatened to leap from my lips. Leonard was right behind the man, ready to strike. Suddenly there was a slight thud as Leonard's foot ran into that damn rock. I held my breath, waiting to see if the man about to kill me had heard the faint noise. For a moment his face was unchanged, and I thought we were safe.

Suddenly the man let out a roar and turned around to plunge his sword into Leonard's stomach.

"Nooooo!" I screamed and kicked the mans legs out from under him. He wasn't expecting this, and fell to the ground with a large thud, dropping his sword. Jumping to my feet, I held my sword to his throat.

I snarled down at him. "How does it feel to be on the other end of the sword," my jaw was quivering with anger. I could hear Leonard gasping for breath from behind us.

The man just looked up at me. He didn't look at all scared so I pressed the sword more firmly to his throat.

"You're friend is dying. You need to help him get medical attention," the man said calmly.

"Fine then, let me kill you first," I could feel the blood still dripping down my face. A drop of blood sprung forth from where my blade met the man's skin.

"You want to fight me again," he still showed no trace of fear.

"Oh yeah?" I snarled.

"This wasn't a fair fight. You know that. Your friend interfered. You get another chance to see if you can best me. You know you want that."

I looked into his eyes for a moment and saw absolutely nothing. I couldn't read him at all. The fact that I hesitated though, showed that what he said contained a grain of truth. "If I let you go, you'll kill more of my people." I needed to decide what to do fast. I could still hear Leonard behind me, the life slowly draining from him.

"I promise that I will not fight another man until I meet you on the battlefield again. You have my word." I could finally read one emotion in the man's eyes: honesty.

I snorted. "That means a lot," I turned to see Leonard staring at me. He nodded. I turned back to the man. "Fine." I pulled my sword away and went over to help Leonard to his feet. When I turned back the man was on his feet. "Remember me," I snarled before we walked slowly past him. When I turned back he was gone.

"You should have killed him," Leonard mumbled as we walked along. We had a long way to go to get to the medic tent. I looked down to see that the cloth he had wrapped around the wound was already saturated with blood. We needed to hurry.

"I thought that was what you wanted me to do," I said with a small smile. It really wasn't a funny topic at all.

"No! The thought of him trying to kill you makes me furious," he was seriously more upset about that than the fact that he had a hole in his stomach.

"The thought of you getting yourself killed while trying to save me makes me furious," I laughed. "But I still appreciate it."

"I know that it's been hard for you ever since Teague died Noble, but you have to use some common sense. That guy was three times your size. I don't want you going out there and looking for a fight that you can't win," Leonard grimaced. He was being completely serious.

"I thought that I could take him," I whispered, not sure if I believed it myself. "Now when I fight him again I'll be prepared." I could see the med tent in the distance.

Leonard shook his head. "I won't let him fight you again Noble. He'll kill you."

"I have to. I want to," I sighed. We were almost there. He was going to be alright. I looked over to see that his face was slightly gray. It had been too close for my liking. Leonard couldn't die. I wouldn't survive.

We walked into the med tent and I sat him down on a cot. Kade came running over and gave me a smile before setting to work. Leonard and I caught each others gaze. Then he finally gave a small smile. I looked down at my feet shyly before smiling back. Then I walked out of the tent and promptly ran straight into Aidan.

When I looked up at him I blushed. He blushed too. Ever since what I liked to refer to as 'the incident' we had both avoided each other as much as possible. I wasn't mad at him anymore, it seemed trivial in consideration of where we were, but I still would rather not have had anything to do with him. Two years was a long time to avoid someone.

"I saw you and Leonard go in and I came over to see if you were alright," he was clearly worried, "I just arrived a few moments ago."

"Leonard got a nasty belly wound, but I think he'll be alright," I answered. I knew that Aidan and Leonard were still very close friends, even though I liked to believe that Leonard and I were closer.

"And what happened to your face?" Aidan asked, raising a hand to touch my cheek.

I flinched, both from the pain and from his unwanted touch. "I got into a nasty fight with a Scarcillian as big as a bear. Leonard actually saved my life," I raised my own hand to the cut. It had stopped bleeding for the moment and some of the blood had dried. I had forgotten about it.

"It should make a pretty good scar. Do you want me to stitch it up for you? It looks pretty deep," he said kindly.

I raised my good eyebrow. "You know how to do that?"

He smiled. "Yeah. Didn't you know that it was me that stitched you up the day that . . ." He paused awkwardly. "Well anyways, you'd be surprised what being a king really entails."

I looked back into the med tent. They looked pretty busy. I turned back to Aidan. I didn't really want to be that close to him, but I knew that I needed to take care of the cut or it might get infected.

"Alright," I smiled. We walked silently back to Aidan's tent where I sat down on his bed while he got the supplies to stitch me up. First he poured the whiskey all down my face and I grabbed the flask and took a swig with a laugh. I was getting used to the sting after lots of minor injuries. Then Aidan stitched up my face with gentle fingers. The lightning between us was still there, but I acted as if I didn't feel anything.

When he was done sewing up both the upper and lower portion of the cut I raise gently fingers up to the puffy skin.

"You know, to tell you the truth, I really don't want a scar," I whispered, not looking up at the king.

He laughed. "All warriors want scars."

I shook my head. "Not me. I'm already manly enough. Scars are less than desirable on girls."

"Do you ever want to return to the life of a female though?" he asked gently. "I guess I just assumed that you'd always stay with us."

I shrugged. "I don't know what I will want to do." There was an awkward silence and I looked up for a split second and caught his knowing gaze. They looked even bluer than I remembered. I couldn't help but gasp slightly. "I have to go," I croaked before walking quickly out of the tent. Things were all far more complicated whenever Aidan was around.

\*\*\*\*\*\*\*\*\*\*

"I'm much too tough to die," Leonard laughed.

I sat next to him on the makeshift medic bed. "You're much too stubborn to die," I smiled. "I hope that you get well soon."

"I'll be back out there before you know it. You just have to make sure that you keep safe until then. I can't save you if I'm stuck in here," he grinned.

"I think that this was the first time that you have ever saved me. And even though I am very grateful, I would like the credit for keeping myself alive for these past two years," I did a fake little bow. It was good to be with Leonard. I was beyond relieved that he was going to be alright. "In fact I'm going back out to fight tomorrow."

"Doesn't that seem a little soon?" Leonard asked with something akin to nervousness splayed across his features.

"Leonard, I was barely even hurt. The cut doesn't even affect my vision. I am in top shape. I'm ready to go back out there and get the man that did this to you."

Leonard shook his head. "Don't do it."

"You know that I have to," I whispered. "You would do the same thing if it was you. Have a little faith in me please."

So, the next day I stood in the front line of men, searching the crowd for a shock of bright red. I didn't see him. I killed, because I had not said that I wouldn't, but I kept my eyes open for the man that I was there for. I was frustrated when I had not found him by sunset.

I didn't see him for two weeks. To this day I'm still not sure what he was waiting for. Maybe he wanted me to be apprehensive; maybe he wanted me to be angry. By the time that I finally saw him I was both.

He was at the front of his army. I could see his confidence rolling off of him from across the field. We held each other's gaze until men ran towards each other, until they ran to meet their fates.

We slowly made our way to each other. I was in a hurry to begin, but I would never let him know that. I wanted him to think that I was as calm and cool as he was. In reality I was hot and ready to show him that I never made the same mistake twice.

"What took you so long? I've been ready to get this over with for a while now," I growled when he was close enough to hear me.

"It will be over soon enough little man. Do you promise that none of your little friends are waiting to save you again?" he smiled down at me.

"I won't need them this time. I'm a fast learner," I smiled back as I pulled my sword from its scabbard. He did the same. "It's a shame that we can't just be friends. If I didn't have to kill you, I might just like you."

He laughed out loud at that. "Princes are not friends with peasants."

"And knights are not friends with invaders," I replied with a sigh. But was it the truth? Wasn't I glad for the war to distract me? "Let's just get this over with."

"Are you scared, knight?" he jabbed playfully at my side. I blocked him without even moving my body.

"Not even a little bit." I raised my sword into the ready position.

The man didn't take any time to feel me out before starting his rain of attacks again. He already knew how I fought. But it was a double sided coin, because I knew how he fought also. From experience, I knew that every swordsman had a weakness. The Scarcillian would have to hesitate in his hits at least once, and that would be my chance. I just had to make sure that I didn't miss the opportunity, because if I did then I wouldn't end up as I had at our last fight.

So, I waited patiently, giving less effort than I had previously. He was good; there was no doubt about that. Every hit was perfectly timed so that I didn't have a single moment to retaliate. His arcs were beautiful, some of the best that I had ever seen. He deserved to beat me, but for once I was glad that life wasn't fair.

Suddenly I saw it, the exact perfect moment to strike. He was bringing his blade back higher than usual, trying to get a heavier hit. It was only a split second of time, but it was all that I needed.

I swung at his side and met flesh while darting away from his angry blade. I danced behind him and plunged my sword through his shoulder. He roared in pain and snapped around to face me, but I was gone again, nicking at him again and again with my blade. He tried desperately to catch up with me, but I had broken his pattern. He had no idea what to do. Finally, it was time to end it. With one last roar, I plunged my sword through his chest. I saw the look of utter surprise paint itself across his face before he fell to his knees. Blood ran down his leg, pooling in the ridges of the dirt.

I wiped my sword on my pants and then walked over to stand in front of him. Looking down at the pain on his face I actually felt sorry for killing him. I felt miserable, but I had to do it. Two years of killing and seeing my friends be killed had taught me that mercy was a luxury I couldn't afford.

He looked up at me and managed a small smile. "I think that we could have been friends. I'm honored to die by your blade."

I nodded down at him and tears pooled in my eyes, but I held them back. He would not want to be cried over. He would want his killer to be proud that they had bested such a man as him.

With one last shattered breath, he fell to the ground.

I heard a Scarcillian somewhere close to me shout. "They have killed our Prince. A knight has killed the Prince!"

**********

The fighting was halted for the rest of the day in honor of our foe. We could hear their wailing all night, and everyone from Bryton wanted to personally thank me. I just smiled graciously, not knowing exactly what to say to everyone. I wasn't used to being the center of attention. I was always in the background, and it was the way that I preferred it.

I had guard duty that evening, even though everyone offered to take over for me. I needed time to be alone and collect my thoughts. It had been an interesting day. It had been an interesting last couple of years. As hard as it sometimes became, I was usually grateful that I chose the life that I had. I couldn't imagine anything else.

I sat perched up against a log, staring out over the fields. The stars were as bright as I had seen them in a long time, and there were no clouds, which was very rare in Bryton.

"Noble," someone called. I rolled my eyes and turned around to see Aidan standing in the moonlight. "Where are you?"

"Over here," I called grumpily. What did he want now? If he was going to thank me again for killing the Prince it was going to put me in a very bad mood.

He came over and sat down next to me. We sat in silence for a few minutes before he spoke. "I'm really proud of you."

I sighed. "Everyone is. The thing is, I don't know what I have to be proud about. I killed a genuinely good man."

"By killing him you saved hundreds of your countrymen's lives," he replied easily.

"Why does everyone keep saying that? Why are our countrymen any more important or valuable than his were?" I sighed again. I seemed to do that a lot whenever I was around Aidan. "I know that they started the war, and they are the ones who invaded us, but humans have a really funny way of justifying everything we do, even if it's wrong."

Aidan just turned to look at me. I sat there for a moment, avoiding his gaze, before I finally turned to look at him. "You are one of the most amazing people that I have ever met, male or female."

"No I'm not," I whispered, "There's nothing special about me."

"You are special," he replied, not taking his eyes off of me. When he said that word I had to turn away. Even though Teague had been gone for two years, it still felt like yesterday when I had held his dying body. "You're everything that I want."

My hand slid off my lap with a thud. Was he saying what I thought he was saying? "You don't mean that," I replied icily.

He reached over and grabbed my hand. I closed my eyes at the feel of his skin against mine. "Yes I do. You're tough and smart. You're beautiful and caring. I could go on and on. For two years I have thought of nothing besides your hands and lips and the way your eyes sparkle when you smile . . ."

I interrupted him. "Aidan, I'm not any of those things. I'm scared and tired. If you think that I'm beautiful then you must be blind," I still sat with my eyes closed even though I could almost feel him willing me to look at him. I wasn't ready for this. I still loved Teague. I would always love him.

To be honest, I wanted Aidan. The lightning I felt when he touched me was thrilling, but it wasn't enough. It seemed as if nothing would ever be enough again.

"You're all that I could think about the entire time that I was away Noble. I just wanted to come back and protect you. I just needed to come and see that you were alright. I should have stayed in Calentto, but I couldn't," he rubbed the back of my hand numb with his thumb.

"Aidan, please stop. I don't understand why you are saying this to me and I'm tired and . . ." I trailed off, trying to find a reason why he should stop. Why not let him go on, my answer would still be the same. The King always got what he wanted; rejection might help to build his character. Of course he was already about as close to perfect as it is humanly possible to be.

"I love you, Noble. Do you understand that?" I finally turned to look at him. There was pure desperation in his eyes. I saw what I must have looked like to Teague and it broke my heart. "I love you."

"No, you don't," I whispered, trying to convince myself as much as him. It was the first time that a man had ever said those words to me.

He nodded. "I really do. I'm actually really frightened by how much I love you," he paused. "I try to deny it or obliterate it but when I'm away I see you in my dreams and when I'm near you I am drawn to every word you mutter and every movement you make."

I didn't want to be with him. When I was with him everything was tangled and blurrily exhilarating. Physical attraction wasn't enough for me. I needed to feel what I felt for Teague before a relationship meant anything. When you feel something like that, everything else pales in comparison.

And yet, in him I saw myself when I told Teague that I loved him. I saw someone who needed me. I couldn't let him feel like I had felt when met with stony silence. There was no good solution to this problem.

"What do you want from me?" I asked wearily.

His face fell slightly. "I want for you to want something from me."

I sighed. It was the moment of a truth. I would never give him all of me. "I do want something from you Aidan. I'm just not sure what it is."

His smile made me smile. "I promise that I'll be everything that you want." He leaned in to kiss me and I gently started to lean forward. The confusing memory of our last kiss came to mind. Our lips were almost touching when we heard a noise and jerked apart. My breathing had quickened slightly.

"Noble," Kade called, "I'm here to take the next shift." I just smiled sadly.

The Scarcillians surrendered the next day.

**\*\*\*\*\*\*\*\*\***

I woke the day after the surrender knowing that we were going back to Calentto. We packed up and burned the minimal dead from the day before. Aidan and I avoided each other as much as possible, which was fine with me. I just assumed that he felt awkward being around me when all the men were there.

We traveled all day and then when we got to a little town we bedded down and the men went inside to enjoy the women, which they had been very deprived of. I sat outside under a tree staring at the night sky. Maybe this time I would actually have some time to myself.

I took a deep breath and let it out slowly.

It would be the first time I had been home since Teague's death. I would have to see all the places we had gone together and know that he would never again experience it. I would be haunted by his memory every day.

It was then that I finally formed a coherent thought about the feelings that had been welling up in me for years.

I would never fully forgive Teague for what he had done to me.

I was so filled with rage about what he had done to me and I never had the chance to tell him. I had feigned forgiveness because I loved him and then he had died, leaving me alone with so much contempt and disgust that I could never share.

It was exhausting, and I wasn't sure that I would ever forgive myself or him for being so weak.

A slow tear trickled down my cheek before I heard a person walking toward me. Reluctantly I looked from the sky and my thoughts to the noise, expecting to see Aidan. I flinched.

Morgan stood in front of me. We stared at each other for a couple of seconds before I spoke, "What do you want?" Morgan and I had hardly spoken in months. He had grown bitter about being passed up for commander of the armies and we tried to avoid each other as much as possible. The mutual hatred ran deep.

"I was just coming out here for a moment alone, but I guess that isn't going to work out," he just glared down at me.

"There are lots of places to sit down Morgan. I don't know why you always have to go out of your way to be cruel to me," I was tired. I couldn't wait to get back to Calentto. I couldn't remember what a real bath or a real bed felt like.

"Why do you go out of your way to make me look like the bad guy?" He asked. There was a touch of actual emotion in his voice. We were the only ones close to the same age. It was unfortunate that we hated each other.

"I think that you're pretty good at making yourself look like the bad guy. You don't need me to help you with that," I shivered in the cool night air. "Do you try and make everybody hate you or does it just come naturally?"

Morgan looked down at me with his jaw clenched. "Don't act like you know anything about me."

"I know that I would have been willing to give you a chance before you made up some stupid worthless lie about me the second day we were at the castle. And I would have been willing to give you a second chance but now all you do is threaten me and stare at me menacingly. I have done nothing to make you hate me, but for some reason you do, and all you do is make my life Hell," I snarled at him. I didn't want to understand him. There was nothing to understand. He was crazy.

"Maybe I just play the part that everyone expects from me," he whispered before turning on his heel and gliding silently away. I stared after him.

As much as I hated to admit it he had a point. When he had been born Merick, Aidan's mentor, made a prophesy that Morgan would take the throne. Morgan had grown up being feared and reviled throughout the nation. It must have been hard on him as a child, but he was a man now, and he ultimately made the decision about how he acted. I didn't feel bad for him. We make our own future, I had learned that.

# CHAPTER FOUR
## Living

We got back to the castle by noon the next day. There were crowds on the street cheering us on. All of us were happy to be back home, but before we could truly relax, that night we had a dinner held in our honor. I was seated next to Morgan and we both chose to remain stiff and formal. I was barely polite. I picked at my food and didn't feel hungry. About halfway through the dinner Morgan left. I was glad and finally started to relax. The dinner seemed to go on forever, and when it was finally over I went to my room and started getting ready for bed. I was exhausted but I knew that there were a few things that I needed to do first, including cleaning my sword. The trip back had seen more than a few hours of bored sword play.

I went to my bed to get my sword but it wasn't there. Frowning, I tried to remember where I had put it. I was almost positive that I had put it on my bed, but I looked around just in case. I tore the room apart but still didn't find it. I was so nervous that I could barely think. Where was it?!

Getting angry I walked into the hall and down towards Leonard's room. Maybe he had taken it for some reason; I burst in with my mouth open to demand if he knew where it was and blushed. Leonard was on top of a slave girl that I recognized. Both of them were naked. He rolled his eyes and tossed his damp curls out of his eyes. I looked away and rushed out, slamming the door behind me. I felt so stupid! I started to walk towards my room when I heard a door open. I kept walking quickly, hoping that it wasn't Leonard or that I would make it to my room before he would make it to me.

"Noble," Leonard called. I turned around and was glad to see that he had at least thrown on a loincloth. He jogged up. "What did you want?"

"Well, I was just wondering if you had taken my sword for any reason. I searched all over my room and didn't find it." I tried to focus on his face and not the memory of his bare ass or the glistening muscles of his chest. It was hard for me to concentrate, but I had to remember that a man wouldn't stare at another man the way that I wanted to stare at him.

Leonard shook his head. "I know that I didn't, but maybe one of the other guys did. I'll help you ask around."

I blushed. "You looked like you were busy. I can do it myself." I looked at my feet. Leonard playfully punched my shoulder. He didn't seem to feel awkward at all.

"I would never place a girl over my best friend! Just give me a moment to get dressed." He turned to go.

"Leonard," I called and he turned to look at me. I blushed once again, "Maybe you should lock your door next time."

He grinned at me and then shrugged as he rushed off and I waited. I watched the girl Leonard was with come out with her clothes slightly disheveled and as she walked away she gave me a little glare. When Leonard came out we walked around and asked almost everyone if they had seen my sword, but nobody had.

The only person we didn't find was Morgan. "Morgan left about halfway through dinner," I added while we were searching. I tried not to let my suspicion show in my voice.

"Well, I hate to say this but your sword had to have been stolen during the banquet and if he wasn't there then . . ." Leonard trailed off. I nodded.

"It had to have been him, but why would he do something like that? He's not an idiot, and he wouldn't do all this stupid stuff to me just for a little revenge," I paused for a moment. "He might be trying to make a point though. Last night we had a conversation about why he acts the way he does."

"Did he explain why he stares at you with that creepy look of his all the time? Never mind, I don't care. Even if he did, now that he's done this, he's gone too far. I know how much your sword meant to you and we will get it back," Leonard was getting worked up.

"Calm down. We don't even know if it's him yet, and even if it was do you think that we're actually going to catch him?" I asked, looking down at my feet.

"I don't know, but we have to tell Aidan," Leonard said and started towards Aidan's chambers. I walked behind him trying to decide whether to say no, or just go on with him. I had only seen Aidan from a distance since what had happened on our last day of combat. We walked on and then Leonard knocked on Aidan's door. It swung open almost immediately.

"Hello Leonard, Noble. How can I help you?" He stepped aside and motioned us in.

Leonard started explaining. "Noble's sword has gone missing and we have not been able to find it. We asked everyone and looked around. The only person we couldn't find was Morgan and he left around halfway through our dinner. Both of us have a sneaking suspicion that he stole the sword!" He was very angry but trying not to let it show, after all Morgan was Aidan's nephew.

Aidan nodded and looked at me; his blue eyes gave away nothing. "Are you sure that the sword is not in your quarters or that you didn't accidentally leave it somewhere when we were coming home?" He sounded rational as always and I wondered if he ever lost his temper.

The most irrational I had ever hear him be was when he was

declaring his love to me.

I shook my head no. "I came right in and then set it on my bed. I wouldn't be making such a fuss, but the sword belonged to my Father and it was special to me," I mumbled. I looked down at my hands. Aidan had no idea who my Father was; if he did, I would not have been there.

"I understand. Elamoneir is like that to me. I don't think that it was Morgan but I can try and talk to him about it now if you want..." He raised his hands as if he were saying that was all that he could do.

Leonard nodded his head vigorously and Aidan nodded. "Leonard, go tell the guard to be on the lookout for Morgan. You can search with them if you want." Aidan went to open the door.

"I think I will search. We have to find him. Noble, we will get your sword back." Leonard patted me on the back. He loved playing the role of my older brother.

"You are such a great friend," I answered with a nervous smile, "But I'll go. You stay here." I wasn't in the mood to deal with Aidan and his infatuation. I just wanted my sword.

"I have to talk to you Noble," the King spoke with authority. I shivered. This was exactly what I had not wanted to happen. I had to fight not to roll my eyes or else Leonard would see.

He gave me a smile before walking out the door and shutting it firmly behind him. I stayed facing the door for a moment. The room was uncomfortably warm and I was aware of Aidan standing behind me, waiting for me to turn. I took a deep breath.

When I finally spun to look at him, his face was unsure. "Have you changed your mind?" he whispered and gave a small, nervous grin.

I couldn't help but smile back at me. He really was in love with me. There was nothing I could do about it except try to hurt him as little as possible. "No, I still want the same things as I did before," which was the truth.

He let go of the air that he had been holding in. "I'm so glad. I was worrying about that the entire trip home, but I was scared to talk to you when everyone was right there." He came closer and grabbed both of my hands.

I sighed, hoping that I never got used to the feeling that passed between our bodies. It was the only thing that was making this bearable. "That's alright. I don't blame you. That's what I figured was going on."

"Do you honestly think that Morgan took your sword?" he asked as he pulled me down to sit next to him on the bed.

I shrugged. "I honestly don't know. I don't see why he would, but at the same time who else could it have been?"

Aidan's hand strayed up to touch the slowly forming scar on my face. It was slightly tender, but wasn't unbearbale. His face inched closer to mine. He grinned.

"Don't worry, we'll find out who it was," he whispered. "Right now, how about we celebrate being back home?"

He leaned in to kiss me. Our lips touched softly and I gasped. Our last kiss had been so long ago, and so different from this soft caress. We both opened our eyes to look at each other. There was shock and awe in his eyes that was probably mirrored in my own.

"I've never felt anything like what I feel between us," he whispered.

"Neither have I," I croaked. We both smiled. I licked my lips and looked down at my hands. They were shaking. Suddenly tears were steaming down my face, salty and warm.

Aidan wrapped an arm around me and I let myself lean against him. He didn't say anything until my sobs had quieted to an occasional hiccup.

"I know that you don't feel the same way that I do, but we were both doing a pretty good job at hiding it until now," he said as he moved back slightly to look down into my face.

I managed to look into his eyes for a moment before looking away. I wiped away the snot that was dripping from my nose. How could this man possibly love me? "I'm still in love with someone else," I whispered.

"Is it Leonard?" he asked sadly.

I let out a genuine laugh which quickly turned back into a small sob. "No," I sighed, "I'm still in love with Teague."

He nodded slowly. "Did Teague know that you were a woman?"

I nodded. "I fell in love with him and he let me believe that he was in love with me too. Then I found out about him and Iseult. We were friends, but it never changed the way I felt about him. To this day I'm still in love with him, and I don't know if it will ever go away." I let out a big breath. "I just . . . I didn't want to hurt you like he hurt me." I glanced over at him for a moment. "I'm sorry."

"It's not your fault," he turned to give me a small smile. "I'm just sorry that I can't be what you need."

"It's not your fault! You are everything that any woman could ever want, and I'm angry at myself for not wanting it," I grabbed his hand. The lighting was warmer than usual. "And I do feel it. I just don't feel . . . it."

We looked into each other's eyes and he knew what I meant, and that I was telling the truth. I felt as if he truly understood me in that moment.

"Maybe, it'll come in time," I whispered and leaned in to kiss him again. He pulled me close and tangled his fingers in my short hair. When we finally pulled apart we pressed our cheeks together and I breathed in the intoxicating scent of his skin.

He was the most human man I had ever met, and somehow in that moment I knew that he was destined to be more than a man.

**\*\*\*\*\*\*\*\*\***

Waking up early the next morning, I heard a commotion outside my door and walked out into the hall to see Leonard yelling at Morgan. I had known that the confrontation had to have come sooner or later.

"Why did you steal his sword? It's his most prized possession but obviously you don't give a shit about that," Leonard said loudly as he grabbed Morgan by the shirt and pulled him up slightly. Morgan was taller than Leonard but still somehow Leonard had him lifted so that he was barely touching the ground.

"I keep telling you that I didn't take it!" Morgan snarled and his hands balled up into fists. I was glad that he didn't lash out like a snake.

"It had to have been you. You left the dinner last night, and you have had it out for Noble ever since the beginning!" Leonard still sounded angry but he let go. Then he turned and saw me. "Noble, I finally found the scum after searching all night." He walked over and stood beside me. I felt bad that I had slept and he had stayed up all night for me. I should have gone out with him; after all it was my father's sword. My thoughts had suddenly become very preoccupied.

"Morgan, did you take my sword?" I asked even though I knew he would deny it even if he had. There really was no point in it.

"No! I feel as if we just went over this," he turned a face filled with mock hurt towards me. It was disgusting to me after I had seen such honesty from him only a few nights ago. It had been a rare thing. This man was a liar; but of course, so was I.

"I thought that you were playing the role Morgan. What do me and my sword have to do with anything?" I asked, growing agitated. What game was this man playing? I took a step closer to him. My fingers were itching to punch his face. I didn't understand what he was doing to me.

Morgan looked shocked. "Little do you know that you have everything to do with a lot of things," With that he turned and walked away. Leonard followed, saying obscene things while I just stood there. Finally, Leonard came back and looked like he had cooled down a little bit.

"I don't understand him at all," he muttered before turning towards the training yard. I followed. We both could use a little sword practice to let out our anger.

When we got there, I stared up into the bright sunlight and felt it warm my skin. I went over to a rack and picked out a sword to use. I finally found one that I thought would be suitable even though it still didn't feel right in my hands.

"Would you like to duel me?" I heard the familiar voice of Kade ask.

"Yes," I said before even turning. I had learned that it was impolite to refuse a duel even if I was bored of fighting with men I could beat. I raised the sword and Kade raised his. Like lightning I brought mine down on my opponent's sword. Kade was a weak man among us, even though his arms were still corded with muscles, and I drove it so close that it almost nicked his nose which was covered by his awkward helmet. He pulled out and swung around to attack, but missed me. I stepped to the left and poked at his side. It hit, as I had known it would. That was Kade's weakness; he never defended his left side. He smiled and I knew he felt a little ashamed. He knew that he wasn't near as good as the rest of us, but it still hurt when he was reminded time and time again.

"You really need to work on that Kade, I don't know what I'd do if you got hurt in a battle because of that," I frowned. In a way, I hated beating my friends because then I knew that they weren't safe on the battlefield. It was hard to acknowledge that your friends could get hurt and you couldn't do anything about it. Teague's face flashed across my mind. I hated thinking about him lying on the ground, so ashen and cold.

"I'm trying, but I get so caught up in attacking that I forget about the defense!" He wiped his brow. It was an extremely hot day. I wanted to strip off my armor like some of the other men I saw were doing.

"Well, it is good to be on the offense but you have to remember that they have the chance to attack also. You are getting better though, at least this time you moved to block me instead of just standing there." I knew that I sounded harsh but it was really just tough love and everyone did it.

Kade nodded before walking off without even a slight look of disappointment on his face. I walked up to Patrick and asked to duel. He nodded and then we fought. This fight lasted longer, but it still wasn't much fun. I had nicked him on his right shoulder, as I often did.

"Duel, lad?" Bran and I dueled a lot because even though he was the superior fighter, we had long, fun fights. I had never beaten him, but I had come so close sometimes that I was still proud. I smiled and pulled my sword out. Everyone crowded around to watch because they would sometimes bet on who would win. I hated letting down the people who bet on me. Bran's sword was already out and he brought it down. I kept it up, with my muscles straining painfully. Bran was a very strong man. I pulled out and then swung to the left, trying to get him into a compromising situation. Out of the corner of my eye, I saw Aidan watching and I smiled. Bran stepped aside and then lunged at my knees. I hopped over his blade and then lunged yet again at his head. He moved to the left and brought himself behind me; I turned and saw him attack out of the corner of my eye. He often circled around when he was fighting because he liked to confuse his opponent. All of a sudden I spun to the left and he was standing in front of me. I brought my sword down on his left shoulder which was his weak spot and it hit him. I immediately pulled away. I had never beat Bran before. He looked stunned for a few seconds before smiling slowly.

"You truly do amaze me, boy," he said and patted me on the back. "But I guess you aren't much of a boy anymore are you?" Then he walked away and I saw Aidan and Leonard beaming at me. I smiled widely and walked over to them.

"You did great Noble," Leonard said, "But I have to remind you again that you are a little weak on your left side. You really should practice with your left hand just in case you're right hand is injured. I've had it happen and it is not pleasant to be defenseless." I nodded slowly while rolling my eyes jokingly.

Aidan nodded. "Yes, it is always good to be prepared." Then he put his hand on my shoulder and the weight of his hand on the metal of my armor made me feel as if I was sizzling inside of the metal case "I'm very proud of you though. Did you have any formal training before you came here?" He smiled at me and I wanted to kiss him so bad that it hurt.

"No, my Father taught me. He always demonstrated with the sword that was stolen. Now that I'm not with my Father I guess the sword was more of a sentiment than anything," I looked across the yard at Morgan. "Morgan said that he didn't take it but I don't know . . ." I didn't finish and looked at my feet.

"I understand. I know that Morgan hasn't been very kind to you but he is a good boy, deep down." Aidan took his hand away and I could tell that he was trying to convince himself that Morgan was good. He just stank of bad will and evil. There didn't seem to be a good bone in his body.

"Do you believe that he will take the throne from you?" Leonard asked darkly and I shivered even though we were in the sunshine.

"No, Merick was a good mentor but I don't really think that he could see the future. I don't believe that any man can do that." Aidan answered the question a little too fast and I was skeptical. I felt as if I knew him relatively well, even though Leonard probably understood him better than I did.

"I'm going to go practice my archery," I smiled before turning to leave. I turned and gasped. Stuck in the far sod wall of the practice yard was my sword. I jogged over and pulled it out. I could hear Aidan and Leonard behind me. I studied the sword and saw that whoever had taken it took the ruby from the hilt. "This is my sword," I turned to tell them, "The ruby from the hilt is missing." I was confused, who would have wanted the ruby out of my sword?

"It must have just been a common thief," Aidan said, "We'll try and find who it was and I will replace the ruby." I nodded and swung it. Was it really just a common thief or had it been Morgan? Why would he want the ruby? How had the sword gotten there in the middle of the day without anyone seeing? Or had somebody seen?

"I still think that it was Morgan," Leonard muttered. I heard Aidan chuckle.

"Why don't you like him Leonard?" asked the King.

"What is there to like?" And with that I heard him walk away.

I turned around and stared at Aidan. "I'm sorry that I blamed him. It's just that he was acting so strange and I didn't know what to think," I looked at my feet, a little embarrassed. The worst thing was that I still believed Morgan was the culprit.

"It's alright," He answered and I saw him smile, "Now, go do your archery."

As I walked away I looked back at him one last time. He stood staring at me with light eyes and glistening hair. He was the most beautiful thing that I had ever seen. I just hoped that it was enough to keep me happy until I got over my heartache. I hoped that he would still want me when I was ready.

**********

The next day Aidan called us all to the Round Table. When we were all seated he stood up and smiled at everyone. He looked good when he smiled. I'm glad that he was smiling more, and was even more pleased because I was the cause of it.

"My brothers, I have good news. Being as the summer days are generally fairly uneventful, in terms of trouble, we have decided that Calentto will hold a jousting tournament in honor of my 34th birthday! All of you will be entered automatically and the winner gets a dinner in their honor and some farmland in the west. It should be a great time for everyone. We have decided that the date will be in late August, giving you roughly three months to prepare. We will open up the field on the right side of the castle for practice. Any questions?"

I sighed and looked around the room at everybody's smiling faces. I could barely ride a horse, let alone joust.

"Well then, if you don't have horses you can find one at the stables. You've all earned some time to rest and relax." He stood up and waited for us all to filter out.

"Won't this be fun?" Leonard asked, while we waited for everyone to leave. His face was lit up like a little boy.

I looked down at my feet, "I'm sure it will be fun for you."

"What are you talking about?" Leonard laughed.

"I don't know how to joust, and you've seen how mediocre I am at riding. . . " I trailed off pathetically.

Leonard looked shocked. "Are you serious lad? You must really have lived a boring life. Riding a horse is like flying. I swear that you will never feel anything like it. If I would have known I would have taught you sooner."

With that he rushed over to Aidan and, as always, I followed obediently. I didn't mind being led around by Leonard; he knew what he was doing.

"Aidan, Noble doesn't know how to ride!" Leonard said, "We will have to have him taught on the kingdom's best horses!"

"No," I said nervously, "I would have enough fun just watching." I smiled hesitantly. It seemed ridiculous that I could fight in a war without a second thought but riding a horse at faster than a walk frightened me.

"Nonsense!" Aidan said and patted me on the back, "Leonard is right. We will just have to teach you to ride efficiently. Let's go down to the stable, I'm sure that we can find you a nice fit." Then we all walked out of the room and towards the right side of the castle. Down one corridor and one turn to the left we were outside in the beautiful May morning. Then we walked across the yard and into the dusty stable. I had always loved the smell of horses and thought that the animals were very majestic.

Aidan walked up to a stall that held a large buckskin. He was the most beautiful animal that I had ever seen. "This is Merick, my stallion, named after my mentor, and my own personal favorite for jousting. He is steady and reliable. He would be a good steed to learn on." I reached in and stroked his nose gently. He sniffed and came closer. Merick nipped at my hand playfully before sticking his nose under my arm. I laughed. "He likes you," Aidan said behind me.

"I like him too," I smiled as I turned around. Aidan was very close. I looked for Leonard but he was out of sight, probably picking out his mount. Then Aidan leaned down and softly kissed me on the cheek. I playfully batted him away.

"What if somebody sees?" I laughed. "We would have a lot of explaining to do."

"He is the perfect horse for you," he said before tweaking my nose.

Then he leaned over to whisper in my ear, "You make me so happy." He leaned back and then said loudly, "I'm going to go get the groom." He walked off and I turned back to Merick. He snuffed my arm and I stroked his silky mane. It was like dark thread that had been washed in honey. I felt honored to be riding Aidan's own stallion.

"I found a horse named Grumpy that I'm going to ride," Leonard came up behind me, but I didn't want to look away from the creature in front of me. I finally turned and saw him leading a white horse that wasn't very large.

"He seems to be a bit small," I answered skeptically.

Leonard laughed. "In jousting it's not size but speed that matters. Grumpy is the fastest horse around!" Even though I doubted his claim I knew that Leonard was a good horseman and I wished the best for him.

"Do you think that Merick here will be a good horse for me?"

His eyes ran over the stallion and then a tender smile crossed his face when he looked at my worried expression. "I think that he'll be perfect."

"Will you please saddle him up, Gerard?" Aidan asked as he came back. A young boy came up and led Merick out of the stall, tying him up to a nearby post with his bridle. Next he pulled a black leather saddle off of the rack. He swung it over Merick and then cinched it below his belly. I tentatively took the reigns and the boy walked off.

"Take him out to the field with Leonard and I will be out in a few minutes with Kin," Aidan nodded and walked past us. Leonard grinned at me and we started to walk back outside. The sun almost blinded me but felt good on my skin. The stables had been very dimly lit.

"Now, riding isn't actually that hard and I'm sure it will come to you naturally." He mounted and made it look so easy. I put my foot in the stirrup and tried to pull myself up. I wasn't nearly as graceful as Leonard and I could hear him laughing at me. I situated myself so that I was comfortable. I actually fit very nicely.

"Good job. Now what you do is hold your reins loosely and gently nudge the horse in the stomach with your heels to get him to walk. You should already know how to do that," he instructed while he demonstrated. I held the reins firmly and softly pressed my heels into Merick's belly. He didn't move. Then I decided that I hadn't pressed hard enough and dug them in again. This time he started to move forward. I had done this a few times before, but usually the horses were being led by someone or in a line of other horses.

The field was a giant, long stretch of land that was bordered by stands on one side and had no protection from the sun. Merick walked up until we were side by side with Leonard and Grumpy.

"Look!" I voiced with mock excitement, "I'm riding . . . Can I go home now?" I liked the feeling of being so high and knowing that the big beast beneath me was in my control, or was at least supposed to be.

Leonard smiled. "You sound giddy as a child. This is just warming the horses up. Next I will show you how to make the horse jog. It isn't very fast but is a little hard on your ass."

We rode in silence and I fell into the easy rhythm of the horse.

"Now, we are going to jog. Just nudge him again a little harder and he should go right into it. You can do it first." I nudged my heels into Merick's side a little harder than last time. Merick went right into it this time and I was bouncing all over the place. Through my rattled brain I could hear Leonard say, "When the horse goes up then lift your butt a little bit out of the saddle. It will make it easier." I followed his advice and jogged for a while, getting used to it. Then I decided that I should probably kick him again to get him to go up to the next level of speed. I did and it seemed like he took off like an arrow. Behind me I heard Leonard call out but I was busy holding onto the reins for dear life. I let out a little scream that was not at all dignified.

Then we reached the end of the field and Merick turned so that he faced back the way that we had come, all the while keeping up his breakneck speed. We passed Leonard who was barely able to stay up on his horse because he was laughing so hard. Then we were almost at the other end and about to crash into Patrick and Bran. I wanted to cry, but I was too frightened.

"Pull back on the reins!" a voice shouted and I quickly did, a little too hard. I was nearly frightened out of my mind. Merick stopped immediately, and I flew forward almost out of my seat onto Merrick's neck. I turned to see Morgan on a big black horse.

"Thank you," I whispered, blushing. I couldn't help thinking that now we were even. It seemed as if we had both saved each others life once.

"You are very welcome, Noble." He gave a smirk and then turned to ride the other way. He was very graceful on a horse.

"Are you all right lad?" Leonard came up beside me, his face still red from laughter.

I turned an icy stare on him. "Yes, no thanks to you!" I nudged Merick softly and then we took off at a jog over to where Aidan was now waiting. Leonard followed silently; I hoped that he was sorry for what he had done.

"I'm sorry Noble but I just couldn't help it. I wasn't the one who decided it was time for you to go that fast!" As much as I hated to admit it he had a point.

"Well, I almost trampled Patrick and Bran because you didn't tell me how to stop! Morgan told me and saved my life," I was almost crying. I wanted to get off of this beast as fast as I could. I was scared to death.

Leonard's face fell. "Alright, calm down, I'm sorry. I'll teach you how to ride properly." We reached Aidan who was walking his horse Kin.

"I think that maybe I want Aidan to teach me," I said cruelly and turned to face my King before I saw the hurt expression on his face.

"I see that you are already doing a lope, good job!" Aidan called to me jokingly.

"Leonard failed to tell me how to stop," I answered as I pulled up alongside him.

Aidan laughed. "The best way to learn is to figure it out for yourself. I taught myself how to ride. I really meant it when I said that you did well though. You seem to have a good seat. Merick was the perfect choice for you."

I smiled over at Leonard sheepishly and patted Merick. We rode around for a few minutes before they tried to get me to lope again. I did, but now that I knew what to expect and how to stop I had a lot of fun. After about an hour I was racing the men and winning a lot of the time. I knew that I was being slightly cocky, but I didn't care. It felt like I was invincible. Merick was an excellent steed and I felt bad that Aidan had given him up for me.

"Isn't this just about the most fun thing that you have ever done?" Leonard asked as we were leading the horses back to the stables.

I nodded and thought about the wind in my hair and the feeling of flying. Riding definitely was very nice. I looked over at his smiling face and forgave him instantly. I just could not stay mad at this man, and it really hadn't been his fault.

"Tomorrow we will teach you how to joust," he said before patting my back and walking off to put Grumpy away. Riding was fun but I wasn't sure about jousting. I didn't especially like the idea of crashing to the ground.

**********

I woke up the next morning with a sore behind. Leonard pounded on my door and I slowly got up to face a day sure to be full of bruises. I put on my lightest outfit, without my armor because it was supposed to be hot again, and went to the stables. I called Gerard to saddle up Merick and rode him out into the field. Leonard was already there but other than that it was deserted; maybe it was because it was barely after dawn. He smiled warmly at me and motioned towards some body padding that was lying on the ground. I saw that he was not wearing his armor either.

"This will be your weapon. I picked this for you because it is not too long or too heavy. Also there is some padding because as you know this is a rather rough sport. Men can die." He held up a lance that he was already holding.

"Fortunately I already know how it feels to be in that position," I grinned.

Leonard laughed. "Promise you are going to take this seriously?"

I nodded and got off to pick the lance up. I was surprised at how heavy it was. I put on my padding and barely managed to get the lance up onto my horse. I could hear Leonard trying to hold back laughter. I knew that I looked silly but it wasn't very nice of him to keep pointing it out. "Now that I got it up here, what do I do with it?" I asked, already growing slightly agitated once more.

"You have to position it over the front of your saddle but out to the side so it isn't hitting your horse on the head." He motioned towards his, which was already perfectly in place. Jousting was only one of Leonard's many talents. "Then we are going to try and let you hit something with it." He turned towards the opposite end of the field. I looked and saw a wooden post with a bag full of something positioned on the side of it, on a long horizontal post. It looked very awkward and not all like what I thought. I thought that I would be hitting a person, not a machine.

"This is a special training device that I like to use." His eyes sparkled. "Charge down the length of the field and try to hit the bag in the center, which is marked. You will need to get a lot of speed and get out of there fast because if you don't you'll get an unpleasant surprise." I just stared at him. I knew that this was a bad idea; I could see mischief in his eyes. I bit my lip and turned so that I was lined up with my target. I knew that men wore full armor when doing this sport and I was nervous. I really didn't want to hurt any more than was necessary the next morning.

I took a deep breath and kicked Merick into a lope. He took off and I watched as my target came closer and closer. I tipped the end of the heavy lance up a bit and prepared myself for pain. I aimed and then my lance made contact with the side of the bag. The handle of the lance drove into my side and then suddenly something hit me in the back and I flew off of Merick. I landed on the ground and skidded. It was hard to breath and a little hard to see. I heard Leonard ride up and dismount. Suddenly his face was in my view and he stuck a hand out to help me up. I grabbed it and slowly stood up despite the searing pain in my side and back. It was still hard to breath. If this was all that the entire day was going to be I wasn't going to be very happy.

"I warned you," Leonard said as soon as I was back up on the horse. I didn't want to get back on, but I did. "You did really well though.

The first time that I tried I didn't even hit the bag." I smiled weakly and lined back up for another try. "Do you want me to show you how to do it before you try again?"

I nodded quickly, anything to prolong my upcoming agony. He lined up and spurred Grumpy into something faster that a lope. When he hit the bag it was dead on and when the bag spun around to hit him he was already out of its range.

"The secret is going faster isn't it?" I asked when he got back. It had been amazing to watch them in their blur of speed.

"Yeah, like I said I picked Grumpy because he is fast. I was at a gallop and it would work well if you tried to do one also."

I hesitantly lined up and sat for a moment. I wasn't really sure if I wanted to try this again. Taking a deep breath I kicked Merick hard and it seemed as if I was going faster than the speed of light. The bag was on me before I knew it and I had only a few seconds to position my lance. This time it just barely grazed the bag but I got out of there faster and I didn't end up on the ground. I noticed that my side was starting to go numb from the impact of the lance against me, and it was only my second time!

When I got back I saw that Aidan was standing beside Leonard and a small smile lit up my face. The smile on his face was even bigger.

"That was good Noble. Merick has good speed and you two seem to be working together well. The only thing that I can tell you is to position your lance when you first start out," Aidan smiled at me and ran a hand through Merick's mane.

"I agree. Also you could try and hold the lance a little tighter against your body. It will hurt a little more but it will also make your opponent hurt!" Leonard lined up and took off again. He hit it dead center again. It was so effortless for him.

"Leonard, you will do well in the competition," Aidan patted Leonard on the back when he returned. Grumpy was so small that the tall man barely even had to reach. "I hope that I don't have to face you. I would end up being sore for sure."

"I hear that you are the best jouster in all of Bryton. If anyone lands on their back it will be me," Leonard replied, "I hope that I don't have to face you."

"Yes, but if I win I will not take the prize but give it to the second best man," he started to walk away, "I will saddle Kin and we will see if you are better than me."

Leonard called back, "Well that should be interesting." I laughed and lined up again. I practiced over the next few months and grew better and better until I could hit the mark dead center every time and avoid the bag most of the time. It was amazing how rapidly I was improving. Aidan and Leonard kept going at it but Aidan always won. He was really as good as all the stories said; he excelled at everything he did.

Eventually I faced Kade and Patrick and was up-seated both times. It hurt when you were hit, like fire for a few minutes, but it was nice when you got back on your horse. I was sore and raw when we all went in for dinner. As usual we all ate like wolves and then wandered the castle. On most nights I found myself walking with Aidan. It was one of the few times that we had alone together unless I snuck over to his room before I went to bed. I was always wary of that though. I was fearful that I would not want to go back to my room to spend the night.

"You did very well today," he said. Then we rounded a corner and he looked around before pulling me into an embrace. He kissed me and I melted into his arms. "You are the most amazing person I have ever met!" He said when he finally let me go.

I always felt like the luckiest person in the world when he praised me. How could such a perfect man adore me so much? It was something that invaded my thoughts constantly.

"I'm nothing special, but it's obvious to everyone that you are," I snuck a look up at him. "There are all these legends about you and somehow you make me believe them all. But at the same time you are so human and normal . . . You're like nothing I've ever seen before."

"I have heard the stories, they say that I am invincible, but I'm not. I'm not different from any other man out there, I have been beaten." His face dropped a little and we started walking again. Whenever I praised him, he seemed to grow quieter. But it was the truth and he deserved to hear it.

"Who has beaten you?" I asked, astonished. It was hard to believe that someone had drawn blood from this man, or held him to the ground at sword point. He was always the one standing over others. I didn't like the idea of him being beaten. I couldn't imagine it and I didn't want to.

"I have been beaten by Morgan once and my Father many times. Father was the best swordsman ever. He was the one that was really never beaten. When he fought it was like the sword had become part of him and they were one. I looked like a shabby peasant boy next to him." He stopped, lost in his memories. I was afraid of my memories but he never was. He was smiling.

I grabbed his hand, hoping that no one was near. "He sounds like an amazing person. I wish that I could have met him."

He smiled sadly. "He would have liked you. He always admired people that were strong. He fell in love with my mother because she was not afraid of anything."

I shivered. "I am afraid of so many things, Aidan. I won't even

---

pretend to be brave."

"I'm afraid, also, Noble but that's normal. I don't think that my Father was ever afraid of anything," he squeezed my hand gently.

"He would have been so proud of you Aidan," I whispered and I meant it with all of my heart. Aidan was a great leader and a great man. I admired him so much and I knew that everyone else did also. He was a hero.

We walked in silence for a few minutes before we came to my room. We looked around before he kissed me good night. I loved it when he kissed me. He smelled of sweat and wool and spices. His lips were always warm and the kisses paralyzed me for a few moments afterwards. Teague had been nothing like that. Those kisses had been filled with tension and secrets, but they had always contained all of my heart. Aidan's kisses were simple and loving. His hand slid up and down my back, willing me to love him, and I wanted to tell him everything. I wanted so badly to tell him about my father, but I couldn't. Not yet. I wanted to tell him that I still cried out in my dreams, but that sometimes I dreamt of him also. I dreamt that I wasn't afraid of his love anymore.

"I love you. I have never felt like this before," he whispered when we broke apart for a moment. Every night he said the same thing. I looked into his eyes and felt like screaming. I wanted to love him back so badly. I wanted Teague to be gone from my mind so that I could move on, but he was always there, making me feel like that same scared girl who couldn't fight back.

I just stared up at him. He gave me a small grin before leaning down to give me one last good night kiss. I sighed. He never expected me to return the words, but he wanted it so badly. He was waiting so patiently.

"I have to go in, someone might see us." He nodded sadly and then ran his fingers through my hair one more time before turning and walking away. I brought my hand to my heart, which was beating wildly.

"Damn it," I sighed, resolved, as I stood in front of the mirror and stared at my plain appearance. Every night I wished that I could say those words. It had been almost two and a half years since Teague's death and I should have been over him after that long. How unfair it all was; unfair for me, and especially unfair for Aidan.

I fell asleep imagining Aidan's voice whispering from Teague's face. I only wished that I knew what to do. I wished that I could stop this unhealthy obsession with a man that it was more than impossible for me to have.

**********

The next morning I woke up and put on my full body armor that Aidan had given me some time before. It had an eagle on the front and had blue adornments. It had been very expensive and I was paying him back in little ways, even though he had intended it as a gift. I had already taken too much away from Aidan.

I went down to the yard and got Merick ready. When I rode him out into the field it was all set up with jousting equipment because today we were actually going to joust each other in tournament fashion. I waited and watched as the others jousted and then Morgan came up behind me on his horse, which I found out was named Lucifer. I wasn't at all surprised.

Every aspect of the man's life was purposefully malicious. Why would he do that unless he was specifically trying to be a dramatic figure, playing that part that was expected of him?

"Would you like to joust me?" he whispered, almost slyly.

"If we must, I suppose," I didn't want to, but I knew that I couldn't refuse. Besides being rude to refuse, I needed to see if I could beat him. We rarely fought and every time we did he was insolent and malicious. I was tired of losing to him.

"I promise that I will be the epitome of chivalry." Then he pulled on his helmet and trotted Lucifer to the other side of the field. I sighed and lined myself up. A horn blew and I assumed that it was time to charge so I spurred Merick into a gallop. I kept my lance low until we were about fifty feet apart and then I raised it so that it would connect solidly with his chest. I knew that I would probably end up on the ground and braced myself. Then I felt my arm explode in pain as I made contact. I gasped as I felt his lance hit me in the leg. His blow was heavy and solid.

Out of the corner of my eye I saw Morgan's black form fall to the ground. I slowly pulled Merick to a stop. It was hard to breath but it was slowly subsiding. I turned and heard everyone cheering. I looked on the ground and saw Morgan struggling to stand up. I smiled. I had actually won a match, and it was even better since it was against the King's nephew! Slowly, I dismounted and walked over to Morgan. He looked up at me with contempt and I was almost afraid but I offered my hand down to him anyway. He took it gingerly and stood up.

"Don't get the idea that you will ever beat me again," he muttered before grabbing Lucifer's nearby reins. Then he walked off towards the stable. I watched him go with a smile tickling my lips, so much for not being rude. But unlike the rest of it, I knew that this time he was truly being genuine.

Leonard came up to me. "You did so well!" Then he clapped me on the back. "I'm so proud of you." I turned to another tap on the shoulder.

Aidan stood there grinning widely. "You did so well, Noble!" I wanted to hug him but it wasn't the time or the place. I would just remember that I owed him one later. I was sure that he would remember, also.

"I owe it all to the two of you, Sirs," I answered, sweeping my gaze back and forth between my two best friends.

"We can only teach you the moves, but you have natural talent. You have to be born with that!" Aidan let out a chuckle.

Then Patrick asked to face me again. I got back up on Merick and gave him a warm pat on his shoulder. I was really starting to like my horse. Patrick's horse was a big chestnut that looked very much of the same disposition as its master. The signal to charge was given and I kicked Merick in the side. We took off and I decided to try and hit Patrick low instead of higher as I had done with Morgan. We were upon each other almost instantly and my lance connected firmly with his side while his grazed my arm. I did not fall off but did lose my balance and drop my lance.

I stopped at the far side of the field and shook out my arm, while waiting for another lance. When a page handed one up to me I held it loosely. Patrick had not fallen off and was waiting at the other end with his body held erect as if he felt no pain. I knew that he must have though because I had hit him more solidly than he had hit me. Patrick was very talented at putting on a good face.

The horn blew and I kicked Merick as hard as I could muster. I did not want to have to do this a third time. I raised my lance so that it was level with his chest. We were both going as fast as we could. We hit each other in slow motion, it seemed. My lance broke and splinters flew everywhere. One hit me in the head and startled me. I looked over my shoulder and saw that his lance was still intact. Aidan had told me that if neither of the knights fell then we were awarded points for our hits and whoever had more was given the victory. I knew that I was doing better because I had hit more solidly and my lance had broken, but I might not make this round because I was growing weary. It was very likely that I would fall off.

I was handed yet another lance and it gave me confidence when I saw Aidan smiling at me from the sidelines. I took a deep breath and let Merick take off again. I kept my lance low. Patrick held his lance high and I knew that he wanted to win.

Even though he was jolly, I had heard that jousting was his favorite and even though he tried to hide it, he didn't like to lose. I understood that, but I wasn't going to give up without a fight. We rode closer and closer and then at the last moment I pulled my lance upward and pushed Merick just a little harder. It hit him square in the chest before his lance made contact with me. He flew backwards while his horse charged on. I stopped Merick as fast as I could and got down to help him up.

He had pulled his helmet off and had started to get up when I got there. I stuck my hand out silently, because I didn't know what to expect. He glared at it and continued to get up on his own. He did not smile as he usually did, or compliment me. I stood silently, wanting to cry as he walked away without a word. I could see in his walk that he was angry at me, or maybe just at himself.

I never had liked it when people where angry at me and always felt awkward, not knowing how to handle the unexpected emotion. I sniffled and wiped my eyes before Aidan, Leonard and Kade walked over. A man would never cry over something so trivial.

Kade put his hand around my shoulder, "I am sure that you will win the tournament." We both knew that it wasn't true, but it made me smile.

Leonard laughed. "He will have to beat me first. I plan on winning."

Aidan raised his eyebrows, amused, "What uses have you for a farm?"

Leonard grinned. "I might just settle down with a pretty lady when I grow too old for the battlefield." We all stared at him in disbelief. He rolled his eyes, in the way that I come to expect him to. "Can't any of you take a joke? I belong on the battlefield, and I'm too much of a player to settle down." We all laughed even though my smile felt false. Patrick's anger had ruined my day.

Aidan noticed. He shook my shoulder. "Don't let Patrick's moods bother you. Even though he doesn't often show it, he has a lot of pride when it comes to jousting. It's a family legacy for him. It was his Father's specialty and his fathers before him. He will be over it before dinner tonight." I nodded and felt a little better. Then we all sat and watched the other men joust. Aidan and Leonard faced each other twice. Neither fell off but Aidan won by a few points both times. I clapped and cheered for both of them, not choosing favorites. I would be glad for whoever won the tournament.

Eventually we all went in and I fell asleep on my bed exhausted and sore. As I lay there, I realized that I really liked jousting. It was kind of soothing, the motion of the horse and then the impact, which you knew would come. And even though you ended up bruised and sometimes with a sore ego, you knew that you could overcome it and face someone else the next time. It was a lot like life.

\*\*\*\*\*\*\*\*\*\*

We practiced every day for the next month, and when we were asleep in our beds we dreamt of practicing. I knew each knight's weakness and strengths. I had discovered that I was weak on my left side and needed to work on that, which I had. I could beat most of the men, but not all, and still had my hopes up that I would win if fate intervened on my side. Kade often helped to boost my morale. Maybe if I won the farm, I would be able to find my father and let him live the rest of his days there in peace.

When the day of the tournament came I woke up with the sun and stretched out all my sore muscles. Then I put on my armor and walked down to Leonard's room. I knocked and he popped out instantly as if he had been waiting.

"Ready to lose to me, lad?" he joked as we walked to the stables. He was in a great mood. I loved seeing him when he was happy. He made you feel like the whole world was smiling.

"I have just as much chance as you!" I answered with my chin in the air and a teasing leer his way.

"Last time you said that we were competing to get here and you were right!" We both laughed and we split when we got to the stable.

I went to Merick and brushed out his inky black mane. He nuzzled my face and got horse spit all over me. I wiped it off and giggled. It was totally un-masculine but nobody was within hearing range and I didn't care. I pulled out my jousting saddle and put all of the tack on Merick, which I had finally learned to do all by myself.

When we were ready I walked out to the field. Hundreds of people from throughout the kingdom had come to participate and I saw that the stands were filled with onlookers. The war had been hard on everyone, and the people were excited to have something lighthearted to amuse them.

Being as I was a knight, I was going to be one of the first to face off. I went over to a list that was posted and was taken aback when I saw that I was going to go second! I was even more shocked when I saw who I was facing. Lord Tremet.

My hand went to my neck when I remembered what a sore loser he had been so long ago. How ironic it was that I was going to have to face this man again more than three years later. I knew that Aidan would laugh when he heard.

I walked Merick back to the sidelines and watched the first couple go. It was a knight against a normal citizen. I watched with butterflies filling my stomach. When the knight won I cheered and then flinched when they called my name out loudly across the field. I rode to the west side, sweating profusely. Someone handed me up a lance and I stared across the field. Tremet was sitting atop a smaller gray horse and was staring at me also. Even though he was far away I saw him sneer and I shivered. He was going to give it his all because I had cost him his place in the fifty. I could sense his hatred for me and mine was almost as great for him.

The horn blew and we both pulled our helmets on. I positioned my lance atop my saddle and took a deep breath. The horn blew again and I kicked Merick into a fast gallop, deciding that the best plan of attack was not to hesitate. He was going a little more slowly and had his lance positioned very high. He was going for my head. I pointed my lance higher and spurred Merick on again. We made impact but I ducked my head enough so that his lance hit only the top of my helmet, it snapped my neck back hard but other than being a little sore and dizzy, I was alright. My lance had hit him squarely in the chest and my arm hurt very badly. I had to admit that the man was skilled. He knew that a good lance blow to the head could kill a man.

I stopped at the other end and positioned myself. Tremet's horse reared up and it looked as if he was the knight and I was just some villager. Resolve made my jaw tense and I could feel Merick shift beneath me in anxiety. We were both ready to defeat this man.

The horn blew and I snapped the front of my helmet down. It blew again and we took off. This time I aimed low and he still persisted and aimed higher, at my head. When we were almost on top of each other I flicked the lance up a hair and my plan worked. My lance hooked him right on the bottom of his breastplate and as I kept going he was forced to slide off of his horse backwards. His lance hit my head, but after he was already sliding backwards. It hurt and my vision blurred for a few seconds before I was able to shake it off.

I turned my stiff neck back to see Tremet once we were passed and he was lying on the ground, on his back. I stopped Merick and almost fell off. A page caught me and helped me stay upright. Then Kade was by my side and helping me walk to the shade that the stands provided. I sat down with a thud on the ground and when he handed me a flask of water I drank greedily.

When I was done I looked up at Kade, "Thank you. I thought that I was going to pass out and that wouldn't have been dignified at all."

He smiled his cheerful little smile down at me. "You did very well out there. It was very rude of him to aim for your head like that. Many men have been killed that way and I was worried about you!" He put a hand on my shoulder, like a big brother would have. In a way I realized that he was a brother figure to me. Kade was always there when I needed him and willing to help.

"Thank you for worrying," I replied with a smile.

He grinned, looking a little shy. "That's my job. After all, I am the unofficial medic, and your friend. I'll go take care of Merick while you rest."

I smiled and then he walked away slowly, back out into the sunlight. I sat in the shade and watched the tournament. I knew that I wouldn't fight again until later in the afternoon. I watched all my friends fight. Kade was out on the first charge of his match, Gair was out on his first also, as well as a few other knights. Other than that, everyone stayed in. We all took a break for lunch and then everyone crowded around the list to see when they were fighting again.

When I managed to worm my way in, I saw that I was fighting first against Gladwin. I groaned. I knew that jousting wasn't his best sport but I could only beat Gladwin part of the time. I went into the stable and saddled Merick back up before taking him onto the field. I went to the west side again and waited. Gladwin sat on his horse Majesty, a white mare, at the other end. He came from a rich family and his armor was solid gold that glinted in the sun, distractingly.

The horn blew and I put on my helmet. It blew again and I felt my insides trembling. I was even more nervous now than I had been against Tremet. I looked back to see Aidan and Leonard wave at me. I hadn't talked to Aidan all day or Leonard since this morning. I nodded and then turned back to the field. The horn blew again and I started Merick off slowly. As we went along we quickly picked up speed and I raised my lance so that I could try the same trick that I had used on Tremet. Suddenly, we were on each other and Gladwin had Majesty swerve just a hair so that my lance missed and his connected squarely with my chest. I held onto my saddle with my legs, but it was no use and I flew off backwards, with Merick galloping on. After I hit the ground, I tried to breath and finally managed to sit up. Then Gladwin was standing over me and offered me his hand. I couldn't help but notice that he was grinning. I was proud of him, but sad for my wounded ego and sore behind.

"I'm sorry, Noble," he said and I could tell that it was at least a little bit hard for him to have beaten one of his friends.

I smiled. "It's alright, that was a very good move at the end," I shook his hand, which I was still grasping to ensure that I wouldn't fall over.

Gladwin laughed, "You always did fit your name, Noble." I still smiled as I watched him walk away. I limped over to Merick. I had landed on my leg wrong and had twisted it. A stable boy held him and I reached out to take the reins. I walked past Aidan and Leonard and they gave me sad smiles. I put Merick back in his stable and slowly made my way back to the field. I sat down off by myself on the end of the stands and watched all my friends. It went on for hours until there was just Aidan and Leonard left. They had both jousted perfectly all day, as I had known they would.

Everyone had heard of Leonard's skill, and the crowds were silent as the two men lined up. I was biting my nails because I didn't know which of my two friends to cheer for. When the first horn sounded I had to stand up. Grumpy and Leonard looked very small compared to Aidan and his gigantic chestnut gelding named Kin. When the second horn sounded, everything seemed to be going in slow motion.

Both horses took off and the sight of their sweaty muscles glinting in the sun as they rode gave me shivers. Leonard was holding his lance low, as was Aidan. They both knew that the other's weakness was in that spot. Then they were on each other and both lances hit their spot in the others abdomen. Both lances shattered and I let out my breath when they headed back to their corners.

The horn sounded again and they rode. Once more, Aidan held his lance low, but Leonard positioned his higher. They collided within seconds of their take-off because both were going at horrifying speeds. Leonard was jarred and everyone held their breaths as he almost fell off, but he managed to hold his seat. I could tell that he was rigid with pain even from so far away.

My stomach was so tense with excitement that I could hardly stand it. It hurt to breath, and I still didn't know how I wanted this match to end. So far, it looked like Aidan would win because of Leonard's falter on that last charge, but things could happen to change that.

The horn blew twice and both men took off for the last time. Grumpy was going so fast that his legs were just a blur, and Leonard kept his lance low. Aidan was building up speed as he went and had his lance high. Then Grumpy gave another burst of speed and Leonard's lance made contact. Aidan flew out of his saddle and slid across the ground when he landed. It was completely silent except for the horses' hooves as they pounded on. Aidan didn't get up. I took a raspy breath with wide eyes. It felt as if my heart had stopped.

I jumped down and ran out onto the field. Kade was right behind me. Kneeling down beside Aidan's barely moving form, I turned him so that I could see his face. I thought that he was crying and my body grew cold, but then I realized that he was laughing. I pulled back as he sat up slowly. He was laughing so loud now that I was sure the people in the stands could hear him. I was sure that he had hit his head and was hurt. He needed to get inside, away from the sun.

"Aidan, are you alright?" I asked as I glanced over his head, checking for any bleeding. He nodded and wiped his eyes. He really did look mirthful.

"You don't know how good it feels to lose something for once!" He sat up and he stopped laughing while he grimaced, "Maybe I could have lost in a less painful way though."

I could feel Kade behind me and turned to look at him. He was smiling. "He's tilt-silly."

I looked back at Aidan.

"You have to be about the craziest man that I have ever met," I said while helping to gently pull him up from the ground. When he was up on his feet I saw Leonard jogging out to help us. He looked almost scared.

"Your Highness, I am so sorry! I just got so caught up in the game that I . . ." He didn't finish and looked as if he might throw up. I smiled but he wasn't looking at me, all eyes in the stadium were on our fallen King.

Aidan stood silent for a few moments. Then he smiled. "Leonard, it is just a game. I am glad that you won because you have more need of the land and the banquet than I. After a few years of having nobody brave enough to beat me, it actually feels very refreshing!" He laughed as he put his arm around me and leaned on me as we limped towards the castle, with Kade and Leonard following us.

I smiled back at Leonard; he caught my gaze and smiled in return. "Good job Leonard, what do you plan to do with your new land?"

"I think that I will just let it be until I retire, which may be soon because Aidan has turned me into one giant bruise!" He laughed and I knew that everything was perfect.

"When will the banquet be Aidan?" I asked as we took him to his room and laid him down on his bed. He was hobbling and whenever we touched him I saw him wince. Leonard wasn't going to be the only purple man in the castle. I smiled; I was going to be the only purple woman though.

"Next week," Aidan grimaced as he rolled onto his back, "You two go back and enjoy your victory, and Noble can help me."

"I'm the doctor though, Aidan. Don't you want me to look you over?" Kade asked.

Aidan laughed, "I want you two to go have fun, Kade."

They nodded and with one last worried look they walked back outside. I bent down and kissed my King. He was still smiling. I was very proud of him; even if he hadn't won, he had acted like a champion. I admired him more than any other man that I had ever met.

"You are such a strange man," I whispered while undoing his armor. He slowly got up so that he could shrug it off. He was drenched in sweat and as I pulled off his tunic he kept flinching away from my touch. I tentatively pulled off his shirt. He smelled of sweat and dust. The sun was setting outside his window, shedding us both with its pink light.

Suddenly, I was very aware that we were standing very close together and that he was half naked. My breath caught in my throat. I backed up a little, keeping my head down. "What are you afraid of?" he whispered as he gently took my hands. I looked up at him. His blue eyes sparked, but he looked very serious and solemn.

"I'm afraid that just because I want you now doesn't mean that it's the right thing to do. I don't want to regret anything between us, and I think that I might, and that's not fair to you," I sighed. His presence was intoxicating. "I don't want either of us to get hurt."

He wrapped his arms around me gently, not even flinching from the massive purple bruises that were starting to appear. "You know that I would never hurt you." He whispered. He said nothing about me hurting him. We both knew that it was almost inevitable.

I ran my hands up and down his warm back and just wanted him to love me. I wanted him to love me enough for the both of us. I pressed my cheek against his warm chest and breathed him in. He lightly kissed the top of my head and I shivered. What was wrong with me? This was everything that any girl could ask for, he was everything. Finally I looked up at him and our eyes locked. I realized that I trusted him. If he thought that this was alright, then I would believe him.

I wanted this moment to be about nobody else but Aidan and I. We had both been lonely for so long, and there was no need for us to be lonely anymore. I had never wanted this more with any other man in my life. Aidan was strong and kind and he loved me. I wanted him.

Our eyes locked, and I nodded at him with a small smile. His face lit up and he squeezed me tighter. Slowly, I leaned forward to kiss him. We had kissed many, many times before, but this kiss was different. For the first time, I understood what true sensuality was. It was if nothing existed in the world besides our lips, and his hands on my skin, and his thighs pressed against mine.

Aidan stepped forward gently, pushing me towards the bed. Backing up without taking my lips from his, I gently sat down and laid back. Aidan pulled away for a moment, and grabbing around my waist, picked me up to slide me back further on the mattress.

I remembered another man throwing me down on the bed.

Aidan straddled me lightly, and his mouth found its way to dance lightly on my neck. His hands slid softly underneath my shirt to my chest, his hands lingering momentarily on the scar he had sewn shut on the battlefield. With his lips and hands caressing me so tenderly, I let out a little gasp of pleasure and reached my hands up to run through his shimmering hair. I tugged on it slightly, to return his lips to mine.

Once more, his hands began to wander, down my stomach to my

hips and thighs. After a moment, they slowly slid back up to my shoulder and then lightly down my arms. Then Aidan grabbed my wrists.

I felt him holding me down. I remembered his body heavy on mine and the panic that there was no escape. His sweat dripping into my face and the fear. I remember his hard penis, ramming into my leg, trying to take everything away from me. I remembered hating him in that moment.

I could feel my heart pounding and suddenly I was gasping for breath. I couldn't stand his body pressed against me one more moment, suffocating me. I tried to sit up but his body was too heavy. It was then that I realized I was crying.

Suddenly, Aidan pulled back, looking into my feverish eyes.

"What's wrong?" he whispered softly as his hand came forward to wipe my tears away. He rolled off of me and sat up, allowing me to sit. I was lightheaded and struggled to take a deep breath.

It was then I lost it. I couldn't hold back the pain and the regret any longer. I buried my head in his chest and began to sob uncontrollably.

"He tried to rape me," I finally choked out. It was the first time I had ever said those words aloud. "I loved Teague and he tried to rape me."

I felt Aidan's body stiffen but his hands still gently stroked my hair.

"I want to be with you Aidan, and I thought that I could" I continued shakily. "I hate him for doing this to me."

After a few more minutes of silence I pulled away tentatively and wiped my puffy eyes.

When I finally dared to meet the King's eyes, I couldn't read them. Breaking away from his gaze, I walked over to face the slowly darkening sky through the window. I couldn't breathe. He came up behind me. Every inch of me was blistering for his touch, but I didn't reach out to him. I was so confused.

Aidan took me by my shoulders and spun me around after a moment. I tried to lean forward and give him a kiss but he turned his head. My bottom lip trembled.

"You know that I would never do that to you," he began solemnly, not daring to look at me. "And I think that if you really wanted to be with me, then it would be enough to help you get over the awful things he did to you, and the good things too. Goddamn it, I hate him for how he broke you."

"I'm so sorry Aidan. I want to, I really do. It was just a mistake. I want you," my voice cracked as I pleaded. I put a hand on his cheek and turned him to face me. The look in his eyes made me realize that I would give him whatever he wanted. I nodded and bit my lip. "I really do want it."

"You don't want me," he whispered sadly. "You want someone to make you forget him, the good and the bad." He just stared down at me a moment.

In that moment, he knew me better than I knew myself.

"Yes," I finally nodded. "I just don't want to feel broken any more."

I wanted him to get angry at me. I wanted him to scream at me. I wanted him to hate me for not being able to let go as much as I hated myself.

Finally, he just nodded. "I'm sorry. I'm sorry for hurting you. It's the last thing that I wanted," he replied and wrapped his strong arms around me.

The tears ran hot down my red face again. "Please, don't just forgive me. I'm sorry that I don't love you Aidan. I'm doing the same thing to you as Teague did to me and I know how much it hurts. It's unforgivable."

He breathed softly into my hair. "Yes, it hurts, but I still love you." He reached up and tenderly wiped my tears away. "I still hope that you will come to love me." He looked down at me and I nodded, I hoped that I would too. "Maybe we weren't meant to be together and if that is the case then I will have to live with it, but will you promise me something?" I nodded. At that moment I would have done most anything for that man. "Promise me that you won't blame yourself for this. What Teague did was wrong, and you can't take that upon yourself."

I looked up into his eyes and saw the man behind them, the amazing and stunning man that made my blood boil and my heart fly.

I looked down at my hand in his. He reached forward and tilted my chin up.

"It's not your fault," he whispered. "I love you, forever and always."

# CHAPTER FIVE
## Glorianna

The tournament took place on a Saturday. Less than a week later, Aidan called us all to the round table. Now that I look back at it, those last few days of that summer were some of the best days of my life.

By the time I walked in to the meeting, everyone was already seated. They all chuckled because I was always late. After sitting down at my spot, I turned to look at Aidan. I was surprised to see a woman sitting beside him, especially considering she was the most beautiful woman that I had ever seen in my life.

Her flaming red hair fell long around her slim figure, and her violet eyes sat behind long lashes. Her nose was small, unlike mine, and her mouth red as a cherry. A green silk dress made her skin appear radiant. I realized that Aidan had never seen me in a dress. The lady looked over at Aidan and he smiled back. I felt my stomach turn. This was the first time I had ever seen Aidan pay attention to another woman.

Aidan started to speak. "My friends and brothers, we are here today to announce two very important things. The first is that as you all know Leonard has won the jousting tournament, and we have decided to host a banquet in his honor on Monday. This corresponds with the other announcement that I have. You have all probably noticed the beautiful Lady Glorianna sitting to my left." I took a deep breath. She was his cousin, or a long lost sister, nothing more. She couldn't be anything more. "The night of the banquet we will also be announcing our engagement to the general public. I wanted you all to know first."

For a moment I couldn't believe that I was hearing him right. It was as if the words had come too quickly for me to process.

"We have decided that the wedding will be held next Sunday. It is very short notice but we thought it best to have the wedding as soon as possible. Besides, we want as few old statesmen there as possible."

"Probably because she's pregnant," Leonard whispered in my ear with a chuckle.

Everyone began to clap and I moved my hands along with them.

"That is all." Aidan said with confidence.

Leonard stood up beside me. "Are you coming with us all to celebrate the news, Noble?"

"In a little bit," I mumbled, not daring to meet his eyes for fear that I wouldn't be able to hide the tumult of emotions inside me. He squeezed my shoulder and then walked out. I waited until everyone except Aidan and Glorianna had left before I stood up.

"Glorianna, could you excuse Noble and I? We have things to discuss," Aidan asked. Glorianna nodded before reaching up to kiss him on the cheek and walking out. I followed her with my eyes, and if looks could kill she would have been dead before she shut the door. I shivered.

I walked over to Aidan, unsure of what I was going to say. What right did I have to be angry? I wasn't even sure that I was angry, just very confused. Why did he want me to love him when now it would mean nothing?

"Why?" I whispered, my voice mirroring my thoughts. My eyes were narrowed and my jaw was clenched. I felt a sob in my throat but I swallowed it down.

"I'm sorry; it was a matter of state. Her family is the most powerful family in the north, and there has always been contention between them and Callento. They are extremely powerful and my father had burned many bridges with them. Since I was crowned I have been working to gain their trust and in the end, the only real way to do that was to marry their heiress. They offered and I could not refuse without ruining all that I have worked for. I had no choice." I knew that it was true, I could see it in his tired eyes.

As much as I tried to rationalize in that moment, I couldn't help but feel betrayed. I felt betrayed to the very core of myself. It was unreasonable, and selfish, but I felt it nonetheless.

"You are the King! You always have a choice!" I was close to shouting. I was being such a hypocrite, but I couldn't stop the words from tumbling out.

He scowled at me, "It's not that simple!" For once in his life he was starting to lose his temper. "You know that. Besides, why does it matter to you, unless you've suddenly fallen in love?"

"It matters because of what you said after the tournament. You said that you loved me. You said that you didn't want to hurt me and yet here you are. You are no better than Teague, just using me for what you want until something better comes along," I choked out. It felt hard to breathe and I started to panic, hysterically.

Aidan grabbed my shoulders. "I do love you but I have to do what is best for the country!" He was trying to remain calm so he could comfort me, but I could hear the frustration.

"Oh sure, it just happens that what it best for the country is marrying a beautiful woman. Well I may not be as pretty as her or as rich but I'm . . . "I faltered, not knowing what I had compared to her. I felt frozen. Hurt too deeply to even cry, I just stood there shivering. I knew that he loved me, but at that moment I had nothing. I raised my chin defiantly. "I'm nothing. If I was you I would do the same thing, except I wouldn't have fallen in love with me in the first place."

He put his hand under my chin and made me look at him. "You

know that's not true, but I've tried to convince you how wonderful you are and you never listen. I don't know what else to say."

Then I realized something. "You . . . you knew by the day of the tournament. You knew and you didn't tell me! You just let me go on believing that everything was going to continue on as it was. You said that you loved me and that would never change. That must have been before you saw her," I stopped and shuddered "At least I found all this out before I fell in love with you. If it hurts this bad now imagine what it would have been like then. But I guess it's not like I haven't been hurt before, right?" I stepped away from him and turned towards the door. I was too tired anymore to fight.

Aidan ran in front of me and stopped me from exiting the room. "You think that I'm glad that I'm marrying Glorianna?! Well I'm not. Every time I think of her up there next to me on that alter and not you I feel sick, like the walls of my life are closing in and I can't escape. This hurts me more than it ever will hurt you! I love you, and you may care for me, but it still isn't the same. All that you feel right now is jealousy and wounded pride, so don't talk to me about pain." With that he turned and walked quickly out of the room.

Perhaps I had imagined it but I thought I had seen the glint of tears in his eyes. My heart crumpled. How stupidly selfish I had been. I held my head high and exited the room even though I wanted to collapse into a heap of self-pity. I wandered the halls as a ghost would. I hated myself for being so selfish.

I didn't have it in me to defend my own actions. I had been wrong.

**********

I reluctantly went to my room that night and fell into a dreamless sleep. I went through the rest of the weekend sluggishly and the only thing that I snapped out of my haze for was Leonard's dinner. I suppose it was because friendship is a bond as close to love as you can get.

On Monday night we were all told to dress in our finest and report to the banquet hall by sunset. I decided to wear an outfit of red and a tunic of black with a golden eagle on the front. Aidan had given it to me right before the Tournament. I hated wearing it, but it was the only thing that I had that was nice enough. I didn't want Aidan to even notice that I was there, much less think I was throwing my self-pity in his face. I had already acted childish enough.

"Noble, if I tell you something that is a secret will you promise to not tell another living soul?" Leonard asked when we were about halfway there. I turned to look at him and then nodded. Leonard was not usually this secretive. His face was almost at the most solemn that I had ever seen it. "I am in love with a lady."

"Well, that is not unusual," I quipped. Leonard was usually in love with at least three women at a time. Still, I could already tell that this one must be special. Usually, he never talked to me about his conquests.

"Well, this time it is real, Noble. Whenever I'm around her I cannot breath. She is the most beautiful thing to ever walk this earth!" He paused and stared off for a few minutes. That was when I knew that it was the real thing. It would have been obvious to anyone who saw him that he had been hit by cupid's arrow. We walked for a few more minutes in silence.

"Who is it?" I finally prompted, dying to know who it was. If I couldn't be in love with anyone myself than I might as well occupy my time with someone else's love affair. It would take up my recently acquired abundant amount of time, if not make me happy.

"It is none other than the beautiful Lady Glorianna! I haven't ever felt this way before, Noble." He put his hand to his chest dramatically. I almost choked on my own saliva. I should have known. It seemed that this woman was ruining everything.

"Leonard," I pulled him off to the side. "You know that you cannot act upon your feelings. That would be adultery, and with the queen nonetheless," I hissed out the word 'queen'. I had never aspired to be Aidan's queen but I couldn't help thinking that it should have been me.

"I know, but she fills my veins. I dream of her when I sleep and when I'm awake I can't help but notice ever word she speaks and every movement of her delicate frame . . . " He looked like a lost dog trying to find his way home, but it was hopeless. I knew the feeling.

"Aidan is one of your best friends; you cannot do that to him!" I shook his shoulders. I was trying to convince myself as much as him. I could not want to be with Aidan anymore. He looked down and I could tell that he was as much at pains about this wedding as I was. "Leonard, there will be more women that you will love. Probably more than you love her; look forward." I was talking to myself now. But I honestly wasn't sure if I was talking about Aidan or Teague.

"It doesn't feel like it. She drives me to speak like a poet . . . me! Before this feeling the best compliment I could give a woman was that she looked good laying on her back." I couldn't help but laugh, even though I knew from his face that he was serious.

With that, we turned and walked towards the banquet again. When we got to the huge long table I stood awkwardly while Leonard took his place at the front. "Come sit beside me," he smiled and motioned at the place to his right. I went over sheepishly and sat down. All of the men and important Dukes and Lords that were in town had been invited, and I felt awkward. We all sat quietly, whispering to each other while we waited for Aidan and his betrothed to arrive. When we finally heard a pair of trumpets play, we all stood and Aidan and Glorianna entered through the double doors at the end of the room.

He was the most perfect thing that I had ever seen in his dark blue outfit with silver and black overlay. He wore his crown, and it was the first time I had ever seen it on him. The sapphires gleamed against the silver background. I knew that he had many crowns but everyone told tales of this one. It was his favorite, and it was said that Merick had it made for him by the most skilled blacksmith in the world.

I hated to admit it but Glorianna looked perfect as well. She wore a long, trailing white gown with silver decorations. Her hair was loose and the half veil that she wore covered the back of her head and made her look like she was adorned with a halo. I knew that even though I would be pained, I could not blame Aidan if he fell in love with her.

I heard Leonard's breathing grow hoarse. I grabbed his shoulder and shook him a little. He turned toward me and gave me a little nod. I could see that his eyes would be only on the Lady tonight. I knew that mine would also constantly wander over to Aidan. When they were seated to the left of Leonard, the serving men all came out bearing lavish plates of food. When they set it down in front of me I started shoving it into my mouth. I figured that if I was willing to partake of the sin of adultery, I might as well treat myself to gluttony as well. Besides, if I was looking at my plate then I would not be looking at him.

When Leonard turned to stare at me with a look that was clearly portraying annoyance, I slowed down and tried to enjoy the food a little bit more. After that course, they brought out one that was a huge whole pig with an apple stuck in its mouth. I adored pork but had always detested the idea of eating something while you could still tell what it was. Nevertheless, I took part of a leg and ate as quickly as I could while still using manners. I looked down the table while I was stuffing my face and saw Morgan glaring at Aidan. I shivered and went back to eating my food.

After that course was done, we were served a simple dessert. I knew that this dinner had been a small one because Aidan really didn't want it to be all about him and Glorianna, but more a simple gathering for Leonard. My thoughts kept coming back to him no matter how hard I tried at avert them. I wanted to hold him in my arms again.

Then, when everyone was done and settling down, Aidan stood up. "Thank you all, friends and family, for being here tonight. First and foremost we are here to celebrate the victory of my dear friend Sir Leonard at our recent jousting tournament." A general round of applause went up, mostly from the knights, because all the Lords and Dukes where only there to hear about the engagement. "Also, as most of you know we are also here for another reason. We are here to publicly announce . . ." I held my breath and hoped, in my heart of hearts, that he would not say those horrible words that would change my life forever. Aidan held his hand out to Glorianna and he helped her stand. I bitterly noticed that I was tall and to his forehead, while Glorianna was dainty and only to his chest. ". . . the wedding of the Lady Glorianna and I, Aidan Penhalion, King of Bryton." A loud strand of applause broke out but my hands barely touched each other. I couldn't believe that he had actually muttered those words. "We will be wed," His voice cracked and became a little softer, "This Sunday. Of course you are all invited." Aidan sat down and Glorianna followed, looking a little unsure of herself, but still beautiful in her shyness.

Everyone started to stand up and mill around. Leonard's hand was shaking when he went to pick up his goblet to get a drink of wine. My lower lip was trembling. I suppose that I hadn't really expected him to do it. I had kept my girlhood fantasy and wanted him to, at the last minute; scream out that he loved me, that he needed me, and that he would never marry anyone other than me, Aceline Banidere. I felt at that moment as if false hope would be the death of me faster than any sword wielded by an enemy.

I stood up weakly and stared down at Leonard. I hoped that I didn't look as bad as he did. I gave his shoulder a tap.

"How about we get out of here and go somewhere a little bit more fun? Perhaps a morgue . . ." I laughed shyly.

Leonard sent one more glance in the direction of the newly betrothed and then looked up at me with an only slightly forced smile. "How about the tavern? Maybe we can even stir up some trouble like old times . . . Remember the horses on the night of the tournament back all those years ago?" His eyes grew a little brighter as he gave a genuine laugh.

I rolled my eyes. "How could I forget? Especially since you puked all over me the next morning. Let's do it again shall we?"

Nobody even noticed as the guest of honor left.

Leonard and I made our way to Mimi's House, reliving old memories as we meandered.

"And what about that time that we replaced Bran's leather polish with indigo dye?" Leonard roared as he slapped his knee.

I had to momentarily stop walking, placing my hands on my thighs to steady myself. "He was so angry," the tears rolled from my eyes. "I have never seen somebody's face get so red in my entire life."

We laughed spastically for a few more minutes, even laughing at the way we laughed.

Trying to regain composure, I wiped my eyes as we walked into the bar.

"Nobody has as much fun as we do Leonard," I said as I motioned for the bar maid to bring us over our usual beverages.

"Agreed. I think we've earned it though . . . We work harder than most people. We have given more for this country than most people," Leonard took a swig from his beer. He didn't sound bitter, it was just a fact.

I took another sip and my thoughts began to drift to all the things that I had given away freely, or had lost, in order to make a difference in Bryton.

I looked over to see Leonard looking deeply in thought.

"Okay no more talk about such serious things," I promptly said with a teasing rigor in my voice. "Tonight we are going to once again revisit the follies of our youth. Let's see who can finish their beer first! Go!"

I put my glass to my lips without waiting for his reply and began to gulp down the slightly warm liquid as quickly as I could manage. Leonard was never one to ignore a challenge and quickly joined in the game. I was thoroughly impressed when he finished his mug a good thirty seconds before I did.

"You always think you can beat me Noble, and then are always so surprised when you lose," he laughed, motioning yet again for the bar maid to bring more beverages. She knew us well though, and this time she brought a full flask of whiskey.

Within the hour the entire room was spinning and I found myself singing off-tune to Leonard's very rapid lute strumming. It appeared that Leonard had never before played the lute, and that he had bought it from the tavern musician for over half a fortnight's pay. This left me with the unfortunate task of having to pay for out overwhelmingly large tab when the owners of the establishment finally asked us to leave well past one o'clock in the morning.

Stumbling down the streets, playing his lute, Leonard suddenly stopped and looked at me.

"Noble!" He yelled, "We forgot to move the horses!"

"What are you talking about?" I laughed until finally I remembered. "Oh right! The horses! Where did they go?"

"I'm not really sure . . ." Leonard trailed off as he spun around, apparently looking for all of our missing horses. His breath steamed in the chilly autumn air and for some reason it looked exceedingly beautiful to me. I crept closer and closer to my friend until finally the steam escaping from his mouth and nose was blowing into my face.

Suddenly Leonard noticed how close I was to him and laughed. "What are you doing Noble?"

"The steam," I giggled. Suddenly I clamped my hand over my mouth. I felt as if the girlish noise that had escaped my lips had resounded through the night, drawing attention to my lie.

"You my friend are very drunk," Leonard smiled and slung his arm around my shoulder.

"And so are you my friend," I breathed a sigh of relief. "Otherwise the truth about me would have just come out."

Leonard suddenly became very interested in the store front to our right. "The truth about what?" he asked absently as he walked over to the door and peered inside.

And then, even though as I heard the words leave my lips I knew they were wrong, I couldn't help but tell my best friend the truth.

"I'm a girl," I smiled shyly at Leonard's back.

"What's that supposed to mean?" He asked with a chuckle, not even bothering to turn around to face me.

For a moment I just stood there. The world around me was spinning so I decided to sit down in the middle of the street.

"I had to tell you, Leonard," I put my head in my hands. "I can't believe that you are the third person to know. You should have been the first. You are the only one that I knew I could trust through everything. You are the best person ever." And then I promptly vomited all over the nicest clothes that I owned.

Finally Leonard turned around. "Okay I guess that means it's time to get you into bed," he said as he leaned down to help me up, smearing regurgitated pork all over his sleeve in the process.

"Didn't you hear anything I just said?" I asked quizzically as soon as I had spit the vile taste out of my mouth.

"Yeah I'm awesome and your favorite person ever, but I've known that a long time," he gave me a roguish grin.

I just shook my head and then turned to throw up over my shoulder once more. When we finally stumbled up to our rooms I had puked many more times than I could remember, and Leonard had joined me more times than he cared to count.

"Do you need help getting into bed?" Leonard asked me as I fumbled with my key. For some reason it would not fit into the lock.

"Maybe just with getting my boots off, they always give me trouble," I smiled as I finally pushed my door open.

I sat down on the bed and Leonard kneeled down on the floor and proceeded to pull my boots off.

"It's probably a good thing that your first sense to go when drinking is your sense of smell," I laughed. "Hey wait a second!" I jumped up and ran over to my wardrobe, leaving Leonard sitting on the floor staring at my rug.

After a few moments of searching futilely through all of my belongings I finally pulled out my newly refilled flask of whiskey.

"One more little night cap," I grinned as I took a couple swigs. The second sense to go when you are intoxicated is your sense of taste.

"Okay but only enough till I pass out," Leonard wagged his finger at me. "Maybe that will keep me from puking my insides out any more."

"Nothing could make it any worse than it is right now," I supplied helpfully as I handed him the flask. He sat there for a few more moments drinking silently. I sat down on the bed, yawning. I glanced out the window and was surprised to see the first pink streams of daylight along the horizon.

"Leonard it is high time for us to go to sleep," I yawned once more. "We aren't as young as we once were and I, for one, am exhausted. I reached down to pull my heavy tunic off and then continued to pull my shirt off. They felt too hot and far too scratchy. Then I tried to lay down but my pants were bunching up around my thighs so I untied them and pulled them off as well. Finally I stood up and snatched the flask away from Leonard.

"You should get to bed," I mumbled as I threw the open flask across the room and offered my hands down to him.

Leonard looked at them as if he had no idea what they were intended for and then finally took hold of them gingerly. It took all my strength to pull him to his feet and even then he was practically laying on top of me. I walked him over to the door and opened it for him.

"Can you make it to your room?" I asked fretfully.

"Oh yeah," he feebly batted a hand at me and slumped against the door frame. I stood him back upright and he turned around and began to walk to his room.

Suddenly I stepped out into the hallway and called after him, "Hey Leonard!?"

He looked back and me and almost tripped over his own foot.

"We have the most fun don't we?" I smiled

His characteristic grin cracked his face. "Yes we do Noble, yes we do." And with that he pulled out his key and stood at his doorway for five minutes, trying to figure out how to open it.

After Leonard was safely into his room I stumbled back into mine and fell onto my bed, completely forgetting what I had wanted so hard to forget.

**\*\*\*\*\*\*\*\*\***

Of course I woke up the next afternoon in a complete panic. The details of what had happened the night before were beyond fuzzy, but all I knew was that I had walked back with Leonard and I had woken up without a decent amount of clothes covering my body.

I also vaguely remembered telling Leonard that I was a woman.

After hours of nervously watching Leonard's door, waiting for him to emerge I finally stood in front of it, ready to knock.

Despite my pounding headache and scratchy eyes I had to know if Leonard remembered my secret or not. I wasn't going to sit around waiting and hoping like I had with Teague, I was going to face my worst fear head on.

Finally my fist rapped a few times on his door and I waited silently, my nausea almost overcoming me.

After what seemed like an eternity the door opened a mere crack and I could see Leonard's matted eyes peer out at me.

"Noble how are you even moving right now?" his voice was raspy as he opened the door wider to let me in. I entered the darkened room as Leonard stumbled back to his bed.

I let out a sigh of relief. If he remembered he would not have talked to me so easily.

"Maybe it's because I really am tougher than you," I grinned, ecstatically happy that I hadn't jeopardized everything for one night of fun.

"Or maybe it's because I have more hair on my chest than you and can drink twice as much as you," he finally smiled, even though it looked more like a grimace. "Do you even remember anything from last night?"

I shrugged. "Some of it . . . It's really patchy."

"Who knows what amazing acts of vandalism we could have committed last night. I'm extremely upset that we can't remember," he laughed.

"Yeah me too," I gulped. "So you don't remember anything?"

Leonard grunted. "I remember that I chugged our first beer faster than you . . . After then the next thing I remember is waking up this morning in excruciating pain. It might come back though, sometimes it does." He rolled over onto his side facing me.

I stood up, scared for him to look at me for too long. "Okay well I just wanted to make sure that you were alive in here. Hope you feel better."

I turned to walk quickly from the room. At that moment, I was glad my biggest problem was watching the man that I could possibly have come to love marry another woman.

Over the next week, the castle was bustling with people preparing for the wedding. It was going to be a huge ceremony, not only because of the wedding, but because they were also going to give Glorianna her crown.

I couldn't help thinking that if things had been different it could have been my crown. Glorianna would grow to love him and he would fall under her charm. They would have babies together and live long and happy lives and I would always be on the outside looking in.

But for the time being, I could not even force myself to look inside the lavish walls of the chapel.

Everyone else had gone in. Even Leonard, after he had recovered from his earth shattering hang-over, had admitted that it was better to know what was coming, but I was so afraid. Afraid that if I entered that room I would lose it. I might break down crying or, even worse, let out all my frustrations and scream until I was hoarse. I knew that I couldn't get out of going to the wedding, because I was scheduled to be part of it with all the knights, but I wanted to avoid facing reality as long as possible. I had already lost Aidan, but I didn't want to lose my fantasies. I still wanted to love him.

I know that it sounds horrible but I found comfort in Leonard's torture, because I knew that it was as great as mine; maybe even greater, because he had not even known Glorianna's love before he had lost it. After our night out on the town he appeared more desolate than ever, hardly ever speaking or eating. I tried to amuse him but the time for that had come and gone. Now all he wished to do was wallow in his own misery.

On Saturday night I could not sleep. I laid in my bed and stared out the window at the moon, but nothing would put my mind at rest. Finally, I got up and began to pace around. I knew that I would not be able to sleep before I had seen the chapel. I had to know. I quickly unlocked my door and walked nimbly through the cold and empty halls. I stood silently in front of the large chapel doors. Was I really brave enough to go in? I still had time to turn around and go to bed. I would have to suffer through a sleepless night, but I could still hold on to what might have been. I could dream of his touch one last untainted time. I wanted to go back so badly.

I took a deep breath and pushed open the large door. When I slipped in I turned and guided the door shut, so that it would not make any noise. When I turned, I was actually not as surprised as I should have been to see him sitting there.

The chapel was filled with fragrant flowers of every color and size. The air was thick with their perfume and I knew that it was the loveliest place I had ever been in. The moonlight shone in through the stained glass window sending the whole room into a colorful darkness. I was too awed by the beauty of it to remember why I was there. His head was bowed as if in prayer. It was all too magical, my heart wanted to break.

I walked quietly up to the front and sat down beside him. He did not move and I wanted to run. I didn't belong there, among the extraordinary scene.

"I don't think that I can do it Aceline," His voice was harsh and it broke the serenity of the room.

I turned towards him and took his hand in my own slowly. He turned to look at me and as I gazed into his blue eyes, I felt tears slip down my cheeks. "You have to," I whispered. "You should consider yourself lucky even. Not many men are asked by their country to marry beautiful women." I let out a sigh, not even heartened by my own attempts at optimism.

"Why do I have to think of this damn nation every time something good happens in my life!? Why can't I think of me for once? I say damn this castle, damn the whole stupid island." He leaned in and kissed me harshly on the lips. "We still have time to run away. We can leave and be together forever. You know that you want that! We both know that every time we see each other we will die inside. I know that I can't survive that, and I think you know that you can't either."

"No," I said, trying to convince myself that this nation was more important than the feel of his lips on mine. I pulled away from him, standing up to distance myself from his warm arms. "You couldn't leave. When we got to the outskirts of this castle, you would freeze and turn back and you would break my heart even more. You have accepted what you know you have to do. I must do the same."

He paused and then looked up at me and nodded. "I know it's over, but it hasn't even had the chance to begin yet. I could picture you and I together forever. We had the potential to be amazing together, and not knowing what could have happened will be the worst pain I will ever have to face. I wanted you to be the woman that I woke up to every morning, the mother of my children."

I sat back down and we stared at the crowns sitting up on the pedestal waiting for tomorrow. Aidan's was the one with blue sapphires in it and Glorianna's was small with rubies set in it. Suddenly, Aidan stood up and walked over to the crowns. He picked up the queen's crown and slowly came back over to me. "This belongs to you, and will forever." He gently reached up and placed it lightly on my head. It felt so right, being beside him with the responsibility of Bryton on me. "You are the love of my life. No matter who I marry I will always remember the time we were together and remember it as the best time of my life. And if my heart could choose, there would be no other Queen."

I stood up. "You don't know how much I wish this was different . . . But eventually you will come to love her and she will be the mother of your children. I just want you to be happy Aidan. I want it more than anything else in the world," my voice cracked and tears started flowing again.

"You will always be my best friend, and you will always be the first woman that I have ever truly loved. Nothing can ever change that," He whispered.

"Aidan," I whispered, "Even though it hurts right now, I'm glad that I . . . that we . . ."

"I'm glad too," he whispered back, even though we could have shouted and no one would have heard.

We inched towards each other, slowly and delicately. When our lips met I gasped. It was long, loving, bittersweet, and everything that a goodbye kiss should be, and yet somehow it felt like the beginning of something. When our lips parted, I buried my head in his neck and sobbed.

He married her the next day.

\*\*\*\*\*\*\*\*\*

I was fine the morning after the wedding. I had a good night sleep, unlike most of the nights previously, and was ready to face the dawn. I would just have to get used to the fact that Glorianna was the new queen. As usual, we all gathered in the courtyard to practice. When I got there I stopped in my tracks. The Queen was sitting on a bench and watching the men fight. Was she going to be everywhere now? I had thought that when we were fighting everyone might forget about the new beauty, but she had even invaded that.

I walked over to Gladwin who was standing by himself. "Why is Her Royal Highness here?" I whispered, once I got close enough.

"It seems that she wanted to see where Aidan is all day. It hasn't been going very well because all the men are focusing on her and not on fighting," he chuckled at this. "And they have all been fighting for only a few moments!"

"Well, how about we show her how real knights fight?" I punched him in the arm and grinned. At least one man was not stunned by the royal beauty.

We both pulled out our swords and turned to face each other. When I saw that he was ready to fight, I lunged at his left side. None of us even bothered to say 'First hit' anymore, it was just an unnecessary formality. He blocked and ducked to the right. Then he swung at my knees.

I jumped over his blade. We hit blades for a few minutes but I soon realized that I was subconsciously moving backwards. I stopped retreating, but he was still being aggressive and kept swinging heartily. I had to back up. Soon I had my back to the wall of the courtyard. I noticed that the sounds of all the other swords had stopped. Gladwin swung at my left side and I jumped to the right. His sword hit the wall above my head and before I knew it, he had his sword at my throat. I took a deep breath, I always lost to Gladwin. Still, the fights were always interesting. Gladwin tried to never fight the same way twice. I knew that there was still a lot that I could learn from him.

Suddenly, there was the sound of soft feminine clapping and Gladwin turned to look. He took his sword away and I looked around his bulk to see Glorianna standing up, clapping her hands. I sighed, for a moment I actually had managed to forget about her.

"That was simply magnificent! Aidan said that you were all very good but frankly, I didn't believe it until now. What are your names?" Her voice was like a beautiful instrument.

"Gladwin," my partner managed to get out. I saw him blush.

"Banidere," I answered huffily. I was mad that just a few moments ago Gladwin had been immune to her charms and now he was just another victim. Was everyone under this woman's curse?

"Those are fine names!" She let out a giggle and everyone, except me, chuckled even though what she had said was not funny. "I suppose that I should let you get back to your work," she chimed before walking back over to the bench, upon which she sat down daintily. The ladies in waiting that stood behind her were fanning her gently. I wished that they would stop and just let her wilt.

"I didn't notice before how lovely she is," Gladwin mumbled.

"She isn't that beautiful," I snapped, even though I had to admit that she was. "Her eyes are too close together." Of course, her eyes were situated perfectly on her perfect head.

"How is it that you are immune to her grace and charm?" he eyed me suspiciously. I knew that he was probably thinking of the time that Teague accused me of fancying men. Everyone had their suspicions about me but no one voiced them. They all had too much respect for me.

"I don't want what I cannot have," I tried not to blush because then he would think that I was lying.

"Alas, that is true," He looked downcast for a few minutes before walking away. I shook my head in disgust.

"Noble, can I talk to you for a minute?" I turned to see Leonard, red eyed and pale.

"Anytime," I replied and we walked over to a corner of the

courtyard where no one was practicing. The dark shadows made my friend look even worse because you could see how hollow his cheeks had become in the last few days.

"Noble, she consumes me," he said loudly when we were there. "It makes me physically sick to my stomach to think of her with Aidan. I torture myself by imagining his hands and his lips on her . . . I can't stop. Please help me!" Why had I ever wanted him to feel this pain? What kind of horrible person was I?

"Leonard, I cannot help you. There is no way to cure love or mend a broken heart. Stay busy, do not look at her. Block her from your mind. Other than doing those things, there is nothing to do but suffer." He looked like he wanted to cry. "I promise though that it will get better."

It seemed to me at that moment that love was the worst thing that can happen to a person. It makes us weak and hopeless. It makes us want to lose ourselves inside of someone else. It makes us forget who we are, in want of the one that we love. At that point in my life I had seen nothing but pain and suffering spring from the name of love. I was growing quite cynical, and I was only twenty years old.

I put a hand on his shoulder. "Come fight me, I will make you forget all about her!" Leonard smiled a small smile, mostly for my benefit. I pulled out my sword and he pulled out his in one swift movement.

I lunged at his right shoulder but he turned left. He swung at my left ankle but I jumped over and raised my sword to bring it down on his back. When I swung down he brought his sword up to block me and I pushed with all my strength down, trying to move his sword closer to him. Suddenly, he pulled out and moved right. I stumbled foreword and then Leonard was behind me with his sword at the back of my neck. I gave a chuckle and turned around.

"Even when down, you are still one of the best swordsmen around," I clapped him on the back.

"Yes, you could give Aidan a run for his money," that horribly sweet voice answered again. I saw Leonard's face light up as he turned to stare at her.

"They are about evenly matched," I tried to keep the snarl from my voice. I couldn't look at her. "Have you even seen your husband fight?"

She looked at me innocently, "Of course."

"I'm sure that Aidan's skill is far above mine," Leonard added. He couldn't take his eyes off of her. He was practically drooling. I finally looked at her. Her smile faded and she looked thoughtful for a few minutes. We all sat in awkward silence as she studied Leonard. Her face was void of all emotion. His face was red and he looked so scared that she would find something wrong with him that I suspected he wasn't breathing.

"You are the man that they call Leonard. I have heard of you," her voice was just above a whisper. "The great warrior from Fraunc that came to England. Why did you come?"

"I was compelled to find a place where my skills would be of use." I knew that he had come to see if he was better than Aidan, but he didn't want to look conceited. Why did love have to make people lie? Wasn't love supposed to be a thing of truth? I realized that my thoughts were contradicting themselves. All that I knew of love was half-truths.

"That is not what I heard." She looked up through her eyelashes at him and I shivered. Leonard's passion was bad enough, but what if she returned his love? I felt a westerly wind blowing and lifting my hair. It could have meant anything, but it felt as if it meant disaster was approaching swiftly.

**********

Glorianna was there with us in the castle for seven years.

Every man in the castle wanted Glorianna for himself and every girl wanted her for a friend. While Aidan was the backbone of the kingdom, she was its beloved darling. At first she was all I ever thought about, her every movement like needles pricking my skin. As the years passed, my dislike and distrust of her never waned, but I was able to continue on and put it aside as much as possible.

Still, I was so jealous that it clouded every word and movement that she made. Whenever she spoke to me, I was brief because I felt deep down that she would hurt us all. Somehow she would destroy all that we had worked so hard for. I hoped that I was wrong and that somehow it was just my envy speaking to me. As time passed, I often questioned myself, but I still couldn't shake my intuition.

So far it seemed that I was wrong. Bryton had become more peaceful than ever since Aidan wed Glorianna. It seemed that since the war had been won, and since everyone loved the royal couple so much, there was no need for fighting. Men came from all over just to see her and women looked at her as the epitome of fashion and beauty. Even though there was a sense of calmness, I knew that trouble had been brewing since the day that she arrived.

Aidan, though still the same man that I had always known, had fallen prey to her charms as well. He would dote upon her and it hurt to see this, but in a way it helped me to know that it was finally over and would never be again. Leonard had pined after her for years, wishing that she was his. Then, he had used his two favorite pass times, wine and women, to drown the pain. Finally, nearly seven years after her arrival, he seemed to be feeling better, and I thought that he was finally getting over her. He rarely ever saw her anymore because she was always with Aidan discussing things that were going to take place, or doing things that I did not want to think of.

One thing that did alarm me a little was that I found that Morgan and I actually agreed on something. It seems that he had a bad feeling about Glorianna also. He was actually brave enough to voice his new opinions at one of the meetings at the Round Table when Glorianna was not there. The Knights all booed him and Aidan glanced at me for a moment, I knew that he saw I agreed. Maybe he even agreed. Even if it was someone that I didn't trust, it felt good to know that there was at least one other person who did not adore the new Queen.

One night when we were walking to dinner, Leonard pulled a piece of paper out of his pocket. "Would you mind reading this poem I wrote for my love interest? I want her to think that I am very literate and I know that my spelling is atrocious." He handed me the piece of parchment and I unfolded it.

"I am glad that you are finally over Glorianna." I smiled. I was glad that my friend wasn't hurting anymore. It certainly had taken him long enough to get over the queen, of course it had taken me almost as long to leave behind the memory of Teague. I had finally stopped dreaming of his face. I had reached the point where I could see that he had never been right for me. I could see his faults. The memory of my birthday had been left far behind me, and I was content to never look back.

"I'm glad that my love is not unrequited. I find it amazing when love has become comfortable and you can talk about anything together. I would never have written her a poem before, but now we know how we feel about each other." He looked so happy.

I read the poem which was full of flowery words that were all spelled wrong and did not rhyme. I did not have the heart to tell him how bad it was, but instead just told him how to spell all of the words that he had gotten wrong. He listened and when I was done, he tucked it back into his pocket. I wondered who Leonard was infatuated with now, probably a maid or noble woman, like the old Leonard.

When we sat down at dinner, I was very anxious to see if the woman Leonard had written the poem for was working at the castle. All through dinner I watched him but he kept his eyes on his plate.

He had had affairs with women in the castle before and he was always ogling them during dinner. There was only one possible explanation and that was that his woman was not in the castle. He was having a hidden relationship and I was dying to know with whom.

Something needed to occupy my time now that Aidan and Teague had finally left my mind alone.

**********

That night I was starving, since I had been too busy watching Leonard earlier to eat. I snuck down to the kitchen and grabbed a big hunk of bread before wandering back to my room, just before midnight. Then, breaking through the still night, I heard voices. They were coming from the hall just in front of me. I moved a little farther foreword so that I could see the people's shadows and then hid behind a statue of a former King. I knew that it was wrong to spy but I couldn't just walk past. The voices were low and sounded secretive. I had always been a little prone to gossip and maybe I could learn something interesting.

"Here, I wrote this poem for you," the voice was low and sensual. I gasped. It was Leonard's voice! Now I would find out who his latest conquest was! There was a moment of silence before the next voice spoke.

"This is the most beautiful poem I have ever read." I choked on the piece of bread I was chewing. I covered my mouth so that I wouldn't cough. Leonard was having an affair with Glorianna! I blinked and tried to clear my head, this couldn't be happening!

Anger shot through me. This woman was supposed to be a role model for an entire nation. Aidan had clearly fallen in love with her, and she was throwing away the love and trust of the most amazing man she would ever know. How could Leonard hurt his best friend and his King like that? If they were found out Glorianna would probably be burned and he would be put into exile. How stupid could they be?

"Well, I mean every word of it. You are my sunshine and I will love you until the end of time!"

I was ready to throw-up. How sickening! I felt as I was the one personally betrayed by this secret relationship, instead of Aidan.

"I love you Leonard, but I must go. Aidan notices if I am gone to long," She was whispering but I heard her meaning loud and clear. Aidan probably suspected that she was unfaithful. He was probably being eaten up by the fact. Of course he wouldn't say anything about it. He had too much good faith in Glorianna to ever openly accuse her of adultery. He also knew what it would mean for the country.

"We must not let him find out. We would be in grievous danger if we were discovered." At that moment, I was very close to hating Leonard. I had given up Aidan, and Leonard should have given up Glorianna. What were they going to do, continue this charade forever?

I heard padded footsteps coming toward me. I ducked down farther behind the statue and saw Glorianna glide past in just her nightgown. I would have spit on her if I had not been hiding. I heard Leonard walk away and then there was silence for a few minutes. I slowly slid out of my hiding place and jumped when I found myself facing Morgan, who was slipping out from behind a statue across the hall.

"We have to alert the King!" He whispered.

"No," I whispered back. I didn't want to hurt Leonard, even when I was mad at him. And yet, he had hurt Aidan. I wished that Morgan wasn't here, and yet I was so glad that he was. I was glad to not have to face this on my own.

"Both of these traitors need to be harshly dealt with! We cannot let this go on," He looked slightly smug and I was ashamed to admit it was satisfying to see that our fears had been justified. "I know that you do not like me, and the sentiment is returned, but Aidan is my uncle and I feel that he must know of this treason." The man sounded almost too righteous. "I hate that woman, and I know that you do, too."

"Aidan is my friend but so is Leonard, I prefer to stay out of this for now." I was so shocked by what I had heard that night that I had to think it over. I knew that no matter what we chose to do, somebody was going to end up getting hurt. For once, I actually wished that I was getting hurt instead of my dear friends. "I have to think about what's best."

"You must know that Aidan loves her! If you do not help me now, then you will be hurting him." He had a point, but I didn't want to do it. "I know that you don't want to hurt him." I looked into Morgan's eyes and for a moment I almost felt as if he knew. I felt as if he knew that I was a woman. I shivered, once again reminded that his face still haunted my memory. After years, I was beginning to think that my impression of knowing him before my time at the castle was just a symptom of my fear for this man.

"No," I turned and walked away. Morgan didn't follow and I thought that maybe he would tell even without me. The thought horrified me. Leonard had been so happy since he and Glorianna had been together and I didn't want to have to choose between my two best friends. I could not sleep at all that night.

**********

The next morning I woke up tormented. I managed to avoid almost all contact for the entire day. I did not talk to any of the three involved in the love triangle and still did not know what to do. I was caught between two bad choices. As far as I could tell, Morgan had not yet told the King. I naively hoped that he was reconsidering, but I knew that if I wanted to avoid hurting the people I loved that I needed to act quickly.

That night I could not sleep and decided to walk in the halls again to try and clear my mind. Snow was falling outside and I could see my breath, even inside the castle walls. I was hoping that maybe I would hear the lovers again and would be able to make a final decision on what to do.

After a few hours of pacing up and down the halls, I finally made a choice. I was going to tell Aidan. First though, I was going to go tell Leonard what I planned to do. Then he would have time to take Glorianna and leave forever. They would be gone and Glorianna would not be able to ruin any more men's lives. I would miss Leonard, Aidan would be angry and I might even be accused of treason, but it was the only way that I could see that nobody I loved was in any danger.

Suddenly, I turned to see a torch in my face. "Noble," Aidan said and I could hear the anger in his voice. I looked past him and saw Kade, Gladwin, Patrick, and Morgan. Suddenly, I knew that he had been told. I had waited too long to make my decision and now I had probably sealed Leonard's fate. Morgan looked at me with a satisfied smile. I hated him more in that moment than ever before in my life.

"Aidan, please don't do this! He is your best friend. He's my best friend. He loves her and he was dying inside," I pleaded with him. He grabbed my wrist, and started walking, pulling me along. I could feel how tense he was.

"That is no excuse, and you have no excuse for not telling me what you knew," he growled and I had never heard so much hate in his voice, let alone directed at me. We were quickly upon Leonard's room and I tried to pull my hand away from Aidan. We stood in front of the door that I was afraid to open and Aidan finally let go. He kicked the door and the whole thing busted open. Splinters flew and I was scared of what he would do once he walked inside. I had never seen this calm man so angry before. When the air cleared I gasped. Leonard and Glorianna were lying in bed tangled in each other's arms.

Leonard's eyes found mine and his gaze darkened. I looked down at the floor. Leonard grabbed one of the bed sheets to cover himself and stood up. "Aidan, I'm not going to apologize or run!" I knew that if it came to a fight between Aidan and Leonard, that one of them would die.

"If you did I would kill you on the spot! You were my best friend and best knight, yet you betrayed me! How could you do this?" Aidan was yelling loud enough to wake the dead. I fought the urge to cover my ears with my hands to keep the words away from me. I squeezed my eyes shut and prayed that I would not burst into tears. "And you, wife of the king of England, have committed adultery against me." Glorianna was crying into a sheet still on the bed. "Tomorrow you shall burn at the stake, and

Leonard you are exiled from this court forever!" Aidan turned and strode out. Leonard lunged at me once he was gone but Kade and Gladwin grabbed him. Before he had a chance to reach me I ran out into the hall.

"Aidan!" I screamed after him. I ran and caught up to him. I grabbed his arm but he pushed me away. He was walking as fast as he could and I was jogging to keep up with him. "Aidan look at me!" he finally stopped and turned to face me. His jaw was set in a firm line. "Please listen to me. You know that you can't do this."

"I can do whatever I want to them because I am the King and I love her!" He shouted into my face, his words hitting me like fists. I took a step backwards. It hurt to hear him actually say those words. I shook away the blow though. I couldn't let this happen to them, even if what they had done had been wrong. I would do anything to save Leonard.

"He is your best friend," I was crying.

"Then why did he do this?"

"He was dying inside. It was wrong, but you would have done the same thing." I knew immediately that I had said the wrong thing. Aidan and I had chosen to give each other up.

"How can you even say that Noble?" The pain that I saw in his eyes broke my heart.

"It hurts, Aidan, I know it does but can you blame them? He did not choose to love her. I'm sure that she didn't choose to want him," I said these words even though I didn't believe them. What Leonard had done was wrong, but I would defend him with every breath in my body. I felt tears running down my face. There was a moment of unsure silence. "Did you stop loving me just because you were married? Not everyone is as strong as you Aidan. I know I'm not."

All of the anger drained from his face and all that was left was weariness and hurt. "Oh Noble, if I could have loved you forever I would have!" He was calm now and he sat down on the edge of a statue. He put his head in his hands and I hoped that he was not crying. I couldn't handle that.

"Don't hurt him, please Aidan, please," I fell on my knees and grabbed his hands. "And don't kill her. Spare them if only because you love me, because you love her. If Leonard leaves then I go with him. I can't just desert him. And then we will be gone and she will be dead."

"What would you have me do then? Should I let everyone in the kingdom think that I cannot even keep my wife? These past 7 years have been some of the happiest of my life with her and the country has been filled with peace and prosperity. But first she hasn't given me an heir, and now this . . . I have to do it."

"No you don't. You don't have to do anything." I bit my tongue.

He had married Glorianna because of duty and now we both knew that he had to do this to Leonard. I had buried my own case.

He looked blank for a few minutes and he sat there listening to me cry. "He can stay, but she will burn. I want her to pay for making me love her." With that, he stood up and walked away. I pulled myself to my feet and wiped my tears. He still did love me or else he wouldn't have pardoned Leonard.

**********

I slept late the next morning. When I finally got up, I felt like it was the end of the world. My only consolation was that I had lived through worse, but not by much. I walked down to the courtyard but nobody was there. As I wandered back through the castle to the banquet hall I noticed that the castle was deathly quiet. Everyone felt the way that I did. I wandered until I was standing in front of the one place that I did not want to be, Leonard's room.

I took a deep breath and walked in through the curtain that had been strung across the doorway. Leonard was sitting on the bed with his head in his hands.

"Where's Glorianna?" I asked timidly. Leonard did not even turn to look at me. I think that he had known I was going to come.

"She's in the dungeon," He sounded like a man that had nothing left to live for, "Thanks to you." I could hear the sob in his words alongside his hatred.

"I did not tell Aidan. I knew, Leonard, and I kept it to myself because of you. If it would have been anyone else, I would have told right away. I was coming to tell you to get out of here," I stood rigidly. My voice held no emotion.

"Then you would have told. You were going to tell weren't you!?"

"I had to, Leonard. Do you realize what you did to me? You split me between the two people I care most about in the entire world!" He didn't even seem to care that I was going to let him get away. His anger at me was deep and he was trying to find more fuel for the fire of his rage.

"Do you realize what you did to me?! I was finally happy. I was finally in love and you ruined it! You had to be jealous of me and her and turn against me. I thought you were my friend and now she is going to die! I will kill myself before I let her die! Now my only loyalty is to her."

I shivered with anger. "You talk of past loyalty when you did that to Aidan!? You were supposed to be loyal to your friend and King! You knew that it was wrong and yet you still did it. I know that you love her but you were being selfish in taking her. It is all your fault that she will burn!"

He looked at me and I shivered. "Don't say that ever again or you are as good as dead where you stand." He sounded as if he really did hate me.

"Are you going to kill me because I speak the truth?" I whispered.

He jumped up, eyes blazing! "I could kill you, don't think that I couldn't! She is more important to me than you are! You were just a stupid little boy who I felt sorry for, and now you are just a weight around my neck."

I took a step backwards, wounded beyond belief. "Well then, go fight a battle with her! Go let her proofread your pathetic love letters. Let her be the one who takes care of you when you've had too much to drink. Let her be the one to see you at your worst and still care, because I won't anymore," I clenched my jaw and walked from the room.

I walked quickly down the halls still trembling. I saw Morgan coming down the hall. I stepped in front of him and he looked surprised. "You ruined everything, you waste of human life," I gave him a look of disgust and spat on his shoe. I had to take my anger out somewhere and Morgan was the perfect person.

"If you would have told, things would have been easier. Then Aidan wouldn't be angry at you and Leonard's hatred would at least have reason. This is as much your fault as it is mine!" Then he spat on my shoe in return. I felt tears prick my eyes and I brought back my arm to punch him. My fist connected squarely with his jaw. He stumbled back a few steps before bringing his fist to hit me in the eye. After a brief pause, I could see again and stuck my leg out to trip him. He fell but grabbed my shirt and pulled me down also. I fell on top of him and grabbed onto his hair and started to pull it as hard as I could. He grabbed my arms and dug his fingernails into them. We rolled over so that he was on top of me. Bits of his hair were falling out and I could feel my arms bleeding. Suddenly, Morgan was off of me and I slowly sat up, dazed. Blood was flowing freely down my arms and I had banged my head on the ground so hard that I could already feel a bump coming up. My ears were ringing.

"What do you two think that you are doing?!" Bran's loud, gruff voice hurt my throbbing head.

"I'm sorry, we were fighting," I barely managed to mumble.

"I don't mind that, but you two looked like a bunch of girls clawing at each others hair and such!" He laughed and I fell back to the ground. My arms were tickled by the blood trickling down them. "I'm going to have to teach you two how to fight for real." With that he let go of Morgan and walked away chuckling.

I slowly got up to see that Morgan's mouth was bleeding and he had bald spots on his head. He snarled at me and then walked back towards his room with his hand up to his lip. I stood up and limped back to my room, glad that I had gotten my anger out, even though I had absolutely nothing to show for it.

**********

Gloriana's trial was swift and the jury sentenced her to death without hesitation. Although she was loved, Aidan's word was the most powerful force in the kingdom.

The morning after, I woke up to someone banging on my door. "You had better get up, Noble, they are going to burn Glorianna, and Aidan wants you to be there." I shivered. I didn't know who the voice belonged to but I quickly got up and washed all the caked blood off of my arms. I pulled on simple clothes and froze at the door. I was a bundle of nerves.

Even though I disliked Glorianna greatly, I knew that I could not let her burn at the stake, no matter how wrong what she had done was. It went against everything within me, but I had to save her. I only had to come up with a plan. After thinking all night, I had finally come up with an idea. I hurried down to the stable and saddled Merick, pulling on my longest black cloak with the hood down low over my head. I checked my side to make sure that I had my blade and rode out into the sunlight.

They were having the execution in the middle of the city, to set an example, so I rode Merick through the city by all the back alleys. When I reached the center of the town, I saw the raised stake on a platform and shivered.

I wasn't sure if I was doing the right thing. For a second I contemplated turning back, but I knew that I wouldn't. For some reason I had to save her. I hated her and I hated what she had done, but I couldn't let her die. I kept seeing how much Leonard loved her and how much he despised me. Teague had been right on that sunny morning so long ago; life wasn't always black and white. I was doing what might have been the wrong thing, and for the wrong motives, but I couldn't stop myself.

Many people had come to watch and it would be hard to get Merick close enough to grab the Queen. Then, I heard the sound of wheels going over the cobblestones. I turned to see Glorianna in a cart. She was dressed in a plain white gown and I thought that even when going to her death she looked beautiful.

I saw Aidan standing up on a raised platform slightly away from the stake and he looked sick. I hoped that he would have them release her and then I would not have to save her, but I knew that he wouldn't. He had his pride. It was the one thing that I could find wrong with him.

She was led onto the platform and offered her arms behind her to a guard. There were at least a dozen guards and I was scared that I would not be able to fight them all. A torch was raised and thrown into the kindling by the edge of the platform. I heard Glorianna wailing over everyone else. "Leonard!" she screamed over and over. I shivered because I could feel her love rippling through the square. It was stifling in its truth.

I knew at that moment that it was the time. I spurred Merick into action but it felt like everything was going in slow motion.

"Move!" I yelled in a commanding voice and the villagers parted like I was a barge cutting through a river. I thundered past them and barely even stopped beside the platform. I raised my sword and brought it down on the stake, cutting the ropes that bound Glorianna. Guards were coming at me from all sides. Merick kept rearing, keeping them off me with his hooves. Glorianna wiggled her feet free and ran over to jump on Merick behind me. After I knew she would not fall off I turned Merick around. I swung my sword at the multitudes of guards and Merick kept wading through them. I knew that I injured at least five men before I got clear of them. They ran alongside us and I had no choice but to cut them. I tried to aim the blows so that they didn't cause more damage than was necessary.

I thundered through the city and kept going, heading for the east gate, knowing that it would be the least guarded. Archers on the walls shot arrows at us, but Merick was fast and we were out of range quickly. I could feel Glorianna shaking violently while she clutched me close and I knew that she was scared, but I couldn't stop to comfort her. They would be after us soon.

I kept my hood down so that she couldn't see my face. We rode for a few hours before we came to the place I had decided to leave her.

We stopped in front of a huge stone monastery. I quickly dismounted and turned to help her down. She was light as a feather and I hoped that Aidan never compared me to her, because I would always lose.

"You'll be safe here. Don't tell them who you are. Stay here for the rest of your life, or I will find you and you will regret it," I turned to mount back up, but suddenly, I felt her hand on my head pulling off my hood. I spun around with a scowl and saw her go wide-eyed.

"I'm sorry Banidere. I didn't think that you were Leonard, but I hoped . . ." Tears filled her eyes. She sniffled a little bit before lifting her chin defiantly. "Why did you save me? I thought you were the one who told Aidan." Her voice was tinged with anger.

I shook my head, trying not to be angry. "It was Morgan who told, but I did know."

"What do you want in return?" She looked suspicious.

"I want you to stay here forever and not ruin any more men's lives," I turned and mounted again. If I never saw this woman again it would be too soon. I wanted the superb image of her cleansed from my mind forever.

I turned to ride but the Lady spoke again, "Banidere!" I turned to look at her again. She sounded close to tears. "Would you please tell Leonard that I love him?"

I stared at her for a moment, trying to decide whether or not I would. Finally I nodded and a look of peace washed across her features. As I rode away she watched me and I hoped that better days would come to Calentto, but I doubted it. The kingdom was more prosperous than ever before, but Calentto was dying. There was too much pain within the walls of the great city now.

Somehow, I knew in my bones that we had reached our ultimate glory in the years of peace and prosperity with Glorianna. There was no way to know what was coming next.

I took all of the back roads to return to Calentto. Every once in a while I would hear the pounding of nearby hooves. I knew that it was futile to hide, everyone would recognize my horse, but I was frightened about what was going to happen to me.

I came in the same gate I had left by, with less fuss than I had expected and walked as quickly as possible back to the stable where I put Merick in his stall and brushed him thoroughly, watching over my shoulder the whole time. I was stalling because I knew that eventually I would see Aidan, and I was almost certain that everyone in the castle knew it was me who freed the Queen. I hoped that he would understand why I had done it. If he didn't, then I deserved whatever my fate would be. If life was fair I would have died a long time ago anyway.

When I got inside, the castle was very busy with people all around . I slipped down the halls back to my room before quickly opening the door and stepping inside. Closing the door quietly, I thought that I was safe. I turned around and felt my heart jump when I saw Aidan sitting on my bed.

"What are you doing here?" I asked even though I knew that answer. I stood by the door, not willing to walk any closer.

"Why did you save her? She ruined what we had together and turned Leonard against you, but you still saved her." He actually sounded amazed.

"Honestly, I don't know why I did it," I went over and sat down beside him, realizing that he wasn't mad. I should have known all along that he wouldn't have been, because he had wanted to do the same thing, he just couldn't.

"Where is she?"

"I'm not going to tell you. All I'll say is that she won't be able to hurt you anymore." I reached up to brush a strand of hair out of his eyes and my hand lingered on his cheek for a moment. "I was going to tell you," I whispered, staring into his eyes.

He nodded. "I know that you and Leonard have been closer than most since the beginning. You would never let anything hurt him. He's the one that . . . ." He turned to look at me. "I will go and tell him that it was Morgan who informed me." He got up and went to the door.

"Wait," I cried at the last minute. There was something that I had to know.  Aidan turned to look at me. "Did you really love her?" My voice cracked. I hoped that he would say no, but I knew what the answer would be. I just had to hear it coming from his lips.

He stood still for a few moments. "I loved her just enough so that we can't ever be the same." His eyes were sad and melancholy, but I trusted him.

I smiled sadly and nodded. When he had shut the door firmly behind him I sighed. I thought about how selfish humans can be. I wanted everything without giving anything in return. I expected everything. When you see what you really are, stripped to the bone, it's a shock and all you can do is try to overcome your nature. Some days you fool yourself into believing that you have evolved into something better than what you what started with. Some days leave you feeling dry and empty, shriveled and old.

**********

The next night, I was sitting out in the courtyard trying to clear my thoughts when Leonard came up and sat beside me. We both remained in silence for a few minutes, just looking up at the night sky. I knew what was coming.

"Did Aidan talk to you?" I finally asked in a whisper. I chanced a look over at him, his words still hurt me. I knew that they had been said in the heat of the moment but still, passion had a way of uncovering people's true feelings.

"Yes," he whispered and we sat for a few more minutes before he spoke again. "I'm sorry about what I said. You are my best friend Noble and by doing what you did you showed me how much you care."

I bit my lip, was it that easy to accept his apology? I wanted to forget everything so bad, I longed for the days before the war, before Teague. I longed for the days of nothing but Leonard with our laughter and our swords. But death and love are hard things to overcome, and once wisdom is acquired it can never truly be forgotten.

"I'm sorry too. Leonard, I shouldn't have waited so long to make up my mind about what to do, but it was so hard. I hated being caught between you two, and then in the end both you and Aidan ended up so close to hating me." Surprisingly, I didn't feel like crying. I just wanted what had to be said to get out. I had to get my friend back. I was nothing without him. I hadn't realized how dependant I had become upon him.

"I'm not mad at you Noble; I don't think that I ever was. I was madder at myself than anything. Noble, I loved her but I once said that I would never put a girl over my best friend and I meant it. I just . . ." he ran his hands wearily over his eyes, "I was so confused about everything. I still am. I wish that I had never met her and yet I'm so glad that I had the time that I did with her."

"Leonard what you did was wrong. It's not my place or even Aidan's to forgive you. First you have to forgive yourself," I sighed.

"But I ruined everything!" He licked his dry lips.

I wanted to grab his hands or wrap him in a hug but I knew that was not something that a man would do at a moment like this. I knew that it was hard for Leonard to show his feelings as it was. "When I took Glorianna away the last thing that she said to me was that she loved you. I hope that maybe that will be enough. I can't stand to see you like this."

Leonard looked over at me. "She might have loved me, but none of that matters now. I don't deserve to be here. I don't deserve to be with you or with Aidan. I knew that it was wrong the whole time and I still did it. That's the worst kind of sin, a conscious one."

"Everybody makes mistakes," I whispered, not knowing what to say. He was right. Should I have lied and said that it was all going to be alright?

"You never would have messed up like this. You always do what's noble," he said it as if he truly believed it.

I laughed. "No, not even close."

We sat there is silence for a few more moments, each contemplating our own problems.

"I'm leaving in the morning," Leonard finally coughed, "I'm going back to Fraunc."

All of the air left my body for a moment. "What?" I finally mumbled.

Leonard turned to look at me. "You know that I can't stay here. Is everyone supposed to just forget? Lines of loyalty would be drawn. The people would either hate me or set me upon a pedestal and I don't want that. I deserve to be the bad guy. I can't look at him every day and he can't look at me. You're the only reason that he even agreed to let me stay."

"Leonard, I did this because I can't . . . I . . ." I didn't know what to say. He had always been there. He was my best friend. He had been there every day for the last ten years of my life. I couldn't imagine him not being there.

"Noble, please don't ask me to stay," he said shortly.

I turned to look into his eyes. I knew that if I asked to him stay he would. I couldn't do that to him. "Fine," I whispered, "Go. If that's what you need to do, then go." I put a hand on his shoulder. "Just don't forget about me alright?"

He cracked a small sad smile. "How could I ever forget about my best friend? We had some good times didn't we?" I nodded, biting my lip. "You're the best man here, don't you ever forget that." I nodded again and stood up swiftly.

"I'll miss you," I managed to say proudly before turning and walking away from him, walking away from the rock that I had leaned on through every trial that I had faced. I wanted to run back to him and throw my arms around him. I wanted to tell him that it would kill me to let him go. I wanted him to know that I loved him.

But I couldn't, because sometimes if you truly love someone you have to let them go.

# CHAPTER SIX
## Treachery

He was gone by dawn the next morning. I watched him ride away from the castle from my window. He needed to get away. I wondered if he thought of me as he took one last look back at the place that had become his home. I hoped that I had made as much of an impression on him as he had made on me.

Someone banged on my door, waking me up once I had finally fallen back asleep. "Meeting at the Round Table," Bran called.

I grumbled as I pulled on my clothes, shivering from the late autumn cold that crept in from the stones. As I stumbled down the hallways to the table my mind flew back to the meeting after I had freed my father. Things had been so different then. I had been so different then.

Ten years was an almost unbelievably long time. Ten years since I had seen my father. Nine years since Teague had died. Seven years since I had last kissed Aidan.

I sat down in my chair and tried to avoid looking over at Leonard's empty spot. It was almost as if I could feel the hole that he had left in my heart. I looked over at Aidan and gave him a small smile. He could see that I was hurting and gave me a reassuring smile back.

Aidan stood up once everyone had quieted. "I'm sure that you have all noticed by now that one of our members is no longer with us. Leonard has returned to Fraunc. There is a civil war raging and he felt that it was his duty to return. I urged him to go. It will provide time for the dust to settle here. I don't know if he will choose to return, but he is welcome back if that day ever does come," he gave a small, strained smile. "Everything else will continue as normal. The country appears to be as peaceful as ever and I see no evidence that anything will change in the near future. If any of you wish to return to your homes and visit your families then I give you permission to do so. If not, go about your normal business."

Then men started talking among themselves immediately. Some of them were fathers and husbands that were eager to get back to their families. I sighed. My whole life was my work; there was nothing else to look forward to. I sat there, lost in my thoughts. I didn't realize that everyone had left until I felt a hand on my shoulder.

I turned to see Morgan. I couldn't help but smile when I saw a huge bald spot right in the front of his hair. "What do you want?" I asked with a sigh. Why did he keep trying?

"Why did you take her? Why did they all forgive you for committing such a crime?" he looked down at me in genuine amazement. "Why does Aidan love you so much?"

I just stared at him for a moment, wondering if that was genuine hurt that I saw in his eyes. "I don't know," I said as I looked away. "I can only answer for myself, and I don't know."

"I wish that I could understand it, but the harder that I look at you the more confused I get. You aren't exceptionally brave, or smart, or kind. You aren't much of anything. At least I let everybody know where I stand," his arms were crossed across his lean chest.

"You don't even know me," I whispered with my eyes narrowed. He had just voiced what I woke up every morning telling myself. There was no reason at all that these people that I cared about should love me. I was afraid that they would wake up one morning and see that too.

"What's there to know? You're a scared pretender who just happens to be good with a sword," he delivered these blows as if he was having a pleasant conversation.

I shook my head at him. "And you are a man who doesn't know where the legends ends and he begins. You told me once that it was just an act. Well I don't think that's all it is anymore Morgan. I think that you believe you're this strong conqueror, but you're just a pale shadow of the villain that you appear to be," I stood up and pushed my chair in.

I started to leave the room and he whispered in my ear as I passed him, "Maybe the hero can't exist without the villain."

I paused for a moment next to him before moving away and walking confidently from the room, even though confidence was the last thing that I felt. I felt as if I had been cut down to my core. I felt as if Morgan might have been the only one who truly saw me as I was.

**********

The next day I rode down into the city. I took Merrick past my old home. I hadn't seen it in so long that it felt foreign to me. I had been but a girl when I had left that place, naïve and scared. I smiled, knowing that a younger me would not have believed where I had ended up.

A wave of longing for my father rushed over me. I hadn't thought of him in so long. I hardly remembered the sound of his voice. Had his eyes been robin's eggs blue or sky blue? I sat there for a moment, lost in my thoughts yet again when I saw a young child rush out from the front door with a hunk of bread in his hand.

His gaze was turned the opposite way and he was heading straight towards Merrick's hooves, which were roughly as large as his head. I quickly dismounted and caught the young boy in my arms before he crashed into my stallion.

His head whipped around to stare at me in shock with eyes as big as saucers. He tried to wriggle free from me, but I wouldn't let him go. "Calm down," I laughed, "Calm down." When the boy finally stopped wriggling I loosed my grip. "Do you promise that you won't run away?"

The little boy nodded up at me. I gave him a look that I hoped reassured him that I wasn't going to hurt him, and let go. "What's your name?" I asked.

"I'm Tommy," the little boy stuck his dirty chin up in the air. "I'm not afraid of you."

I smiled. "I'm glad. My name is Noble," I pointed past the boy, "That used to be my home, a long time ago. Is that where you live?" He shook his head. "Then where do you live Tommy?"

I had no experience with kids. I had not grown up around them and since I had joined the knighthood the only people that I had dealt with were grown men. Most women my age were married with children of their own. I had no desire to have kids, even if it would have been possible. The idea was completely terrifying to me.

"I live on the other side of town with all of the other boys," he grabbed my hand. "I'll show you."

I smiled. It wasn't like I had anything planned for the rest of the day. "All right. Would you like to ride on my horse with me?"

The boy craned his neck to look up at my horse with wonder before nodding excitedly. I stood up and lifted him up onto the horse before swinging myself on behind him. He was almost trembling with excitement. I turned Merrick and we started to wander along the streets and every once and a while Tommy would direct me when to turn.

"How old are you Tommy?' I asked as we ambled pleasantly along. The sun was warm on my back and the boy's thin body was warm pressed up against mine.

"I'm the second smallest boy," he sighed sadly.

"How many brothers do you have?"

"They aren't my brothers."

"Does your mother take in boys?" I asked, starting to realize what was going on.

"I don't have a mother, none of us do," he answered proudly. "We all take care of ourselves. One time I even brought in enough food to feed all of us for dinner."

"How many of you are there?" I asked, trying not to frown.

"I dunno," he mumbled. "We're here."

I looked around. We were in an alley, surrounded by wooden walls. The sun was blocked out by laundry hanging from ropes between the buildings. There was a disgusting stench. I saw a shanty made of splintering wood and dirty linen leaning against the wall. I slowly dismounted and then pulled Tommy down beside me. He stayed holding my hand.

We walked over and I leaned down to walk into the little shelter. It was pitch black and I almost tripped over a child that was lying on the ground. There was a small fire going, but it was reduced to almost nothing but dull red coals. Horror raced rampant through my mind. How could these children live like this?

I rushed out of the shanty, pulling Tommy with me. He looked up at me, beaming with pride. "Did you like it?" He was proud of that place. He was proud of surviving as long as he had.

I nodded. "Yes, but now it's only fair that you see where I live," I smiled encouragingly. The little boy nodded.

I pulled him onto the horse again and we rode back to the castle. The boy grew more and more excited the closer that we came, until when we finally rode through the castle gates and he exclaimed, " You live in the castle?!"

I smiled. "I'm a knight."

"You are! I want to be a knight when I grow up," he said dreamily.

"Would you like to meet some of my friends?" I asked.

"Are you friends with the King?" he asked, sounding as if he might jump out of his skin at any moment.

"Yes, the King and I are very good friends. Would you like to meet him?" I could feel him nodding. "Do you promise to behave?" Again, he nodded.

We dismounted and I led him through the castle until we reached Aidan's quarters. I knocked on the door and after a moment he opened it with a big smile. His eyes drifted down to my new friend.

"Aidan, I would like to introduce you to my new friend Tommy," I smiled as Aidan kneeled down and held out his hand for Tommy to shake. The boy took it gingerly.

"Hello Tommy, my name is Aidan," he glanced up at me for a second, and I could tell that he saw what I hadn't seen until I reached the boys 'home'.

"Everyone knows who you are," the boy stuttered. "None of my friends are going to believe that I met you."

Aidan laughed. "Are you hungry?" he asked as he stood up. Tommy nodded and we both followed Aidan into his room. Aidan grabbed an apple off of his table and handed it to Tommy. The little boy looked at it like it was the greatest treasure that he had ever received, and it probably was. I couldn't even imagine what life must have been like for this boy. He couldn't have been more than six or seven, and he was already his own provider.

"Thank you sir," he smiled before tearing into the apple. The sweet juice rolled down his face in clear, sticky streams and I looked up to see Aidan smiling sadly down at the little boy. He looked up and caught my eye.

"Noble, can I speak to you for a moment out in the hallway? Tommy, feel free to sit down if you wish," the King walked to the door and opened it for me. We stepped outside and then he closed it firmly. "Where did you find him?"

"I was visiting the part of town that I used to live when I caught him stealing. He offered to show me his home. I just assumed that he was a normal boy living with his family. They live in a little hut leaning against the wall of a dark alley," I sighed. "It's horrible."

Aidan shook his head. "I thought that our city was better than that. I thought that maybe I was a better King than to allow that."

"Aidan, I know that you aren't that naïve. Every city has poor and run down people. Now that we're aware of it we can try and help," I crossed my arms. "Maybe we could build an orphanage."

"I've thought about it before. Would you help me build it Noble?"

"Of course,' I smiled. "Now let's hope that he hasn't stolen anything from your room."

\*\*\*\*\*\*\*\*\*\*

Bran, Gladwin, Kay and I pushed the wall up into place, each of us with groans of exhaustion and sweat pouring down our faces. The plans for the orphanage hadn't been elaborate, but we were trying to get the building up as quickly as possible. The snow would be coming soon. We could all feel it in the chilly air.

I wiped my hands on my pants and pushed my sleeves even further up my forearm. "It's starting to come together," I patted Gladwin on the back and he smiled at me.

The building was a simple two room shelter with only one window and two doors. One room would be for the children to sleep in and the other was for cooking and eating. The orphanage was being built right outside of the castle walls. An elderly couple and their grown children were going to cook and clean for the children. They were considered castle staff and were going to be paid well. I was glad that everything had come together so nicely.

Tommy had been living with me ever since I had met him. He was enjoying being as pampered as a prince. I had learned that his parents had died a few years ago and he had been wandering the streets, alone and cold when he met his best friend Bill. Bill was the biggest boy in the group, and he was the father figure. From the way that Tommy described him, the leader couldn't have been more than ten or eleven.

I took Tommy back to his 'home' and let him describe to the boys about what the orphanage was going to be. Some were hesitant, scared of being ripped from what had become the usual for them. Others, mostly the younger ones, were excited about having hot food and a soft blanket to sleep with every night.

All of their faces were so tiny, and their features so beautiful. I wanted everything to be better for them and was proud of the work that we were doing. I wanted for everything to be ready as soon as possible.

The night before we were ready to move the children into their new home, Aidan and I looked everything over one last time by the light of the setting sun. The walls were sturdy and the food was all ready to fill the hungry boys' stomachs. I sighed with pleasure as we took one last look before heading back to the castle.

"You seem to have gotten really attached to these children," Aidan commented as we strolled through the gates.

I shrugged. "They deserve the same things that everyone does, and I want to make sure that they have them. You, and Kay and Bran and Gladwin have done just as much as I have," I looked up at the sunset. The sky was a bright orange with streaks of pink running through it. It was beautiful. Lately I hadn't taken any time to notice things like that.

"They didn't have to put up with Tommy every second of every day," he smiled. "That boy adores you."

I blushed. "I don't know why. I have no idea what I'm doing with him. I have no idea what time children should go to bed or what they should eat. I talk to him like he's an adult and most of the time he doesn't understand what I'm saying."

"Do you ever want children Noble?" he asked softly. I shook my head. "Why not?"

"I'm selfish. I like doing things for me, and I would be so scared that I would mess up and raise horrible little beasts," I smiled down at my hands. They felt tight from the cold.

"I think that you would do a fine job," Aidan replied. "I'll have to have children someday."

I paused. "Do you actually want them?"

He shrugged. "I don't really have any choice in the matter, but I suppose that I would want them if I ever met the right woman to have them with. Glorianna and I tried for so long . . . maybe it's not a possibility for me."

"Don't give up so easily," I gave him a reassuring smile. "While we aren't as young as we used to be, there is still plenty of time."

He smiled back at me. "I feel practically ancient. Almost too old to be raising children. But at least Tommy has been some good practice the last couple months."

I nodded. "You really love him, don't you?"

Aidan smiled. "He's a brave and smart boy. He actually reminds me a lot of you. I imagine a younger you as a almost exactly like him, except for being female of course."

I turned to look at him. "Really?" He nodded. "I don't see it at all, but I take it as a compliment. He's a pretty good kid, all things considered."

"So are you, all things considered," he grinned down at me. I rolled my eyes playfully. "I mean it. You might not always do the things that I want you to do, but in the end what you do always turns out alright. I have faith in you."

I grunted. "I don't know why. I don't have a lot of faith in myself most of the time."

"And I don't understand why you don't believe in yourself. Obviously everyone else does. We all love and respect you. It's amazing how far you've come," we went into his quarters and sat down next to each other on his bed. He grabbed my hand between his two larger ones.

I closed my eyes for a second. I had forgotten how good it felt to touch him. When I opened them he was staring at me. "If I'm so amazing then why doesn't anything ever work out for me? Don't I deserve to be beautiful and love someone who loves me in return? Seven years is long time with no love . . ."

"You are beautiful," he replied as his gaze swept over my face,

"I'm only beautiful to you because you love me," I replied coldly as I pulled away from him and went to stand at the window. Now he would see how depressing and awful I really was. Now he would see the real me.

"I love you because you're beautiful, inside and out," he said as he came up behind me and wrapped his arms around me. I wasn't sure if he meant a platonic love or a romantic love. I wasn't sure what I wanted him to mean. I was finally over Teague. I thought that Aidan was done with me. It had been so long since he had held me like this.

"Aidan, no matter how many times you say that, it won't change how I feel about myself. I think that I know myself better than you do," I sighed as I leaned my back against his chest.

"You're right," he whispered, "I can't make you happy if you don't want to be happy."

I whirled around to face him. "That's not fair!"

He threw his hands up in the air. "What?! You think I'm lying when I tell you something other than what you think, and when I agree

154

with you, you get mad." There was a look of frustration across his handsome features. My eyes strayed to his full lips.

"That's not true. You said that because you knew that it would make me mad. You're either too nice to me or you're horrible to me. Can't you just . . . be honest?" I pleaded, rolling my eyes to the ceiling to keep from crying. His eyes felt like weights upon me. "I'm sorry. I don't mean to make you out as the bad guy when you aren't. It's been really hard for me since . . . I've tried to keep busy with the orphanage, but now we're almost done with that. . . " I stopped, not knowing what to say.

Finally, his gaze strayed.

"Do you wish that you would have gone with Leonard?" he asked and looked up at me for a split second before looking back down at his hands.

I didn't answer for a moment. He was really asking who I loved more. It wasn't a fair question. They were such different men, and they meant such different things to me. "No," I finally whispered, "He needed to get away from all of this, including me." I avoided the answer that he really wanted: was it him or Leonard. He wanted the lines drawn, and I was right down the middle, but I wouldn't budge. I would let them cut me in half if it came to that.

He just looked at me for a moment with smoldering eyes. Finally he took a step forward and cupped the back of my head in his hand before kissing me deeply. I didn't move forward or backward, I just absorbed the moment. Could I love him? Could I be with him now that Glorianna was gone? He had said that we would never be the same. What we had before had just been the start of something, there could be so much more. Did I want that with him? Did he truly want that with me, or was he just trying to sway me to his side permanently?

When he pulled away I looked up into his eyes. I didn't have to say anything, he already knew. He probably knew more than I did. He knew that every morning when I woke my first thought was that I should have gone with my best friend.

**\*\*\*\*\*\*\*\*\*\***

"No Tommy, never drop your sword during a fight, ever. It gives your opponent an extra moment to think, or attack," I said as I lunged softly at the young boy with the blunt wooden sword. I stabbed it gently into his soft tummy. The boy had gotten sturdier and sturdier ever since his arrival at the palace, but in the afternoon it was time for him to go to his new home.

I looked down at his precious face. He had a small gap between his two front teeth and his cheeks were dotted with tiny freckles. His sandy brown hair was messy as always. I would miss him. I almost hated to admit just how much I would miss him. He had made life bearable over the last few months.

"Noble," the boy began, "Are the people at my new home as nice as you and the King, and all of your friends? I don't care if there's food and all my friends as long as the people are nice. I'd never met any really nice grown-ups until I met you." The boy had a tendency to ramble, and I waited until I was sure that he was done.

"I assure you that these people are far nicer than me, and they will help you to grow up into a strong, kind, and intelligent young man. Besides, it's not like we won't see each other. We're neighbors, and we can go see each other whenever we want," I smiled as I gave him a hug. His tiny arms wrapped around me and he buried his head in my shoulder.

"Do you promise?" he sighed sadly when he finally pulled away. I nodded solemnly. "Alright,' he smiled at me. At that moment I wanted the world for him. I wanted him to have the kind of life that men dream about.

That night Tommy and I stood in front of his new home. The sounds of happy boys and the smell of beef stew drifted in the air. I looked down at Tommy's little hand locked in mine. His eyes were wide, either from anticipation or wonder. I smiled down at him.

"Are you ready to go?" I asked. My voice cracked with sudden emotion and I coughed to try and hide it. I blinked rapidly so that the boy wouldn't see the tears in my eyes. He was only going to be right next door, I told myself. There was no reason to act all emotional and soft.

"It looks beautiful," Tommy whispered. "Thank you Noble," he said before letting go of my hand and running over to open the door. A warm soft light filtered out. Tommy turned to give me one last wave and then he walked inside, shutting the door behind him.

I definitely wasn't cut out to be a parent.

**********

The week after the orphanage was finished, Aidan threw a party, trying to get my mind off of how empty my days had become. I sat in the corner gulping down whiskey. I was tired of the women making bets to see who could bed me first. It was a game. Little did they know that it was a game that none of them would win.

I let out a sigh. Kay was even dancing with a tall plump redhead. Everyone looked like they were having a wonderful time. I wished that it was that simple for me. I thought about what Aidan had said. Maybe I just wasn't made to be as happy as everyone else. Maybe I was meant to fall every time I was just about to reach the top of that wall. Sometimes I felt like I should just stay on the ground.

"Why aren't you out there dancing Noble?" a voice asked from even deeper in the shadows than I was. I turned to see Morgan leaning against the wall. His eyes were scanning the crowd. He raised a flask to his lips and a drop dribbled down his chin. He hastily wiped it away.

I turned back towards the party, "Dancing isn't my strong suite," I replied taking a sip of my own drink. I was nearing drunkenness.

"Mine neither. I would have thought that one of those harpies would have pulled you out already though," he took a step forward so that we were beside each other.

I laughed. "And why haven't they dragged you out into their dancing frenzy yet Morgan?"

"Everyone's afraid of me," he answered heavily. There wasn't a moment of hesitation.

I turned to look at him. "I'm sure that not everyone is."

He turned to give me a sneer. "You're afraid of me, why shouldn't they be?" He took another huge swig of his drink. I could smell the alcohol oozing from his flesh.

"Who says that I'm afraid of you?" I asked. We both knew that I was.

"No one needs to say it. I can see it in everyone's eyes. Most of the time I like it, but sometimes I hate it more than anything. Sometimes all I want is for someone to look at me and see something good," his voice had dropped to a raspy whisper.

"You're a good fighter," I offered weakly.

Morgan laughed. "I don't know if that can really be construed as something good."

"Of course it can! Think about how many lives you've saved," I drained the rest of my flask. I couldn't believe that I was defending Morgan.

"You do it to protect your country. I have my own reasons," he turned to look at me, and I trembled under the weight of his black eyes. "If I could choose one person to love and respect me, I would choose you." My mouth dropped and every muscle in my body tensed. "It hurts when you look at me with all the hatred and disgust you can muster." I could see a feverish gleam in his eyes. His eyes twitched. Then he leaned in close so that his mouth was right next to my ear. "I knew your father Aceline."

I stood as still as I could through my trembling. I could almost feel my blood freezing in my veins. Then he was gone. I looked around and he was nowhere to be seen. My knees almost gave out and I leaned against the wall, my breathing shaky.

I jumped when somebody laid a hand on my shoulder.

"What's wrong Noble?" Aidan asked with hardness in his eyes. "What did he say to you?"

"Aidan, he knows," I whispered and without waiting for him to answer, fled to my room. He was too shocked to run after me.

I didn't sleep at all that night. I kept hearing Morgan's voice slithering through my head, squeezing the breath from my lungs. I had no idea what to do. How could he know, and for how long had he known? How should I act around him? Why hadn't he told anyone yet?

I finally dozed off for a few minutes and woke up in the morning tangled up in my sheets. I was starting to dress when I heard a knock on my door. I quickly pulled on a shirt and opened the door to see Aidan. He looked as if he had gotten about the same amount of sleep as I had.

"Just act normal," Aidan said as he brushed past me into my room, "Don't let him know that you are upset or nervous. Avoid him as much as possible, but don't make it obvious that you're avoiding him. . ." Aidan put his head in his hands. "He's the last person that I would want to know."

I shivered. "You have no idea." Our eyes met and I gave him a small smile. I couldn't bring myself to tell him anything else that Morgan had said to me. I just couldn't say it. To have any of those words come from my mouth would have been completely unnatural.

"I just wonder how he found out," Aidan mused. "I thought that you were doing a pretty good job about keeping it a secret. I mean, it's been over ten years and only two people had found out until now. I don't know what we'll say if he tells anyone."

I sighed. "Aidan, if he does tell anyone, I don't want you to be involved. I want you to pretend like you didn't know anything about it. You can't afford to be implicated in something like that so soon after what happened with Glorianna. "

Aidan shook his head. "No. I won't leave you to face the wolves without someone at your back. You know that."

I smiled at him. "I suppose that I do. Now, I don't know about you, but it's time for my daily workout." I picked up my sword and walked towards the door before turning to look at him again. "Try not to worry about me too much. I'm sure that it's all going to be fine." I tried to sound confident, and Aidan tried to pretend like he believed me.

Surprisingly though, for a time at least it appeared that I was right. Morgan and I spoke to each other as little as possible, and things were no more awkward than they normally were. In fact, Morgan had kept to his room even more than normal. It was rare to see him at all. Still, I held my breath. There was no part of me that ever trusted him. But as time passes, most things are easy to forget, and you can't live your life based on one moment. I almost forgot.

That is, until Morgan turned his attention to something much larger than a girl trying to make her way in a man's world.

**********

"There's a major force gathering on the east coast. It wasn't identified who they were, but they were obviously dangerous, and obviously ready to move," Morgan reported.

Aidan looked down at him with narrowed eyes. "How did you gather this information Morgan?"

"I'd been hearing rumors of trouble brewing and I sent out a few men to take a look. I would have gone through you, but I heard it from unreliable sources. I figured that it was nothing, but my scouts just arrived. It's going to take all of us knights," he shook his head. "I'm sorry that I didn't tell you sooner Aidan."

Aidan nodded slowly, "It's alright Morgan. I understand your reasoning. Did your scouts report how many?"

"Not enough to call out our army, but it won't be easy to put them down," Morgan replied. "I think that you should lead all of us down there. The men are itching for a fight anyways."

Aidan nodded again, "I'll go and wake everyone up." He flew out of the room. He was excited too. We had all been cooped up in the castle for too long.

I turned slowly too look at Morgan. He was staring out the window, lost in thought. He never seemed to be quite present anymore. His eyes were always distant. I was glad that he wasn't trying to converse with me.

I stood up and started to walk towards the door. I had to get ready to go.

Suddenly I turned, "I don't believe you, you know," I whispered. The words had just flown through my lips. I felt as if I hadn't even thought them before I said them.

Morgan turned to look at me, slightly startled. Then a small smile crept over his lips. "Why not?"

"I don't know," I stuttered.

"Women's intuition I suppose," he smiled pleasantly before turning to look back out the window. I shivered and walked out of the room as quickly as I could.

The men were running around, getting things ready to leave. The looks of excitement that lit up their faces was brilliant. This was exactly what these men needed. Who was I to take that away from them? Besides, all I had was a feeling, nothing tangible. For all I knew I was just mad at Aidan for still trusting Morgan.

I turned around when someone clapped me on the shoulder.

"Isn't it wonderful?" Kade asked, barely containing his excitement, "I was getting so tired of just waiting around. I know that I'm not a fighter, but I wasn't meant to just sit around the castle getting fat either."

I smiled. I knew exactly what he was talking about. "I never thought that I'd be looking forward to a fight," I replied.

Bran walked over. "I told you that you'd get used to it someday. A man can't truly hate what he excels at."

"I wouldn't say that I excel," I laughed, "More like hold my own."

"I wonder if you truly believe all that modest bullshit that you say," Bran said as he put his arm around my shoulder and gave me a squeeze, "Or if you are just playing us all for fools."

I grabbed my heart in mock pain. "Oh how you grieve me brother! I am mortally wounded by your mistrust." We all let out a laugh. I hated it when people put me on the spot like that. I knew that I was good, and I felt like I did deserve praise every once and a while, but I didn't feel like that meant that I was conceited.

My father always used to tell me that a true lady accepted compliments with grace. I didn't even have that. Any trace of femininity that I had was slowly being washed away.

Aidan broke me out of my thoughts. "You had better hurry and get all of your things ready Noble," he smiled, "We're leaving after midday. We want to stop these rebels as soon as we possibly can."

I nodded, trying to tell myself that the sinking feeling in my stomach was just something bad that I had for breakfast.

**********

Of course, even though it had been sunny all morning, it started snowing as soon as we were out of the city gates. It reminded me of my first fight, the first time that I had ever killed a man. It seemed so long ago.

I had been a completely different person. Back then I had been naïve and hopeful. I wasn't that way any longer. I was hard and cold and tired. There were still similarities of course, we were both idealistic and headstrong, but that was almost it. Now I had to pretend to shave every day. I could no longer hide behind the excuse of youth. I was full grown, had been for quite some time.

We camped that night, and it was miserable. I sat in my tent that I shared with Kay, staring out into the cold night. My breath came out in clouds. Kade's snores were some of the loudest I had ever heard. He always had been able to sleep through anything, thus preventing everyone else from any sleep at all.

"Noble," someone called from right outside my darkened doorway.

I wrapped my cloak around my shoulders and stepped outside, letting the flap close behind me. Morgan stood there in all black. His white skin glowed beneath the pale glow of the moon. His lips were red. I looked around; all the other tents were dark.

"Aren't you supposed to be on look-out Morgan?" I asked impatiently.

"Come keep me company," he smiled, "It's not any fun to be cold and lonely."

"Have you ever had fun in your entire life? And what in the hell makes you think that I care about whether you're cold and lonely?" I asked throatily.

"Because I care, and what I want happens to be in your best interest," he smiled again. His sparkling eyes looked enormous in the darkness.

"I'm not going to play stupid," I replied as I swallowed, "But I'm not going to be your lap dog just because you know things."

"What things might I know?" Morgan asked innocently.

I just stared at him coldly. "You think that you're so smart, playing all your little games? Well all I see a fool who thinks that he can intimidate me. Let me tell you something," I whispered before I leaned in so that my lips almost touching his ear. "If you plan to hold what you know about me over my head, then one of these days you're going to lose yours."

I felt his skin warming with my breath. I held myself there for a moment, just breathing. He smelled like cinnamon. It was slightly intoxicating, and it made me braver. "Do you still want me to come with you Morgan?" I said softly before pulling away.

As I pulled back I saw an open vulnerability in his eyes for a split second. It was as if he was just a scared boy, trying to claw his way out of a whirlpool of secrecy and blackness. Then it was gone, back into the mask that gave nothing away. I was used to dawning that face myself.

"Do you honestly think that you can frighten me? I'm a better fighter than you. I'm smarter. I'm more decisive. I'm everything that you're not," he started to circle me silently. "Don't pretend that you're important in any way, shape or form to me. You're just as dispensable as anyone else here."

At this I let out a dry laugh. "Don't fool yourself. I don't know why, but for some reason you're the one that keeps seeking me out. Why is that Morgan? What is it about me? Don't keep me in suspense. If you see something worth a damn thing then please let me know." I snapped around to look at him.

We were almost the same height, he and I. He was of a slighter build, but he was probably stronger. He was fueled by something that I couldn't put a finger on, but somehow understood.

"You want to know why you interest me?" he asked.

"It's not that hard of a question," I snapped. I could feel myself loosing control of the situation very quickly.

He just stared at me for a moment. Then he shook his head. "I honestly have no idea."

That wasn't near good enough for me.

"That's a lie. Everything that you say is serving some master plan that you have. You never say anything honest," my jaw was clenched and I was trembling. "Every time that I see something true and honest you just hide it away. Are you incapable of feeling anything? Are you incapable of showing anyone who you really are? Do you want me to tell you the truth of why I'm not going to kill you right here?" Suddenly I lost the strength that I had been desperately holding on to for years. Tears were rolling down my face. I saw him, but he wasn't there. In my head it was just me and the truth. "When I look at you I see all the things that frighten me about myself. When I look at you, I see all the hurt and fear and loneliness that I shove back every day. I hate you because you remind me of all that I could so easily become; I hate you because you are all the things I hate about myself," I choked through the pain. We stood there for a minute before I finally looked up at him.

His face was crystal clear through my veil of tears. "I can't let myself become you, and yet I can't bring myself to truly hate you," I finally whispered. It broke my heart. It shattered every bone in my body and seared my flesh from within. I trembled and started to crumble to the ground when he caught me in his arms.

For a second I just let him hold me. But we had never touched like that before and it felt wrong. My body seared, as if I was getting ready to be burnt alive.

I jerked away swiftly and wiped my eyes, not daring to look into his eyes until I had composed myself. I was trembling though and it took a few seconds for my breathing to stabilize.

Slowly I looked up at him through my lashes. He was staring down at me and the look on his face took my breath away yet again.

"I love you," he whispered more to himself than to me. He looked completely shocked by the realization. "I always have."

I just stood there like a child, looking at a person they trust to make everything better, pleading with them. My eyes pleaded with Morgan for him to not say another word. I was too exhausted and too confused.

He understood.

"You do know that I'll tell them about you one day," he finally whispered. "That I'm going to use you."

"I know," I whispered, "Just don't expect me to be happy about it."

"Is there really such a thing as happiness?" he asked before turning and walking away. I stared after him until he ducked into his tent without another glance at me.

I have never felt so lonely in my entire life.

\*\*\*\*\*\*\*\*\*

In the days that followed there was nothing more than a deep ache. I was anxious to arrive, fight, and leave. It wasn't that the world was dull, it was me that lacked all luster. I saw the same in Morgan.

Finally, we stopped for the night, knowing that we would reach the rebels the next afternoon. Everyone sat around the fire laughing and cleaning their already shining blades.

I stared into the flame absently. My mind was a blank slate with only the constant crackle of the flames and the laughter of my friends.

Someone sat down next to me. "What are you thinking about?" asked Gladwin with a sigh.

I turned to look at him. There were wrinkles at the corners of his intelligent eyes and there were threads of silver running through his curly red hair. It was the first time that I had truly looked at him in a while.

It made me sad to see that he had grown old before his time. It made me sad to know that we had grown apart over the years. I hardly knew him anymore.

"I actually wasn't thinking about anything," I answered with an honest smile, "Now I'm thinking about how fast these last few years have flown by. Soon we won't be young anymore."

A smile lit up his face. "I realized that a long time ago."

"Well, I'm not half as smart as you, and I haven't been around you enough lately for it to rub off," I turned back towards the fire.

I missed the way that things used to be. I missed how it was in the beginning. I wanted the days before I learned about love and loss. I longed for my innocent friendships with these men. Now I was so jaded that hardly anything felt real anymore. It was as if I was a seed being tossed around on the wind, and wherever I landed was only rocky ground where I could begin to grow before being ripped away again onto the gales.

"None of us are as close as we used to be," he supplied, knowing exactly how I felt.

"I really miss that," I sighed, "I miss waking up every day knowing that the world was beautiful and that my friends would always be everything that I needed."

I could feel his stare. "While we all grew old, you were still growing up," he stated. "I'm sorry that it had to happen that way. You deserve more than any of us have to offer."

"But I don't want anything else," I shook my head slightly. "I wouldn't have any of this any other way."

"The thing is, you think that we're the best, but we're not. All of us are broken and hard. We run towards death. You are better than this, and that's why we all need you around. For some reason you chose all of us drunkards and slobs. It means more to us than you'll ever know. All of us have been outcasts our entire lives. We are so lucky to have you."

"No," I whispered, "I'm lucky to have all of you."

I had completely forgotten that it was my 27th birthday.

**********

We woke up the next morning well before dawn. The game plan was that we would travel just until we reached a grove of trees that circled the rebel's camp. Then we would spread out and attack them from all sides. They would never see it coming, and there would be no direction for them to escape. We expected it to be a speedy victory with as little injury on both sides as possible. After a few hours of riding, we reached our destination. We split up in pairs and set off into the woods.

Aidan and I were together. We didn't speak a word for fear of being heard. Soon, we could hear the sound of voices and the trees began to thin. We stopped and waited. I glanced over at Aidan with a small smile and he grinned back at me.

After a few minutes Aidan let out a loud bird call, our signal to attack. Aidan and I rushed forward, swords held high. I could see the others on both sides of us, ducking in and out among the trees.

When we finally broke the tree line I gasped. There were not just a few rebels. Before us was an army in full armor, standing in battle formations. They stood in a wall, shoulder to shoulder. They had been waiting for us, and there was only one guess who had alerted them of our presence. Perhaps the same man who had called them to come there to fight us.

I saw a few of the men falter, not sure what to do. None of us were prepared for this kind of opposition.

Aidan was in front of me, with his sword still raised, growling a war cry. I followed, not hesitating. We were here to fight. We would not run now. It would be hopeless, and this way nobody could ever say that we were cowards.

We crashed into their wall with all that we had.

These men were good, whoever they were, but we were better. We were slicing through their defenses fairly easily, and they were falling back.

I stabbed a man through his gut and then beheaded him before scanning my surroundings. Most of our men seemed to be holding their own, but there were bodies strewn everywhere.

Suddenly there was a loud bugle call.

Every sword in the clearing fell silent as we all turned to see where the call had come from.

Somehow in the commotion Morgan had found a horse and was sitting on it, making him head and shoulders above the rest of us. The bugle that he was holding dropped to his side.

I glanced over at Aidan. I could see from his furrowed brow that he was trying to think of any other explanation for what was happening besides the obvious. There was no misunderstanding it though. Merick's prophecy was coming true.

"I thought that everyone could use a rest," Morgan bellowed, using the same sarcastic tone that he always did. Then his head flew back and he let out a laugh that was unlike anything I had ever heard before. It was so crazed that it barely sounded human. Once more, I pictured something trying to claw its way out of Morgan, but this time it was pure evil. When he was done his head turned so that he was staring at Aidan. "Unfortunately for you uncle, you've spent your whole life resting, and now your going to have to fight for what you've always taken for granted."

"What are you talking about Morgan?" Aidan asked slowly.

"Haven't you figured it out yet?!" Morgan threw his arms up into the air. "I'm fulfilling the prophesy! Only instead of being the villain, I'm the savior. I'm saving them from the opulence and complacency of you." His eyes were wide and gleaming.

"Morgan . . ." Aiden began as he took a step toward his nephew.

"NO!" Morgan roared, "It's my turn to talk now."

Aidan froze mid-step.

"Callento has already been sieged by my men, and by now, uncle, the rest of my men have circled this little clearing. You've lost. For the first time in your pampered and privileged life, you have been bested. You always did underestimate me and now it has cost you everything you have ever loved," Morgan smiled briefly. "Any last words, Aidan, former king of Callento?"

Aidan just stared at the crazed man in horror.

"I didn't think so," Morgan snarled before raises the bugle to his lips one more time.

There was a roar as hundreds of men streamed out of the trees that we had been hiding in only moments before.

My mind was racing and my heart was pounding but there was no time to think.

Two men ran at me at once, both roaring ferociously. I swiftly stabbed one through the shoulder. The other managed to slice my hand open before I could turn to face him. He swung wildly at my left shoulder and I deftly moved out of the swords arc. Then I lunged at his right leg, slicing deep into his thigh. He fell to the ground with a cry of pain. I didn't hesitate to slit both of their throats.

I looked up to see Morgan riding away through the mass pandemonium. On the back of the first man that I had killed was a bow and a sheath of arrows.

I grabbed the bow and quickly notched an arrow, aiming it at the center of Morgan's back. I tried to steady my shaking arm and took one shattered breath before letting the arrow fly.

I knew as soon as I let it go that it wasn't going to hit him and I let out a curse. It flew past him close enough so that he turned to look behind him. Even through the crowd his eyes met mine. In them I could see nothing but a feverish glow.

I heard a noise behind me and swiftly turned to see an enemy running at me. I stepped forward and with a savage roar decapitated him. I whipped back around to fire another arrow at Morgan who was still staring at me with a mocking grin. He knew that I was possibly the worst archer out of all the men. He knew that I would never hit him.

I began to run towards him, mowing down anyone who tried to stand in my way, but he never seemed any closer. Finally he turned his horse and rode away through the trees. I let out a groan of frustration, but I had no choice except to stay and fight.

The senseless slaughter went on for hours. Morgan's men were trained, but not to the point of expertise, and thus were slightly challenging to fight. The greatest difficulty came in the sheer multitude of them. It seemed as if the battle would never end.

Finally, the sun began to set and I looked around me, exhausted and bleeding from various wounds.

There were very few men left standing.

"God damn it," I whispered and wiped a tear away as I began to wander through the heaps of dead bodies. Even the war hadn't held this much gory slaughter in any single battle.

There was the noise of someone approaching and I lifted my sword wearily before turning around. I wasn't sure how many more fights I had in me.

I let out a ragged sob when I saw that it was Aidan.

Running towards him I threw my weary arms around his neck. He pulled me close.

"What in the hell happened here Aidan? What . . ." I couldn't even finish because I had no idea what to say. It was all so horrendous. "I thought you were dead."

"I don't know what has happened Noble," he whispered into my hair. "I honestly have no idea. How did I let this happen?"

I pulled away and grabbed his face. "This is not your fault!"

"What kind of King can't see that an army is being raised against him within his own city?" he was on the verge of being hysterical.

"One who has faith that his subjects aren't venomous, treacherous bastards," I hissed. "I'm going to kill him Aidan. I am going to rip him limb from limb and then peel the flesh from every inch of his body."

I stepped away from him and tried to keep myself from shaking.

Aidan wiped a tired hand across his eyes. "First we have to . . ." he paused and took a ragged breath, "We have to see who is still alive. Lets comb the field."

I nodded tiredly and walked away from him. I looked among the bodies for hours, trying to find any one of our men who was wounded.

I found Gair and Gerard both slaughtered, as well as about half of the other knights. I could only hope that the rest of the men were on their way back to our camp.

Of course Morgan and his men had taken all of our horses, so Aidan and I had to walk miles back to the encampment despite our exhaustion.

The camp had been ravaged while we had been busy fighting, but we weren't the first of our group to make it back there alive.

When I saw Gladwin, Kade and Patrick it was all that I could do not to weep. Bran made it as well, but had been seriously injured in the process. Kade was afraid that he was going to lose a few fingers.

Only twelve of us had made it back alive from the massacre.

\*\*\*\*\*\*\*\*\*\*

"We must retaliate and we must do it swiftly," Aidan was trying to sound as calm as possible.

"Agreed," Bran replied, "But he probably has thousands of men surrounding Callento by now if the numbers of this little skirmish reflect how many followers he has."

Aidan nodded slowly. "We have to plan on facing the worst possible circumstances when we arrive."

"How are we ever going to find enough men to stand a chance against him? Gladwin asked.

"The majority of the country must still be loyal to the true King," Kade snapped testily.

"Yes, but even so there is no way that we can assemble them all without being noticed, and it will take time . . ." sighed Patrick.

"We can use the time to our advantage," I mumbled, "Make him wait. He must know that it's coming. Let him squirm."

"So we watch and wait . . . But we still don't have enough men," Gladwin wiped his eyes wearily.

"We can spread out throughout the country rounding up all of our willing and able men," Aidan replied.

"There's something else that we can do as well . . ." I began, looking at Aidan. "We have allies . . ."

His eyes flicked up towards mine. He already knew what I was going to suggest.

"We could send a message to him at least . . ." I continued unsurely. "He must have some friends at court and maybe they can be persuaded to send their army to help us. Please just consider it . . . It wouldn't take any longer than rounding up the men and getting them ready for battle, and it could greatly boost our numbers."

His eyes bore into mine and I looked down sheepishly.

"Would you want to be the one to go?" he asked softly. All eyes were on the two of us.

"No," I answered hastily. "I mean not if you didn't want me to."

He stared at me for a moment more before nodding his head slowly.

"We will all set out on different paths tomorrow and come together again a month from now on the eastern shore," Aidan said as he gazed into the fire.

**********

I stood on the deck of the ship looking at the approaching shore.

The last few days we had been at sea. It had been my first experience on the water and I had been sick for the duration of the time. Besides my stomache being ill, my heart had been ill as well.

I was so nervous that I couldn't sleep at night and all I could think about while I was awake was his laugh and the twinkle in his brown eyes.

I was so excited and yet as nervous as I had ever been. I wasn't sure what to expect.

My mind drifted to when he had said goodbye. I had expected to never see him again. At that moment, I had taken stock of him as if it was the last time I would ever look upon him. Now I was imagining how he would have changed over the last few months.

I foolishly wondered if he would even remember me.

When I stepped foot on Fraunch soil for the first time I was naively surprised that it didn't feel any different than Bryton had.

Being as I was a foreign ambassador, I was treated with the upmost care and concern. It was lucky that at the time of my visit the King and his court had just moved to his palace by the sea. I was shown directly to my quarters at the castle.

Once I was in my room I fell back onto my bed in a sigh of exhaustion and closed my eyes for a moment. I had been assured that I would have an audience with his Majesty within the day, and I needed to be as fresh as possible.

Suddenly there was a banging on my door. I hopped up, hoping that it was the servant boy that I had sent for to draw my bath. I felt sticky, and every movement was almost crunchy from all the sea water that I had come in contact with.

When I opened the door I just stood there in shock for a moment staring at my best friend.

"Leonard!" I managed to smile before he wrapped his arms around me in a crushing hug. I allowed myself to lean against him for a moment, breathing him in before I pulled away to look at him.

His hair had grown longer and his cheeks a little thinner but other than that it was still the same Leonard, my Leonard.

"When they told me that you were here I couldn't believe it," he smiled and placed a firm hand on my shoulder. "I wasn't sure that I would ever see you again."

I let out a small laugh. "I wasn't sure either," I said as I turned to sit back down on my bed. Leonard came and sat beside me. "How have you been?"

"Absolutely miserable," Leonard grinned. "After Callento where everyone is friends and there are no formalities this place is so exceedingly stuffy that I feel like I can't even breathe. The people are all awful and the soldiers unbearably conceited. I can't stand it." He shook his head wearily. "How are things back home?"

When he called Callento his home I had to swiftly blink back my tears.

"It's awful," I began. "I've come here to beg your king for help against Morgan. He's raised an army and taken over Callento. He lured us out of the castle and slaughtered almost all of us. " I wiped my hand across my eyes. "Gair and Gerard are both dead and Bran might lose part of his hand. I have no idea how it even happened . . . It was all so sudden." I turned to look at him.

His eyes were blazing with fury. "I'll kill him," he said through a clenched jaw.

"Well you'll have to beat me to it," I managed a small smile. "He's ruined everything." I tried to keep the sob out of my voice but I couldn't. I didn't look over at Leonard while I let a shattered breathe out.

Leonard sat awkwardly beside me while I regained my composure. "I'm sorry," I laughed shakily.

"Don't ever apologize to me Noble," Leonard replied as he looked me squarely in the eyes.

My breath caught in my throat for a moment. I had missed him so much. My eyes swept over the creases extending from the corners of his eyes and the laugh lines curled around his lips even when he wasn't smiling. I blinked rapidly, trying to stop my heart from beating out of my chest. Why was I shaking so badly? It was just Leonard . . . He had seen me at my absolute worst. Why did I find myself worrying that my hair was sticking up and my lips were cracked?

Luckily he spoke again. "I have some pull with the King. I'm pretty sure that between the two of us we can persuade him to go and help Aidan. And even if he doesn't Morgan doesn't stand a chance with you and me back together again," he smiled as he nudged me in the side.

I chuckled. "I don't know how he got so many men without us knowing," I shook my head.

"Morgan's a sly little bastard," replied Leonard, "but we will get him in the end."

"I hope so," I replied, "I don't know how Bryton would survive with him as a ruler."

There was a knock on the door and I stood up to answer it.

"I was sent up to draw you up a bath sir," a young boy announced with a slightly superior air. Everyone here acted slightly superior.

I turned to look at Leonard. He was looking out the window and the light shining on his profile made his hair shine and his neck look long and powerful.

When he twisted to look at me his lips were slightly open and his eyes looked as if he had been dreaming of places far away. I blushed and looked quickly down at the floor.

"I'm going to take a bath before I go before the King. I don't want to be completely disgusting," I mumbled. "Will you come with me when I go in front of him?"

Leonard stood up and walked towards me. He playfully grabbed my hair and yanked my head up to look at him. "Don't let things be different between us," his brows were furrowed over his warm brown eyes. I had almost forgotten that they had flecks of gold in them. "You're still my best friend. That won't ever change, at least on my side of things."

With that he breezed past the little boy and walked away.

I stood there trembling. He was right, it was absurd to think that anything between us had changed.

**********

"Your majesty, this man who has taken the throne will drive Bryton into the ground. All of the progress that has been made under the rules of Aidan and Umber will be obliterated under his madness. We're begging you for your help," I pleaded with my chin held high. It went against everything within me to beg, but Aidan had told me to appeal to the Fraunch King's world renowned pride.

The King looked down his massive nose at me.

"King Aidan is a great man your highness," Leonard supplied, "And he will be sure to return the favor tenfold whenever you have need of his assistance."

"This is a rather large undertaking," the King sighed as he rubbed his chin. "Let me consider it overnight, and talk to my advisors. Come back tomorrow and I will have an answer for you."

With a bow I followed Leonard out.

Once the doors were shut behind us Leonard turned to me with a huge grin. "We've got him."

"Are you sure?" I asked with a smile. "We really need his support if we have any chance of winning."

"I can almost guarantee it," he grinned as he put an arm around my shoulder. "Now what do you say that we go celebrate?"

"It's been a long time since we have been out wreaking havoc on the masses," I laughed.

We went to a little Fraunch Inn that Leonard apparently frequented and began drinking and laughing over old times. Within an hour we were both gone to the wind.

"Do you remember that time that we convinced Bran that if he rubbed that plant on his head all his hair would grow back," I was laughing so hard that I couldn't breathe, "And his entire head was dyed bright red!"

Leonard was wiping tears from the corners of his eyes. "What was even better was when we shaved off all the men's eyebrows while they were sleeping because we wanted to prove how drunk they always got. It took them weeks to get over being mad at us for that one."

"But I didn't care," I finished off my eighth mug of beer, "They deserved it and even if they weren't talking to us it was worth it to see how ridiculous they looked with no eyebrows. Especially Patrick because he looked like a little old woman!"

"And what about that time we covered the stairs in butter so that Gladwin would slip, but that poor fat cleaning lady came down first instead and slid all the way down on her stomach!" I could barely even understand what Leonard was saying, but I was laughing all the same.

Every time we would start to regain our composure we would look at each other and bust out laughing again.

Finally I had to excuse myself to go to the bathroom. When I came back, Leonard was kissing a scantily clad girl who was sitting on his lap.

I stood there and just stared at them for a moment, leaning against the wall in order to steady myself.

After taking a deep breathe I slowly made my way over in order to grab my cape.

"I think I'm going to head back to the castle," I smiled without looking him in the eye. I could see the girls foot brushing against his leg.

"No, Noble please stay. We're having such a great time," Leonard smiled. "Meet my new friend Katrina."

"Hello there Noble," the girl purred.

"Hello ma'am," I mumbled. "I really have to go Leonard. Tomorrow is going to be a big day." I turned to leave.

"See you tomorrow," Leonard called as I walked out the door.

I started to walk down the street.

"Hey Noble wait!" I suddenly heard him call as the door swung open. I turned to look at him. "I'd almost forgotten your almost uncanny way of leaving just when things start to get fun."

I grunted. "I'm sorry that screwing some sluttly tavern girl isn't my idea of fun," I rolled my eyes. "Why can't it just be enough for you to be with me for one night? I haven't seen you in months and you can't even stand for it to be just us two."

"Why do you have to be so bizarre?" He spat at me. "I mean you are 27 years old and I don't think I have ever seen you look twice at a woman? What's wrong with you?"

"Well I . . . I just," I couldn't find the right words. My excuses on the subject were growing thin. I looked up into his confused and hurt eyes. Suddenly the tears started to roll down my face. "Leonard, I'm a girl."

I couldn't blame it on the alcohol or my heightened emotional state, it was just time for him to know. I should have told him years ago.

For a few agonizing moments his face didn't change. Then his eyes narrowed and he took a step backwards.

"What are you talking about?" he asked quietly.

"I'm a girl, Leonard. This whole time I've only been pretending. My real name is Aceline," I held my hand out towards him and took a step closer. "For years I've wanted to tell you . . . I actually have told you before but you didn't hear me. I undressed in front of you and you didn't even notice!" I didn't realize how much that had hurt me until that moment. Leonard would screw any woman that had half of her teeth and yet he hadn't even remembered the sight of me practically naked in front of him.

But none of that mattered anymore. All that mattered was being voluntarily honest for the first time in my entire adult life.

"You're the only person I've ever wanted to tell Leonard. But I was so scared because I need you to be there for me and . . . I'm so sorry that I have lied to you for so long," I blinked back the tears. "I just couldn't lose you too, having you leave Callento was so much easier than the possibility of you eventually hating me when you discovered the truth."

I let out a weary breath. I wasn't sure how he would react but at least he knew now.

"That can't be . . ." he mumbled as he ran his hand through his hair, "How in the hell could you have gotten away with it all these years?"

"With a whole hell of a lot of luck," I laughed but he wasn't smiling. "Teague and Aidan both found out by accident . . . And Morgan recently revealed that he knows."

"Morgan knows?!?!?! Teague and Aidan both knew and they never told me? I can't believe that . . . Aidan would have told me . . . He would have . . . Oh shit," he trailed off and looked up into my eyes for the first time since I had uttered my secret. "You really are telling the truth aren't you?"

"Why would I lie about something like that?" I asked quietly.

"But why the hell would you do that? I mean the life you have led has been painful and frightening . . ." now he couldn't stop looking at me. He must have been thinking about all that we had gone through, all of the strange things that I had done. It was all clicking in his head, all of it was starting to make sense.

"Do you remember that prisoner that someone let escape when we first came to Callento?" I whispered hesitantly.

"That was you?!" he was clearly shocked. "What the hell is the matter with you?"

"The prisoner was my father . . . I figured that the only way that I could save him was by becoming one of the knights. I realize now how naïve that was, but I'm so grateful because I love my life now. I planned to leave right after I freed him, but I couldn't make myself do it. This life is everything that I have ever wanted and more," I rambled on, trying to make him understand why I had done it. "And it may seem ridiculous to you, but I wouldn't change it for anything in the entire world." I stuck my chin up defiantly.

I remembered the day that I had let those men barge into our home and take my father from me. I no longer recognized that girl. Now all I recognized was how desperately I needed Leonard to forgive me. I would plead and I would beg, but I would never give up on him like I had my father.

Leonard slowly walked towards me and I felt my breathe freeze in my chest. He lightly placed a hand on the side of my face, rubbing his thumb gently up and down the scar on my cheek.

"I think that it's the most amazing thing that I have ever heard," he gave a slow and whole-hearted smile. "We always knew that there was something strange about you Noble."

I looked down sheepishly for a moment. "Hopefully strange in a good way," I finally smiled as I looked back up into his face. The look in his eyes was different. I felt as if he somehow now saw me as more than I was. He was close enough that I could feel his breath on my forehead.

"Strange in the best possible way," he grinned and punched me in the shoulder. Then he let out a little gasp. "Sorry . . . I didn't mean to hit you . . ."

"Leonard just because I'm a girl doesn't mean I'm breakable," I laughed. "I thought you of all people would understand that. Please don't look at me any differently."

"I can't help it," he laughed as well. "I've always needed to protect you, and now I know why."

"I don't need protecting," I replied. "And why does everyone say that? I've earned my place here just as much as anyone else."

His gaze was soft. "Of course you have," he smiled slowly. "Come on now. Let's go back inside and finish our drinks and you can tell me everything."

\*\*\*\*\*\*\*\*\*

"God damn it why is it taking so long to assemble his men? Doesn't he realize the importance of this situation? I don't know how you could have managed to live here most of your life Leonard. I'm going mad," I paced around my room, pulling at my hair. "All of the woman are gaudy and the men unbearably pompous. I haven't found a single person that's worth my while to converse with . . . Besides you of course. And all the while that we are sitting here playing parlor games, Aidan is waiting for us and Morgan is destroying Bryton little by litte. I can't stand it . . ." I trailed off and turned to look at Leonard. He was sitting on my bed grinning at me. I let out a sigh and a little laugh.

"It's just the way the King works, he's absolutely worthless," Leonard replied as he laid back. "It's the way most men in the world are, but here especially. Why do you think I left?"

"To satisfy your ego that you were a better swordsman than Aidan," I grumbled as I sat down beside him. "Why in the hell hasn't anyone managed to overthrow this ridiculous facade of a King yet?"

Leonard laughed, "Everyone is too busy having sex and throwing parties to try."

"Well I can't wait to go home," I flopped down on my back. I rolled over to see Leonard grinning at me. "What?"

"I just think it's funny that you don't even mind laying here on the bed with me," he replied.

"Does it bother you now?" I asked softly. I bit my lip self-consciously.

His eyes ran over my face for a second before I rolled to look up at the ceiling.

"No . . ." he began, "It's going to take some getting used to is all. I mean you have told me everything and I understand it but now whenever I look at you I see something different. All of the pieces are finally clicking together the way that they should."

"You probably won't ever see me as a real girl though will you . . ." I stumbled over the words. "I mean not like you see other girls."

"I don't know Noble, I mean you know that I don't treat women as well as I probably should . . . I wouldn't want to treat you like that. I'm actually really embarrassed about all that now. I should have acted as more of a gentleman. I should have acted with at least a shred of decency . . ." He threw his hands up and pursed his lips. "I'm really sorry about all of it and . . ."

I cut him off with a laugh. "You have nothing to apologize for! All of those women you had over the years deserved to be treated that way because that is how they allowed themselves to be treated. They liked it, and they liked you. While it wasn't pleasant for me to watch at times, you have absolutely nothing to apologize for." I sat up and looked over at him with a smile, prompting him to feel alright.

He sat up too and looked down at his hands. "I guess what I mean is that I would never treat you like that. So if that's what you mean by me seeing you like a girl then I guess the answer is no." He cleared his throat.

And while I knew that it was silly for me to feel offended, I couldn't help but wish that he could have just said a simple yes.

But instead of saying that I stood up and walked over to the window.

"Well I appreciate that I suppose . . ." I trailed off. "When is that goddamn King going to give us a goddamn answer?!"

Suddenly there was a loud knock on the door.

"Right on cue," Leonard laughed as I practically ran to fling the door open.

There stood the same boy who had come to draw my bath, still with that ridiculous look across his youthful face. "The King requests your presence in his throne room," he stated crisply before turning to walk away without waiting for a reply.

"Thank you young man!" I called down the hallway to the boy's rapidly disappearing back, barely able to mask my disgust.

"I don't know how you lived here for 30 years," I grunted as I turned back to Leonard who was wearing his customary grin. "I should probably put on some more suitable clothes in order to please his High Majesty."

"I guess that's my cue to leave," Leonard said as he stood and walked past me to the door. "Even though didn't you mention something about undressing in front of me before?"

My face turned bright red. "Well . . . I . . . I was really, really intoxicated," I stumbled over the words, trying to figure out what I was even trying to say.

"Noble," Leonard laughed and I looked up at him despite my better judgment. "I was just joking. It's kind of what we do . . ." With one last shake of his head he shut the door behind me.

I let out the huge breath that I had been holding inside, wondering why it was incredibly easy for me to sound like such a raging lunatic since I had been there. Leonard didn't seem to care that I was female, so why was I preoccupied with the fact that he was undeniably male, and undeniably handsome.

I quickly changed into the outfit that I had hastily bought at a local merchants shop. Everything was so tight and the pants were far shorter than I was accustomed too. I felt like a preening peacock.

When I opened the door I was surprised to see Leonard leaning against the wall waiting for me.

"You ready for this?" He asked. I nodded. "He's going to expect you to be beyond grateful."

"I'm prepared to literally kiss his feet as long as he gives Aidan the help he needs," I mumbled as we neared the doors to the throne room. The guards to the door let us in, knowing us on sight.

As we entered, everyone already in the room turned to stare at me as if I was some alien creature. Leonard and I made our way to the front and finally bowed down to the pompous bastard that sat on the throne.

"Courageous Knight Banidere and respected defender of France Leonard, I have thought long and hard of the proposition you brought to me concerning my aid to our ally Bryton. After much deliberation I have had the army mobilized and the navy prepared to escort you across the channel. You will leave for Bryton within the fortnight," the King let out a sigh and tilted his head back slightly in appreciation of himself.

"Thank you your Majesty," I bowed once more. "As I have said before, King Aidan and all of his loyal subjects greatly appreciate your generosity and plan to repay you with our alliance if you ever find yourself in a time of need."

Leonard bowed as well. "They will tell tales of your generosity for generations to come your Highness. Your name will surmount all others in the annals of history."

I rolled my eyes slightly.

The King however looked pleased. "But I'm not doing this merely for the fame and glory that accompanies such a deed . . ." he trailed off, peering down at the dozens of rings that adorned his plump fingers.

"Oh of course not your Majesty and we are insinuating no such thing," I replied hastily. "Of course you do this only through a deep respect for honor and charity. Anyone who says different is a fool and clearly does not understand the philanthropic nature of your reign."

"But of course the driving factor of your assistance is your inherent love for what is good and righteous. You want the world to live in such an enlightened and virtuous society as your own," Leonard supplied with one last flourish.

I couldn't beat that one. Leonard was never so elegant as when he was jesting.

The King was thoroughly tickled pink. He tilted his chin up and pursed his lips thoughtfully. "The two of you may dine with me tonight. In honor of our new union."

I barely had time to open my mouth before Leonard replied. "Your Highness we are deeply honored by your polite invitation, but we beg your pardon to be excused from supper this evening. We request a few days to journey to my old home and see my family before I must once again leave for Bryton. This time the farewell will be forever."

The King let out a sigh of agitation before shooing us away with his hand as if we were merely some insect that was buzzing in his ear. It didn't matter that we had only moments before been praising him to the heavens. We were once more not worth his bother.

Leonard and I exited the room without another word. Before the doors even shut we could hear the merriment behind us commencing.

I looked over at my best-friend. "Do you really want me to go and meet you family or was that just an excuse to get out of this hell hole?"

"Well I mean I want to go and say good-bye to my family but . . . Yes I want them to meet you," now it was Leonard's turn to stutter.

I glanced over, surprised to see him blushing. It made me blush in return.

"Anyway," the confidence had returned to his voice. "It's going to be a long ride tomorrow if we want to get there before nightfall so we should probably pack and get to sleep. I will come get you at dawn tomorrow morning?"

"Only you could get me up that early," I laughed. "See you tomorrow."

As I shut the door behind me I couldn't help but grin. I was important enough to meet his family.

**********

The next day everything was just as it always had been. There was no awkwardness as we rode all morning and the afternoon stretched into dusk. We joked and remembered the good times. He explained to me that his mother, younger brother, and youngest sister all still lived in the home he had grown up in.

"My father left us when I was seven," Leonard supplied. He couldn't keep the bitterness out of his voice.

"Well all I had was my father," I supplied quietly. "I imagine that with seven siblings you weren't ever lonely at least. As wonderful as my father was, I realize now that there was no way he ever could have been everything I needed."

Ever since the night when Morgan had told me he had known my father I had been struggling with the idea that he had been a traitor. Perhaps he had been with Morgan in the earliest strain of his rebellion. As much as I loved my father, I now saw all of his flaws in a clearer light. If he had betrayed Aidan, denouncing his King, I could no longer defend him to myself. As much as I loved Aidan as a man, I was not choosing the man over my father, I was choosing the ruler, the legend.

"We didn't have time to be lonely," Leonard laughed, but I could tell that he wasn't joking. "We had to run the farm. My mother was a frail woman, scared of everything and as near to completely useless as one can be. We've all had to take care of her our entire lives. I don't blame my father for leaving her, but I do blame him for leaving us."

"But obviously you turned out alright," I smiled lightly. "So something in your childhood must have been good."

I was shocked that it seemed as if Leonard had to pause to think of something that had at least been decent in his youth.

"My siblings were good. They tried the hardest that they could," he finally supplied.

"I bet you are excited to see them."

"Yeah . . . I always feel guilty though. Bernadette and Louie are the only ones that had it in them to stay, the rest of us fled as soon as we were old enough. They don't blame me, but somehow every time I look at them I feel this overwhelming sense of shame. It's like I gave up and left the despair for all of them to endure, but I just couldn't do it anymore . . ." He trailed off. "Maybe this was a bad idea."

"No!" I cried. Leonard turned to look at me quizzically. "I just mean that they are your family and no matter what they are important to you. You owe it to yourself and to them to say goodbye, especially if you don't plan on coming back for . . . A while." I wasn't trying to hint at what Leonard had told the King but I couldn't just ignore what he had said. I wanted him to come back to Bryton with me, and I wanted him to stay.

"I know," Leonard sighed. "Still . . . I can't help but wish that things were different." He became lost in his thoughts for a few moments. I could see a light off in the distance.

"Is that it?" I asked wearily.

Leonard nodded. "I'm glad we got here while they are still awake. Otherwise we would have had to sleep in the barn. It's not a pretty place."

"I'm sure we've slept in worse," I laughed. "And I'm so tired I wouldn't even notice if I was sleeping next to a family of pigs."

However hard I tried though I couldn't make him crack a smile.

"This was a bad idea," he muttered. "I should have left you back at the castle."

I pulled my horse to a halt, staring at him. "Do you really think that I will embarrass you that badly?" I asked, deeply offended.

Leonard stopped his horse and turned around to face me. "You? No . . . I'm the one who is embarrassed. Please promise me that you won't think any less of me once you see where I come from. I didn't choose it." I could see pain mixed with firm resolve in his normally warm, brown eyes.

"There's no way that I could ever think any less of you," I whispered truthfully. "You're my best friend and nothing could ever change that."

Leonard nodded and swallowed harshly. "You are the only person that I would ever show this to."

"Then I am honored," I smiled gently. His eyes flicked up to mine and for a moment we just looked at each other. I saw how the shadows filled the deep lines etched into his face and there was a spot from a scar where his beard refused to grow.

I wanted to know every thought he had, every memory from his past and everything that was to come in his future.

Suddenly I ripped my eyes away. "We should probably hurry. Even though I'm more than fine with the barn I would prefer to sleep inside if at all possible. I can smell snow in the air." I nudged my horse to walk on past Leonard.

"Noble," Leonard whispered. I stopped but couldn't bring myself to look back at him. "I'm more proud of you than anything else in my life. That's why I wanted you to come here. To show them how far I've come."

I let out a shattered breath. Nobody, not my father, Teague, or even Aidan, had ever said anything that touched me as deeply as those words.

I was important. I was special. I was worthy.

"Race you to the house?" I laughed, not waiting to look back at my best friend before I took off.

Leonard never was one to refuse a challenge.

\*\*\*\*\*\*\*\*\*

We spent the next three days at Leonard's family home. I had never before in my life felt so domestic.

I woke up early to the smell of tea and before the sun was up I went out to help collect the few eggs from the scrawny hens that pecked the frozen ground. Then I would help milk the solitary cow. At first I had been reluctant, but as it is with all things, convincing myself to begin was the hardest part.

The rest of the day would be spend out chopping wood in a small grove. Once the winter snows set in, it would be dangerous to return to the forest, and so all the wood to last the winter had to be felled before the first large snowstorm.

The exercise was good and the crisp air gently burned my straining lungs. Every once in a while I would look up to see Leonard split a large piece of lumber, his muscles straining and sweat dripping down his angular face.

At night the five of us would sit around a small fire, eating our meager but filling supper, and then within the hour we would all fall into an exhausted slumber.

On our last night, Leonard's mother prepared a simple chocolate cake to celebrate the time we had spent together.

"I was so pleased to have the two of you here," she smiled giddily. Leonard had gotten his exuberance for life from her, but that was where the resemblance stopped. While the woman tried her hardest to contribute, very little that she did was considered helpful. Watching over her and catering to her slightly addled ways was a chore in itself, and a delicate one at that. The woman could snap at the drop of a pin and begin crying or screaming. I had seen it both, and all the children could do was stand there apologizing until the fit would pass.

Leonard's younger siblings, however, were far more like him than they were their feeble mother. Bernadette was already sharp as a tack. Though she had received no formal education her humor, was biting and highly amusing, much like her brothers.

Louie was far more somber than his siblings, but his kindness and patience were astounding. While Bernadette was the youngest and felt obligated to stay, Louie had recently turned 35 and yet was still catering to his foolish mother's vapid delusions. Out of all the children, he was the only one who had enough compassion to not abandon his mother to a lonely old life.

Leonard assured me that he sent more than enough money for his dwindling family to survive on, and yet for his mother it never appeared to be enough. He told me not to be fooled by his mother's cheery disposition, inside her heart was bitter and shriveled, completely destroyed when their father abandoned her.

And yet somehow, despite all of his embarrassment, Leonard could not help but look upon them all fondly. They had shared the hardest times of his life together, and for that he owed them a debt of gratitude. For that he had come to say a proper good-bye.

When it came time to say good-night, I slipped outside, leaving the family to have a moment alone. Light, small snowflakes drifted down, softly coating the hard ground with a sparkling coat of white. I was glad that I had been able to help Leonard's family come up with enough wood to last the winter, it looked like it was going to be a long, bitter season.

The door opened and Leonard walked out, crossing his arms against the cold. When he saw me he walked closer with a smile.

"You must be freezing out here," he laughed. "I appreciate the alone time with the family but you could have at least gone into the barn."

"It's beautiful out here though," I shrugged. I glanced over at the snowflakes melting slowly in his hair. The light from the moon caught them, making his hair glisten. His cheeks were flushed and his eyes looked heavy. "I want to appreciate it all one last time before we have to go back and fight. As hard as I know this was for you, it's almost like another world here for me. I wouldn't change my life for anything, but . . .

Somehow this was like a pleasant dream that I will be sad to wake up from. All of this here with you . . . I can't help but feel like it was just a dream."

"Somehow I think I know what you mean," he replied. He teeth chattered and suddenly he reached down and grabbed my hands from my sides. I looked up at him as he just stared down at my hands, rubbing them gently between his two larger ones. "You're freezing."

My heart was thudding so heavily that I was almost sure that he would hear it. If it would have been Teague, his hands would have slid up my arms and down my back, and if it would have been Aidan he would have pulled me in and kissed me deeply. But it wasn't Teague or Aidan. It was Leonard, and I wasn't sure what he would do.

It was at that moment though that I realized what I wanted him to do.

I wanted him to love me as much as I loved him, and that was all. I didn't want passionate embraces or romantic declarations of love, I wanted him just the way he was. I wanted his infectious laugh, his undying loyalty and his large, rough hands holding mine. And I wanted it for forever.

Holding my breath, I just stared up at him, unable to speak.

Leonard looked up from our entwined hands to meet my vulnerable eyes. I couldn't mask the feelings that I experienced in that moment, and I didn't even try.

Without dropping my hands Leonard let out a laugh, but I couldn't bring myself to even smile.

"Bernadette confessed to me tonight that she thought you were the most handsome man she had ever seen," Leonard's face crinkled in amusement. "She told me that if the knights here in Fraunc were half as gallant as you, her virtue would already be shredded to rags! She was quite besotted with you. I think that she might even fancy herself to be in love with you." He laughed on, still not dropping my hands. When he saw my mouth drop open slightly he rambled on. "I told her that while you were indeed a very handsome lad, she would have to fight half the women at court back in Callento if she wanted a chance to marry you."

It was hard for me to breath. Out of all the things he could have done or said in that moment, nothing could have hurt as much as those words.

"Besides the noticeable lack of facial hair you do trump most of the rest of us beastly men in the looks department," Leonard continued on obliviously. "And of course all women love scars, and you have more than enough of them that are visible and even more hidden. My sister also complimented how muscular you were, but at that point my mother warned her to behave like a lady and that was the end of that."

Finally he paused to take a breath.

"I'm glad you find that so amusing," I finally replied as I gently pulled my hands away from his. "I think we had better turn in since we have to leave early in the morning."

Turning to walk into Leonard's childhood home, my lips quivered as I blinked back the tears that threatened to slip down my cheeks.

It wouldn't have been at all manly for him to see me cry.

**\*\*\*\*\*\*\*\*\*\***

"Are you alright, Noble?" Leonard asked after a week of my near silence.

"Why wouldn't I be?" I still could hardly bear to look at him. We had been trapped inside of the castle since we had returned from Leonard's home. Thankfully we were scheduled to leave for Bryton the next morning at dawn.

"That's what I'm trying to figure out . . ." he trailed off. "I know that something must have upset you. I hope that it wasn't something that I did."

I bit my lip. How much longer could I deny how badly I was hurt? I wasn't mad at him, I knew that he had not meant to be cruel, but I couldn't help but hear those words ringing in my head over and over and over.

There was no way that he would ever love me, not when he saw me in that way. The shift for Teague and Aidan had been swift and decisive. As soon as they had known my true gender, they had realized the possibility that I presented. I didn't want to admit it, but I had expected the same reaction from Leonard.

However, I saw then that Leonard, even though he knew that I was a woman, would never see me as more than he always had. I loved him for it. I loved that all along he had given me all of himself that he could share. I loved that our friendship was so important to him that he couldn't see past it.

And yet I couldn't help but feel repulsive and unworthy. While I realized that it was because he loved me that he didn't want to be with me, another part of me was haunted by the fact that if I looked like Glorianna all of the things that I wanted for the rest of my life could have been obtained.

Because of all this I couldn't bring myself to tell him that I loved him, despite the fact that he was my best friend and I had shared almost every facet of my life with him for the last decade.

I just continued to stare out over the castle wall. Leonard took my silence as agreement that he had done something wrong. Suddenly he let out a deep breath.

"Why don't you stop acting like such a little girl and actually tell me why you are upset with me?" He finally asked.

I let out a jagged breath and slowly turned to look at him.

"Does it amuse you to keep reminding me that I'm not dainty and coy and undeniably feminine?" I finally asked, much more abruptly than I had intended.

"That's not what I was doing . . ." Leonard started to reply, but now that I had started I was not about to stop before I had finished.

"Don't you think I know that even if I do make it out of Aidan's service alive no man will ever look at me and think that I am beautiful? Do you think I'm grateful that once I'm worn out and tired enough to leave Callento, I will forever be alone with my scars and my decaying muscles?" My voice was jagged with self-depreciation. "Not that I had much chance of attracting anyone from across a room before, but now I don't even have the hope that it might happen someday. So to answer your question: no, I'm not mad at you. I'm mad at myself for having that hope in the first place and daring to think that maybe even despite my ugly masculinity I was good enough for somebody to desire."

I turned back away from him, too tired and scared to meet his eyes.

"I like that you're manly," Leonard said softly after a long pause. "I wouldn't have it any other way."

I let out a devastated laugh. "Of course you wouldn't, and that's why I could never be mad at you," I said, hastily wiping away the tears that pooled in the corners of my eyes.

"I didn't mean . . ." He began hastily.

"It doesn't matter," I interrupted yet again. "Can we just forget the whole thing? I can forget about your sister being in love with me and you can completely forget that I ever told you my secret. After all, you have once before."

And then I walked away without looking back at him. I slept deeply that night, and awoke the next morning wanting to go home desperately. Leonard and I boarded one of the 3 ships that the King had filled with soldiers without speaking one word to each other. I couldn't tell if he was angry at the show of emotion I had indulged myself in the day before or if he was just as weary as I was.

When we arrived at Bryton I let out a sigh of relief. It felt good to be home, and I could see thousands of men in the distance preparing to fight to win Aidan back his crown.

The second that Leonard and I stepped off the ship we were smothered by all of our friends. Once I had greeted Bran, Gladwin, Patrick and Kay I finally stood in front of Aidan.

I walked forward with a shy smile and wrapped my arms around him. He held me tight and seemed to not want to let me go.

Finally he pulled away and looked down at me, still holding onto my shoulders.

"I was almost frightened that you weren't ever going to come back," he grinned.

"Aidan I hated it over there so much," I laughed back. "I couldn't wait to come home."

"As long as someone was coming home with you . . ." he trailed off as he looked past me. I turned around to see Leonard standing there uncertainly. I turned back to face Aidan with what was probably more like a grimace than a smile.

"Aidan he knows . . ." I trailed off, not sure what to say.

"And what did he say?" He asked softly.

"Nothing too important," I mumbled. Not wanting to look up at his curious eyes.

Aidan let out a deep breath. "That answer is not at all satisfactory and even though I know you don't want to talk about it, we are going to have a long conversation about this later. However, right now I have to go say hello to our friend."

Aidan let go of me and slowly made his way over towards Leonard.

He held out his hand for his old best friend to shake. While holding hands they looked up at each other and nodded.

I couldn't help but smile. I wanted for them to be the way that they used to be.

Leonard looked up at me and my breath caught in my chest. He looked as if he was pleading with me to forgive him. Did he still not understand that he didn't need my forgiveness?

Within hours all of the Fraunch soldiers were off of the ships with their tents set up. They needed their sleep if we were going to be preparing for battle the next day.

"I think that we have more than enough men to wage a successful attack if we go in with the right strategy," Aidan began that night as all of us knights sat around one of our many campfires. "I don't want this to turn into a war. I want it to be quick and decisive."

"Does Morgan have men posted around the outside walls of the city or only within them?" I asked as I took a bite out of an apple. The air in Bryton was so much fresher than it had been in Fraunc and it made me hungry.

"He has a few thousand men posted around the city gates and probably another couple hundred that have been reported within the walls to protect the castle specifically," Bran reported. Kay had managed to make sure that his fingers were saved, but his hand was still heavily bandaged.

"Well then," Leonard began, "We let the Fraunch and the majority of our less trained soldiers take Morgan's men in a head on attack while us knights and a few more sneak into the city and take the castle. I have no doubt that the outside defenses will be easily defeated, and then the soldiers can rush the city to come to our aid if need be." He looked over at Aidan for approval.

"It's really the only option," Aidan agreed. "We just have to hope that Morgan doesn't have too many more reinforcements waiting somewhere for the orders to attack."

"Even so our numbers are far superior now," Gladwin supplied. "I don't see any way that he could have that many more men stashed somewhere. We searched the entire country."

Aidan ran his fingers through his hair wearily. "I know you're right, but I just want to be prepared for anything."

"Completely understandable," Patrick smiled. "I say we attack at the beginning of next week. We need time to prepare and at this point Morgan isn't going to be able to adjust his defenses much more than he already has."

"Do we know if Morgan is aware that we have brought Fraunch allies?" I asked.

Bran shook his head. "We have tried to keep the knowledge of all plans only among us knights and we now have guards posted a mile outside the perimeter of the camp in all directions. It would be a miracle if he someone found out."

"Well then I only hope we can get these Fraunch bastards to listen to orders," Leonard laughed.

Aidan smiled. "It hasn't worked out too well for me so far."

Kay stood up and stretched. "I'm ready to go get a good night sleep," he yawned and as he walked by me he patted me on the shoulder. "Nice to have you back Noble, Leonard."

I looked up through my lashes at Leonard. He was staring at me, but when my eyes met his he hastily stood up.

"It's been a long day for me too," he faked a yawn. "I think I'm going to go turn in as well." With a nod at Aidan he swiftly walked away into the night.

I let out a deep sigh and my shoulders fell into a defeated slump. I rested my head in my hands and closed my eyes wearily. I could hear all of the other men laughing and slowly making their way back to their tents.

"Let's go out for a walk," Aidan finally said. "I bet the stars aren't near as pretty in Fraunc as they are here."

I stood up slowly, knowing that there was no way to avoid telling Aidan what had happened. He gave me a gentle smile and we wandered slowly until we were outside the massive labrynth of tents that filled the vacant meadow.

"Now tell me what happened, from the beginning," Aidan said assertively.

I opened my mouth to speak a few times before I finally just came out and said the words that I had yet to utter.

"I'm in love with him," I blew out my cheeks and grabbed my hair in frustration. "I don't know when it happened or how but I can't stop thinking about him and every time I see him I notice some new little detail that takes my breath away and . . . I just love him."

I was completely surprised when Aidan let out a deep laugh. I turned to look at him as he stopped and doubled over, his laughter echoing through the night.

"I don't know why nobody seems to take me seriously anymore," I finally grunted. "I'm really not that amusing."

"I'm sorry Noble," Aidan said as he finally straightened up and wiped his eyes. "It's just that I can't believe that you are just figuring that out now."

"That I'm not amusing?" I asked, getting annoyed that I had just uttered some of the most important words I would ever say and he was laughing at me.

"No," he shook his head with a gentle smile. "That you love Leonard."

I blinked, furrowing my eyebrows. "What are you talking about?"

"I've known since the last time we kissed. There were no more Teague or Glorianna to stop us from being together, and yet you still didn't want to be with me. And when I pulled away I could see it in your eyes. I knew that through it all, even when you loved Teague and me, Leonard would always be first for you. Leonard would always be the one person who you valued above all others." All I could do was stare at him. "At first that love manifested itself in your friendship, but I knew before you left that it had changed to something more."

I slowly turned to face him. "Why didn't I see it before?" I finally asked myself in soft amazement. "I mean it's so obvious now."

Aidan laughed yet again. "Part of your charm is that despite how observant you are about others you very rarely notice things concerning yourself."

I grinned and looked up at him. He was still the most amazing man that I had ever met.

"Aidan . . ." I started, having one last thing to say to him before I finally had the strength to tell him what had happened in Fraunc. "I want you to know that I really did come to love you. And after everything that did happen with Glorianna and Leonard leaving, I wanted it so badly to be the way it was before . . . I'm sorry that things went the way they did between us. I was often childish and selfish and I regret some of the things that I said and did. I may not have acted like it, but through it all I really thought that we would end up together."

"That's another part of your charm," Aidan laughed. "You are always apologizing for things that you have no need to." Then his eyes became serious as they roamed slowly over my face. "I will love you until the day I die Noble," his voice cracked softly as he managed to give a small smile. "But as much as I still wish that we could have a fairy tale ending together, I know that we were never meant to last forever. It wasn't my fault, and it most definitely was not yours. All I want now is for you to find all the happiness that a world like this one has to offer, and I know that Leonard is the one that can offer you that."

"Except for the regrettable fact that he doesn't love me," I said with a small smile that was a thin mask, which I knew Aidan would see right through.

"Of course he does," Aidan replied as if it was the most obvious thing in the world. "What happened in Fraunc that has both of you so obviously upset?"

I ran a tired hand over my eyes. "Nothing happened . . . It's just obvious that he still doesn't see me like he sees other women. He even said so himself. Like you said, my feelings for him have evolved into something more than friendship but his are always going to be stuck at that level."

"That's ridiculous," Aidan stated. "He kept stealing glances at you all night. He couldn't keep his eyes off you."

I shook my head. "That might be true but it isn't because he thinks I'm beautiful or he's in love with me. It was probably just because he can tell I'm upset and he thinks that it's because of something he did."

"Well . . . it was quite obvious as well that you were avoiding looking at Leonard almost as much as he was looking at you," Aidan ventured.

I rolled my eyes. "I was not avoiding him. I just . . ." I let out a deep sigh. "Okay I might be avoiding him, but it's not because I'm angry. It just hurts to look at him knowing that he will always just see me as his best friend who is 'handsome, well-muscled and covered in scars,' and just happens to be a girl. And at the same time I'm looking at him wanting him so badly that at time's it's all I can do to stop myself from reaching out and touching him or even just saying his name."

"Did he say those things to you? Is that how he described you?" Aidan asked gently.

"Well not exactly, but he told me that his sister was in love with me and he just played right along with her, talking me up and agreeing that I was all those things. And the worst part is that he was holding my hands, staring into my face and didn't even notice that he had just basically ruined my life," my voice rose in volume and I started talking faster and faster. "There wasn't even a glimmer of recognition in his eyes. And then it took him a week to even notice that I was upset. And then he had the nerve to tell me to stop acting like a girl and just tell him what was wrong. What in the hell did he think was wrong?! And when I finally told him how I felt so hideous and unlovable all he could manage to say was that he wouldn't have me any other way! I could have killed him right there! But instead I just walked away . . . Feeling like an idiot who is so angry at herself that she wishes she could just melt into the floor and disappear forever."

By the time my rant was finished I was a little short of breath. I finally looked up at Aidan who had his mouth half open in the most infuriating smile that I had ever seen.

"I don't think it's yourself your mad at," he finally said, biting his lip to hold back his smile. If looks could kill he would have dropped dead on the spot. "We all know that Leonard says things without thinking more often than not. I'll talk to him about it."

For a moment I just stood there staring at him.

"That's not going to change anything," I finally muttered.

"Well even if you do feel that way then there's absolutely no harm in it," he smiled. "And since I am your King I would do it even if you told me not to."

Now it was my turn to smile. "Yes, you are the King, and you will be for decades and decades if I have anything to say about it. I won't let anybody take that away from you."

And with the moonlight shining down on Aidan, I could picture the crown sitting upon his head that night in the chapel. I had never been surer that he was the best King that had ever lived.

That moment is the way that I like to remember him best. It will haunt me and inspire me until the day that I die.

\*\*\*\*\*\*\*\*\*\*

I woke early the next morning, wishing that we didn't have to waste precious time assimilating the new reinforcements.

As I walked out into the blinding sunlight, I attached my scabbard to my belt. It would feel good to use my sword again. I hadn't so much as looked at it the entire time I had been in Fraunc. When I was used to fighting every day, even if it was just sparring with my friends, a month was a long time to go without that little ounce of normalcy.

I walked over to where a make-shift mess tent had been set up. I was starving. The night before I hadn't eaten, my stomach still being too unsettled by our aquatic journey. The sea did not agree with me.

As I grabbed a hunk of bread to gnaw on and walked over to where all of the men were slowly assembling, I felt as if everyone was staring at me. Whenever I turned though the men would quickly turn their faces away, and continue what they had been doing with feigned fervor.

I saw Kay and smiled hello. He just blushed and walked away swiftly.

I rolled my eyes. Something was wrong, and I could only guess that Aidan had something to do with it. I needed to find him right away.

I assumed that he would be leading training exercises for the new allies, showing them the routine for how we fought, laying out for them the way that we undertook a battle.

From what I had seen the Fraunch soldiers were well equipped, but I still doubted that their King was competent enough to have them trained well. I would have asked Leonard how well he deemed their skills but . . .

As I approached the men I saw Aidan riding slowly around on Kin, studying the Fraunch men as they sparred. I watched briefly as I made my way through them towards the King.

The soldiers all had beautiful form, the lines of their bodies were straight and their lunges were perfectly timed. Actually it all seemed a little too perfect.

I had wanted to ask Aidan first about if he had said anything about me to Leonard, or anybody else yet, but as soon as I reached him I couldn't help but comment on the soldiers.

"Aidan," I said as I absently patted Kin's soft nose. "All of these soldiers are following a scripted set of moves."

Aidan nodded. "I know," he let out a deep sigh, "Fraunch has always been known for their tenacity in battle but with these men . . . They would lose to Morgan's army without so much as a moment to surrender."

"It's all just staged fighting, engineered to look pretty for the court," I shielded my eyes from the burning sun. It was unusually warm for a winter's day.

"There's no doubt that they have balance and technique mastered, but if it snows even that will be worthless. We have less than a week to try and save some of these men's lives," Aidan dismounted Kin.

190

"Well who better to teach them how to fight like Brytons than us?"
I grinned.

Aidan turned to me with a smile as well. "I'd say that we have a
fair chance of sending these men home to their families. It's going to take a
hell of a lot of work though. . . Long hours and late nights."

"Music to my ears," I laughed. "After all I wouldn't want you to
think that I've gone soft."

"Oh I never doubted you for a second," He replied assuredly.
"Now go out there and teach these guys a thing or two."

"My pleasure," I smiled as I walked up to a man who was standing
idly.

"What's your name?" I asked.

"Willis," the man replied. He looked bored to death.

"Well Willis, I'm Noble, one of the knights. How about we make
sure you have what it takes in order to get off this island," I smiled.

The man grunted. "This petty little skirmish will be over within 24
hours, and then all of us will go home and forget all about this little pity
mission."

"Well I sure hope your right," I replied. "Because we all want you
here far less than you want to be here. But how about you prove how well
you fight right now, just to be sure. If you are as good as you say you are
then you should have no reason not to fight me."

"I suppose that I have nothing better to do," the man replied
casually.

"First blood," I replied. This man needed to bleed in order to
discover how serious this situation was. I was trying to save his life.

I swung my sword down heavily towards Willis's left shoulder. He
caught me high, and I pulled out swiftly, lunging towards his now exposed
mid-section. He jumped deftly to the right at the last second. I swung at his
right leg, not daring to give him a moment to get a hit in.

My blade snagged the fabric of his ridiculously short pants, but
didn't hit flesh. Willis saw his chance to lunge and took it, coming with an
upward arching jab at the level of my chest.

Sadly for him, the blow, although beautifully executed, was far too
slow. While I moved to the left, I slashed his right side with a low thrust.

For a moment Willis just looked down at his side, which was
slowly starting to drip crimson drops of blood. It almost looked as if he
didn't understand what had just happened.

"You didn't use the Rochefore defense mechanism," he muttered.
"Any good soldier would have used that defense on the attack I just
presented you with."

"Well then all these 'good soldiers' you have been fighting with must have had the creativity of a doorknob," I replied with a laugh. "Let me just warn you that the man who is trying to take over Bryton is a far superior swordsman to me, and his followers aren't going to know all the technical terms or fancy combinations of moves, but they are going to know how to kill you."

"I'm just a little rusty," the man replied as he stuck his nose up in the air, in exactly the same way that everyone from Fraunc had done to me since the minute I had set foot there.

"Okay you may have had time at home to fluff your enormous ego, but here we do things a little differently. You owe it to the people you left back home to come back to them, and the only way that is going to happen is if you think outside the box a little bit and give your pride a little rest," I jabbed at him with my sword and slashed where I had already cut him again. He let out a cry of pain. "I don't want you to get hurt out there, so I'm going to make sure right now that you are prepared. You need to be ready for anything. We are trained to be ready for anything because here, there will always be something working against you. If it's not the snow, then it's the mud or the sun in your eyes. The terrain is usually rocky, but we will be fighting around the castle so that shouldn't be much of a problem this time." I went to jab him in the other side but he brought his sword up to block me. At least he was a fast learner.

"Why don't you cut it out . . ." he started.

"No," I cut him off. "You are going to listen to me now if you want to survive this. You clearly are a strong man so your hits will be hard enough, but you have to speed them up a bit. If I had enough time to move out of the way and slice open your side you should be worried. We're used to guttural fighting, we use our surroundings and we never hold anything back. Now are you ready to fight me again or do you need a medic?"

"I don't need anything from you," He spat at my feet.

I couldn't be angry at him, simply because I knew that I was better than him.

"I don't want you to need anything from me," I replied with a grin. "I just want you to be able to fight me."

"Well then your prayers have been answered," Willis grumbled as he swung his sword at my shoulder. His form was still perfect, but his agitation fueled him and his movements were more decisive, more passionate.

I hadn't planned on my attitude causing him to fight with more purpose, but I wished that I had. It was a good idea.

This fight lasted far longer than the last one had. Willis was still slower than I was, but his form did lend itself to cleaner defenses and less hesitation.

In the end, I still nicked his right leg with my sword.

I was surprised when the man let out a little laugh as he put his hand to his new wound. I just stared at him for a moment before he finally looked up to meet my eyes.

"That was actually kind of fun," he finally supplied. "No thanks to you."

I couldn't help but smile. "I think my work is done here. Good luck Willis." I started to walk away.

"Wait!" I heard him call and I turned back around to face him. "Can you show me that move you used when I swung at your left and you feigned right again?"

"You're a smart man," I smiled. "I'm sure you can figure it out on your own." It was more than a little rewarding. I genuinely hoped that he would be one of the one's who made it out.

I walked on to the next man. We were going to have our work cut out for us.

*********

The week that I had been dreading as time wasted flew by faster than I could have imagined. I was kept busy, moving from one man to the next. Some of them were extraordinary swordsmen. A few of them even beat me. Those were the ones I didn't spend too much time on. I knew that they would be fine without my help.

It was the ones who had the most pride that took the longest to help. They refused to listen to my advice until I had proved to them that they were wrong. I understood where they were coming from, but at the same time I also knew that every once in a while it's healthy to be wrong.

I tried to keep myself distracted from certain thoughts that kept trying to worm their way into my every movement. It was utterly ridiculous. I knew that defeating Morgan was the most important thing, and that it would take all my concentration and talent, and yet I couldn't seem to keep myself from looking for Leonard wherever I went.

He was just as busy as I was though, and I could tell that he was avoiding me just as much as I had been avoiding him. I would feel him stealing glances at me, and then turn away just as I finally found the courage to return his stare.

We weren't openly awkward around each other. We pretended as if everything was fine around all of our old friends. At times I almost forgot about everything that I had felt, but then he would turn his head or let out a raspy laugh and I knew that I would never be able to just be his friend ever again.

Finally it was the night before we were scheduled to attack. I had never felt more ready for any battle before. This needed to be settled. Aidan needed to reclaim his throne.

The sun was starting to set and I was ready to go to sleep early. I wanted to rise before dawn in order to make sure that all of my armor was at it's finest.

However I had skipped supper earlier in order to help a younger Fraunch boy with some last minute adjustments to his defenses, and my stomach was growling. I wanted to grab something to eat before I turned in.

As I made my way to the mess tent, I noticed that the camp was eerily silent. In a place where thousands of men are living, it tends to always be noisy, with men running around at all hours. However there was hardly anyone walking around, and everyone who was, yet again, was avoiding my gaze.

I had been too busy the entire week to let it bother me, but I had still noticed that all of my friends had been treating me differently. Whenever I walked past hushed conversations would cease, and congregated men would scatter as if on an urgent errand. Kade had been going out of his way to avoid me. Bran and Gladwin were barely speaking to me, and Patrick would just stroke his mustache nervously without ever meeting my eyes.

It was getting to be ridiculous. My only hope was that they would give up whatever was wrong before we were forced to fight side by side against Morgan.

Even though defeating Morgan was always my main concern, I couldn't help but feel a preoccupied worry regarding how everyone was treating me. There was only one thing I could think of that would cause everyone I knew to treat me so differently than they had for the last decade of my life.

They knew my secret.

And I could only guess that it had been Aidan that had told them. Normally I would have been so furious and confused that I wouldn't have been able to think straight. I would have felt betrayed beyond belief and I would have approached him days before.

However, I had reached a point in my life where I wasn't sure that my secret was the most important thing.

What was the most important was keeping Aidan on the throne.

All of my life I had worried about myself first. Even when I had been acting on behalf of others, such as my father or Aidan, I had always calculated the outcome for myself.

While I didn't regret any of the decisions I had made, I was tired of living that way. I needed to focus on something bigger than myself with all that I had, no matter what the consequences.

That was how much I believed in Aidan. He had inspired me to be more than I was.

When I finally reached the mess tent, I saw Aidan leaning against the tree just outside of it.

When he heard me approaching he turned around and gave me a warm smile.

"Somehow I knew that you would come here," he laughed.

"You know me too well," I replied. "Do you know where everyone is? It's like a ghost town around here. I mean it's a good idea for everyone to turn in early but I must say that I am surprised by this level of dedication." I let out a laugh.

Aidan just stared at me. "Come with me."

I let out a sigh. "Aidan, whatever you are doing isn't important right now. What is important is being ready to fight well tomorrow. I don't need to be distracted right now."

Aidan reached down to take my hands in his. "This isn't a distraction Noble, this is your life. You have fought for me to have the life of a King for your entire adult life, now it's time for me to fight for you to have the life that you deserve," he gave me a small smile. "It's time for you to come with me."

I followed him silently through the tents. As the sun fell beneath the horizon I noticed a glow continuing to come from the field on the outskirts of the camp. I began to shake, as much from apprehension as fear. Whatever was going on was big, and whether it be good or bad I was scared to death.

Finally, as we passed the last group of tents all of the breath left my body.

The field was filled with hundreds of burning torches. My friends, the men who I had shared my life with, stood among them, lining a pathway.

"Aidan," I whispered, "What is this?" Tears were springing to my eyes.

"If there is anyone who deserves a fairy tale ending, it's you Noble," I could hear the tenderness in his voice.

I turned to face him, tears streaming down my face.

"I don't understand . . . and I don't deserve this . . ." I began, unsure of what to say.

"Stop saying what you do and do not deserve," Aidan said abruptly. "We have given it to you. It is yours."

"Thank you," I choked out as I hastily tried to wipe away the tracks of my tears.

"It wasn't my idea," Aidan smiled as he wrapped his arms around me and pulled me close. I just stayed there in his arms for a few moments, savoring the feel of him, his electricity and his warmth. "Now you have to go out there alone. I can't go with you for this part."

"I have a feeling that you will always be with me Aidan," I said as I slowly pulled away. Straightening my clothing I took a step closer to whatever was awaiting me. I took one last look behind me at Aidan, and his smile wiped away all of my fears.

I took a deep breath and walked out into the glowing field.

First I saw Kade and Bran.

"This took a lot of planning Kid," Bran grinned. "Hope you're grateful."

"More than you know," I replied as I punched him in the shoulder.

"One hell of a punch for a girl," he replied with a guffaw.

I continued on. Patrick, Gladwin and a few of the other knights all greeted me warmly.

But it wasn't them that I was looking for.

Finally I saw him standing in the midst of the torches, at the end of the path. Out of all the men that I could have loved, forever and always I knew that it was him.

The rest of my life was held in the balance of that moment.

Even from yards away I could see that he was shaking. He was the only one not holding a torch.

I slowly made my way to him, holding my chin high, but I was sure that he could see that I was shaking just as much as he was.

Finally I stopped in front of him, my heart yet again threatening to pound it's way out of my chest. After one more deep breath I brought my eyes up to meet his. I was so uncertain and so afraid. But in that moment all of the men and the candles faded from sight and there was only him.

For the rest of my life there would be only him. My best friend. My role-model. My hero. My entire world.

"It's beautiful," I finally whispered.

He swallowed deeply. I could see the fire gleaming in his eyes.

"Noble, I'm not an eloquent man. The moments that matter the most never seem to come easy to me. I always say the wrong thing or am just an instant too late to make the right impression. I know that I leave a lot to be desired. I'm course and unthinking and proud. I'm almost as stubborn as you are, and so much of who I am is only layers upon layers of scar tissue. But I have always known who I am and I have never apologized for it." He paused for a moment as he moved forward to take my hands into his. I instantly stopped trembling when I felt the calluses that covered his hands. Their strength gave me strength. "You make me want to be more than that though. For your sake I wish that I was all of these things, and yet I know that you know me better than I even know myself. You see all of the flaws and the ugly truths, and yet you're still standing here in front of me after all these years. You are the only person who has ever seen all of me, and not abandoned me. You've given me so much. Every day I can wake up and wade through the mess I've made of my life because I know that you are always there at the other end waiting for me, and making it all worthwhile. You have been there for me through everything. You've seen me at my worst and at my best. My entire life I've seen things and I've taken them, but they have never made me happy," he swallowed deeply. "You are the only thing that has ever made me truly happy, Noble."

I raised a hand to place it on the side of his face softly. I tried to speak, but the words wouldn't come.

"I'm sorry that I can't say all of the beautiful words to you that you deserve or give you nice things, but I want to give you everything that I have to give," his voice was thick with emotion as he stumbled over the words. "All of the moments that I have wasted without you in my life are a reminder that I need you more than I have ever needed anyone before. Every ungraceful movement, and misspelled word and badly timed confession of love that I make are only because you have inspired me. And the future is now worth contemplating because I will forever have a lifetime of loving you to look back on and be proud of."

He took a deep breath. "So here it is. I love you. I love your courage and your strength. I love your vulnerability and your fearlessness, your laughter and your tears . . ."

"Stop," I interrupted softly as I brought my other hand up to lay lightly on his chest. He gave a small nervous smile. "All my life I've needed confirmation of my worth from everyone around me, but not now. I've spent my whole life searching for something to help fill this hole that always been there inside of me. There have been times when I thought I had filled it, but at the end of the day it was never enough. But no matter how bad it got for me, you were always there." The tears pooled in my eyes. "It's been you since the moment I first saw you, and I was too busy running away from my fear and my loneliness to ever see it. But I see it now, and all I want is to be there for you every day, and hold your hand through the messes that we make and the moments that take our breath away. All I want is to love you forever."

And then it was the moment that I had been unknowingly waiting for my whole life.

Slowly, I brought my lips slowly to touch his. The breath that passed between us in that moment was enough to last me for the rest of my life.

And as I pulled away and looked into his eyes, we both broke out laughing.

"I think that might be the longest speech I have ever made in my life," he grinned as he pulled my body against his, burying his face into my neck.

"It was beautiful," I chuckled as I ran my fingers through his hair. "And I promise you will never have to make another one as long as we live."

"Thank God," he said as he pulled away to look at me again. "I've never been so nervous in my entire life."

"Kiss her again!" I heard Bran call loudly. All of them men joined in. "Kiss her again! Give her a good one!"

"It took over an hour to get all of these torcheses lit," Leonard grinned as his hand snaked around to hold the back of my head. "I think it's only fair that we oblige them."

"I'm always one to please," I grinned as he slammed his lips down on mine.

When he finally pulled away again, his lips were starting to swell and he couldn't keep the grin from his face.

"You and I are going to have everything we have ever wanted Noble," Leonard smiled like a little child. "We are going to fight until we can't fight any longer and then we are going to move out to that farm that I won and grow old together. And every night you are going to be in my arms and I'm going to protect you and keep you safe."

"Well as flattered as I am, I don't need anybody's protection," I said as I playfully punched him in the shoulder. "I might even be able to beat you."

"I'll let you do whatever you want to me," he replied as we slowly started to meander back towards our tents. All of the men had put out their torches during our last embrace.

I blushed and rolled my eyes. "Well tonight I just hope that I can sleep through your deafening snoring. It's a big day tomorrow . . ."

Leonard let out a sigh as he laced his fingers through mine.

"It's going to take everything that we have to defeat Morgan."

I nodded. "I'm scared."

"Now come on Noble," Leonard stopped and pulled me to face him. "You know that with me and you back together, and now highly improved, they don't stand a chance."

I felt a grin creeping up my face. He had always made me feel so safe.

"You know it is still pretty early," I looked shyly up at him through my lashes, as I rubbed the back of his hands with my thumbs. "We don't have to go to bed right this instant . . ."

His face lit up and we resumed our walk back towards his tent. He lifted the flap for me and I ducked unsurely inside. As I stood there in the near pitch black, I realized that once more I was trembling.

Once Leonard stepped inside and tied the flap shut behind him, he turned to look at me slowly and gave a nervous chuckle.

I smiled shyly as I sat down on his bedroll and licked my lips, once more too scared to look up at him. I was hoping he would show me what to do . . . I couldn't imagine it being anyone besides him.

He slowly sat down beside me and took my hands in his. After what seemed like an eternity of awkward silence I couldn't stand it any longer.

"I'm nervous," I whispered, not sure what needed to be said. I brought my hand up to rest on his face. It was scratchy with stubble. My thumb reached to brush gently against his lips before I pulled it away.

He grabbed my hand in his own and entwined my fingers with his again.

"Have you ever ummmm . . ." he finally stuttered. "I mean did you and Aidan or Teague ever . . ." He grunted in frustration.

"No," I smiled shyly.

I could see his chest rising and falling more rapidly. Slowly he brought both of our hands up to rest on my thigh. I could feel my heart racing and I started to shake.

Leonard raised himself up and rolled over so that he was holding himself above me. We just laid there for a moment staring at each other before I reached up and pulled him down by a leather thong he was wearing around his neck.

As his body touched mine I stopped shaking. He brought his lips closer and closer to mine until finally I felt as if I couldn't stand it any longer. I could feel his breath flowing into my mouth and my eyes fluttered shut.

Suddenly though he pulled back slightly and I opened my eyes to look into his.

"These last few weeks this is all I have thought about," he finally whispered as he looked deeply into my eyes. "It's all I have wanted. You're all that I have wanted."

"Me too," I replied honestly. "And there is nobody that I would rather be here in this moment with than you."

"It's just . . . I've been with so many women Noble and I'm ashamed of that now. I wish that it was only you," he sounded embarrassed to say the words out loud. "I'm so honored to be the only man who will ever make love to you."

"I want you just the way you are Leonard. You never need to feel ashamed or embarrassed with me," I gently pushed a curl out of his eyes. "I trust you."

I reached up to kiss him but he slowly pulled away once more.

"I would never hurt you. You know that right?"

"Yes," I whispered with a small grin as I looked up at him.

He kept inching backwards, father and father away from me. I felt every inch of his absence.

"And you know that I love you more than any woman I have ever know and any woman that I will meet for the rest of my life?" he slowly pulled my shoes off of my feet. Then he began to unlace my pants.

"Yes," I replied.

He stopped pulling off my breeches and looked up at me.

"And you know that even though I never knew it, I have been waiting my whole life for this moment with you?"

"Yes."

"Then nothing else matters."

# CHAPTER SEVEN
## The Fate of a King

Dawn seemed to come extremely early the next morning, but at least it was Leonard's deep voice that woke me up as pleasantly as possible.

"It's time to save a kingdom Noble," He whispered into my ear as he slowly unwrapped his warm arms from around me.

I sat up slowly, clutching his blanket around my exposed body. It was surprising that I could still be embarrassed even after what had happened between us the night before.

"Well I have no idea why we didn't start doing that years ago," I managed with a nervous laugh.

Leonard pulled on his breeches and grabbed my face, turning it so he could kiss me tenderly.

"Well let me tell you that it's not always as good as that," he grinned back. "But promise me that you won't be distracted today now."

I rolled my eyes. "It wasn't that good," I let out a laugh as he turned to me with an mock hurt in his eyes. "Okay, that's a lie."

He just stared at me for a moment. Then he reached forward to brush a strand of hair away from my face. "It's always been easy with us Noble."

I grinned as I reached down to pull on my pants. "The easiest. But the thing is that we definitely deserve it to be easy for once."

"Well after today we will have that at last," he shook his head wearily.

I finished pulling on my clothes and we exited the tent together.

The camp was buzzing with energy. Everyone was more than ready to begin.

I saw Aidan and gave Leonard's arm a quick squeeze before I jogged over to join the King.

"So thanks again for everything," I smiled as I caught up with him. He was walking briskly. "That definitely went above and beyond what I was expecting when you said you were going to talk to Leonard about me."

All Aidan could manage was a small, almost pained, smile. "Well like I have always said, you deserve above and beyond." I could hear the exhaustion in his voice. The night before he had been so full of life, but now he seemed flat and stagnant.

I rested my hand on his shoulder. "Everything is going to be okay Aidan. You deserve above and beyond too, and you have a whole army behind you making sure that's going to happen."

He wouldn't even look me in the eye, but I saw his jaw clench. I was having trouble keeping up with his long, swift strides. He didn't appear to be heading to the mess tent, or back to his own personal tent.

"Where are you going?" I finally asked after a moment of awkward silence.

"God damn it Noble I don't know!" He stopped and turned to stare at me, throwing his hands up in the air. "Why do you always have to assume that I have all the answers."

I looked up at him for a moment, searching his eyes with mine. He barely met my gaze.

"Aidan I know that you are under a lot of pressure right now, but we all believe in you . . ." I began.

He let out a strangled laugh. "But why?! My whole life people have blindly followed me through all of my triumphs and my mistakes alike. But nobody ever acknowledges all of the mistakes, and so I have to bear the memories of them all alone. I'm stuck trying to live up to this Golden Man who saved a nation, and I have no idea who that person is. All I see when I look in the mirror is be a man who sees everything and everyone that he has ever cared about slip through his grasp."

I had never heard him sound so desperate or alone. I had seen this side of him before, but I had never taken the time to understand it. I too often fell under the spell of the King and neglected to see the humanity of the man. I had only seen glimpses of his complexity that adhered with my opinion of what he should be.

"I'm sorry for not understanding that until now," I replied softly. "But you haven't lost everything. There are so many things that you could never lose, because you are the man that you are today. It's not the title or the legends that governed a kingdom or conquered an army, it was you."

"I did those things once upon a time," he scoffed. "But now there is nothing to show for it. I have failed all of you, and even now you refuse to see it."

I grabbed his hands. "Look at me," I ordered. "You have not failed me, or any of these men, because if you had then none of us would still be here risking our lives to stand beside you."

"You say that Noble but it all sounds the same to me," He pulled his hands away swiftly. "And all it does is make me lose faith in your ability to judge a man's worth."

I couldn't believe what I was hearing. Yes, I understood how he felt, but I knew that he had the strength to get past it. The fact that he was choosing weakness over strength was infuriating. I had given my life to this man. If he didn't feel like he owed it to himself to continue on, he at least owed it to me.

"We don't have time for you to stand here and feel sorry for yourself," I replied icily. "You have an army to lead."

"Don't you realize how ridiculous that sounds coming from you," he replied evenly.

I stuck out my jaw. "And what is that supposed to mean?"

He leaned in slightly closer. "I mean, think about all the years I spent watching you feel sorry for yourself. You still would be if I hadn't fixed the mess that you made with Leonard. I'd at least think you'd have the courtesy to understand when a person is dealing with legitimate, important problems."

"How can you be such a hypocrite?" I asked softly, almost shocked beyond words.

"And how can you be so disgustingly ungrateful?" He stared frankly back at me.

"Oh yes because the man who apparently has nothing thinks that he has given me everything," I retorted. "I thought you were smarter than that Aidan. You can't win a war when you're fighting on both sides."

"And now who's the hypocrite? You can't say that I'm the one worth fighting for and then just sit there on your high horse pointing out every flaw I have the honesty to reveal," he gave a cold grin. "Especially when you have never been honest a day in your entire life."

"How can you say that?" I asked with raised brows. "You have no idea the strength it takes to carry around the burden that I have carried, and then to finally rip all of the masks away for everyone to see. You have no idea what I have been through."

"And now I'm supposed to feel sorry for you again? Well I can't do it anymore Noble. I'm done with it. All this time I have been the one who is wrong. You don't deserve to be up on that pedestal I have put you on. You deserve to be down in the dirt with the rest of us," he turned and started to walk away.

I reached forward and grabbed his arm, yanking him around to face me again.

"I never asked to be on that pedestal, and neither did you," I replied holding back tears. "After all these years how can we still not really see each other?"

For a moment I saw his face soften, but then it was gone.

"Well now it's just you who has that problem," he yanked his arm away. I didn't even try to hold him. "I finally see all of it for the sham that it is, and I don't want to be part of it anymore."

He turned and started to walk away once more.

"But Aidan you can't just walk away," my tears caught in my throat. "What are all of us supposed to do?"

He paused for a moment and glanced over his shoulder.

"If Morgan wants Bryton than he can have it. It means nothing to me anymore."

I felt as if I couldn't breathe. Where was the man that I had chosen to follow as long as I lived? The man that I had once loved? The man who inspired a broken nation? The man who was walking away wasn't him.

"There was a time when I knew without a doubt that you were a better man than Morgan," I choked. "But in this moment I can't see that. What happened to you Aidan?"

He didn't even pause this time. I watched him walk away, desperately hoping that he would turn around, but he didn't.

\*\*\*\*\*\*\*\*\*\*

"What the hell happened to him last night?" I bellowed as I paced back and forth in front of all the knights that I had called together.

"Can you please stop yelling?" Bran moaned holding his head, apparently his celebrating the night before had not taken into account the battle that was to be fought the next morning. "I've never in all my years met a woman who could roar the way you can."

"I'm sorry," I replied as I ran my hand through my hair. "It's just that we are supposed to be attacking Callento now, and our King and Champion has all of a sudden decided to turn his back on everyone and everything. I would call this a crisis worth roaring over!" My voice escalated in volume as I continued.

"Does anybody even know where he is right now?" Kade asked.

"He just walked off into the field somewhere," I growled. "I mean what does any of this even mean? And why the hell is he acting like this?"

"You keep asking that, but none of us know," Leonard said softly. "I say that first we focus on how to attack today."

"But we attack a kingdom without a King behind us," Patrick replied.

"Well as soon as someone can talk some sense into Aidan we will have a King behind us. But since nobody knows where he is right now I say we continue with the plan and attack today. Morgan doesn't deserve to have one more day sitting on the throne of this country," Leonard supplied steadily.

"Leonard is right," Gladwin chimed in. "I have known Aidan my entire life and I know that he loves Bryton more than any King that has come before him and any King that will come after him. Whether he agrees right now or not we need to save this country from Morgan and place him back on the throne as soon as possible."

All of us sat there for a moment in silence, digesting the plan.

"Then each of us can lead an attack on a different gate," I finally whispered. "We have enough men. Nobody enters the castle itself until all of us have breached the walls and we can attack together."

"Are you sure it's a good idea for all of us to spread out?" Patrick asked.

"We have the advantage of numbers, but we aren't sure the skill level of Morgan's men," Leonard came to my defense. "We need to spread his defenses as thin as possible."

Bran stood up. "I will go divide up the men. It's time to end this fiasco as swiftly as it started."

All the men stood up and walked out.

Finally it was just Leonard and I left. He wrapped his arms around me and I let him hold the brunt of my weight.

"It's going to be alright Noble," he whispered into my hair.

"I'm worried about him Leonard. You didn't see him, something was very wrong," I couldn't hold in the tears anymore. "I've seen him at some of the worst times in his life , but today I just stood there. I didn't know what to say to make it better. He's one of my best friends and I have no idea what he's feeling or where he is." I sobbed into his chest.

"Shhhh . . . We both know that Aidan will be fine," he rubbed my back. "Is that the only reason you're upset?"

"He hates me," I sobbed even louder, not even caring that snot was getting all over Leonard's shirt.

"Oh come on," Leonard let out a small laugh. "We both know that could never be true."

"He told me that ever since we met he has had me up on a pedestal, but now he sees that all I do is feel sorry for myself and that I belong down in the dirt with everybody else," I hiccupped.

"Well wouldn't you rather be down in the dirt if you get to be here with me and all the rest of us disgusting old men?" Leonard smiled.

I finally looked up at him and attempted to wipe away some of my snot and tears.

"In all seriousness," He replied softly, pulling me back close to him. "Last night Aidan told me that letting go of you was the hardest thing he ever had to do, and that you are one of the reasons he still believes that it's worth it for him to get up every day and be the man that he is. Now tell me if someone who says things like that could ever hate you."

I let out a deep breath. "But that's not what's important . . . Something must be really wrong for him to turn his back on all of us, and to just let Morgan get away with ruining the country that he has spent years building into one of the strongest nations in the world."

"I agree," Leonard replied. "But we have time to figure that out later, right now we need to take care of Morgan."

"I don't know if we can do it without him," I answered softly.

"As much as he has earned every ounce of our respect and loyalty Noble, Aidan is just a man," Leonard pulled away slowly. "I'm sure we will do him proud."

I nodded slowly.

"You always did know what to say to make me feel better," I finally gave a small smile. "I just like it better when there's kissing involved at the end of it." I leaned forward to gently touch my lips to his. "Sorry I'm kind of snotty."

"I wouldn't have it any other way," he laughed as he pulled me in again.

After a few minutes of complete bliss I let out a sigh.

"I suppose we should go out and lead the revolt now," I grinned as I grabbed his hand and we walked out into the early morning sunshine together.

We promptly saw Bran motioning us over to where he was standing.

"We didn't want to interrupt the love fest, but the men are ready," he said with a knowing grin. I rolled my eyes. "Leonard you are going to lead the majority of the men through the main gate at the north. Noble you will take the southern gate. I will come in from the west and Gladwin at the North with Patrick and Kade attacking the two remaining service roads. Those are all the marked entrances, but we will have a few men left guarding the perimeter. We are assuming that Morgan has all of his forces inside the gates but we can't risk the chance of anybody escaping."

"And the men have all been briefed on the plan? We attack until we reach the castle together and then they guard all entrances while the knights enter the building alone unless we call for reinforcements," Leonard directed as his eyes scanned the masses of men that we were leading towards possible death.

"Wouldn't it be smarter to have half of the men come into the castle with us? Our numbers are highly depleted and Morgan will be heavily guarded . . ." Bran trailed off.

"No," I replied firmly. "This is personal. We need to do this ourselves."

Bran nodded though I could visibly see that he was biting his tongue.

We all went our separate ways to prepare for the battle.

As I stood in my tent pulling on my armor, I remembered the day that Aidan had given it to me. I couldn't help but smile at the memory.

Even after all that had been said earlier that morning, I knew that Leonard was right.

Aidan was still the man that gave me that armor. He was still the man who pulled me from my stubborn-headed hatred and made me into the person that I had become. Wherever he was, he was still a man worth following.

Before I knew it I was sitting atop Kin, leading hundreds of men towards the Southern gate of Callento. I was all alone, and yet I wasn't scared.

I felt completely competent. I felt ready.

We were quickly approaching the gate. As soon as Leonard was in place he was going to going to give three short blows on the bugle. Each of the 6 of us would reply with two short blows and then Leonard would give one long bellow when we were all finally ready to attack.

There was no reason anymore for subtlety. Morgan knew we were coming.

As soon as we were in position I turned to look at the men that stood behind me. I had never led anyone before, I wasn't sure what to say to give them courage. I didn't have it in me to be a leader.

"All of you will forever be remembered for your courage and your loyalty to the true King of Bryton. Now remember that there are numerous places for Morgan's men to hide inside the gates of the city. Even if we appear to have defeated all defenses immediately inside of the gates, we must keep our guards up until we actually reach the castle itself," I called out, growing more sure of myself as I continued.

"Well that's great to boost morale," someone called out from the ranks. I scanned the men and couldn't help but chuckle when I saw that it was Willis, the first man that I had helped from Fraunc. "I'd listen to her though, she knows what she's doing."

"That's a girl?" Someone asked, sparking hundreds of other men to ask the same question. "Why are we taking orders from a woman? Why is she even here?"

I blushed, not sure what to say.

"This woman knows more about fighting than the rest of us put together," Willis called out again. "There's no one here I would rather take orders from."

Suddenly I heard Leonard's bugle call, followed by four more. I gave the final bugle call as all of my men once again gained their composure and pulled out their swords. There were twenty men out front holding a felled tree that we were going to use as a ramming device. There was no other way to breach the heavy wooden doors.

Our archers brought up the rear, ready to provide cover for the men from enemy archers as long as possible.

Finally, Leonard let out one long and thunderous horn call.

"For Bryton!" I cried as the front men gave a thunderous roar and charged the entrance. On the first blow the gates gave a thunderous crack, but did not appear to budge. On the second attempt splinters of wood showered the men. By the fifth try the lock was shattered and the doors flew open.

I took a deep breath. "Forward!" I called as I urged Kin into a gallop. The men behind me took off running with adept speed, roaring their own battle cries as we neared the entrance.

Suddenly enemy arrows were raining down on us. I raised my shield at the last moment to catch a flaming bolt that would have pierced Kin's skull. Behind me I could hear men falling to the ground with cries of pain, but I could not turn to help them.

And then I was through the gate with my army behind me.

I was met almost immediately with a wall of heavily armored men.

I charged headlong into them, cutting as many as I could with the advantage of the height I gained with Kin. He was also useful, smashing men's skulls and legs with his powerful hooves. Some of the men I killed I recognized from Callento, or even from the castle itself.

I paused for a moment after over an hour of slaughter, glancing around me at the destruction. The ground was filled with trampled dead bodies, and yet the square seemed no emptier of soldiers than it had previously.

Suddenly, I heard a loud thud and Kin gave a pained scream before toppling over with an arrow in his neck. He was dead before he hit the ground. I gave a cry of pain as he landed, pinning my leg beneath his enormous weight.

"Damn it," I grunted as I clenched my jaw, hoping that my leg wasn't broken.

I pulled my sword from my scabbard, prepared for someone to try to kill me while I was trapped.

After one last deep breath I dug my elbow into the ground and tried to pull myself out from underneath the horse. I gave another scream of pain as I heard a loud pop come from my hip.

I wiped away a tear that leaked unbidden from the corner of my eye.

Suddenly I heard footsteps behind me and tried to twist so that I could see the person coming, holding my sword as high as I could manage.

The man that came at me was a guard that I recognized from the castle. I saw his face flicker with uncertainty before he swung his heavy blade at my head.

With no other choice, I swung my blade with as much force as I could, trying to chop through his legs.

He moved at the last moment, jumping back far enough to avoid my feeble swing.

With a wicked smile he raised the bow that he had slung across his back and pulled out an arrow to notch it. At such close range there was no way that I would be able to dodge the arrow even once.

I started shaking, but continued to stare the man straight in the eye. I would not beg for forgiveness. I would not even give him one word.

And then without warning an arrow struck the man in the throat. His hands flew to the wound, trying to stop the blood spurting from his body, but he fell to the floor without another sound.

I once more tried to turn myself to see who my savior had been. Maybe they could help me get free.

And there, standing amidst all of the smoke and chaos was the King.

As soon as our eyes met he gave a small smile and ran over to me.

"Aidan where did you come from?" I asked as he crouched beside me.

"That doesn't matter now," He answered as he surveyed the situation. "Alright I'm going to try and lift him enough so that you can slide yourself out."

I nodded and braced myself. Aidan took a deep breath and grabbed Kin by the saddle, lifting his mid-section enough so that I was able to pull myself out as swiftly as I could. Aidan set the dead horse down with a grunt.

I pulled myself up to a sitting position and slowly bent my leg. At least it wasn't broken, even though it was screaming with pain. I wasn't sure how long I would be able to walk on it before it gave out.

"Are you going to be alright to fight?" Aidan asked and he stood and offered his hand down to help me up.

"Of course," I replied, trying not to grimace as I put all my weight on my feet. "I'm just sorry I got your horse killed." I managed a small smile. "But I still want to know what you're doing here."

Aidan wiped his eyes as he looked at the carnage all around us.

"Did you really think I could let you fight my battle for me?" He slowly turned to face me.

"After this morning I thought that was exactly what was going to happen," I replied evenly. "I mean obviously I'm grateful and glad that you're here, but what happened? What made you walk away in the first place?"

"I had a visitor last night," He started slowly.

"Who?" I asked, as I took a sip from my water jug and offered it to Aidan.

"Your father," he replied before raising the container to his lips.

For a moment I stood there, not knowing what to say. I had never told Aidan the true reason that I had come to serve him. I had not known that my father was even still alive. How had he come to visit Aidan?

"What are you talking about?" I whispered.

"He snuck into the camp last night and was waiting in my tent for me," Aidan replied slowly. "Of course I remembered who he was immediately. He had tried to assassinate me days before I had him arrested for treason. He shot an arrow from a local window while I was riding in a parade celebrating my coronation."

"That's why he was arrested?" I asked as I began to shake. Why had I never bothered to ask why he was accused of treason?

"Yes," Aidan continued. "What I didn't know was that he was merely following orders from Morgan and his mother, my sister, who had been his friend and confidante for years. It was also brought to my attention that Grosipan had a daughter, and that her name was Aceline as well."

That was how I knew Morgan. Suddenly I could see him sitting at the table with my father, their heads leaned together whispering. Of course, Morgan had been young then, but he was always accompanied by an older woman. I realized now that it must have been his mother, Aidan's sister, who had been banished from court years ago. Back then, she had been the mastermind, but it was clear now that Morgan was in charge.

I was always sent to bed before he arrived but I often would peer at them through the crack in the door between our two rooms. Once I had accidentally made the door creak. My father had looked up and stormed over, throwing it open.

That was the first time that the King's nephew had stared into my eyes. How could I have forgotten that cold stare when it was obvious that Morgan had known who I was all along?

After that night he never came back.

"He told me how he was freed by his daughter after she dressed up as a man and impersonated a knight."

I couldn't bear to meet his eyes.

"He told me without him being free, Morgan would never have been able to raise enough support to take over the Kingdom."

"Aidan . . . I don't know what to say," I began, trying not to let my voice tremble.

"And then he told me that if I attacked every single one of my men would be slaughtered except you, because you had earned a place at Morgan's side."

All of the breath left my body and I stumbled, but Aidan caught me. Slowly I looked up to meet his eyes.

"And finally I told him that Morgan could have all of it. He could have my country and my crown. He could have my knights and my castle. And if he still wasn't satisfied with all of that, then he could have you, because I couldn't bear to look at any of it again."

"Then why are you here?" I managed to breathe.

"Because somewhere along the way I think I turned into the person all of you thought I was all along," He smiled gently. "And that person would never walk away from his country or his knights. And no matter what, he would never walk away from you."

"Aidan I'm so sorry I never told you he was my father," I leaned forward to sob into his chest. "But I had no idea that he was part of all this. I thought that it must have been a mistake that he was arrested . . . If only I had known. This is all my fault!"

"This is Morgan's fault, and we are going to make him pay for every drop of blood that has been spilled because of him," Aidan replied icily.

I took one last breathe to calm myself and pulled away.

"I'm ready," I unsheathed my sword. "I'll follow wherever you lead, my King."

He nodded and we surveyed the battle raging around us once more.

"Well then let's end this ridiculous charade," he replied as he charged into the fighting. I followed right behind.

**********

We were fighting until dusk. While our men had fought valiantly, Morgan's numbers had matched if not surpassed ours and they had the advantage of preparing on the site of the battle. There were hardly any of us left, but we had tried to take as many captives as possible.

Silently we made our ways through the streets of the city that I had been born in, the city that I had lived in my entire life.

It was barely a ghost of it's former glory. It seemed gray and lifeless, even in the smoky pink sunset. The city had started to reflect the man who was ruling it.

When we finally reached the castle, we saw men wandering in from all directions.

The first knight that we saw was Bran.

"They put up a hell of a fight," he mumbled. I saw that he had a large gash running the length of his arm. "We'd better hope that he doesn't have that many men left inside, otherwise we might be in over our heads."

"Have we heard from any of the other groups yet?" Aidan asked.

"Nice to have you back by the way," Bran smiled as he punched Aidan in the shoulder. "I knew you would come through, even if it was at the last possible minute." Aidan grinned sheepishly. "You two are the first I've seen."

"Well then I'm glad to be third," a voice chimed from behind us.

We turned to see Leonard. A relieved smile covered my face as our eyes met. I hadn't doubted for a second that he would make it.

"The plan to spread out worked well on our end at least," he supplied. "While the men were tough there weren't nearly as many as I expected. I still have more than half my men."

"I think you are the only one that fared that well," Aidan replied. "The rest of us are left with only a few of the best."

Leonard blew out a deep breath.

I noticed a man I didn't recognize walking towards us. I gently tapped Aidan's shoulder to catch his attention.

"Who are you?" The King asked.

"Sir Kade asked me to come notify you if he . . ." the young man trailed off. "He didn't want all of you to wait for him unnecessarily."

For a moment we all just stood there, not quite comprehending what had just been said.

"Is he injured?" Bran finally asked abruptly.

The young man shook his head no.

I looked down at the ground, trying to compose myself. I had already cried far too much that day. I needed to stay focused.

"I see," Aidan replied slowly. "Well thank you for your service today young man."

Without another word the messenger walked away.

"We shouldn't have let him go in by himself," I whispered.

"He's been fighting his own battles for years Noble," Leonard said as he placed a hand on my shoulder. "Nothing we could have done would have saved him."

"I'm going to miss that funny little man," Bran mumbled.

"I think we all will," Aidan agreed. "But the best thing we can do right now is to stay focused. Kade deserves to be grieved properly, and we can do that as soon as Morgan has been brought to justice beneath my blade."

"Aidan's right," Leonard replied. "We all need to eat something and drink some water while we wait for Gladwin and Patrick."

We all sat silently on the steps leading to the castle, trying to regain some of our strength. We appointed groups to take turns monitoring the castle and surrounding area for activity while the others rested.

Finally, long after the sun had set, Gladwin stumbled in and not long after him Patrick. We gave them a few minutes to recuperate as well and then we all met to discuss our plan of attack.

"There are only 10 knights left after Morgan's initial attack and the battle today," Gladwin mumbled through a mouthful of bread. "Are we sure that we still want to go in alone? Especially after the strength his forces have already shown?"

We all turned to look at the King.

He slowly nodded. "We will leave half of the remaining men in the outer courtyard and then the other half stationed just inside the castle walls. That way we can call for backup if we truly have need of their assistance. Till then we have to face this alone."

"Well I'm ready to get started," Leonard said as he jumped to his feet. "It will make my day to kill a couple more heartless traitors."

"Let's just get this over with as soon as possible," Patrick said wearily as he stood to join Leonard.

We all grabbed one last chunk of bread and one last sip of water before-fastening all of our armor and pulling out our swords.

Slowly I walked over to Leonard and clumsily wrapped my heavily armored arms around him.

He gently kissed the top of my head.

"Do you promise to be safe in there?" He asked quietly. "I might not be there to save you this time."

"I'll be alright as long as you are alright," I gave a small shrug. "We both know that neither of us can make any promises right now."

"It's okay to be scared, Noble."

"I am scared," I nodded jerkily. "He has always scared me more than anything else."

"I know," he pulled me closer and tilted my head back so that I was looking up at him. "Don't let any of the guys know but I'm scared too."

I grinned. "Always worried about your reputation."

"Yours in the only opinion that I really care about," he beamed back. "I need you to come out of this alright."

Looking into his warm brown eyes I leaned forward and kissed him tenderly.

"That doesn't get to be a goodbye kiss for us," he replied forcefully. "Promise me that wasn't a goodbye kiss."

"Like I said I can't make any promises about that," I replied deliberately. "But I can promise you that I will love you for as long as I live. And I hope that's enough."

"It's more than I could have ever asked for," he brought his hand up to lay it gently on the side of my face.

Aidan cleared his throat behind us. "Are you two ready to go?" Leonard pulled away and turned to face the King.

"Let's go kill the bastard," he responded.

Everyone crept quietly into the ghostly inner courtyard of our once beautiful home. We all stood silently, listening for any signs of life, swords raised. Only moments after we entered a group of guards sprung out at us from the hall. We were prepared though. Morgan knew how strong we were, and thus he would have insight on how to defeat us. He was capitalizing on the element of surprise he held.

A guard I knew jumped out in front of me and snarled. I swung at his left but he ducked and swung at my right. I moved backwards and then brought my sword down hard on his helmet, he was not wounded but I knocked him out. I held my sword over his chest, wondering if I should ram it through his treacherous heart. Finally, I reluctantly drove my sword through his chest. I couldn't run the risk of him killing Aidan or Leonard because I wanted to be kind.

When all of the guards were defeated we made our way wearily forward. The halls of the castle were so silent that our footsteps sounded thunderous as we walked. It was as if there was no one in the world besides our small group of people.

After what seemed like an eternity of anticipation we stood in front of the throne room. Somehow without even speaking, we all knew where we would go. Aidan stood with his back to us and his hand on the handle of the door. I held my sword at the ready. I was prepared to attack. The real King threw the door open.

Though we knew that he surely would be, we were all still shocked to see Morgan sitting on the throne. He was wearing the crown that Aidan had worn to his wedding with Glorianna, except that one thing had changed. Instead of a sapphire on the front there was a large ruby. I gasped; it was the ruby from my father's sword, the sword that was now one of my most prized possessions. I looked down at the empty place that the ruby had once filled and looked up again at my enemy, bitterly.

An old foe of mine was by his side. Lord Tremet snarled the minute he saw me and pulled out his sword. I froze with fear. I did not like that fact that he was on Morgan's side. My gaze swept downwards to the men that surrounded the dais where the throne sat. There must have been over a hundred of them.

"I knew that you all would come!" Morgan's voice scared me. He sounded as if he had become ever more unhinged than before, with a certain leer to his voice that made him almost sound like a rabid animal. There was a crack and we turned to see that the doors were shut. There was no way out. We should have left someone outside in case we had needed to call for reinforcements, which it was now apparent we desperately needed.

"I always knew I was clever. But I never considered myself a genius until now. This happy little reunion seems to be coming together perfectly," He was breathing heavily.

"Morgan," Aidan called evenly. "If you were any other man I would offer you one last chance to repent before you are brought to justice, but you are not. You are my family! The betrayal that you have made against me shows me that you will never repent, your madness will not allow it. And even if it did, I'm not sure that I could ever be a big enough man to forgive you. And so, remember this moment because it will be your last on earth."

Momentarily there was silence as the two held each other's gaze.

And then Morgan slowly brought his hands together to clap.

"Bravo!" He laughed, the noise sickly grating. "That final monologue will make your death even more tragic." He sat there for one more moment, his lips curling in a snarl. Then softly he growled, "Attack."

Suddenly, the men in front of us all jumped towards us with madness in their eyes that almost matched their master's. One came at me and I jabbed up under his breastplate. He fell to the ground immediately. I pulled my dripping sword out. I could only hope that the rest would be that easy to kill.

Another guard came at me. This one had yellow eyes that grew wide as he swung at my head. I ducked and spun around to hit his left side. He blocked and pushed my sword back. All of a sudden he pulled out and made a gash on my back where my armor didn't cover. I screamed and put a hand to it. I heard him laugh and in rage I swung wildly at his knees. My blade cut the through the calf of both legs and he fell with a sickening thud while screaming. He kept screaming for a long time, until his voice finally faded into death. I didn't feel kind enough to end his misery. Somehow all my compassion seemed to have gone missing. All that mattered was pulling Morgan from the throne and throwing him beneath Aidan's blade.

I looked over my shoulder to see that I was bleeding heavily. I knew that I would have to keep fighting even with the wound. I hoped that I wouldn't lose enough blood to hinder me in any way. My leg was already shooting pain up my entire body. Hopefully the energy of the fight would be enough to keep me alive.

It appeared to be, for a while at least. I killed 6 more men before the room finally started to thin out. I stood there for a moment, catching my breath and willing the blackness that was creeping into the corners of my eyes to stay at bay.

Abruptly, I was grabbed from behind. The man pinned both of my arms behind me and was dragging me roughly towards the front of the room. I screamed and tried to fight my way free, but the man had arms as thick as my thighs and was at least a good head taller than me.

I still held my sword in my hand and I tried to hit his legs with it, but I couldn't cut him because of the angle that I was at. My feet clumped along the ground as he pulled me up the steps leading to the throne. Then he threw me on the ground and I laid there stunned for a few seconds before sitting up. Immediately, my eyes went to my sword. It was a few feet away where I had dropped it when I had been thrown. I gazed down to see a room filled with bodies. The only men I knew left standing were Aidan, Leonard, and Gladwin. I stopped breathing for a moment and when I finally did again it came in ragged gasps.

Hot tears rolled down my grimy face. My eyes swept the floor and I saw all of my friends scattering the bloody floor. Bran was lying next with an axe in his head. Patrick was right next to the door. He had been one of the first to die.

The grisly sight of the room before me and my own hot blood running down my back made my stomach turn, and the blackness that I had been trying to hold back threatened to overwhelm me.

But I wouldn't let myself pass out. I had never before left my friends alone in their time of need, and they needed me now. I tried to stand up but the man who had grabbed me back-handed me across the face and I fell down to the ground once more. I spat blood all over the smooth stone.

Finally, I turned my head enough to see Morgan staring at me. I shivered, but couldn't make myself stand. His eyes ran over my body, and grew brighter with a feverish gleam. He reached over and grabbed me by the neck. Then he pulled me so that I sat in front of him. I didn't resist.

I shivered as my gaze swept the room again.

Once again my eyes lingered on the grisly deaths of all of the people that I had built my life with. I almost didn't believe that they were there, lying dead in the place where we had once joked and laughed about death. They were invincible. Some had been mutilated and some you could still see the horror on their faces. Tears flowed down my cheeks. I wanted to scream! I wanted to kill this damned man who had done this to these noble friends.

Morgan was running his fingers through my hair. "Don't you love the smell of blood? It is nice to know that I caused all of this to happen. But don't worry, you did your fair share to help too." I leaned over and retched. "You and your beloved Father of course. He was one of my minions, one of my play things. When Aidan is dead no one will protect you and you will be my play thing also." His fingers trailed down my neck. I couldn't move. I lifted my eyes to stare at the only friends that I had left alive. Aidan had won his fight and was surveying the damage all around him. Then he turned towards me and our eyes locked. I could see the horror on his face. Gladwin's man fell and Leonard's fell shortly after. Then they all turned to look up at Morgan and froze when they saw me at his side. I heard the sound of a sword being pulled out of a scabbard and then the blade was pressed to my neck.

"If you want her come and fight for her, Aidan," He laughed.

"Aidan no!" I screamed but then Morgan pressed the blade more firmly to my neck and I was forced to stop my desperate plea. I felt a thin stream of blood trickle down my chest.

Aidan took a step forward, keeping his eyes locked on Morgan's.

"Do not hurt her," his voice was low and dangerous. Leonard and Gladwin stood behind him with their swords drawn also. My eyes met Leonard's for a minute. He looked almost as scared as I felt.

"Make your men go outside," Morgan ordered. When Aidan did not move he spoke again, "Make your men go outside!" Gladwin turned to leave but Leonard stayed where he was. Gladwin grabbed his arm and hissed something in his ear. Leonard still wouldn't move.

Morgan let out another terrifying laugh. "So I see that Aidan's not the only one who loves the bitch anymore. I shouldn't be surprised. I thought I loved her once too, but now I realize I just want to use her for the slut she is."

"I will cut out your heart!" Leonard screamed as he jumped forward. "I will rip your limbs from your body until they are just shreds of meat!"

Both Gladwin and Aidan grabbed him to hold him back.

"You're not worth my time, Leonard" Morgan replied evenly. "Only Aidan is worthy to fight me." Morgan pulled the sword away from my throat slightly. Then he leaned down to whisper in my ear. "If you make him leave right now, I will let him live. And then when I've had my fill of you and I have cut off both his hands, I'll let you retire to that ridiculous farm and you can take care of him for the rest of your pathetic lives. You have my word."

Slowly I looked up at Leonard, trying to stop my tears.

"Go," I finally whispered.

"I can't leave you," he started, his jaw clenched.

"I'll be fine," I replied shakily, trying to smile. "If you don't leave now he's going to kill you and that will kill me. So please, if you love me, go."

I watched his face slowly fall. He ripped his eyes away from mine and stormed out of the room, Gladwin following right behind him.

I let out a sigh of relief.

Now all I knew was that I did not want Aidan to die because of me. He was a King and I was nothing.

"Come down and fight me," Aidan yelled. He took another step closer.

Morgan let go of me and pushed me to the side. I felt Tremet's hand grip my shoulders tightly, but my hands were free and I readied myself to use them. I eyed my sword again which was about four feet in front of me. If I leaned forward I could almost grab it.

Morgan stood up, disembodied as a spirit and it seemed as if he drifted rather than walked until he was about five feet away from Aidan. All I could do was sit and watch as they circled each other.

They whispered something to each other that I could not hear and I knew that one of them would die before their duel was over.

There was no other way that it could end.

Morgan was the first to lunge at Aidan's left. Aidan ducked right and then spun around to try and hit Morgan's uncovered neck. Morgan's sword intercepted Aidan's blade and he held him there for a few seconds before he pulled out and swung to the right. Aidan stepped back and took a full powered jab at Morgan's stomach. Morgan swung under to try and stop it but it made contact and Morgan barely pushed it out of the way before he was seriously injured.

They had their bodies pressed together and their swords up in the air. When they came apart Aidan had blood on his stomach. With a gasp, I realized that it was Morgan's blood. Aidan ran to the left, away from Morgan. I wondered what he was doing. I hoped that he wasn't running, but I trusted him and I knew he was fully capable of beating Morgan. The only thing that kept flashing through my mind was that Morgan had beaten Aidan once before. I could only pray that he would not beat him once more.

When Morgan was close, Aidan leaped onto a statue and jumped down onto Morgan. He was on the enemies back with sword ready to kill when Morgan threw him off. I gasped as Aidan hit his head on the floor with a loud thud. Morgan walked over to him with his sword raised, and Aidan only slowly getting up.

" Aidan!" I screamed before Tremet grabbed my throat. Suddenly, I knew that I had to help Aidan. I took my elbow foreword and then brought it back as hard as I could right into Tremet's crotch. He gave a loud yelp and let go of me. I grabbed my sword and then ran towards the King. I knew that if he lost, without me at least trying to help, I would never be able to live with myself.

Morgan was almost right over Aidan with his sword raised and I didn't know if I was fast enough. I was about twenty feet away when

Tremet grabbed my legs. I fell to the ground, hard, hitting my head on the stone.

Then, as softly and swiftly as a breath, Morgan stood over Aidan and plunged his sword into Aidan's chest.

"NO!" I screamed with a sob. I kicked Tremet in the head with all my strength. I heard his neck crack and he fell lifeless to the floor. Morgan was still standing over Aidan and suddenly Aidan sprang to his feet like lightning. Morgan stood with wide eyes for a moment before Aidan raised Elamoneir high and plunged it all the way through Morgan's heart. Morgan stood for a few minutes looking at his bleeding chest before saying his last words as a King, "The throne was mine." Then he slumped foreword and fell to the floor with Aidan's sword still rammed through him.

Aidan stood breathing heavily. He looked over at me and then tried to take a step towards me before falling to the floor.

I stared at him for a moment in shock before trying to stand up. I heard the last remaining guard behind me, and in one swift movement I turned with a roar and slit his throat.

Then I turned and ran to be at my King's side.

I quickly fell down beside him and pulled his head onto my lap. "Aidan, Aidan you did it. You killed him!" I had tears of cold fear streaming down my face. His eyes were still open, but they were starting to get cloudy. At that moment they were the most amazing blue that I had ever seen in my life.

"Morgan is dead!" He swallowed hard before letting out a cough that let blood dribble down his chin. "Elamoneir is yours, Noble." I grabbed his hand which was growing colder by the second.

"No, it's yours," my voice cracked, and I was afraid, "You'll be alright. Leonard will come and help you. You're strong. Please just hold on." We sat for a few minutes as his breathing grew raspier and slower. Then I knew that he was not going to make it and I wanted to die with him. "You are the best King that has ever lived, Aidan Penhalion," I whispered as I pushed his hair back from his forehead. He was so beautiful.

"Don't forget me, Noble." His hand slowly fell from mine and his blue eyes closed for the last time.

I stared down at his face in horror. I lifted his body to mine and rocked him back and forth, sobbing into his hair.

"Nobody will even forget you," I wept, not sure that the world could even go on without him.

********

The mist curled around the boat as it rocked gently upon the relatively still surface of the lake. I helped lift his still body onto the boat and stared down at his face for the last time. A shattered sob escaped my lips even though I tried to keep it inside my broken heart. I gently pressed my lips to his forehead before stepping back onto the dry sand of Lake Avalon. I knew that it would be the last time that I would ever see him.

At that moment, my life changed completely. You only see his kind of beauty once in a lifetime. The lady at the head of the boat turned to give me one last look before giving the signal for the boat to be pushed off.

The ladies of Avalon would take him to a secret burial place, hidden in the mist. He would never again be the burst of sunshine and gold that I had always known him to be. Now he would be a memory, etched in stone and surrounded forever in the fog that is mystery and legend.

I grabbed Leonard's hand because I knew that I could not stand on my own. We stared in silence as the boat soundlessly drifted away. Finally, we could not see it through the dense mist. I slumped to sit in the sand. Leonard crouched beside me.

"What are we supposed to do? It seems as if there is nothing left. I'm not sure I know how to live anymore," I whispered softly, leaning against him.

"I know it hurts Noble, but this isn't the end for us," He replied gently. "There's still so much we need to do. The new King is going to need all of our support. We can keep busy. And at least we have each other."

I turned to give him a small smile.

"At least we have each other," I nodded slowly. "And we have the memories. I won't ever let anyone forget what he gave for this country, what all of us gave."

"And of course we always still have our farm," he nudged me gently.

"Are you two ready to head back to the castle?" Gladwin called from farther down the beach. "We have a long ride ahead of us."

"But of course that can wait till we are old and tired," I replied with a genuine grin.

"Of course," Leonard replied as he leaned in to kiss me once more before pulling me to my feet. He turned and started walking towards Gladwin.

I paused one last time to look out at the lake. The waves gently lapped the gray sand and I could still hear the Lady's oars gently dipping into the green water.

"Goodbye Aidan," I whispered, speaking his name aloud for the last time. "My one true King."

220

## Chapter Eight
### An Old Woman's Epilogue

Of course that isn't the true ending to my story.

Leonard and I fought many more battles together for many more Kings. Most of them were just, and some of them were unquestionably noble.

When we found ourselves growing creaky and stiff, we did make use of the farm that Leonard had won. Neither of us ever stopped moving though, and we found an incredible peace there together.

He finally died in his sleep shortly before I began writing this history. While his death has been a catalyst for my story, I am not writing it for him.

I am writing it so that the world will never forget the one true King that Bryton has ever known. And I am writing it so that perhaps you can truly know me.

So now you know what it was like to walk among men that were true heroes. It took a long time to realize that I might even be a hero myself. There will never be another man like Aidan, but there will be more heroes.

Once more, I cannot draw a conclusion concerning the worth of my life or my actions. I will leave that to others if they choose to make such judgments.

Besides a possible verdict on the value of a life, I hope there is one thing that can be taken from this telling of the life of a normal girl thrown into abnormal circumstances.

Being brave isn't wielding a sword or defeating a foe. Being brave is seeking happiness even when it seems that there is only darkness. Being brave is to live.


THE END

## Acknowledgments

First and foremost, I would like to thank all of those who helped me by reading and editing my manuscript numerous times over the past ten years: my mother Janet, father Michael, brother Travis and family friend Daniel Pritt. Without their support and assurance, this novel never would have been published.

Secondly, I would like to thank Amazon for providing such a wonderful platform for aspiring artists to utilize. It is truly an amazing opportunity, and one that I am exceedingly grateful to have.

I would also like to thank the talented and generous Tara Cosby for the beautiful cover art. Neither of us imagined back in 2011 when we did the photo shoot that it would be used for this purpose, but I'm so glad that I am able to convey the tone of my work through her unique gift.

Finally, I would like to thank my love, Adam Meyer, for supporting me completely through the publishing process. His confidence in me gave me the confidence to share my novel with the world.

Made in the USA
San Bernardino, CA
27 July 2015